THE BOYFRIEND GOAL

LAUREN BLAKELY

Lauren Blakely Books
powered by Argo

COPYRIGHT

ABOUT THE BOOK

A forbidden romance with my brother's hockey teammate wasn't on my to-do list when I moved across the country...

Neither was getting locked out of a friend's place wearing next to nothing.

Or spending the night with the sexy stranger who rescues me.

But I'm trying to get out of my comfort zone so getting out of the rest of my clothes with him seems like a good way to start.

In the morning, I learn the filthy-mouthed man with the talented hands is not only the hotshot new hockey player on my brother's team: he's also – wait for it – **my brand new roommate.**

I'm a good student turned good librarian. A rule-follower. I'm not the kind of girl who does complicated flings. So we agree to another rule: *friends-only*.

It's not easy though. Wes is bossy, flirty and generous.

He gives me rides to work.

Pitches in at my library's fundraiser.

Takes care of me when I get hurt.

And looks at me like I'm the only one.

Soon, I'm falling hard for my brother's teammate.

Especially when Wes comes to my door and tells me exactly how he'd like to break our rules.

Every single one.

Tropes: forbidden romance, all the feels, teammate's little sister, roomies-to-lovers, hockey romance, forced proximity, she has a list!

DID YOU KNOW?

To be the first to find out when all of my upcoming books go live click here!

PRO TIP: Add lauren@laurenblakely.com to your contacts before signing up to make sure the emails go to your inbox!

Did you know this book is also available in audio and paperback on all major retailers? Go to my website for links!

For content warnings for this title, go to my site.

THE BOYFRIEND GOAL

By Lauren Blakely
Love and Hockey #1

1

WHEN A SCARF'S NO LONGER A SCARF

Josie

Don't look now, but everything is going perfectly today.

This never happens so I'm going to savor every single second. My flight into San Francisco arrived early. My black-and-white leopard-print luggage was the first to land on the carousel. And the town car my older brother sent for me—since his wife is fifty-nine million months pregnant with twins—cruised along the 101 and into the city easily without hitting any traffic, even on a Sunday afternoon.

The car pulls up in front of a charming yellow building in Hayes Valley that my college friend Maeve has been secretly renting from a trapeze artist, who's been subleasing it from a foot archer (I didn't even know that was a thing), so somehow this game of six-degrees-of-circus-separation brought her to this vibrant neighborhood. And it brought this neighborhood to me, since I'll be couching it here this week until I move into my own short-term rental on Friday. My new job begins on Tuesday. I'm so excited to start this next phase of my life.

Right now.

The car stops and the driver hops out, hustling to my door and swinging it open for me. "Here you go, Josie. Can I help you with anything?"

I smile brightly at the man but decline. "I've got it," I say, since I can't let myself get used to drivers or special service. That's my brother's world—not mine.

I'm a do-it-yourself kind of gal, and my meager bank account thanks me for it. When the driver unloads the suitcases on the sidewalk, I thank him then take a beat to note what's on this block. A cute café, a record shop, a noodle diner, and a sea of people swimming through the city.

It's a little overwhelming, but in a good way. It's also nothing like the quiet little town in Maine where I've lived most of my life. But I'm getting out of my comfort zone. I'm starting my first job post master's degree, and I've even got my list from my fabulous aunt Greta.

The list I've held onto for two years. The list I will definitely, absolutely finally tackle. Though maybe not item number one. That's way out of my comfort zone. But the other things on the list are fine.

Well, mostly fine.

We'll see.

For now, I say goodbye to the driver, then send my big brother a text. Christian still worries about me, so he'll want to know I navigated the wilds of the big bad city safely.

Josie: I'm here and all is well.

He doesn't reply, but I'm not worried since he and his wife are about to have their hands full, which will be doubly hard since hockey starts at the end of this week, and it's his second season as the team captain.

I drag my bags—bought secondhand at a thrift shop, naturally—up the stoop. After checking the front door code that Maeve texted me, I punch it into the keypad, then head up three steep and cardio-inducing flights of stairs to the fourth floor, searching for B4.

Note to self: no need to join a gym this week.

I find the door—it's purple, which doesn't surprise me but does delight me—and I try the code Maeve sent again. It doesn't work. Which, knowing Maeve, also doesn't surprise me.

The second I rap on the door though, it swings open inside and there's a half-blonde/half-brunette tornado. In a mad dash, Maeve's doing up the final button on a starched white shirt, then stabbing a chopstick through her curls of light brown hair, streaked with blonde.

"Ahhhh! I'm the worst. I'm late for a last-minute catering gig for a Dark Futures exhibit at this gallery I'm dying to get my paintings into—the Frieda Claiborne Gallery. It's a mile away. Meet me there at ten and we'll grab food."

Ten? What, are we still in college? I like to be in jammies at nine-thirty on the dot while enjoying a cheap merlot and debating the best book-to-film adaptations of all time in a Reddit group.

But I smile and say, "Sounds great."

She's hugging me in a blur, then racing out the door as I barely catch my breath to call out, "Good luck. You'll wow this Frieda, I just know it."

She shudders as she walks backward toward the stairs. "I hear she's tough."

"So are you," I say, as she spins around, but...wait.

I point to the purple door I'm holding open and the keypad on it that I'll need to use the next time I return to this place. "Maeve, what's the door code for here? It's different than the one downstairs."

She waggles her phone. "It's long so I'll text it to you." She wheels around, then turns right back, lifting a finger. "If you hear a funny noise on the windowsill, don't freak out. It's just the pigeons banging."

Okaaaay. "Didn't have pigeon sex on today's bingo card but thanks for the heads-up."

"And the showerhead is kinda short, so you might have to, well, duck."

I make a mental note. "Short shower. No problem."

She winces, a guilty look in her hazel eyes. "Also, you can't face forward on the toilet seat since it's wedged right against the wall."

I'd hate for her to feel bad when she's opened her home to me, so I say, "I love acquiring new skills, like peeing sideways."

"You're the best," she says, then blows me a kiss and races down the hall, jumping gracefully over the top step. "Watch out for this one," she warns and is gone in a cloud of sweet plum perfume and tardiness.

I turn around, take a big welcoming breath, and survey the tiny one-bedroom. Yup. This is definitely the Maeve I met my freshman year of college. Her stuff fucks like horny rabbits and multiplies. Paintbrushes are scattered in the kitchen sink, plants grow wildly from the windowsill, and homemade lamps crafted from old liquor bottles and castaway rhinestones sit on the table.

But it's home for the next few days till I can move into my own temporary place. I check the clock. It's four. Which gives me plenty of time to explore the neighborhood before I meet Maeve. That just makes good sense. I like to research everything before I do it. That way I'm always prepared for whatever comes my way.

* * *

I need to stop.

Truly, I do. I came to San Francisco for my first job as a librarian, not as a pigeon pornithographer.

But holy balls. Maeve did not lie. Not only is pigeon sex loud, it's like a freaking pageant. I adjust my phone screen as I record the show. Big Bird over there has been strutting his stuff on the windowsill, cooing and sashaying for Ms. Peck, who keeps scurrying around in circles. Tittering. She is definitely tittering. Then, he hops up on her back.

That's how pigeons do it? Like they're forming a cheerleading pyramid? I had no idea, but I can't look away. The dude is perched there. Now, he's flapping his wings. And five seconds later, he jumps off.

Talk about a quickie.

"Not impressed, Big Bird," I say, then peer behind me into the apartment, like I need to check to make sure someone didn't just watch me record birds doing it.

Nope. It's just me here. The pornithographer.

Best to get on with my evening. I hit end on my invasion of pigeon privacy and head into the bathroom.

Oh.

I stop abruptly. It's like the size of a high school locker. But no matter. Maeve is giving me a free place to stay. Who cares if I have to squeeze into the bathroom?

I head to the toilet where, as promised, I have to pee sideways. Fun fact about peeing sideways—your knees bang the sink.

There's a little scrape now on my left knee.

Fine, my life isn't quite as perfect as it seemed an hour ago, but a shower will cure that. I strip out of my travel clothes and hop under the hot water, where I pretty much have to do a squat the entire time I'm under the spray. When I get out, my thighs are burning. But bright side and all—this building is a life hack, and I get cardio and strength training here.

The good news is there's *almost* enough room in the bathroom to do my makeup.

A half hour later, my hair is dried and I'm wearing my oversized white T-shirt with an off-the shoulder neckline (cut by yours truly), my aunt Greta's signature scarf to hold back my hair, my black-and-white cat-eye glasses, and a pair of pink fuzzy slippers. My face is lotioned and potioned. In the tiny bathroom, I finish slicking on mascara, then blush, as I google directions to the Frieda Claiborne Gallery while listening to a podcast about the history of San Francisco. The gallery is just down Hayes Street, so it's not too far away.

I'll just switch out of this shirt and pull on jeans and a hoodie, then take off. No need to dress up since I'm not actually attending the Dark Futures exhibit. Maeve's texted the code so I'm good to go. As I head to my suitcase, set neatly by the ratty green couch, there's a knock on the door.

Hmm. It's not my place to answer it, but what if Maeve's expecting something and forgot to tell me? I scurry to the door, setting down my phone to check the peephole. A woman with red hair and freckles flying across her pale skin stands in the hall, frantically bouncing a baby on one hip and balancing a package on the other. And is that a little toddler wandering in bored circles behind her?

"Hey, Maeve. They dropped off your mail for me again," she says, sounding like sleep has eluded her for a millennia.

Must be her neighbor. I swing open the door.

"Oh. You're not—"

"I'm Josie. Maeve's friend," I say as the baby whimpers. "But let me take that. You look busy," I say, reaching for the package, then setting it on the table right by the door inside the apartment.

The woman looks down at the baby with a heavy sigh. "She's hungry. Eats constantly. But I have to go meet her father for a playdate."

She doesn't sound thrilled about the playdate. I bet the playdate she really wants is with her pillow. I so get it. My pillow and I are tight.

"Mom, I want an ice cream," the toddler whines, making airplane arms as he spins in a circle. "Please. Now. Please now."

"And we're leaving any second," she says in that *I'm so exhausted but I'm faking it for you* voice when her purse slinks down her arm, then careens to the floor in a heap.

Airplane boy seizes his chance and wings out, propelling down the hall toward the wobbly step. Tired Mom is grabbing her purse, so without hesitation, I rush on pink fuzzy feet, lassoing the boy with my arm before he tumbles down a flight of stairs.

Got him!

The mom gasps. "Oh my god. Thank you."

In seconds she's next to me, clutching him while thanking me profusely as the baby wails.

Note to self: say no, albeit nicely, when Christian asks me to babysit.

But I don't share my child-free thoughts with the stranger. Instead, I just smile. "Glad to help."

On another effusive thank you, the harried mom takes the boy's hand and heads down the steps. I whirl around, returning to the purple door, which must have fallen closed. I lift a finger to punch in a code...

A code I don't know.

Since it's on my phone.

On the other side of the door.

I groan in frustration.

Don't look now, Josie. But nothing is going your way.

My good luck must have drained down the short shower stall.

Still, there has to be a solution. Every problem has several. I just need to find one. That's all. I head along the hall, scanning for the mom, peering down the stairs, but she's already gone. I look back at the apartments on this floor, considering meeting my temporary neighbors. I could knock on doors and ask to borrow a phone.

But I don't have Maeve's number memorized anyway. Come to think of it, I don't even know my brother's number by rote. Even if I had a borrowed phone, I don't know who I'd call.

I stare forlornly at B4, wishing the door would magically open. But there's only one person who can let me back into this place and she's at an art gallery at 814 Hayes Street.

I glance down at my getting-ready outfit. A baggy T-shirt that hits me at the scraped knees and my pink fuzzy slippers.

Great. Just great.

But I shrug. Desperate times call for do-it-yourself measures. I undo Greta's scarf from my hair, tie it around my waist, and turn my shirt into a not-at-all-fashionable T-shirt dress.

Then, chin up, I venture forth into the wilds of the city on my slippered feet without a phone.

Or even a bra.

2

MY PLUS-ONE

Wesley

I know what's coming before my dad even asks.

"Yes, Dad, I had the high-protein jerk chicken breast with quinoa and lime cucumber salad for lunch," I say to him on the phone as I stride through the sleek, state-of-the-art kitchen of my townhome in Pacific Heights, the black plates washed clean from the lunch he made sure the meal planner prepped and sent over to me.

"Good. Because it's a recovery day and tomorrow you'll have—"

Does he actually have the meal plan memorized? Wait. Stupid question. Of course he does. And so do I, since I knew this was coming too. I had my phone's text-to-speech app read the meal plan out loud till I learned it by heart. "The chicken and squash bowl."

"You got it," he says, pleased, like I've answered the right question in class. "You know what top nutrition leads to."

"Top performance on the ice." I finish the thought easily having heard it since I was in youth hockey.

His voice crackles through the line, persistent and unwavering. "You need to fuel your body right, son."

"I'm like a Bugatti, Dad," I say, attempting to lighten the mood.

"Good. That's what we want on the ice. The better you fuel yourself, the lower the chance of injury. The lower the chance of injury, the more ice time..."

The better the chance for a great season and so on. I don't really disagree. I've just heard it before, and there's no mood lightening with Mister Serious, so I let it go.

"I know," I say, as I leave the kitchen and head into the living room, staring longingly at the TV and the video game controller. A round of zombie slaying would be real nice right now.

"Are you heading to the gallery? Your walls were almost bare the last time I was at your place."

So much for destroying the undead. Or seeing some of my teammates. I was *this* close to a round of pool with Max, Hugo, and Asher when Dad swooped in earlier today with his request. No, his insistence that I attend his new conquest's—sorry, his *girlfriend's*—art gallery show.

"On my way, Dad," I say, as upbeat as I can manage about checking out the exhibit Frieda's created called Dark Futures—whatever that is. But it feels fitting—the future of this night is dark, even though I'm still meeting my guys—just a little later now. I'm going to need to detox after an evening at an art gallery.

I glance at the handful of framed concert posters I hung in the townhome I bought when I was traded to this team last February. "What's wrong with the art I have?"

"Tame Impala? Wesley, you're not a rock critic or a beat poet," he says.

Are concert posters the de facto art of beat poets? I scratch my jaw. "Is anyone even a poet anymore?"

It's another attempt to lighten the mood, but Dad sighs heavily. I can picture him in his office in Los Angeles, where he works half the time—thank god he's most of the state away. I bet he's pinching the bridge of his nose.

"That's not the point. The point is it's a contract year, and you need to manifest an attitude of success. Remember what I've told you?"

Repeat after me. "Be the whole athlete," I say, and it's empty but he won't be able to tell.

"It's a mentality, Wesley. And Frieda is expecting you so you should go."

Well, I'd hate to disappoint his flavor of the month. "I'll manifest a new persona as an art connoisseur."

"Perfect."

My sarcasm was entirely lost on him.

I hang up, then head to the garage, passing a sleek mirror in the foyer on the way. Wait. I can't wear a polo shirt. Frieda will tell Dad, then he'll say I'm not looking the part.

Having your father as an agent is no joke. But the dude is sick with contracts, and a beast in negotiations, so I change into a tailored sage green dress shirt I usually only wear on game days with a suit.

I hop into my electric car and take off for the gallery at the edge of Hayes Valley, where I snag a sweet parking spot. When I get out, I check the gallery address once more. Passing by quaint cafés and designer boutiques, I picture the season ahead. Our training camp has gone well. Our first game is in less than a week, and if chicken and squash bowls do the trick for me on the ice, then fine. Bring them on.

When I pass The Scoop, a small-batch ice cream shop though, I try to manifest a hatred for ice cream. But my manifesting skills are not *that* good. My mouth is watering for a salted caramel cone.

No way is that on the meal plan.

I jerk my gaze away, then head down the block, weaving through the evening crowds, bracing myself for an encounter with Frieda with her slicked-back hair and fake British accent. Maybe I can avoid her. Perhaps she'll be so busy entertaining clients, I can pop in, go *eenie, meenie, miney, moe* at the walls, and then head to the bar with my friends. I'll be in and out in a flash, like a break-away shot to the net.

And I'll still get credit for having shown up.

But when the gallery comes into view, the tall, bird-like woman is staring down her nose at...what in the ever-loving fuck is that *other* woman wearing?

I peer more closely at the subject of Frieda's disdain. A brunette with wavy hair, dressed in a long T-shirt and fuzzy slippers with a flowery black scarf tied around her waist. That's not what people wear to art galleries. That's what people wear when it's laundry day.

Is she down on her luck?

As I come closer, I catch pieces of the conversation.

The younger woman places her hands together in prayer. "I just need to get a passcode from one of your caterers. I swear, it'll take one minute, and I'll be done."

Frieda's tone is faux warm. "I desperately want to help you. But Frieda has made out a list, and you need to be on it. See? I'm in a quandary."

She's pretending she's not Frieda? Give me a break.

"Yes. Same here! I'm in a quandary too," the woman in the makeshift outfit says desperately, clearly hunting for common ground. "I'm locked out of my friend's place without any of my things. I'm new in town, and I just need to get back in there."

"I would think your phone could be useful," Frieda offers oh-so-helpfully.

Gee. A phone. Why didn't that occur to her?

"My phone is in her place. If you could just tell Maeve that Josie is here," she says, begging Frieda, "I'll be out of your hair in no time."

Frieda pastes on an *I don't give a shit* smile. "I wish I could help, truly, darling. I do. But I can't. Frieda has made it clear. You need to be on the list." She pauses, sighs, then frowns apologetically as she stage whispers, "Plus, we have a dress code, love."

Oh, hell no.

The woman in the T-shirt—Josie, she said—turns around, and her eyes are shining with the threat of tears behind those cute glasses.

Well, if Frieda has made it clear you need to be on the guest list, I can make some things clear too. I stride right up to the woman in need and flash her a helpful grin. My dad might think I have zero taste and a lack of focus, but one thing I do have? My improv skills are unparalleled.

"Hey, sweetie. Glad you could make it. I love your dress. You're so fashion-forward, I can't even keep up with you," I say with a smile that I'm sure gleams.

The brunette whips her gaze to my eyes and the breath is nearly knocked out of me. Her lips are pink and glossy, her chestnut hair is wavy, and there's a faded, pink jagged line on her chin—a scar somehow makes her even prettier.

Her blue eyes are bright and full of question marks. But it doesn't take long for her to connect the dots. In seconds, she's figured out my plan and she pops out a hip, showing off her outfit with a no-big-deal wave. "Oh, thanks, I just threw it together. A little DIY."

"You look...incredible," I say, and that's not a lie. It's the whole damn truth. Smugly, I turn to Frieda, then fasten on my most apologetic look. She already thinks I'm an idiot anyway. She'll buy this next lie easily. "My bad. Did I forget to put my date on the list?" I tap my forehead, like details are just so hard for this guy. "Josie's with me. My plus-one."

"Your plus-one, Wesley?" Frieda's lips twist into a doubtful scowl as she glares at me, then stabs a finger suspiciously in Josie's direction. "I thought you were locked out of your friend's place?"

"Oh, I am." Josie looks up into my eyes and floors me again with the intensity of her stare. Then she flashes the sweetest, most apologetic smile Frieda's way as she says, "And I was in such a rush to leave because Wesley likes to surprise me with his fantastic date ideas, so he told me to meet him here. I'm excited for the show."

Frieda's false warmth recedes. She's an iceberg now. "Of course. Enjoy the exhibit, Wesley," she bites out, smiling so falsely that it's a goddamn pleasure to watch her try to keep her shit together.

"Thanks, Fri," I say since she hates nicknames and effectively blowing her cover with Josie. "Appreciate your generosity."

I offer an arm to the woman in the T-shirt and slippers, and walk her into the gallery, all thoughts of seeing my teammates later as far from my mind as the chicken and squash bowl.

3

WHEN THE ART SPEAKS

Josie

I clutch the cocktail napkin with the door code like it's the gold the hero hunts for in a pirate's tale. "Thank you," I say to Maeve after telling her the tale of my misfortune, down to my impromptu plus-one.

"Girl, thank you. For giving me a hell of a story. You are a determined tiger, walking through the city like that," Maeve says, eyeing me up and down in my ragtag clothes that make me look like, well, like I was sleepwalking. She tips her forehead to Wesley, standing a few feet away and studying a painting of what looks like a vampiric ant. "Also, he's not *too* unattractive."

I laugh at her dry humor. "Yeah, he's definitely not too bad at all. But he was just helping."

"Right," she whispers, her eyes darting to him again. "Hope you have *fun*."

"It's not like that," I insist since I don't want to assume anything.

But with a wink that says *you lie*, Maeve whirls around, balancing a tray of sparkling champagne flutes, offering them to the crowd. I turn back to the stranger who saved the day as he turns back to me. Scruff lines his chiseled jaw, his light brown eyes twinkle with amusement, and his full lips curve into a very playful grin. He wears a silver chain that draws my attention to the fair skin of his throat, and inexplicably makes me wonder how he'd taste if I kissed him there—right there by his Adam's apple. Does he wear cologne? Would it go to my head?

Get a grip.

He's a stranger. I shouldn't lust after a stranger. Instead, I brandish the napkin like it's a prize. "I've got it," I say, with more relief than I've ever felt.

"Now protect that, Josie," he says.

"With my life," I say, and I'm about to stuff it in the safest spot possible—my bra—when I remember that I'm not wearing one.

I just fold it, curling my fingers around it. He's probably ready to take off and, I dunno, study the art here or whatever people who go to art openings do. "Thank you, Wesley," I say since I heard Frieda the Wicked Witch use his name. "That was amazing. And I seriously appreciate it. Is there anything I can do for you?"

I genuinely want to thank him. I also maybe, possibly, don't mind looking at him because this man is...unreal. He's six-foot-fifty, and his shirt is hugging his pecs, and cuddling his biceps that go on for days. And his wavy, wild, dark brown hair is just a delicious mess. The kind of mess I want to drag my fingers through.

Focus, girl.

"As a matter of fact, you can help me pick art," he says.

I was not expecting that. But it makes sense. We're at a gallery after all.

"You want me to help you choose something?" On the one hand I'm grateful for the chance to repay the favor, but on the other hand...I gesture to my get-up. "I hate to break it to you, but I'm wearing a T-shirt and slippers. They did want to bar me from entry for all eternity."

"And they failed. So, wanna help?"

I don't really want to wander around a gallery half-dressed after walking a mile like this already and feeling like the biggest fool. But the man swooped in and saved the day, so I owe it to him to help, even with my free-range boobs. "I hope you're ready for my exquisite taste," I say.

"I'm always ready," he says with a confidence that sends a zing down my naked chest, "for anything."

And the zing spreads farther.

Ready for what, the too curious side of me wants to ask. But I keep that to myself. With my slippers slapping against the polished blond wood of the floor, we check out paintings hanging on stark white walls.

And wow.

I don't want to be rude. I'm a librarian not an art historian.

But these paintings look like my nightmares. They're all apocalyptic. Like that one of fish with wings flying over a desolate cityscape.

Wesley gestures to it. "Would this look good on my walls?" It's asked seriously.

I study his handsome face, trying to read him as he crosses his arms and stares at the huge canvas taking up way too much space. "It depends where you live," I say diplomatically.

"An underground bunker," he deadpans.

I smile. "Perhaps then."

But I don't entirely want to insult his taste in case I'm reading him wrong, so I'm careful as we head to the next one—a black painting with a skeleton horse riding across a desert landscape toward an alien, whose face is melting off.

Wesley studies it intently, tilting his head one way, then the other. Oh god, does he really like that monstrosity?

"What do you think?" I ask enthusiastically, trying to be nice.

He hums for a beat, then leans closer to me, his shoulder bumping mine. A charge rushes through me. From his shoulder. I've never been a shoulder girl, but I'm reconsidering that stance tonight. Nope. I'm revising it. I'm officially a shoulder woman.

"I feel like this painting is telling me to shop at another gallery," he whispers.

I breathe out, relieved. "Thank god you said that."

He tilts his head. "Did you think I liked it?"

"I was hoping you didn't," I whisper.

"Josie." He tsks, his clever eyes holding my gaze in a way that makes my chest flip and reminds me of item number one on my list, which makes no sense, because item number one is not my style, not at all, not one bit. "Don't you know me better by now, *sweetie*?"

No, but I kind of want to—want to know him as more than just my spur-of-the-moment fake date. "You're right. This is totally not your style, *honey*."

"Exactly." He pauses, looks around. "But what about that one?"

I furrow my brow. He's not gesturing to a painting. "Which one?" I ask, confused.

He lifts his finger higher, his lips tilting up, his irises gleaming with mischief. He's pointing to the exit sign.

I grin. I can get behind that plan. "That's a sign...to sneak out the back door," I say in a low voice.

He glances around, looking for Frieda perhaps, then pushes open the door by the exit. "I'll cover for you."

Without giving it a second thought, because he's too fun, too handsome, too helpful, I slip past him, my arm brushing against his firm chest. He's right behind me, and we're pushing out another door that opens into the alley while we're laughing like we've made our great escape.

When I catch my breath, the thrill of our swift exit seems to vanish, and I feel empty already. Because it's probably time to say goodbye. I have my code, and surely he's ready to move on with his night.

With a resigned sigh, I stick out my free hand, the one that's not holding the napkin. "Thank you again, Wesley. I seriously needed this. All of this."

He takes my hand, shaking it. "Happy to help."

"I should head home," I say, tipping my forehead in the direction of Maeve's place. "It's a mile in slippers."

He doesn't let go of my hand. He's silent, but his eyes seem to flicker with ideas. "Can I walk you?"

Briefly, I weigh the risks. He's a stranger, but he's a stranger who saved me. Plus, I'm walking anyway. And the streets are full of people.

"Sure," I say. He lets go of my hand. As we leave the alley and turn onto Hayes Street, we walk a few blocks and chat about the city. But a question nags at me. "Did you really want to buy art tonight?"

"Not from there. I'd rather hang a poster from a concert I've gone to, or pics of my sister's dog, or just something funny. But I kind of had to show up. My dad wanted me to check it out," he says, but his light tone disappears, telling me he doesn't want to talk about his father. "Do you hang fancy art like that? Or terrifying art?"

"I haven't really done it before. I'm more of a photos girl—of the people I love," I reply, ignoring the slight pang in my chest when I think of one person I love who was taken from my life too soon.

We pass an ice cream shop and he glances at the window—a little longingly—before turning his gaze back to me. I file that information away in my mind under Things Extremely Built Men Want But Can't Have. I shift gears. "And do you usually save women trying to infiltrate art events?"

"That was definitely a first. Do you usually infiltrate art events in your..." He lifts a curious brow, checking out my absurd clothes.

"My getting ready outfit?"

"Yes, that."

I pluck at the oversized shirt, then wince. "No. It's sort of fitting, the art was nightmarish. Walking around half-naked is kind of a nightmare."

Instantly, his mirth vanishes. His brown eyes are serious as he scans the block with assessing eyes. "There's a shop a couple blocks away. I saw it when I was driving. Let me get you something to wear."

My lips part. My brain stutters. Is he for real? Who is this generous? "Are you serious?"

"Yes."

It's said like the simplest answer ever. And it's no longer just a fleeting thought. This sexy stranger is definitely making me rethink item number one on my list.

4

VERY SINGLE

Wesley

"I'll pay you back," she says, as I hold open the door to Better With Pockets.

Hell no. I shake my head vehemently. "Nope."

"Seriously. You don't have to buy clothes for me," she says as she walks past me into the boutique.

"I know. But I want to," I say firmly, letting the door fall closed.

"You really want to shop for me?" The question resonates in the sweetly scented air of the shop—the smell is feminine, berries maybe. It's a contrast, or really, a complement to Josie's scent, which is a little like cinnamon. Pop music pumps through the speakers, Sabrina Carpenter's tune matching the colorful array of trendy clothes that line the racks.

A woman from behind the counter nods our way. "Let me know if I can help you with anything," she says in a warm, husky voice.

"We will," Josie says, then turns back to me, still studying my face like she needs to make sure I meant the offer.

"Are you worried that I don't like shopping?" I ask, trying to understand her.

She seems to give that some thought for a few seconds. "No. Well, maybe. But mostly, it's so generous of you. But you totally don't have to. I'll be fine. My friend's place isn't that far."

She says it all upbeat and cheery, like she needs to exonerate me from the offer.

Maybe she's not used to people doing nice things for her. But is helping her out of a jam *that nice*? It just seems like the right thing to do. Besides, it's rare when you can truly help someone. When you can give them what they need when they need it. Usually, help is like the old toolbox you find in your grandfather's attic. It has a flat-head screwdriver when you really need the Phillips-head.

In my case though, I have the right tools for Josie. A wallet and a willingness. I pin her with a serious stare, so she knows I mean every word. "Let me help you, Josie."

"Let me pay you back, Wesley," she says, staying strong.

"One, you're not paying me back. It's a gift that I want to give. Two." I glance around the shop, gesturing to the racks and shelves bursting with clothes that women her age usually like. I mean, it's not like I picked a Dress Barn. "What's it going to be? Pants, shorts, shirt, or dress?"

She laughs. "You're bossy."

I resist the urge to make a naughty joke. *Mostly*. I mostly resist it. "I am."

She breathes out in a sort of relaxing sigh, like she's relenting. "Thank you. And shockingly, I'm not picky right now. I'm at the *I'll take anything* stage of dressing." Her pretty lips curve up in a curious grin. "But tell me, Mister Bossy, what would *you* pick for me?"

I seize the opportunity to get to know her. "I'll pick, but on one condition."

"What's that?" It's asked with a little challenge, one that says she likes to hold her own.

I wiggle my fingers in a serve-it-up gesture. "I need a clue or two."

"A fashion clue?"

"Exactly. I'm a good shopper but..." I take a beat, so my next words land right where I want them to. "I don't want to pick an orange sundress when it turns out your... boyfriend hates orange."

Her eyes sparkle. "Wesley, was that your way of asking if I have a boyfriend?"

I scoff. "Please. I'd never be that obvious," I say, then give her a look like *I'm waiting*.

She straightens her shoulders. "My boyfriend, who's the head of the San Francisco mafia, would probably like to personally thank you for making sure I don't roam the streets half-naked while he's off working at *the docks*."

I shoot her an *I'm impressed* smile. "Making concrete shoes, I'm sure."

"Of course. It keeps him quite busy." She pauses, then asks, "And will your girlfriend who speaks five languages, looks beautiful without makeup, and saves endangered animals like to give you any fashion tips over FaceTime for me?"

Fuck me. She's perfect. "Actually, she's going to come join us. That work for you?"

"It works perfectly," Josie says, and if I was looking for

a distraction from my father tonight, the universe delivered.

But even though we were both clearly messing with each other, I don't want there to be any questions about my status. I set a hand on her bare arm, briefly savoring the feel of her soft skin as I say, "Josie, I'm single." And because she's so damn pretty and so flirty and so quick on her feet and because we haven't talked once about hockey or calories or exercise, I add for emphasis, "Very single."

She doesn't fight off a smile. "I'm very single too."

"Good." I roam my eyes over her in her makeshift dress. "And while I suspect you look good in anything, I'm picking pants."

"Why's that?"

"I'm betting you want to feel different than the way you feel right now. Pants would be the fastest way to that."

Her smile is sexy and smart at the same time. "Get me some pants, please," she says, and hell if I don't hear *get into my pants*. Or really, I want to.

I nod toward the rack near us and flick through some options. "So, what's your favorite color?"

"Guess."

"Fine." I stop hunting and take a beat, traveling up and down her frame, adding up clues, then give it my best shot. "Black."

She blinks, clearly surprised. "Um, close."

"Gray?" I ask with a laugh.

"It's black and white actually," she says.

I crack up. "Dude, you picked two colors."

She squares her shoulders. "Maybe I'm an over-achiever."

"Maybe?" I arch a brow. "Sounds like you are."

"So how did you know?"

I lift a hand, pointing in the direction of her glasses. "There's a little black and white checked pattern on the arms."

"Oh," she says, then touches them gently, like she's reminding herself. She tucks a strand of chestnut hair over her ear. "You're right."

"Yeah. I noticed them earlier," I say, and it's an admission that I've paid close attention to her.

Her cheeks pinken in the most alluring blush ever. She swallows, then looks around, getting her bearings maybe. For a few seconds, a sense of déjà vu slams into me. Have I seen her before? She feels vaguely familiar, but I see a lot of people at hockey games. It's possible I've seen her or someone like her once. Besides, I'm pretty sure I'd remember her if we'd met.

I'm definitely sure I don't want to talk about hockey though, so I don't go fishing in the *do we know each other* waters. Instead, I return to the clothing hunt and wait for her to go next.

"So what's yours?" she asks. "Your favorite color?"

"Do people still have favorite colors?"

"You just asked me mine! Are boys not allowed to have a favorite color?"

I smile, shaking my head as I find a cute pair of pants and lift the hanger from the rack. "I don't really have one."

"Everyone has one. Some people are just more aware of it. For others it's subconscious. So what's yours?"

I consider her heart-shaped face, her pink lips, her bright-eyed attitude. Her mouth that hasn't met a question she doesn't have a comeback for. Then, her eyes. They caught my attention from the second I saw her outside the gallery. "Blue."

She freezes for a second, like my answer's sinking in,

then maybe it hits her, because she rolls her lips together, then says crisply, "Noted."

Jerking her gaze away from me, she turns to the black pants I've grabbed, taking them from me.

Hold the fuck on. Did I read her all wrong? Maybe the blush was because I embarrassed her? Maybe she legit needs help, the *very single* convo aside. I home in on that and give her the Phillips-head screwdriver she needs. "Let's get you a white top to go with that, and some new shoes."

Quickly, I choose some options and hand them to her. She heads to the dressing room, the door clicking shut. I wander around the store, getting a little distance as I chew on the best way to figure out where her mind's at when the door swings open again.

I spin around.

She's standing in front of it in a pair of pants that flare at the bottom and a white sweatshirt that slopes off the shoulder and shows off a sliver of pale flesh. And a sparkly belly button ring I want to lick.

My mouth goes dry. My mind goes haywire.

She juts out a hip. "What do you think, *honey*?"

Like she said to me back at the gallery when we were role-playing. Maybe I didn't read her wrong. "It's very, very you...*sweetie*," I say.

"Good." She takes a deep breath, then her voice pitches up as she adds, "Because I would love to wear it to take you out for an ice cream right now. To say thank you."

That is so very specific. It's not the typical *let's have a drink*. Not that I'd say no to a drink with her. "Ice cream?" I ask, my improv skills flying out the window, because it's a little surreal, her question, given where my mind was earlier.

She swallows, then nods. "Do you hate ice cream?"

"No. God no." My brow creases. "Who hates ice cream?"

"Ice cream haters?" She sounds nervous.

"Not me. Definitely not me. I'm just a little freaked out that you're reading my mind."

She breathes out a sigh of relief. "I had a feeling since you were kind of into the ice cream porn earlier. When we walked past The Scoop a while ago, you stared at it like it was the source of all your fantasies."

Pretty sure she is my fantasy right now. "Let's get ice cream. But on one condition."

"Okay," she says, a little tentative.

I step closer and set a hand on her arm once again, watching as her breath hitches her chest. "It's a date."

Her smile sends a shiver down my spine. "It's a date."

I set a hand on her back and walk her to the register, making a mental note to text the guys and let them know I'm bailing. When we leave, with her old clothes in a bag and her new ones on, I barely give a second thought to my car, several blocks away. I can get a parking ticket for all I care. I'm not doing a damn thing to throw a wrench in the first date I've looked forward to in more than a year.

That's the real surreal part of tonight.

5

BIRDS DO IT

Josie

Just because I haven't been on a lot of first dates doesn't mean I don't know the basics. Research queen here. And a queen needs her phone, especially since I'm going to put my location tracker on for Maeve.

I soldier on for another half mile of free-range boobing as we walk till we reach my friend's yellow building. "I'll just grab my phone and be right back."

"Take your time," Wesley says, then pops in earbuds and leans against the railing as I unlock the door.

Buzzing with excitement, I rush inside, then wrap my arm around my chest as I hurtle up the three flights of stairs in my new flip-flops till I reach B4. I uncrinkle the napkin I've been clutching all night, then punch in the long code lightning fast, and hallelujah!

I've never been so happy a door opened in my life.

I set down the bag with my T-shirt, slippers, and scarf, then grab my phone. I clutch it tight. "You naughty thing,"

I say, admonishing it, but really...*me*. Even though it wasn't my fault. I was a hero earlier, saving that kid from sliding down a wobbly step. And look where it got me. A date with a hottie. I slide open my phone, finding a text from my mom, then one from my brother, responding to my *I'm here* message. I open his first as I hustle to my suitcase to grab a bra.

> Christian: Hey, J! Glad you made it safely, and welcome to San Francisco. Sorry it took me a while to reply. Liv was having contractions but they turned out to be Braxton Hicks.

> Josie: OMG. Did you go to the hospital?

> Christian: No, but she was swearing and cursing at me while I dialed the nurse on call.

> Josie: Aww, I feel so bad for you getting yelled at.

> Christian: Funny thing—she has no sympathy for me either. Anyway, do you need anything? I can send over groceries if you want. Or some takeout. You name it. But be careful when you're walking around the city, K? Stay alert. Or better yet, I could get you a bodyguard?

I roll my eyes at my overprotective brother as I tug off the sleeves of my white top.

Josie: Do you have a bodyguard for Liv? If not, I don't need one.

Christian: I'll send over some mace and a pocketknife. Like she carries.

Josie: Stop worrying about me! Worry about Liv! How is she doing now?

I slide on my bra at the speed of sound as I read his reply.

Christian: Let me check. Hold on.

Christian: She says she's the size of Alaska and to get the F away from her.

Josie: Yep, she's definitely in the "don't do this to me again" phase of pregnancy. Good luck!

Christian: Mace is on its way.

I stick one arm back in the sleeve as I spot my mom's note.

Mom: Did you hear Liv had Braxton Hicks? Is she OK? Should you go see her?

To do what? Help her give birth to babies that aren't ready to come? But that's typical of Mom to focus on Christian. As I pull my sweatshirt down, I dictate a response.

> Josie: If she needs someone to read to the babies, I'll be right there!

Next, I send a quick text to Maeve as I rush through the living room.

> Josie: I'm getting an ice cream with the hottie who saved me. But I can still meet you later!

I yank the door open, then stop, spinning around to grab my scarf from the bag. For good luck. I toss it around my neck jauntily since that's the *only* way you should toss a scarf, then take off down the steps. I slow at the ground floor when my phone pings with her reply.

> Maeve: I'm sorry, ma'am. But did you say you're getting banged by the NOT UNATTRACTIVE hottie who saved you?

> Josie: Ice cream, Maeve. We're getting ice cream.

Maeve: New slang, obviously. Also, I was right, I was right, I was so, so right.

Josie: It's just ice cream. Also, I'm turning my location tracker on for you.

As I'm nearing the door, her reply lands.

Maeve: I can't wait till it shows you're on the couch in my place having fun.

Josie: Maeve!

Maeve: Also, I can entertain myself tonight. Don't worry about me walking in on you. I'll go to that 24-hour bookstore while you're busy. Just watch out for the spring on my couch. It's loose and might stab you in the ass. Solution? Have him bend you over the back of the sofa. Sex is just better like that anyway. And that's your sex tip from your girl, Maeve.

I exit the building and when I look up from the phone, I'm grinning as I shake my head. Wesley's on the stoop where I left him, checking me out with curious eyes. He pops out the earbuds and stuffs them into his jeans pockets. "Something good?"

I am definitely not telling him what No-Filter Maeve said. But I can give him a little something. "I was telling my friend about you."

His smile feels like it's the same vintage as mine. A

robust *I want you too* wine from this year. No, from today. Harvested this evening. "So she knows your whereabouts?"

"Yes, but also..." I pause. Am I really doing this? Yes, I am. "But also because she likes to be right."

"About what?"

"I'll tell you if it happens," I say, teasing him.

"Can't wait," he says, and his voice is dripping with undertones.

We head down the steps, but we don't go to The Scoop. Instead, I tell him there's an ice cream shop a couple blocks away. "I just looked it up. There's one called The Hand Dipper nearby," I say, then...it hits me. "That sounds vaguely dirty."

"Just vaguely?"

"Okay, completely."

"Perfect then," he says, and along the way we pass the record shop I spotted earlier, where he tells me he bought the new Ben Rogers album. I have no idea who that is, but I say "cool" and make a mental note to look them up later.

We reach The Hand Dipper quickly. The name is etched into the glass along with a tongue darting past a pair of lips, licking a cone.

"Definitely not vague at all," he says, holding open the door for me like he did at the clothing shop earlier.

As we walk to the counter he sets a hand on my back. A possessive one that covers the fabric of my sweatshirt and my exposed skin. That makes me shiver too. When we reach the case and check out the tubs of mouth-watering desserts, he murmurs, "Yup. Ice cream porn all right."

"You should be happy then."

"Very happy," he says, in the same confident, raspy way he said *very single* earlier.

We check out the flavors—balsamic strawberry, lavender honey, cinnamon and champagne. I'm definitely not in Kansas anymore. He turns to me. "Want to try a bunch?"

I want to try him. But first, I need ice cream courage. "What do you think is good for a first night in town? I just moved here."

He gives me a quick once-over. Something he's been doing a lot tonight. "You definitely need the cinnamon and champagne then."

"Perfect. I'll have a single scoop in a cup." I shouldn't be licking a cone in front of him like it's a sweet, icy dick.

"You don't want to try it first?"

I shake my head. "No. I'm taking a leap."

"A woman who knows her mind. I like it."

He catches the attention of the man behind the counter with a "Hey there." The guy is wearing a Renegades cap for one of the city's football teams.

"Hey," he says to Wesley, furrowing his brow, like he's studying him. "Are you...on the football team?"

Wesley laughs politely but shakes his head. "No, man. I don't play football."

"Sorry," he says. "You just looked familiar."

"No worries. It's all good," Wesley says. "I'm in the sports business though. On the assets side."

The server's brow pinches like that doesn't compute. "Ah," the guy says, then satisfied, perhaps, with Wesley being in finance rather than on the field, he returns to rinsing a steel scoop.

And Wesley resumes looking my way. This is probably where I should say what I do for a living. But all the dating research I've done says focusing on someone's job—theirs or yours—is a red flag that you're boring, or just into money, or that your question might remind them of an annoying co-worker.

I follow his lead and keep it simple with, "I'm in the book business."

There. It's true, and we can move on.

"Cool," he says, then does exactly that by asking, "Have you spent time in San Francisco before?"

I could tell him my brother lives here. That I've been to a couple Sea Dogs hockey games over the last few years, though not that many since I've been so busy with my master's in library and information science. But I've spent most of my life in my big brother's big shadow. I don't need to spend tonight talking about my semi-famous sibling. We might wind up in a convo about asset management in the sports business, and that might put me to sleep. Besides, knowing those details might compromise the integrity of item number one on the list—which is starting to look more and more like a possibility. The less we know about the other, the more faithful I'll be to Aunt Greta's list. Best to just be fun, talk about hobbies, and the moment. "I have. But I was usually fully dressed before."

Wesley laughs, and I pat myself on the back for a perfect deflection. "I'm glad to hear that. Not that you don't look great in slippers."

"I rock a pair, don't I?"

"You do. But wait till you see mine," he says, and that feels promising too since his slippers are—just a guess—at his home.

In his bedroom.

If I get another couple signs he's game for more, I'll go for it. I'll jump even though it's been a while since I've been on the horse, and I've only ever ridden in one saddle. But I've seen a lot of saddles on screen. And read about them in books. My imagination is not lacking.

The server finishes scooping and sets down a strawberry balsamic cup for Wesley, then the cinnamon and champagne for me. I reach for my phone to pay, but Wesley covers my hand with his. My breath stutters. His skin is warm. His hand is strong. How would it feel on my back as he bends me over the couch? Damn that Maeve.

"I lied when I said yes to your offer. I lied because I'm buying," Wesley says.

"But you've already been so generous," I say, though I know it's a feeble protest.

Especially when he lifts a brow playfully but says nothing, like he's letting me imagine other ways he might be giving.

Oh I'm imagining, universe. I'm definitely imagining.

With an uncommon speed, he whips out his phone and taps it on the screen to pay, then gives a tip that doubles the amount.

"Thanks, man," the Renegades fan says.

"You're welcome."

The sports asset management business must be a good one.

Wesley picks up both our cups, then heads toward the counter by the window, pulling out a white metal stool for me. We both sit and he lifts his cup like he's offering it to toast. "To your friend being right."

Tell me you know what she said without telling me you know what she said.

"I'll...lick to that."

"Me too," he says with a smirk, then holds my gaze

with so much confidence that my stomach flips. A blast of heat rushes through my body.

We "clink" paper cups, then he takes a spoonful of his ice cream and I do the same. He watches me the whole time with those warm brown eyes, flecked with gold. More specifically, he watches my mouth, and I like it.

When I set down the spoon, he says, "Your scar is fucking hot."

He's fucking hot. And blunt. I run a finger across the indentation on my chin. No one has complimented it before. Certainly not John, my longtime college boyfriend who became my post-college boyfriend since inertia kept us together till we finally petered out. "Thank you. I fell off a bike," I say.

"When you were learning to ride?"

"Yes." I don't tell him I was chasing Christian as a kid. That I was trying to keep up with my big brother. That I felt like I'd tried to be like him for so long in everything. That I even tried to play hockey to be like him. But I'm not athletic. Besides, books were, and are, better companions than athletic gear. "I'm not particularly sporty, but I did end up learning how to ride."

"So you got back on," he says, his deep, steady voice thrumming through me, turning me on.

"I did," I say, then take another spoonful. He does the same, then offers me his.

"Wanna try?"

"Sure," I say, then hand him mine.

I take a lick of the balsamic strawberry. "It's sweet, and a little tart."

He licks the cinnamon and champagne off my spoon with an approving hum. "A little like you, I suspect, since you smell like cinnamon."

Warmth blooms in my chest. "You noticed," I say, but he's a noticer, so this shouldn't be a surprise. It's nice though. "It's my lotion."

"It's got a little kick to it," he says.

Do I have a kick to me? In some ways, I probably do. In other ways, I don't entirely know. But tonight is for boldness, so I add, "Like me."

That earns me a heated grin. He takes one more bite, like he's savoring every ounce of the treat. "And yours tastes...a little forbidden," he says, and arousal builds in my belly. I don't know why ice cream is forbidden to him. I don't even really care. I just like the way he talks to me and looks at me. Like he wants to know me and eat me up.

He gives me back my forbidden cup, then says in that same heated voice, "What do you think of San Francisco so far?"

The air between us crackles. "I'm liking it," I say, my skin tingling. We're not talking about the city.

"Yeah, me too," he says. "And your first night here? Is it what you imagined?"

"Nothing has been like I imagined," I say playfully, flashing back to Big Bird and Ms. Peck. "Even the pigeon sex."

But for the first time in a while Wesley looks thrown off. "Okaaaaay."

Shoot. I'm pretty sure pigeon sex is not on a list of acceptable date topics. I shake my head quickly. "It's not like that." But what do I even mean by *it's not like that?* I scramble to explain myself better. "I meant I took a video of two pigeons banging..." Nope, that's not better.

No wonder I haven't attempted the first item on my list before. I am a hot mess when it comes to flirting.

But Wesley doesn't let my comment go. "You recorded the bird portion of the birds and the bees?"

"I did," I say with a wince since it's too late to take it back. "Do you want to say goodnight right now?"

His hand comes down on mine again, covering it, squeezing it. "No. I want you to tell me how they do it."

With a smile and a fresh surge of adrenaline, I give him a quick overview of pigeon copulation, and soon he's laughing. When the laughter subsides, he says, "I'm not sure how to top that. I was going to say we could check out the Golden Gate Bridge or the Palace of Fine Arts. But once you've seen pigeons fornicating, everything else is downhill."

Except...

I can't believe I'm about to do this. I can't believe I'm using my pornithography as my lubricant. But what do I have to lose?

I take a deep breath...

But he goes first, speaking in a quieter, bedroom voice. "You're blushing again, Josie. You did that in the store."

I know what moment he means. I know what I was thinking about then too—item number one. I was weighing if I was going to do it or not. "I did?"

"Yeah. It's pretty when you blush. Just like your blue eyes."

That's why he said blue's his favorite color.

No time like the present. No night like tonight. Get out of your comfort zone. I already did that when I walked half-naked around the city. This next step should be easy. I take one more bite of my ice cream for courage, then set it down.

But Wesley is faster once again, asking, "Can I try your ice cream a second time?"

He really does like the dessert. I hand him the cup, and he takes it with a quick thanks, but then sets it down on the counter.

I frown, confused. "You didn't taste..."

He rises from his stool, closes the short distance between us then leans in, dipping his face close to mine.

The air whooshes from my chest. A shiver runs down my spine. For a long, delicious second—or several—he waits. Like he's letting the moment ripen. His gaze drops to my mouth, then he lifts his hand. I expect him to cup my cheek or thread it through my hair.

Instead, he presses his palm against my collarbone, under the scarf, spreading his fingers wide against the exposed flesh. I go hot everywhere. It's possible my panties are on fire.

He drops his mouth to mine, our lips connecting at last. His kiss is soft, heady, a little on the sweet side. Then it's tart, from his ice cream.

He kisses the corner of my mouth, then slides his hand up the side of my neck. His thumb glides over the hinge of my jaw as he deepens the kiss. I part my lips for him, my mind popping, my skin tingling. As he kisses me, his scruff rubs lightly against my skin, the sandpaper scratch of it making my knees weak. I feel like my bones are melting right along with the ice cream as he kisses me more—the kind of kiss that's so much more than a taste.

I part my legs slightly.

I'm keenly aware we're in an ice cream shop. But I'm pretty sure I've stopped caring since I invite him a little closer. He moves in, nudging my knees a little wider so he can stand between my thighs. Good thing I'm sitting because the move turns my legs to jelly.

Our tongues skate together. He presses more firmly on

my jaw, tipping my head back the slightest bit. The move makes me shudder.

And that seems to turn him on more, judging from the passion in the kiss, the wrap of his arm around my back.

He murmurs as he kisses me, a desperate kind of growl that sends me spinning. I lift a hand and grab at the open neckline of his dress shirt. He kicks up the kiss a few notches. Then, like it costs him every ounce of control, he ends it and yanks himself away. His eyes are dark. His breathing is staggered.

"How did it taste?" I ask.

"I might need to try it again...and again...and again."

Same here. This is it. This is absolutely it. He's item number one. "There's something I've always wanted to do but never have," I say, and nothing is going to stop me now.

His irises say *go the fuck on.* "Yeah?"

I pause, then find my courage as I tackle the first item on my list. "Have a one-night stand with a sexy stranger."

6

THE FIRST CHECKMARK

Josie

It's a weird thought—*my aunt would be so proud of me*. But it lodges in my brain as we take off, Wesley grabbing my hand and threading those long fingers through mine.

He holds it tight, possessively. I like it.

On the street, Wesley says, "Your place, mine, or a hotel? And the hotel's on me."

From the clothes to the ice cream to the room, I'm sensing a pattern with this man. He's...*giving*. Part of me wants to do the polite thing and decline, but I'm mixing it up tonight big time. "Since I'd rather not get stabbed in the ass with a couch spring, let's do the hotel."

He gives me a *what the hell* look.

"My friend has a couch with a bad spring," I quickly explain. "But do you have condoms and are you...safe?"

I've read plenty of articles, including "Top Twenty Tips for Having a Great One-Night Stand" on *The Dating Pool* website. Being safe in all the ways is one of them.

"Yes. Negative. And I have condoms."

"Me too. The first, that is," I say.

Ten minutes later, he's at the front desk of The Resort, a nearby hotel. I give him some space to check in, since it seems eaves-droppy to be right next to him as the clerk informs him of the mini-bar costs and how much incidentals are.

I hang back next to a waterfall structure, with a gurgling stream sluicing against a black stone wall, as Wesley chats amiably with the man behind the counter. Wesley's that kind of guy. He has an easy, friendly way about him with everyone from the guy in the ice cream shop to the clerk.

As they chat, I text Maeve.

> Josie: I'm at The Resort!

> Maeve: I know, my little tiger! I know! And I can't wait for your report.

> Josie: Don't wait up.

> Maeve: Best words ever, bestie. Especially since it's way past your bedtime.

Yup, I'm definitely getting out of my comfort zone tonight with Mister Asset Management. Once he's checked in, he strides across the lobby, flipping the key card between his thumb and forefinger over and over. He doesn't miss it once. Those are some nimble fingers.

"Ready?"

"Very, very ready," I say, repeating the adjective he used earlier.

"That's very, very good."

A minute later, the elevator door whisks closed, and it's just us. He turns to me, then tugs on my hand, jerking me against him. "What do you like, Josie?"

I like the outline of his hard cock against me right now. I like his scruff. I like his firm chest and his biceps that go on for millennia.

"In bed," he adds, when I don't answer right away. But he's not pushy. "So I can give it to you. What you're into."

Is this a thing guys do? Ask what you like? Hunting for an answer, I swallow, flashing back to the porn I've watched, the scenes I've read, the fantasies I've played out.

I keep coming back to Maeve's suggestion. I'm not really the most experienced girl when it comes to, well, what I'm into. But what I lack in experience I, evidently, make up for in gusto tonight. *Here I go, San Francisco.* "Can you bend me over the bed and fuck me hard?"

He breathes out in a rush of air, full of arousal as his eyes flash, like he's won the jackpot at the slot machines. Then, in a rasp of a voice, he says, "Josie, I can and I fucking will."

He seals his dirty promise with a hot, deep kiss that has me seeing stars.

When he breaks it, we're at the tenth floor and soon, at the room. Once inside, he kicks the door closed then reaches for me again, jerking me against him, and with a quickness I've never experienced before, he lifts me up.

I wrap my legs around him, laughing. "You're strong. Must be all those assets you lift."

"You're quick with that mouth. Must be all those books

you read," he says, then somehow, some way, he kisses me as he carries me koala-style to the bed. Talk about multitasking. He's like the hero in an adventure tale—he can lasso the prize and leap across raging waters. Can he deliver orgasms in a single bound?

Turn the page and find out, gentle reader.

When he sets me down on the bed, I kick off my flip-flops and unwrap my scarf, tossing it on the floor. Greta will understand.

He toes off his shoes, then climbs over me. I expect more kisses, but instead, he pushes up my sweatshirt. "This has been driving me crazy since I first saw it," he says, then presses a hot kiss to my belly, flicking his teeth across the ring. Oh, I think I'm into that. Gasping, I arch closer to his touch.

"I was hoping it meant you wanted to be kissed all over," he says.

"Try me," I tease. "And find out."

He grabs the hem of the sweatshirt he bought for me, whisking it up. "Looks great on." Tugs it over my head. "Looks even better off."

He drags his teeth over his bottom lip as he roams those sinful brown eyes over me. I shiver under his hot stare. That seems to excite him, my reaction, judging from the hiss in his breath. The heat in his irises. The bulge in his jeans.

"Josie, Josie, Josie," he repeats, shaking his head in admiration. Then, he's all determination and desire as he kisses me thoroughly, starting at my belly button, traveling up my stomach, stopping to lift his face and say, "Yeah, drives me crazier."

I smile, then sigh happily as he pays a visit to my tits, then frees them.

"Perfect," he murmurs as he cups my tits, then buries his face between them. But he doesn't stay there long. He moves to my right breast, flicking a delicious circle around the nipple, then drawing it into his mouth. Then nipping me lightly.

"Oh god," I say, but it's more like a half-moan, half-yelp.

"You like that." It's less a question, more a statement.

"I think I'm into it," I tease.

"Let's be sure," he says, then bites a little harder. I arch into him in answer. He moves to the other one, and yes, I'm very into having my tits played with, as it turns out.

And he's into playing with them. He squeezes and kneads, sucks and kisses, then lets out a long, hungry rumble. "Fuck, you taste good everywhere," he says as he rises up and meets my face.

His gaze is borderline feral, and I love it. But he's wearing too many clothes. He's too sexy to be clothed.

"I wonder if you do too," I say, then I push up, ready to discover.

"Find out," he says.

In no time, I'm unbuttoning his shirt and he's shrugging it off, and holy fucking hell. His muscles have muscles. His biceps are ripped. His abs are illegal. A blue bruise decorates the side of his stomach, and a small scar travels across his right wrist. "I bet you didn't get this falling off a bike," I say of the scar.

With a laugh, he shakes his head, then lets me explore him more.

The best part? The ink that crawls down his arms. Sunbursts on his shoulders and biceps, a couple music notes on his forearms, and a line drawing of a cute dog on his wrist. That silver chain I was drawn to earlier gleams around his neck, thick links resting against his skin. I can finally find out how he tastes right there, and the prospect makes me giddy. My hands journey across his pecs and up over his collarbone, my fingertips playing with the cool metal against his skin. I lean in and press my lips to his throat. He growls, a low sound as I savor the woodsy, clean scent. Like the forest trees from my hometown in Maine. Like a mountain stream.

Like a stranger who saved me tonight.

I lean back and stare a little longer. My eyes have never feasted so well. "Where did you get this body? Did you order it from the Department of Abs and Pecs?"

His smile is pleased. A bit proud but not cocky. "I work out a little," he says dryly.

"Liar," I say as I run my nails down his sturdy pecs, carved from, I dunno, titanium maybe. I travel down to his abs. "I mean, you've never skipped core day."

"True," he admits.

"And these arms," I say, exploring them from forearm to shoulder. My jaw might be on the floor. It's possible I'm drooling. "I'm sorry but I'm totally objectifying you right now."

"I'm not sorry. But fair warning, in about one minute I'm going to tear off those panties, spread your thighs, and taste what I've done to you tonight."

I know what I'm into now. *His mouth.* "First, can I objectify your cock with my mouth?"

Dragging a hand through his hair in slow mo, he stares like he can't quite believe he found me outside a gallery dressed in slippers and a T-shirt. And like he can't believe his luck. He bends, cups my cheeks, and presses a hot kiss to my lips. "Yes."

I'm not sure who's inhabiting my body tonight. I'm not sure I've ever felt this...*forward*.

But I am sure I've never been this turned on, this excited. In no time, he sheds his jeans and his boxer briefs, freeing his cock. It's as sexy as the rest of him. Thick, hard, and with a drop of liquid arousal beading at the tip.

I push him down on the bed and climb over him, then right when I'm about to have some fun with his dick, I remember...my glasses.

I pop up. "Just a sec."

I crawl across the bed to set them down on the nightstand, then he tackles me by the waist. "Can't stand these clothes a second longer," he says, then he's flipping me onto my back and undressing me.

Skimming my pants down my legs, then my undies.

Everything's happening so quickly, and for a few seconds, I'm no longer the bold girl. I'm vulnerable. Completely naked in a hotel room with a stranger. A sexy stranger, but still a stranger.

A stranger who's...

Oh.

Oh god.

Oh, my.

Oh, fuck.

Wesley's objectifying me right now. With his talented mouth. With his wicked lips. With his fantastic tongue. The man has slid between my thighs and is spreading me open. He's groaning and sighing, flicking his tongue up and down my center, then sucking on my clit.

He laps me up as he glides his big hands under me, scooping me up, squeezing my ass, bringing me even closer to his mouth.

I feel like his dessert. Like I'm the ice cream porn he was really craving all day. Like The Hand Dipper date was part of the foreplay.

For a second, he stops. "Put your hands in my hair. It's more fun that way. You can control the pace," he says.

Oh, right. Good idea. I slide my fingers through his strands and jerk him close. He rumbles against my pussy, then blows on it. I suck in a breath that turns into flames inside me.

His mouth is back on me in seconds, and he eats me thoroughly. I'm tugging on his hair as he's squeezing my ass. He kisses and sucks and *worships*. And it's so decadent. It doesn't take long at all till I'm rocking against his scruffy jaw, then gasping, crying, screaming.

I come hard and fast. And loud. So loud that when he finally stops, he's chuckling. "I'm going to need to hear that again. It's good for my ego," he says.

"And my pussy," I say, still catching my breath.

His smile burns off. "That's it." He reaches for my hand and tugs me up and off the bed. My feet hit the floor. "Time to fuck you hard."

I frown. "Isn't it my turn to objectify you?"

But he's no longer in the mood to indulge me, it seems, since he spins me around and bends me over the mattress. "Hands on the bed. Ass in the air," he instructs.

Something in his voice has me scrambling. My generous, helpful knight in shining armor is a little rough in bed, a lot dirty. He presses a big hand to the small of my back, pushing me down.

A flame sparks higher in me. Then hotter when he grabs my ass cheeks and squeezes them appreciatively. "The things I want to do..."

Is Wesley an ass man? Am I an ass woman? I don't

even know, but my body likes whatever he's doing to me since my bones are dissolving.

But he lets go. Bends over, pushes my hair to the side. "Be right back."

What? "Where..."

"Stay here."

Um, I wasn't going anywhere. Curiosity has got a hold of me so I crane my neck and watch him retreat, and yup. I'm an ass woman. That is one fine backside. Firm, and big.

He strides into the bathroom. A second later, water streams into the sink. Then stops. He returns, roots around in his jeans, and brings out his wallet. Then he fishes out a condom and meets my gaze. "You like watching me, don't you?" he asks with a cocky rise in his lips.

"I do," I admit, my eyes locked on him.

He holds the condom in one hand, then drops the other to his cock. Gives it a stroke.

I swallow.

His lips curve up.

He gives it a rougher tug.

I clench my thighs.

"Bet you'd watch me if you saw me jerking it to you."

It feels like a filthy game we're playing. Like we're testing out scenarios in our one-night. "Bet you'd do the same," I taunt.

His smile is full of wicked approval. He gives another shuttle of his fist till he's squeezing out a drop of pre-come from the head of his cock. I squirm. He reaches closer, offers it to me. "Suck it off," he says, a clear order.

And yes, I'm into that too. I part my lips, and he slides his thumb into my mouth. He tastes like clean hands. He washed his hands before he put a finger in my mouth. That's some swoon-worthy attention to detail. I close my eyes and moan around his finger.

"Show me," he says. "Show me how you wanted to suck my cock."

This man keeps me on my toes. I open wider, saying, "More."

He gives me another finger, and I suck harder on both. He groans, and I shudder.

After a few more seconds, he eases out. Smacks my ass lightly, then rolls on the condom. Nudging my legs a little wider, he notches the head of his cock against me, then sinks in.

I bow my back. Grip the covers. Moan.

"Yesssss," he murmurs as he pauses, takes a beat. Then he sinks all the way in, filling me up.

I'm stretched. The pressure is intense. But so is the crackle of pleasure. The sharp, hot jolts that rush through me. Slowly, like a tease, he eases out almost all the way, leaving me wanting more.

But he doesn't give it to me. He takes his sweet time, fucking into me slowly, inch by inch, then easing out. After he's done that four or five times, I'm panting and begging.

"Wesley," I moan, needy.

"Yes, baby?"

"Harder," I demand.

"Ah, that's right. You wanted a good, hard fucking tonight," he says, then he slams into me.

I cry out from the intensity. "Oh fuck."

He stills. "Okay?"

"That was a good *oh fuck*," I say, my breath already shallow.

He grips my ass tighter and drives into me, his hips flush against mine, then eases out again. Making me ache for more. Making me beg.

"Please," I gasp.

He sinks into me again, filling me till there's no room left. Then he covers me with his body, his chest to my back, his arm banding around my tits. His mouth against my neck. His teeth nipping at my flesh.

It's intimate the way he's holding me, and aggressive the way he's using me. I feel held and used all at once, and it's so damn good. This is a kind of hard, rough sex I didn't know I was into.

But it turns out, I am.

I'm clawing at the sheets as he pounds into me. I'm moaning and gasping. He's grunting and cursing. My cells light up with each thrust. When I'm close, obviously close, he lets go of my tits, moves that hand up the back of my neck and into my hair.

He tugs on some strands, and that's it. It sends me over the cliff. My brain blanks out. It goes offline as my body shakes.

The orgasm hurtles through me, a burst of pleasure and light and fire. I'm calling his name as he drives into me, then stills, jerks and groans for days.

Another slow pump. Another moan. Then he slumps over me, brushes my hair from my neck, and presses a tender kiss there.

He's somehow filthy and sweet. And the way he fucks me is the best welcome to San Francisco ever.

* * *

A little later, we're cleaned up and in bed, flicking through the channels, but finding nothing exciting to watch. Since, well, it's regular TV.

I'm not sure how this works—hotel sex. Do we stay the night? It's not even midnight. It's eleven. And the day feels like it's been ninety-six hours long and I'm tired, but I haven't had dinner, even though the ice cream was real good. My stomach speaks up, growling.

Rude bitch.

He laughs. "You hungry, Josie?"

"That's a yes."

"Let's get some food."

I frown. "Do I have to get dressed?"

He scoffs. "No way."

Soon, we're dining on sushi in bed from a nearby restaurant, and he's telling me about his favorite cafés in the city and the best place to get a latte, and I tell him about the places I want to see. But we don't trade numbers. Or last names. We don't say *I'd love to see you again*. And we don't make plans.

Still, there's one very important thing I want to say. My aunt gave me a list of the top things she's never regretted, and since I've *finally* started tackling the items on the list, and making them my own, it seems right to let number one know how I feel. I draw a soldiering breath then say, "That thing I wanted to do?"

He adopts a perplexed look. "What would that be?"

I swat his biceps. "Have a one-night stand with a sexy stranger."

"Ah, that thing. Yes, I recall it now."

He's making this so easy. Still, it feels important to get this right. When someone you love gives you instructions before they go, it seems like you should handle them with care. Wesley's part of the list now. Part of this new history of me. The first checkmark. So I meet his eyes and say, "I'm glad it was you."

He dips his face, smiling. When he lifts it, he locks his gaze with mine again, then says, "Me too."

There's an intensity in those warm, soulful eyes that makes my stomach flip. That makes me wonder what it would be like if he was more than a stranger. Briefly, I toy with the idea of asking if he wants to hang out, but there's no item on Aunt Greta's list or mine for anything more than one night. My new job starts in two more days—on Tuesday. My new life.

Best to be true to the plan.

We're both quiet for a beat, and maybe he's unsure of what happens next when he says, "So the night ended better than it began?"

"It really did," I say, then I yawn, fighting to stay awake.

"Go to sleep," he says, on a yawn too. "Sleep makes a perfect one-night stand even more perfect."

I take off my glasses again. We dim the lights, slide under the covers, and crash into slumber.

I'm dead to the world until I get up to pee early in the morning. When I trudge back to bed, I fumble around for my phone to check the time and squint at the screen.

Christian: Get ready to be an aunt! Liv is in labor for real, and the babies are almost here!

Then he sends me the address to the hospital.

I bolt upright, wide awake despite the fact it's five a.m. In a flurry, I jam on my glasses, yank on clothes, find a tube of toothpaste and smear some on my teeth, then hunt for a pad of paper.

Finding one, I scribble out a note, thanking Wesley.

Then I go, leaving him behind and taking the sexiest memory of my life with me into the early dawn.

7

GLASS SCARF

Wesley

The fading scent of cinnamon drifts past my nose. That's a real nice way to wake up. But there are even better ways to rise. I stretch an arm across the bed, reaching for Josie. She's adventurous. Maybe she'll be up for one more round.

"Hey," I murmur, my voice gravelly from the last remnants of sleep.

She doesn't answer. The room's quiet. My hand makes contact with...a pillow. My eyes float open.

Pushing up on my elbows, I tilt my head, listening for any sounds of a shower perhaps. It's dead silent. My shoulders slump, but I'm a glutton for punishment, since I swing my legs out of bed and pad to the bathroom. Just in case she's, I dunno, quietly applying hotel lotion.

But it's empty too. I take care of business, then hunt around the room for my clothes. I pull on my boxer briefs before sitting on the end of the bed, more contemplative than I like to be first thing in the morning.

Or, really, ever.

I drag a hand through my messy hair, missing Josie's hands in it making it messier.

Fact is, I wasn't just hoping for another round with her. I was hoping to get her number. To ask her to hang out again. Sure, we said it was a one-night stand. But some one-night stands should turn into two nights. Or three.

I'd been planning to suggest as much when we woke up. It's been a while since I met someone I clicked with so easily. Someone who wasn't into me for the number on my back. Or, on the flip side, someone who didn't hate what it represented. Though hate may be a strong word for my ex's feelings about hockey. Anna looked down on it, it turns out—and me. "You need a life beyond hockey. The sport won't last forever, you know," she'd said.

Really, it won't?

"But you don't like anything besides hockey," she'd said. "You never want to discuss the world or ideas. You don't even read the articles and think pieces I send you."

No shit.

I'd rather take a puck to the chin than read a fucking essay.

And this trip down Romance Memory Lane was brought to you by The One-Night Stand That Ended Too Soon. But...it's for the best. Just because Josie and I had one great night doesn't mean we'd vibe beyond ice cream and the bedroom and random conversations that were—let's face it—easy to have, given how we met. It's not hard to talk to someone who's wearing next to nothing as she bargains to gain entrance to a snooty art gallery.

Besides, my ex wasn't all wrong. Hockey is my life. I

eat, breathe, and sleep it when the season starts, and that's what's happening in a few more days. Resigned to not seeing Josie again, I push up from the bed, get dressed, and return to the bathroom to scrub some toothpaste on my teeth. After, I splash water on my face.

That done, I return to the room, looking for my wallet when I catch sight of a white notepad by the entrance to the room.

Huh.

I head over to it. The notepad is propped up next to the door. My name is on the first sheet, with an extra flourish on the Y. She left it there, so I wouldn't miss it, and my chest pounds with excitement.

I grab it in record time, turning the page. Her handwriting's neat, with plenty of space between the words, and I'm grateful for that.

Once upon a time, I moved to San Francisco. My first night in town, I met a guy who reminded me of a book.

No one has ever—in my whole life—compared me to a book before. That's like comparing a truck to a blanket. They don't go together. With some skepticism, I flip to the next page.

Because he fucked like a page-turner you didn't want to put down.

And I crack up. A deep belly laugh first thing in the morning. That's so her. You think she's going to say something sweet, then it turns out she's a dirty girl. With a genuine smile, I turn one more page.

Maybe I'll see you around the city. It's big, but it's small too. You never know...

XO Josie

Is it just me or does this note feel a little like a clue? Like she's a siren in a video game, darting down a passageway, saying *come find me*.

I'd follow her. I'd look for her. I'd chase her and catch her. Maybe that's what this is. A little treasure hunt. A riddle, perhaps.

But that's stupid. If she wanted to get together, she'd have left her number. Not a series of clues. It's fine she didn't. Just fine.

I take the three pages, rip them off carefully, and fold them in half, then quarters. I resume the hunt for my wallet so I can save these.

Wait. Where the hell is it? Did she take off with my wallet? Is that why she's gone?

My skin goes cold. There's no cash, but my ID and credit cards are in there. What if last night was some long con into identity theft?

You've seen too many movies, man.

Or maybe not enough. My pulse spikes as I search the room, but then it slams hard against my rib cage in relief when I spot the vegan leather wallet on the floor by my side of the bed.

I kneel to grab it when I catch sight of a swath of black fabric. Is that...?

I grab it from under the bed.

I am not responsible for the smile that takes over my face. Fate is. Because yeah, it's a motherfucking clue. This scarf she left. This note she wrote.

This scarf is a glass slipper, and I'm taking it. I know where she lives—in that yellow building on the block by the record store.

I check out of the hotel and walk several blocks to my car, which is littered with tickets, and I don't even care.

I've got a damn good excuse to see my Cinderella again.

* * *

That afternoon, I'm racking the bench press next to Asher in the Sea Dogs' weight room when Max comes in, all glower and attitude. The grumpy goalie travels with his own storm cloud. "You missed last night, Newman." He grunts as he passes me, heading for the free weights.

At the start of practice today, Asher gave me a hard time for being a no-show at pool, even though I texted those jackasses last night while I was waiting for Josie outside her place. Told them I wouldn't make it. But Max is wired to give me a hard time. And to use that awful nickname.

"I wouldn't really say I missed it," I remark as I add one more plate.

Like a dog who just heard the dinner bell, Asher sits up on his bench, pausing his preacher curls. He's suddenly more interested in a story than a workout. "You ditched us for *Hannah*, again, Newman?"

I roll my eyes. "Fuck off."

"Is that what you told Pamela last night?" Max goads as he grabs a couple barbells, pronouncing it like *palmella*.

"Yes. That's exactly what happened last night. I told my hand to fuck off."

"And your hand said *oh, oh, oh*," Max says, pumping his hips, because we're all immature like that. But it's also impressive he can do it while holding weights.

Still, I scratch the side of my face with my middle finger, then lie on the bench, briefly flashing back to the convo with Josie last night when I said, *I work out a little.*

For a second, a sliver of guilt wiggles through me. Was it rude not to tell her what I do for a living? I mean, she didn't really tell me what she did. Just said she was in the book business. Probably works for a publisher or at a bookstore. But still, I talked around my job way more than she did.

Was that misleading?

Of course it was misleading.

But was it wrong to hide it the way I did? Well, I can rectify that if she says yes when I figure out how I'll return the scarf.

As I settle in and wrap my hands around the bar, I nod to Asher. "Spot me, Callahan," I say, using his last name, rather than his nickname—Pretty Boy. Not that it isn't fucking amusing to call him that. I'd just like them to stop calling me Newman for being the new guy. The less I say Pretty Boy, maybe the more he'll call me by my last name —Bryant.

Asher comes behind the bench, standing watch. "I got you," he says. He's a winger, and he's ferocious on the ice.

The opposite of how he looks off it. He has the kind of smile that gets him all sorts of sponsorship deals.

As Max shifts into flies, his blue eyes scan the room, clearly looking for someone. "Hey, where's Winters?"

That's a good question. "I didn't see him on the ice."

"Me neither," Asher remarks.

"He never misses practice," Max adds, then his brow knits, like maybe he's figured out the mystery of our missing captain. But he says nothing. I don't either as I lift the bar again.

"Too bad you didn't make it last night, Newman," Asher remarks as I lift. "Max was off his game big time. Huey and I cleaned up."

That's Hugo, one of our top defenders. I saw him earlier when I arrived, but he hit the athletic trainer's room after practice.

Max scowls. "It's all part of my strategy. To take you for everything next time."

I scoff. "Keep telling yourself that, Lambert," I say as I lift the bar one more time, my muscles straining.

"So how was your night, Bryant?" Asher asks. Thank fuck we don't use nicknames all the time.

"Don't tell me a miracle happened and you actually found a woman in this city willing to sleep with your ugly ass," Max says dryly as he sets down his weights.

Breathing out hard, I put down the bar, then sit up and meet my jackass friend's eyes. I smirk like a cocky fucker as I think of last night. "I don't kiss and tell."

Asher gives me an approving look. "Nice, man."

Max just shrugs. "Even a broken clock gets lucky once in a while."

I laugh, shaking my head. "Dude. The saying is even a broken clock is right twice a day."

"That too," he says as the slap of sneakers in the hallway grows louder. A teddy bear of a hockey player fills the doorframe.

"Give it up for Daddy Winters," Hugo calls out, then strides into the weight room, wielding his phone like it's Simba. He brings it to us and we crowd around it. There's a picture splashed across it. It's our team captain, Christian Winters, looking overjoyed as he holds two of the tiniest people I've ever seen.

"Holy shit," I say, smiling at the sight of one very happy new dad. That's why he's not here.

"He has two little boys. Looks like we've got some Sea Pups," Hugo says, and he's the softie of the bunch. Probably because he's already a dad. He and his wife have a little daughter.

"We need to get them skates, stat," I say.

"And helmets," Hugo adds.

"And sticks," Max puts in.

"The pucks are on me," Asher adds.

Hugo lowers his phone. "And he said he deputized me to handle any problems. So, guess I'm acting team captain." He puffs out his chest. Power-hungry teddy bear. Which means we need to give him hell.

Asher must feel the same way since he shoots him a doubtful look. "Shouldn't Weston be the acting captain?" Asher asks.

Weston is Chase Weston, a center and the former captain who stepped down right before I joined the team. He'd been captain for a few years though, earning mad respect from the guys for his calm, focused, and outgoing style. But he'd said he wanted to spend more time with his wife and their dogs. Which I get. If I had dogs, I'd spend as much time with them as

I could too. But it's hard when you're on the road to have a pet.

"Dude, Weston said Nacho had an agility tournament. He said it like an hour ago when we left the ice," Hugo says to Asher, shaking his head.

I can see the play before the puck even comes my way. I lunge for it, clapping Asher's shoulder as I say, "Remember? Weston said he was taking off for the tournament, but that Winters had planned to take us all to dinner tonight. To our favorite hot pot place."

Asher's eyes twinkle. "Right. That was it."

Max strides over, then in his deep voice adds, "The one in Japantown."

What a beautiful, clever bastard. That's the priciest hot pot.

"For team morale before our game," I add with my nice guy smile.

Asher flashes Hugo a satisfied grin. "He told us to round up the other guys."

My brow pinches, like I'm momentarily confused as I ask, "So that would mean dinner's on you, right Huey?"

Hugo snaps his fingers. "Dammit."

* * *

When I leave that afternoon, I check my phone on the way to the players' lot. There's a message from my sister.

> Natalie: Dude, you're in trouble. I heard you didn't get any artwork. How could you refuse the chance to decorate your walls with a skeleton horse?

. . .

Ah, hell. I'd nearly blocked that art gallery out of my head. I'd also gone almost a whole day without thinking about my dad. But I'm back to my meal plan, my workout routine, and everything else. Which means I'd better order mushroom broth, veggies, and lean chicken tonight at hot pot. But really, I can't complain.

> **Wesley:** What's even more mind-boggling is that he told you.

> **Natalie:** I was caught in the crossfire when he called me today about his trip here at the end of the week when the season starts. Anyway, I think Frieda was devastated that you didn't buy something from her gallery, so she gave Dad an earful, and Dad gave me an earful. But enough about them. WHO IS THE WOMAN IN THE T-SHIRT?

> **Wesley:** Shit. She told you?

> **Natalie:** Well, she told Dad. And Dad told me. And now he wants to know who you're dating.

I groan as I click on my seat belt. Of course he'd try to get it out of Natalie first. He's not a shrewd guy for nothing. Natalie loves all things romance, so...

Wesley: Is he asking to see if he thinks she'll be a distraction or an asset?

Natalie: Well, it is Dad. But this is me, and I want to know because I love you. Details!

Wesley: There's not much to tell, Natalie.

Natalie: Liar.

Wesley: I swear. We're not dating.

Natalie: Really? Frieda made it seem like you guys were together.

Shit. There is that issue to contend with now. The *I lied to Dad's girlfriend* issue. But maybe it won't be such a lie soon enough.

Wesley: I'll explain it next time I see you. But trust me, we're not dating. I gotta go.

She says goodbye, and I set the phone down, then pull out of the lot while mentally revising that last statement. We're not dating *yet*. When I get home, I flop down on the couch, fire up my laptop, and pay my parking citations. Happily.

* * *

Do I walk past Better With Pockets a couple times this week? Yeah, I do. Do I hope on some off chance I'll run into Josie there? Abso-fucking-lutely. Do I? No, I am not that lucky.

But men who rely on luck don't get far in life. Dating is like hockey. You need a plan. You need a strategy. You need to know what you're doing. On Thursday I head into a store on Fillmore Street called Effing Stuff. The place sells little tchotchkes, mugs, coasters, and magnets. I walk up to the counter where a woman with box braids and a nose ring says, "What can I help you with?"

"Hey there. I need a gift bag. For a girl."

"A girl you like?" the woman asks.

"Yes."

"What's her favorite color?"

"Black and white," I say, feeling a little smug that I know the answer. Hoping the answer leads me to another yes from Josie with no last name.

8

CACTUS ATTACK

Josie

Three days into my new job at a small branch of the San Francisco Public Library, and my stomach didn't growl embarrassingly during my meeting today, my teeth didn't become a net for lettuce when my new boss took me to lunch at a nearby salad bar yesterday, and I didn't trip and fall on my face, ass, or knee at all this week.

Not that I am prone to those things. But I am human after all. And I've read enough books where the heroine has a Very Bad Day during the first week on a new job and thus needs to drown her sorrows in chardonnay and cookie dough that weekend.

I'm counting the fact that I don't need a double dose of food and wine sympathy as a big win.

Bonus points I'm giving myself? I didn't once try to massage the kink out of my ass, neck, or back while at work. This might be the biggest victory of all since that loose spring in Maeve's couch is no joke. I'm so convinced it's out to get me I've named it The Kid. As in, The Kid from Shel Silverstein's *The Giving Tree*—also known as the greatest villain in all of literature.

The Kid is sharp, pointy, and merciless, and my body is paying the price. But I'm moving into my short-term rental tomorrow after work, and I refuse to complain about another night on the floor (since The Kid was so vicious last night, I moved to the hard wood at Maeve's, hence the migration of said kink to my back and neck.)

Besides, I'm all about looking on the bright side after my week kicked off with the world's greatest one-night stand. My string of good luck then continued. My new boss, Thalia Rosenstein, is super cool. She told me there's a guy named the Great Grimaldi and when he comes in to use the library's recently opened digitization center I should jump at the chance to help him, since he's digitizing his old magic shows and you can learn the coolest things. She also spilled that Eddie, who handles the city's research collections, likes to nuke tuna fish in the microwave every day at 12:01 so the break room is best avoided then, and the rattling noise in the stairwells isn't a ghost but a raccoon, who may or may not be living in the walls, but who occasionally has been spotted in the ladies' restroom on the third floor.

Thalia also set me up with real projects on my first day —not just busy work. Thanks to a newly established grant the library won from The Violet Delia Foundation for Library Digital Empowerment, I'm here at this branch in the Upper Haight on a three-month position to work on its digitization initiatives. That includes teaching some classes to patrons on how to best use online resources and helping the public digitize their own materials, like cassette tapes, Super 8, and floppy disks. I'll also work on managing the library's existing digital collections and promoting them to the public. Since digital archives was a key focus for my master's degree, I jumped at the chance.

As I'm packing up behind the second floor desk, I turn to Thalia, who's taking a pile of books from the returns tray.

"Thanks again for the raccoon tip. I'm not sure if I want to *only* use the third floor restroom or *never* use it now," I say. "I mean, raccoons can be cute."

"It's a real dilemma," she says dryly, then swivels away from her desktop, and lifts a finger, covered in silver skull rings that match the silver bracelets jangling up and down the light brown skin of her arms. How she wears bracelets and types all day is a mystery to me, but the bracelets sound like pretty bells so I don't mind the intrigue. "Oh! One more thing, Josie. On Fridays, Dolores from the children's wing brings her special brownies."

I pause, digesting that nugget. When I hear *special* and *brownies* I think of the ones some of my friends made in grad school—special as in laced with a little something extra to make the day, or night, feel real chill. I arch a curious brow but keep my tone even as I ask, "Special in what way?"

"As in they're made with melted dark chocolate."

Oh, that's a relief. "What time do I need to be here to make sure they aren't all gone?"

She nods approvingly. "I knew you'd understand." She looks around furtively, then whispers, "Eight fifty-five. The vultures from circulation descend at nine. Also, tomorrow afternoon we have a training session on how to help people experiencing homelessness. Might last into the early evening since there are often lots of questions."

"I'll be there," I say, glad the library is tackling this

important topic since any library staff member these days needs to work compassionately with the unsheltered, as well as patrons with substance use disorders or mental illnesses who come through our wide open doors.

For now though, I'm happy to leave work behind. Because this little information specialist has a project and a plan for her Thursday night.

After I sling my bag over my shoulder, I grab the tiny cactus I picked up last night at Welcome to the Jungle, a plant shop over on Fillmore Street run by a retired hockey star from the Sea Dogs. I smooth my free hand over my white button-down blouse, then along my black pencil skirt and head to the circular stairway. My flats click clack with a loud but satisfying echo through the weird little library that's quickly become my home away from home.

I reach the exit, then walk past the fire station next door. Some of the guys who work here are out washing their cherry-red truck. I smile a hello, and the three of them smile back. I continue on in the San Francisco evening. It's warm since it's October, but I still instinctively reach for my scarf to wrap it around my neck. But of course, it's not here. A pang of sadness hits me every time I do this phantom move. I realized when I left the hospital on Monday afternoon, after cuddling my little nephews as much as I could, that I'd probably left the accessory behind in the hotel room.

But when I popped into The Resort that evening to see if it was in their lost and found, the clerk checked and then frowned an apology.

"Sorry, Greta," I say to the sky, since that scarf was her favorite. It was the scarf I'd played dress-up with as a little girl when I'd stayed with her. I'd wrap it around my head, put on her glasses, and pretend I was a granny. Or we'd dress up her rescue Labrador, turning Lulu Blossom into a cowgirl with it, or Rosie the Riveter.

"Scarves are the unsung heroes of the fashion world. They add personality to an outfit, they add flair, and they add a certain *je ne sais quoi*," Greta had said, then tucked a finger under my chin. "And you, my love, are a *je ne sais quoi* type of person, so wear it that way."

I'd like to think wearing it as a belt on Sunday night was so very *je ne sais quoi*.

And if I had to lose the scarf, leaving it at the scene of my night in sex heaven seems the perfect place to let that part of me go. I straighten my shoulders and walk like I'm still wearing it. I'll find another one. I'll hit the thrift shops this weekend once I move into my new place. Once I'm settled, I can tackle the rest of Greta's list in earnest. I've already started researching the second item she left for me to do. Now that I've tackled the first one, it'll be easier —I think—to work my way through the list.

But even though I'm researching item two, I can't stop thinking about item number one.

The way Wesley touched me. The way he teased me. The way he talked to me. A hot shiver slides down my spine.

And the way I see it—I was faithful to the list when I checked that first item off. It was a one-night stand with a sexy stranger through and through. Since I completed the task so perfectly, I figure I'm free and clear to see him again. *Not* as a one-night stand.

I mean, the logic holds up. That is, if I can find him again. My stomach dips with nerves and hope.

I'm almost tempted to tell my mom I started doing the list her sister gave me before she died. Mom hasn't seen the list, but she knows it exists. She's asked me a few times

about it. Right now though, she's way too focused on her
athlete son's babies. Understandable. Truly it is. Though,
she's always been focused on him. She's a former athlete,
so I get it. My dad is too. Mom played college volleyball
and won an NCAA championship, and Dad ran track, so
they've always just had their bond with their firstborn
who skated before he walked. It's fine. I'm used to it.
Mom's flying in this weekend to help out for the next
week.

As I walk, I text Maeve since she knows about my plan
to try to find Wesley tonight.

Josie: I'm doing it! I'm on my way.

Maeve: I know, my little tiger!

My brow knits. She knows? I voice dictate my reply as I
weave past early evening crowds in the Upper Haight.

Josie: How do you know?

Maeve: You're on the corner of Webster
and Hayes. You're almost there!

Dammit. I never turned off my location tracker.

> Maeve: Also, looking at your location history, I see you went to Elodie's Chocolates today at lunch. I'm hoping you got me some. But I'm most interested in this visit you paid last night to my favorite "toy store" after work. I thought you were just going to the plant shop. Did you go into Risqué Business and pick up a battery-operated gift for your girl? You holding out on me?

Red splashes across my cheeks. Of course Maeve would notice that. She was the devil to my angel one Halloween in college after all.

> Josie: Yes, but your toy is so big it's requiring a forklift. Hope you can carry it up the stairs!

> Maeve: Now that just makes me want it even more!

I put the phone away and check the numbers on the storefronts. The gallery's on the next block. As I walk the final fifty feet, I steel myself. Frieda didn't like me when I begged her to let me in on Sunday. There's a very good chance she won't help me tonight. A great one, in fact. But this is my only recourse. If I can convince her to give me Wesley's last name, I can track him down. The Internet and me are tight, and I can find anything on it.

All I need is that one tiny detail.

I'm prepared, though, to bargain with the ice queen. I researched Frieda, learned she studied art history in London, she loves fine wine (I don't have the budget for that), fine art (definitely don't have the budget for that), Antibes (as if), and cactus plants.

Yay, plants! I picked up a tiny bunny ears cactus and I'm hoping to use it as an apology gift, and, well, a lubricant. After all, when I first met Frieda, she pretended to be someone else so as not to have to deal with me.

When I arrive at the gallery, I gather my nerves and head inside the sterile place with futuristic art. My shoes clack louder than they do at the library, echoing around the white walls, adorned with nightmarish visions.

"I'll be right there," she says warmly in a somewhat British tone from a back room.

Butterflies flap in my chest as I say, "Thank you" as cheerily as I can.

But when Frieda emerges, her expression turns stony, a brow elevating in disdain as she sizes me up. "I see you discovered the existence of clothing stores."

I absorb the blow, deflecting it. "I did. I wanted to thank you. For letting me into your event the other night."

Her right eye twitches. Like she doesn't want to say it wasn't her choice. "I do so hope you were able to locate your phone. Maybe consider a lanyard or a crossbody bag to attach it to next time. That's what parents do for young children," she offers with so much false kindness it's as impressive as the white pantsuit with the plunging neckline that she wears.

"Great tip. I appreciate it," I say, trying my best to appear upbeat and undeterred. "I'm here to offer a little thank you gift."

"You're going to buy a piece of art? How lovely. Come on now, darling. I'll show you around."

"Actually, I can't."

"Oh, why not?" It's asked with so much concern.

Because each piece of this horrid art is over five thousand dollars, you snob. "I don't have the budget," I say honestly, then brace myself for the toughest ask of all. It feels like scaling a ten-story wall. In Louboutins. "I was hoping you could give me Wesley's last name."

She blinks, peering at me first with utter confusion then villainous delight. "Your date? Your plus-one? The one who likes to surprise you with his fantastic date ideas, so he told you to meet him here?"

She parrots my words back to me so precisely that my stomach twists. I knew this wouldn't be easy. I didn't know it would be this hard. Make me feel this small. But she has the moral high ground and the information, so I can't argue with her. "Yes," I say, swallowing roughly. "Do you think you could give me his last name?"

I hold out the plant in a peace offering.

"Do you not have it, darling?" Her tone is dripping with concern.

Sadly, I shake my head. "I don't."

"Let me see if I can remember it. Hmm." She sighs, taps her chin, stares at the ceiling. "It's coming back to me." She lowers her face, smiles serenely, and says, "His name is..."

I hold my breath. She's not an evil ice queen after all. She can melt.

"Wesley," she continues, then mimes typing on a keyboard. "*The guy I met at a gallery who doesn't want to see me again.* There. Just put it into Google. Just like that."

I feel two feet tall. Talk about a slap in the face. I'm

reeling as she crosses the distance in her spiky heels, sticking out a bony hand, reaching for the plant. "The bunny ears, please."

Briefly, I fantasize about flicking my hair, channeling the scarf power even though I'm not wearing it, and saying ever so coolly, "You can find it online. *Just search for unkill-able plants that even I could kill with my bitchiness.*"

But I don't. Instead, I yank the plant closer to my chest, spin on my heels, and get the hell out of there, race-walking away from her gallery, powered by my own frustration.

It was stupid of me to think that could work. Just foolish to believe I could pull off that kind of request. What's the point anyway? Frieda's smack back is probably a sign the one-night stand is supposed to stay a one-night stand.

As I unleash an annoyed sigh, my phone rings. I'm reaching for it when I realize too that my chest feels a little strange—a bit scratchy and uncomfortable. But before I can figure out why, I check the screen. It's a 415 number from Johnson Properties—that's the place I'm moving into tomorrow. The landlord probably wants to give me the passcode or something.

"This is Josie," I answer.

The rough, gravelly voice on the other end says, "Hey, hey, hey, Ms. Winters. This is Barry Johnson. I have some good news and bad news. Which do you want first?"

Probably a broken pipe. Possibly a toilet installed upside-down. I can handle either. "Bad news, of course," I say.

"Cool. I'll start with the good news," he says.

Why did he even ask? "Okay."

Barry wastes no time. "So it's more like world's greatest

news since I just signed a sweet deal to sell this building. Ten percent above asking price."

This is worse than I'd imagined. I feel like I was just dropped out of a plane without a parachute. My stomach bottoms out as I say weakly, "The bad news is I don't have a place to stay?"

"You are sharp, girlie," he says with a whistle, like he's genuinely impressed with me adding up two plus two. "But the other good news is I have a buddy, Donny, who's got a deal for a short-term rental, just for my referrals. He can lease a one-bedroom to you at a bargain."

There's hope on the horizon! "Where? When can I move in? How much?"

"Russian Hill. Sunday, and a helluva deal at $3999 a month."

My eyes bug out. "I can't afford that on my starting salary." I wouldn't be able to afford that for many years. If ever.

"No worries. He thought you might say that. More good news is this—he's got a one-bedroom that you can share with three other people as long as he doesn't disclose how many are on the lease. Plus, there's a bathroom down the hall for you all to share."

I stop, lean against the wall of Better With Pockets, and close my eyes for a beat. When I open them and look down, my chest is bleeding right above the neckline of my shirt. Great. Just great. The cactus has pricked me.

"Thanks, Barry. But I'll have to pass," I say, then hang up.

My throat tightens as my chest bleeds into my white shirt. Tears well behind my eyes. From Frieda's insults to the cactus attack to the terrible news, I can't deal anymore with my upside-down luck that seems to flip-flop by the day.

My eyes sting, but I suck back tears and stab my brother's name. I hate doing this. I truly do. Especially now when he has his hands full.

I call my brother.

* * *

Christian's blue eyes are tired but also pleased. The gold flecks in them almost seem to be twinkling. Which is a weird reaction to me telling him my sob story on the back deck of his spacious home on California Street, overlooking the Golden Gate Bridge, as he holds Cooper while Caleb nurses inside with Liv. But I try not to read anything into his reaction—he's a new dad and is also in the starting lineup for tomorrow's season opener. He has a lot on his plate. Which is why I wish I didn't have to come to him.

"Don't worry, Jay," he says, reassuringly. "I'll help you out."

I look at him with still-wet eyes. I can't believe I'm crying over a lost rental. But it's not only the rental falling through. It's how much I want this job. I'm three days in and I already love it. I don't want to lose it simply because I have no place to stay. Jobs like this are hard to come by. Cities like San Francisco, though, are even harder to live in.

Maeve volunteered to let me stay with her, but her place is too small. And, well, The Kid haunts it. So here I am, with a Band-Aid on my chest, a bloody shirt, and an attacking cactus, asking my brother for help. I hate asking anyone in my family but my aunt for anything.

But I have no choice.

9

A SECRET ROOM UNDER THE STAIRCASE

Wesley

The scarf in the bag is safe and sound on the backseat of my car. I've got a plan to drop it off tomorrow morning at the yellow apartment building. Saturday seems like a good day for something like that, when it's late morning and the sun is up. I can leave it in the foyer with other packages at her place.

It'll be the perfect morning activity after we win tonight since I fully plan for us to leave the ice victorious.

I've been eating my quinoa and squash, been following my exercise regimen, been working on strength and conditioning all summer with the performance coach my dad hired. Hell, Dad and I met with him *again* today after the team's morning skate so Dad could go over my workout routine with him for the season.

This will be your breakout year, he likes to say. *Let's set you up for long-term success.*

Translation: let's get you a no-trade clause.

Hell, I'd love a no-trade clause and the security that would come with it. I *thought* I'd had job security in New York. My stats were solid there, where I played for four and a half years. The trade surprised me, but I rolled with it. After a strong second half of the season last year when I joined the Sea Dogs as a winger, I want to show the coach on my new team why I belong on the first line.

For now, I go through my pre-game rituals. I'm parked in a chair in front of my stall, taping my stick, and chilling with the guys. I've been debating with Max and Asher whether we should get tickets for the Chappell Roan concert next week, since we're all a little obsessed with her tunes, when Christian strides into the locker room looking like he's got something on his mind.

Even though he just had kids earlier in the week, he's playing on the first line for tonight's game. That shouldn't surprise me—him being here or playing well—since I don't think he missed a game all last season. Guess he's captain for a reason. The dude shows up and plays hard. He sets an example every goddamn day. I respect the hell out of him. I want to have a career like his.

Resting his arm against a stall, he clears his throat. "Good news. My sons are awesome. The three of us took a pre-game nap together today."

Those are a must on game days.

Chase pumps a fist. "Starting the hockey training from day one," he calls out from in front of his stall. "Well done, Winters."

Christian nods then takes a deep breath. Yup, my instincts were right. He must be gearing up for a season-opener speech, and when he says, "Listen guys," I'm sure he is. "I've got some more good news."

He scratches his jaw, overrun by a five-day growth he

probably hasn't bothered to shave. "Great news, actually. My sister's rental fell through," he says, and he sounds pleased in a Machiavellian way. "And I couldn't be happier. Her place wasn't in a good neighborhood," he says, then names the area. I cringe. My reaction does not go unnoticed by the captain. "You wouldn't want your sisters staying there either. You'd only want your sisters staying someplace safe, right?"

There's a collective yes from maybe half of us—the half of us who have sisters. Natalie and her girlfriend live in a nice place in Noe Valley, so I don't worry about her.

But Ryker Samuels nods toward Christian, a grim look on his face. "That's why I made sure Ivy moved into my place when I moved out way back when. Well, back when she was single."

"Same," Hugo puts in. "I always look out for my family."

"My point exactly," Christian says to our top defenseman. "Anyway, I warned my sister against it when she rented it, and now that it's fallen through she's finally listening to me."

"So she's staying with you?" Max barks out from next to me as he tugs on his chest protector.

Christian scoffs. "Dude. No. Liv and I are just a little bit busy with the twins, we have a baby nurse staying in a guest room, and my mom is coming and staying in another room. There's no space for Jay." He points to the group of us filling the locker room. "Which brings me to the great news. Which one of you guys wants to do me the biggest favor ever and let my sister stay with you for the next three months? I want her to live in a safe neighborhood, and I know all you assholes live in Pacific Heights or the Marina District so that'd be perfect. She's quiet, keeps to herself, and spends most of her time reading or working. You won't even know she's there. And you'd be doing me a solid."

Asher smacks my shoulder. "Dude. You have that secret room don't you? The one under the staircase, right?"

I laugh. "Yeah, it disappears and reappears whenever you need it."

Asher tips his forehead to me. "Fucking Newman didn't even know when he bought the place that it had an extra room."

I hold out my hands wide, shrugging, like it's no big deal. When I was looking for a place to buy after I was traded, I checked out a bunch of townhomes in Pacific Heights, where most of my friends on the pro teams in the city live. Some had two bedrooms, some had three. I picked the one I liked most, barely paying attention to the details. It's an investment more than anything. Who knows how long I'm here, but I'd rather own than rent, since I can. Turns out, I own a three-bedroom when I'd thought it was two. But it's like finding a slice of pizza you didn't know you had left in the box. "It was like a bonus room when I moved in," I say, then I meet Christian's gaze and lift a finger. "Happy to help out."

Christian breathes the biggest sigh of relief. "Perfect. I'll send you her contact info, Bryant." He whips his phone from his pocket. "And I'll tell her I found her a place and that you'll be reaching out." He pauses, then adds, "Now."

As if I'd do anything else but reach out right away. "Of course," I say.

"I already told her to come by at the end of the game so I can introduce the two of you. She has some training thing that's running late at her library."

Chase whistles at Christian. "You already told her to come by? Before you even asked us? Damn." The golden-haired former captain turns to the rest of us, arms out wide. "That's the kind of attitude we all need to manifest on the ice. A winning attitude."

He's not wrong. The rest of the guys nod in agreement, and I grab my phone and click on the contact card Christian just fired my way. Jay. I send her a quick text then meet his eyes.

"Done," I say.

"Suck-up," Max mutters under his breath.

Christian cocks his head Max's way. "What did you say?"

Max swallows, then shrugs as nonchalantly as he can. "I said, that was so nice of him to help out."

"I thought so," Christian says, then walks to me and offers a hand. "I owe you." We shake, then he adds, "Just keep your hands off her."

There's a collective laugh in the locker room. Then a collective *no shit.* Like I'd do anything to rock the team boat. "I got you, man."

"We all know *that rule*," Asher adds.

It's the golden rule of being on a team. You don't bang a teammate's sister. Well, unless you plan to marry her.

As Christian heads to his stall to get ready for the game, my phone pings with a text from my new roomie.

10

MY NEW ROOMIE

Josie

Is that a raccoon tapping on the bathroom door while I pee? With my luck, it'll be a ghost planning to haunt me for the next three months.

The scratching sound feels more corporeal though.

But is there really a raccoon in the library? While I now know they can live in walls, that usually happens in older homes. They're resourceful little critters who shimmy into chimneys, attics, and crawl spaces. I looked them up when I heard the raccoon story from Thalia. This building is modern and seems less likely for a raccoon home invasion.

So, that leaves me with...yup, a ghost.

Of course.

I pee as fast as I can, flush, and hustle to the sink to wash my hands. I need to get back to the training session anyway. Maybe Christian wrote to me. He should be at the rink by now. He said he'd be in touch before the game started. But when I turn around to check my phone as I leave, I stop in my tracks, startled. That's not a raccoon. That's a cat. A big, beautiful seal-point Siamese cat.

He's parked at the door. And I do mean parked. He's barn-cat size and it's like he's guarding the exit, tail swishing, big blue eyes lasered right at me.

"What's your name, buddy?" I ask.

He doesn't move. Just flicks his tail. And stares at me without blinking. "I kinda need to get back to the meeting," I say.

Yes, this is now my life. Anxiously waiting to hear from my brother about a place to live while negotiating with a giant cat.

The feline is impervious to my dilemma. I advance toward the door he's guarding like a sentry, but he makes no move to let me by. Am I going to have to pick him up and move him? Right as I'm contemplating my cat removal options, my phone buzzes in my skirt pocket. I grab it like it's on fire and read the new text from Christian.

My shoulders relax. My whole body relaxes. Christian found someone—a guy on his team named Bryant. He's attached the contact card.

Then I spot another text. From a new number and name.

> Bryant: Hey! Christian said you need a place to stay. I have a sweet guest room under the staircase.

My heart sprints.

> Jay: That sounds like something out of a book!

> Jay: Also, thank you! I am so grateful. You won't even know I'm there!

> Bryant: Happy to help.

> Jay: My brother said I should come by after the game and we can meet. Does that work for you?

> Bryant: Yup. See you then.

I'm about to slide my phone into my pocket when it pings once more.

> Bryant: Also, you can move in whenever. It has sheets and pillows and stuff already.

> Bryant: The decorator did it. Not me.

> Bryant: So it's not like it's black sheets and chrome.

I laugh at his reassurances that it's not hyper manly even though I wouldn't care if it was designed in every single shade of gray.

"Buddy, you need to move," I say, pleading with the fluffy beast with the implacable gaze.

The cat refuses to budge though, so I bend down and scoop him up.

"Oof. You weigh thirty pounds," I blurt out as I lift the big boy, then open the door with a pretty impressive combination of elbow and butt maneuvering if I do say so myself.

"I see you met Raccoon."

It's Thalia on the other side, bracelets jangling as she heads my way.

"Raccoon?" I ask.

"Our library cat. We found him in the wall and he stayed. But don't body shame him," she says with a wink.

"My bad," I say, then gesture toward the floor. "Okay to put him down here?"

She waves her arm around to the shelves, her bracelets chiming. "He has run of the place. Leave him wherever. He's why we have no mice," she says as I set him down and in a heartbeat, he makes like a cat and hightails it far, far away from me.

On my way back to the conference room, Christian sends me one more text, telling me a woman named Everly will meet me at the arena whenever I arrive. He drops me her number too. I thank him, then return to the conference room, feeling like I can breathe easily thanks to a room under the stairs in some hockey player's home.

When the session ends an hour or so later, Thalia suggests we all grab a drink. Since I have time before the hockey game ends, I join them. She takes us to The Spotted Zebra, and I learn that I'm the first new librarian at this branch in years, and it's also the first time this little branch has landed a grant for any position.

"You're our unicorn," Thalia says.

And unicorns are cool, so I say, "Achievement unlocked."

When we're done, she offers to drop me off.

I say yes and text Everly on the way. Once Thalia reaches the rink, I thank her and hop out of her little Honda, hoisting my bag up on my shoulder as I walk toward the main doors. I pass the huge lit-up marquee for the Sea Dogs—their mascot is a fearsome canine who looks like he can brave the icy waters of any North Sea ship. I haven't had a chance to google this Bryant guy, but I can do that when I'm inside rather than when I'm walking outside at night. Safer that way.

When I arrive at Main Door G, there's a tall blonde with her hair pulled back in a sleek ponytail. She's polished and put together in black slacks and a royal blue shirt, the color of the team. Her fair skin is dotted with a few freckles, and her brown eyes are warm.

"You must be Christian's sister," she says, then offers me a hand. "I'm Everly. I work in publicity for the team, and he asked me to take you down to the locker room."

I balk at that last word. "Um..."

"Oh," she says, shaking her head with an amused smile. "You probably don't want to go into the locker room."

Not with my brother there. Not with any of them there, to be honest. I love my brother. But I've never crushed on his teammates. Not in high school, not in college, and not while he's been in the pros. I'm more into geeks and nerds than athletes, so the idea of standing around a bunch of big, sweaty guys does nothing for me.

"I can wait in the hall," I say helpfully.

"Of course," Everly says, then whisks me past security and through the concourse. "So you just arrived in the city about a week ago, Christian tells me. What do you think so far?"

That I never know if I'm going to step into a mud pit or a garden of flowers. "It's great," I say, since there's no need to tell her the details about my topsy-turvy experiences here. "You never know what each day holds."

"Sounds like working here. I never know if I'm going to have to wrangle a pack of ornery kangaroos or not," she says, then whispers playfully. "Usually it's ornery kangaroos."

I think I love her. We speak the same language. "I hope you wear armor then."

"Part of the job, along with fetching sisters for the captain and, oh yeah, organizing publicity," she says as she guides me through the upper concourse, past chichi food vendors peddling organic and sustainably grown food, and toward the lower level. I've been here a few times, including for a game last season. But it's still helpful to have a guide so we can move quickly past the throngs of exiting fans. "But tonight the pack of kangaroos-slash-dogs will likely be happy since the Sea Dogs beat the Coyotes."

"Oh! That's great," I say. I hadn't even bothered to check the score. But that's great news for my brother and my new roomie.

"Ah, and there they are," Everly says as we round the corner toward the locker room where my brother's waiting outside in his post-game suit, and he's standing next to a tall, broad, ridiculously handsome man.

My heart stutters.

Then stops.

I can't breathe. I'm a computer that just beach-balled

as I come face-to-face with the guy I tried to track down last night. "And that's Wesley Bryant," Everly says.

I cough. I part my lips to try to speak but wheeze out a question that I already know the answer to but have to ask anyway, "Wesley Bryant?"

"Yes, and he got an assist tonight so he'll probably be in a very good mood," she says.

I'm not so sure about that.

When he turns toward our voices, his brown eyes lock with mine. It takes a beat for his brow to furrow. Then it goes tighter, then tighter still.

When Christian sees me he says, "Hey, Jay! Here's your new roomie."

Wesley's jaw comes unhinged.

Just like mine.

I guess I was dead wrong about not liking athletes.

11

FATE HATES ME

Wesley

I don't believe in luck. I believe you make your own luck through work and practice and skill.

But what in the ever-loving fuck is this bullshit? Does fate hate me? Is this my comeuppance for eating ice cream five nights ago when it's not on my meal plan? That's a helluva price to pay. Maybe this is the universe's payback for the time I didn't read *To Kill a Mockingbird* in school, but looked up the SparkNotes instead? Then did the same for every other book that followed.

If so, karma has a funny sense of humor, but I'm not laughing.

Hold on. I know what this is. This has to be a prank. A fantastic, elaborate prank. Like the time Max and Asher loosened the top on my water bottle before my first game last season, and the liquid spilled all over me while I was on the bench. The ESPN cameras were on me and caught the whole thing.

I laughed it off then. Except I'm not laughing now as I rasp out, "Josie?"

When...shit.

I'm not supposed to know her name. Christian's only ever called her Jay, clearly a nickname based on her first initial. But he must not notice the way her name is strangled by my throat since he claps me on the shoulder and says, "Thanks again for helping out. Always knew you were a good one, Bryant."

He yawns, checks his watch, and says, "I gotta go."

He strides over to the flirty, outgoing brunette with the scar on her chin and the cat-eye glasses. She's wearing a black skirt and a white button-down shirt, unfairly sexy. I jump back in time to before the game when Christian was telling us about her. How the hell could he call her quiet? There was nothing quiet about Josie. Especially when she asked me to bend her over the bed and fuck her hard.

Christian wraps her in a big bear hug. "Bryant lives in a safe 'hood," he says, then lets go and flashes her a satisfied grin. "Guess that means I won and you got yourself a bodyguard after all."

Right. He wants me to look out for her—not date her.

No shit, Sherlock.

Still, my help-a-teammate-out vibe has never been so flattened like a pancake as it has been tonight.

"Yes, a bodyguard," Josie repeats, clearly flustered, but Christian doesn't seem to pick up on it.

Everly does though. Tilting her head, she lifts a brow curiously, studying Josie's reaction, then mine. But she's our PR woman, and I don't want her thinking I don't want to help. Or worse, figuring out I've already fucked my teammate's sister.

That'd be bad.

Christian is so by the book. So rules oriented. I straighten my shoulders, adopt my media grin, then close the distance to...my new roommate. I stick out a hand in the world's most awkward handshake. "Hey. Nice to meet you," I say, the lie sailing off my tongue as easily as *of course I read To Kill a Mockingbird* did in eighth grade.

Josie's pretty pink lips twitch for a few seconds till she says brightly, "You too." She pauses before she adds, "Wesley."

"All right," Christian says, brushing one palm over the other. "My work as the problem solver is done." He shoots me a stern stare with his steely ice-blue eyes, colder than his sister's, more calculating. "See you at morning skate on Sunday. And don't forget what I told you earlier."

I fight off a grimace and paste on a smile. "We're all good."

As Christian heads to the players' lot exit, Everly rolls her eyes, then says, "Let me guess what he told you earlier. Is it the antiquated, sexist, *don't touch my sister* rule?"

She asks it like she wants to step on that rule and stub it into the ground with her heels.

"Um, yeah," I say, embarrassed on behalf of testosterone and its stupidity.

"Men," she says with a heavy sigh. "Seriously." She turns back to Josie. "Listen, if there's anything you need, I'd be more than happy to help out."

"You don't have to," Josie says.

"I want to," Everly adds, boss mode activated completely. "I work with these guys every day. They can be—"

"Ornery kangaroos?" Josie offers.

I shudder. "Kangaroos can be mean."

Everly lifts a finger. "Precisely." Then to Josie she says, "Text or call anytime. We can talk about survival tactics."

For the first time since she spotted me, Josie smiles. "That would be great."

Everly gestures down the hall. "I'm off to the media room. Thanks again for taking a few questions earlier, Wesley."

"Anytime," I say, and when she takes off, I'm left alone with the woman I wanted to ask to hang out again. The woman I wrote a note for. The woman I've been obsessing over all damn week.

"We don't have to do this," she says quickly, her eyes flickering with worry. Fear, too, like I'm going to yank the offer out from under her.

No way. She needs a place. Just like she needed pants on Sunday night. "It's cool," I say, and I'm about to reassure her further when Max and Asher stream out of the locker room, followed by Hugo.

Ah, hell. I'm not in the mood for a group introduction. I drop my voice. "Want to get some food and talk?"

She nods, and I point toward the players' exit before they can head there. My dad came to the game tonight, but I already talked to him right when it ended, so I've done my part.

Josie and I walk together to the door, but the coach exits his office as I pass it. I straighten my shoulders the second I see Noah McBride. He's dressed in a charcoal suit, his short hair is neat, and his expression is intense—it's only ever intense. The man does not mess around.

"Hey, Coach," I say.

He chin-nods toward me. "Good game, Bryant. Keep it up."

It's said evenly, without emotion or a clap on the back.

But I don't need an *attaboy*. Those six words are more than enough.

"I will, Coach."

Then he nods toward Josie. "Evening, Ms. Winters."

Holy fuck. Even Coach knows she's Christian's sister?

She smiles his way. "Hello, Mr. McBride. Good to see you again."

With a crisp nod, he heads the other way, and I lead Josie to the exit. I'm tempted to put a hand on her back as we walk.

But I don't.

I can't anymore because...*karma.*

12

THE ROOMIE RULE

Wesley

I have so many questions. But first things first. I open the car door for her when my gaze swings to the backseat and the evidence of my intentions on it.

That won't do. As she's sliding into the front seat, I quickly yank on the door handle for the back, then grab the bag, muttering, "Just a sec."

"No worries," she says.

As she buckles in I fish out the now pointless note. I stuff it into my back pocket.

That letter she left on hotel stationery wasn't a clue after all. It wasn't a treasure hunt, like I'd mistakenly thought the morning after. She's just a girl who's got a lot on her plate and legit had to jet in the morning.

It's fine. Really, it is.

I slam the door harder than I'd expected, then head to the driver's side. Once I'm in the car, I hand her the bag.

"Here you go," I say, then turn on the car and cruise through the lot.

"Oh my god," she gasps. "Wesley!"

Fuck me. That excited sound. The smell of her perfume—cinnamon and my dirty dreams. Her lush chestnut hair. This is harder than scoring on the New York goalie.

"You left it behind," I say in a statement of the obvious. But hell if I'm going to let on how goddamn excited I was to find it the other day.

"Thank you so much. I went back to the hotel that afternoon to the lost and found. But they didn't have it."

She went back to check on a scarf? But not to ask for my name?

Like the hotel would give her your name. Get over yourself.

She hugs the scarf to her chest. "My aunt gave this to me. I'm really glad to have it back."

"Glad I could help," I grumble, a little annoyed.

I'm annoyed because my plans are shot. I'm annoyed because I'm going to be living with temptation. And I'm annoyed because...well, she didn't come looking for me.

Which is the stupidest reason of all to be irritated. Still, I am.

I focus on heading to the nearest salad and grain bowl spot instead. Nope, scratch that. I don't want to run into fans or, worse, teammates. I take a detour to a place in Russian Hill instead, since that's kind of, sort of on the way back to my place but far enough from here. Along the way, we make uncomfortable small talk about food, the hills in the city, how light the traffic is at this hour. It's painful.

I pull up to Garden Kitchen and park. Once inside, I order something acceptable—sliced chicken, avocado, cherry tomatoes, and no cheese—while she orders a veggie and cheese bowl.

We snag a table but keep ourselves busy getting napkins and water. Once we sit and a server brings the food, the elephant in the room is tromping around. Getting louder and noisier. Best to deal with it, stat, even though there are so many questions I have. "So, your brother calls you Jay?"

"Yes, he couldn't say Josie when I was born, so he's always called me that." She pauses, her expression resigned. Maybe frustrated too. "And I guess he calls you Bryant."

"Well, yeah. It's a thing we all do."

"I know," she says, like she wasn't born yesterday. Of course she knows we use last names. Hell, she knows the coach.

But there are more elephants to deal with. "And you're in the book business?" That came out a little bitter.

"Yes, I'm a librarian," she says. "And I guess you *are* the sports asset rather than being in sports assets."

I feel a little called out—rightfully so. But facts are facts. "Yeah, I guess players are assets," I say with a shrug, like it was no big deal to tell her that.

"I guess so," she says, distant.

I mull over her tone as I take another bite from the bowl, then ask, "You're pissed I didn't say I played hockey?"

She shakes her head. "No." She pauses, though, like she's not done. "I mean, I get it. I sort of wish I knew, but I also understand why you didn't tell me."

"Why do you think I didn't?" I'm not sure she could know my reasons, but I'm damn curious what she thinks they are.

Her blue eyes hold mine as she says, "Because you probably just wanted a night to be...sort of someone else?"

She nailed it. She might not know the exact reason why, as in my dad likes to control everything I do since my career is everything to him, but she figured out enough.

"Same for you?" I ask, though I suspect since she wanted to have a one-night stand with a stranger she probably *also* wanted an escape from her regular life, just like I did.

"Same," she says, then spears a forkful of tofu, chewing thoughtfully. When she sets it down, she adds, "And also, I was deliberately vague about my family because people tend to kind of geek out when I mention my brother, so I didn't want to say that I'd been to San Francisco a few times for his games. I went to one last season."

"And you met the coach then?"

"Christian introduced me to him briefly. That guy has a good memory," she says.

"No shit," I say, but that's Coach in general. His mind is a steel trap. But then, so is Josie's. "You do too."

She shrugs. "I'm good with names."

"I'll say." Then, I freeze with a bite of chicken midway to my mouth, my mind tripping back in time. "This is going to sound weird, but for a moment when I met you I thought you looked vaguely familiar. But not in a way where I could place you. Maybe I *did* see you at a game? The one you went to last season?"

She smiles apologetically. "Maybe? I was in that same hallway I was in tonight. Meeting Christian after a game."

I set down my fork with a heavy sigh as the déjà vu feeling crashes back into me, but it's more clear this time. Yeah, now I remember seeing a pretty woman with Christian one night. But I never met her, of course. And I never thought twice about it, really. "Just my luck," I say sarcastically.

She laughs. "I've been saying that a lot this week."

Ah, hell. She *has* had a bad week. And I have been kind of cold tonight. I try again to be civil. "So your place fell through? The one you got locked out of?"

"No. Another one. That was just my friend Maeve's place. The woman I talked to at the show?"

"Right. I guess I figured you were living with her," I admit.

"I get that. You would have no reason to think I wasn't. Anyway, I had a short-term rental, but the landlord sold it at the last minute so I turned to Christian for help, and well..."

I manage a smile I don't entirely feel. "Here we are," I finish for her.

"Here we are," she echoes, then takes another bite of her veggie bowl.

I try not to linger on watching her eat. Even though I really like her mouth. Picture her pretty lips as she said she wanted to objectify me five nights ago and...yeah, things are gonna be real hard with her in my house.

I wipe my mouth with a napkin and take a drink of my water. I'm not even sure what to say next. I should say I'm sorry I didn't tell her what I did for a living, but neither one of us was very forthcoming about details that night. At the time it was deliberate. We only gave as much info as we wanted to. She didn't even come back to my place. And in retrospect now, it's clear what the other night was—and what it wasn't.

It wasn't the start of a new romance, like I foolishly had hoped when I woke up. It wasn't the beginning of our dating season, like I'd tricked myself into believing this week and not only because she's my team captain's little sister. But because she meant what she said that night— she wanted one night and one night only.

I pat the note I'd planned to leave with the scarf, making sure it's safe and sound in my pocket. It is. It won't ever see the light of day.

Then I draw a deep breath and do the right thing—I move on. "You're good with this, Josie? I don't want you to be uncomfortable, but I'm truly happy to have you living with me," I say, meaning it since I hate the idea of her out there in a dangerous neighborhood when I have the tools to help her. "For as long as you need."

Her blue eyes are etched with gratitude as she asks, "Are you sure?"

She sounds so vulnerable. So worried. I feel like a dick for having been, well, a dick tonight. "Of course. I volunteered. I'm happy to help." But I'm really going to sound like a dick when I say the next thing. Still, I have to say it. We need to lay down the rules. "Guess it's a good thing that night was a one-and-done."

I cringe at the way that sounds all casual and cool. Like I'm a playboy when I'm not.

"Totally," she says quickly, sitting up straighter as she smiles.

Way to punch me in the gut, Josie.

"Right?" I say with a big laugh. A goddamn gregarious one. "And obviously, what happened has to stay between us."

"Oh my god, clearly," she says, agreeing easily, like we're totally sweeping the other night under the rug together.

"Look, it's a dumb rule. Like Everly said. But it exists

for a reason—the good of the team," I admit honestly. "You need to go to war every night with these guys. You need to trust your teammates, and if you're sleeping with their sisters, and things go sideways with that, then…"

She nods vehemently. "You don't have to tell me twice."

That's the thing. I don't need to convince her about why this golden rule exists—for the good of the team. I don't need to win her over to it since she's already on board. It's like Sunday night never happened. I definitely don't need to convince her.

She adds enthusiastically, "Especially since we're roomies now and it's just a bad idea to—" But she swallows whatever she was going to say—sleep with your roomie? Date your roomie?

I don't even know, so I nod, because whatever she was going to say I'm sure I agree with. "Yes. Exactly. The roomie rule."

"And we'll follow it," she adds.

"We absolutely will."

We finish eating, and rather than ask her out for another night, I'm asking a more surreal question: "Want to see your new room?"

"I do," she says, then adds with a smile, "roomie!"

She says it brightly, like that's all she wants to be. That's going to have to be fine with me.

13

I'M A PRICK

Josie

Wesley parks outside Maeve's place so I can get my things. "Be right back," I say, cheery and upbeat.

I'm done with my brief bad mood over dinner. That was rude of me anyway. There's no need to be sullen about Wesley not telling me he chased pucks for a living the night we met. Not when he has the thing I need most—a place to live in comfortably for the next three months. And dammit, I'm going to be the best roomie ever, just like I try to be the best second-born child ever.

I fly up the stairs to Maeve's place, grateful she's out at a catering gig so I can hustle quickly. Once inside, I grab my suitcase—pre-packed this morning, just in case. Then, I rush to the bathroom to check the shower—which I won't miss. Then the vanity.

All good. I didn't leave anything behind. I'm ready to go. I text Maeve on my way to the door.

. . .

Josie: I love you madly, and I am so, so, so grateful you let me stay here for the week! Also, we're going to need a major debrief tomorrow. Like the biggest debrief of all time. For tonight, I am heading to...

Josie: Wait. I think I'll make you guess!

Maeve: Admit it—you love that I track you.

Josie: You weirdo.

Maeve: Um, check your weirdness at the door, girl who left on her tracker for five days. Anyway, can't wait for the debrief.

I do like the tracking. Maybe because no one cared that much about my whereabouts when I was younger. I still haven't turned it off.

I grab the doorknob but my gaze catches on Prick. After snagging the cactus I named, I hold it gingerly then head downstairs, lugging my suitcase, and avoiding the wobbly step. Won't miss that either. When I hit the first floor, I march as fast as I can to the door. Wesley's leaning against the car, looking relaxed and, well, climbable.

Shame.

He's wearing his post-game suit, which I appreciated far too much during our dinner. But he's shed the jacket already, so now he's lounging against the car in tailored burgundy slacks that hug his strong legs, a creme button-down and no tie. The cuffs of his sleeves are rolled up, revealing a hint of ink on his forearms—the line drawing of the dog and the edge of a music note.

He's holding his phone in his hand, listening to music presumably, giving me a few seconds to think about the real weirdness.

I'm going to live platonically with the guy I tried desperately to see again. Hell, I implored Frieda the Witch for his last name. She might have even told him I practically begged, bribed, and bought art for that last name. But I'll deal with that another time. For now, I have a place to stay, and so what if it's with a man who saw me naked once?

Wesley clearly just wanted a one-night stand, and that's fine with me. I wanted the same with him. Well, I did at the time. But it's not like I'm going to let on to him that I wanted more once it was over. He might think I'm clingy or worse—a stalker. Trying to track him down again at an art gallery is kind of a lot. My stomach churns at the memory from last night.

When Wesley makes eye contact with me, he hits stop, then pops out his earbuds and sets them in his pocket as he trots up the steps to grab my suitcase. "Let me help."

"Thanks," I say brightly, shifting into Super Roomie mode as he hoists my luggage easily into the car even though it weighs fifty metric tons. Once he's shut the trunk, I thrust the cactus at him. "Here you go! I got you a housewarming thank you present."

His brow pinches. "Already?"

"Well, Christian said he'd find me a place," I say, then I want to kick myself. I'm re-gifting the plant to a guy who's been generous enough to open his home to me. *Real classy.* "But it's okay. I can get you something else. What do you like? I mean, besides ice cream and records?"

And giving me orgasms.

"Plants are cool," he says, but it's like I've handed him a baby when he's never taken care of one.

"They don't need much. It's a bunny cactus. Just a little water. I call it Prick though. Since it attacked my chest last night. Made me bleed," I say, and *wow, what a great gift, girl.*

His lips twitch. "Prick?"

I wince. "I'll get some ice cream tomorrow."

He curls his hand around the little terracotta pot, shaking his head. "Prick is perfect."

He sets it gently on the floor of the backseat, then holds my door open for me. Once inside, a new reality hits me as he starts the car and eases into traffic. "I don't have anything besides my clothes and books. You said you had sheets, but do I need to get anything else? Towels? Toilet paper? Hangers?" I wave a hand. "I'll just go to Target tomorrow. I can take the bus."

As he buckles in, he smiles, the confident, in-control kind of grin he gave me the other night. "Josie, it's furnished. And I have all those things already."

Of course it is. "Right, right," I say. "The decorator. You mentioned a decorator."

He scratches his jaw. "Decorating's not my thing."

What is your thing? Besides saving half-naked women with clothes and now saving fully-clothed women with homes?

"Well, I'm excited to see it," I say, playing the Super Roomie role perfectly, since he's clearly a Super Landlord. Which brings me to another point—something I should have asked Christian. "What is the rent?"

Wesley scoffs.

I wait for his answer.

But he's silent.

"Seriously? What is it?" I ask again, hoping it's affordable. I'm sure it is—that was the point of me asking Christian for help. Still, I want to know.

"Josie, I'm not charging you rent."

"I can pay. I have a job. It's only for three months, but still, I have one. How about I pay whatever I was going to pay for the short-term rental?"

He shoots me a quick look before he changes lanes. "How about you don't?"

"Wesley," I plead. This man is so generous. But I can't keep taking from him. "I want to pay. *Something.*"

"Josie," he says, his voice as stern as it was when he told me to bend over the bed. "I own my home. *Outright.* I only want you to be a guest."

Now is clearly not the time to argue with this bossy and generous man—and that's a lethal combo. *Lethal to my panties.* "I'll find a way," I say, and maybe I can plant some seeds for the next time this comes up. "I can cook, I can make coffee, I can water plants, I can help...and I can shelve books according to the Dewey Decimal System."

"How about you do your own dishes and keep things neat, and we'll call it good?"

I can tell that's as far as I'm getting, so I drop the topic, saying, "I won't miss the spring on Maeve's couch."

He tosses me a look as he slows at the lights on Fillmore. "The one that was going to stab you in the ass?"

I groan privately. I told him about the evil spring the night we slept together. *Way to move on, Josie.* "Yes. That one. And it definitely attacked me. I have the bruise on my butt to prove it," I say, and that probably doesn't help either—all this butt talk. I quickly pivot. "So, if you don't have black sheets, are they...Sea Dogs colors?"

"They're navy."

"That's in the same family as Sea Dogs colors," I point

out as he drives.

"The Sea Dogs color is royal blue," he says.

Okaaaay. This isn't awkward at all, discussing the precise hue of his team colors instead of the attack spring. "Right. Of course," I say, then hunt around for safe topics. Not hockey. Not Sea Dogs. Not the other night. What do roomies discuss? House stuff. "So you have a room under the stairs? Is it like a cupboard?"

He shakes his head. "No. It's a room. It sort of extends past the staircase. It even has a window. And a nook."

My mouth waters. "A reading nook?"

"I guess you could use it for that."

"What else would someone use it for?"

He shrugs as he drives past shops I'll want to check out soon, like An Open Book and Bling and Baubles. "I don't know," he says. "I don't use it. Honestly, no one has even stayed there since I moved in. Guess it's a virgin room."

That doesn't make me think of sex either.

He flicks the turn signal and turns onto Jackson Street, full of modern homes with Scandinavian designs, square-like structures in cool shades of gray, with metal and wood accents that give them a modern, minimalist feel. Every yard is well-kept, every porch is pristine, and every home screams money.

I hate that Christian was right, but this area is the opposite of the one the short-term rental was in. Wesley pulls into a tiny driveway, then hits a button for a sleek garage. Once inside, I step out of the car into a neat, clean space. Is Wesley neat and organized? I'm dying to know simply because I want to know him.

But I shouldn't want to know him. He's just a room-mate—that's all. He pops the trunk, then grabs the suitcase from the trunk before I can. I snag the cactus from the floor of the backseat as he punches the code into the door and swings it open.

"After you." He flicks on a switch. Everything is light and airy. Clean and quiet.

We head up a short flight of stairs to the main floor, where he sets my bag down. "Let me show you around."

I try not to gawk. Really I do. I've seen nice homes before. My brother has a nice place. But Christian's five years older and he's always felt twenty years my senior. Wesley feels like my generation, and it's strange for someone my age to have a place this upscale.

"How old are you?" I ask, instantly wishing I could take it back. I've been trained not to ask people's ages. You're not supposed to do it at work. I shouldn't do it with Wesley. Even though I *could* find all his info online since he's a pro athlete.

"Twenty-seven," he says, saving me from Google as I set down the cactus on a table in the foyer. "I grew up in Denver. I was drafted at eighteen. Played in college. Then in New York for four and a half years. Was traded last season in February. I studied marketing in school," he says, then shrugs. "Yeah, it's the jock major, I know."

But I wasn't going to say that. "I don't think it's the jock major," I say earnestly.

He shrugs casually. "It's cool. It is. At least it was at my school. And I took rocks for jocks, dinosaurs for jocks, planets for jocks, and so on."

I feel terrible now. "I didn't mean to make you feel like you had to give me your CV. It's just really nice—your home. I'm not used to that from people my age. I'm twenty-six." Since we're both course-correcting from the other night, I add more. "I have a master's in library and information science. My undergrad was English. And hey, I took physics for poets," I say, and that makes him laugh as he leans against the doorframe leading into the living room. It's a good look. One I cannot, should not, and will not linger on. "And English was the nerd major."

"Your words."

"I like words. And nerds. Which I am obviously one of," I stage whisper.

Wesley holds my gaze for a long beat, his eyes going darker, his lips curving the slightest bit, almost like he wants to say something, but then must think the better of it, since he says, all businesslike now, "Let me show you around."

He walks me through the living room. There's a huge U-shaped couch, a flat-screen TV with a game console, and a record player on a table. We head into the kitchen, which is man-magazine-style worthy. I can't resist. "Hey, it *is* black and chrome," I tease, rapping my knuckles on the marble counter.

"Yeah," he says, scratching his jaw, like he's taking it in. "But I don't mind. I don't use it a ton." He strides to the Sub-Zero fridge, so gleaming it could double as a mirror. Patting it, he says, "I'll make some room in the fridge for you. It's full of prepared meals right now." He sounds apologetic, but whether it's for the meals or the lack of fridge space, I don't know.

"You cook in advance? Because I can definitely help with that," I offer, hoping, truly hoping, he takes me up on it. "My aunt taught me to cook. And I can do healthy stuff too, like you had tonight."

He gives a quick shake of his head. "I have a meal service."

"Oh. Okay," I say, a little defeated, but I'll find some

way to help. "That sounds fun too."

"My dad set it up. The meal service," he says, lowering his voice, like it embarrasses him.

He mentioned his dad that night. That he'd sent him to the art gallery. I'm about to say something along those lines to show I paid attention, but I think the better of it since I don't want to bring up Frieda and maybe summon her somehow. She'd probably descend in a black cloud of vengeance and Chanel and tell Wesley I've been creeping on him, so I say, "Sounds cool."

"It's whatever," he says, and that *whatever* is doing a lot of work in telling me how he feels about his meal plan and perhaps his father. He guides me down the hall, gesturing to the staircase leading to the second floor. "I'm up there."

"Got it. The main bedroom suite," I say, then playfully —or so I hope—add, "I'll stay away from it."

His jaw ticks briefly, then he moves on and says, "And there's a room at the end of the hall. It's a gym."

"Makes sense."

"But I usually work out with friends instead."

"Cool."

He turns around and opens the door under the stairs, and I moan in pleasure. The cutout-style white door leads into a cozy room with a peaked roof. He gestures for me to go first and I head inside, whimpering in happiness as I look around. There's a dove gray area rug with cute geometric shapes in different colors on it, and a full-size bed with a navy comforter. The best part, though, is the window seat. It's covered in white and blue pillows, and my heart does a jig. "It's the cutest thing I've ever seen," I say, bringing my hand to my chest.

"Yeah?"

"It's so cute I could cry," I say, then impulsively, I fling my arms around him. "It's the first thing that's gone right for me since I arrived," I say into his neck, where I catch his scent. It's the way he smelled the other night. Like the forest trees from my little town in Maine, and a mountain stream. I save these details in my Wesley file. He has a favorite cologne. Maybe even a lucky one that he likes so much he keeps it at home and at work.

I draw a furtive inhale and once again, he's my sexy stranger. The man who plus-oned me into an art opening simply to help me, who took me shopping so I wouldn't feel foolish without pants, who bought me ice cream on our date, who rented a hotel room to fulfill my wish for a one-night stand.

For a second, he seems unsure what to do with my hug, then his strong arms wrap around me. His muscles mold to my body. Images flash wildly through my mind.

His arm locking me into place when he fucked me hard the other night.

His hands on my ass when he went down on me.

His lips coasting over every inch of me, including my belly button ring.

When he breaks the embrace before I do, his eyes drift over my body, stopping at my stomach. Is he remembering my belly button piercing too?

He clears his throat, but he looks...blank, almost stony, as he says, "There you go. Good night."

He's gone. Leaving me alone in this room. It's only when I sit down on the bed that my last words echo.

It's the first thing that's gone right for me since I arrived.

I groan. I've already insulted my new landlord. I'm the prick.

14

MY WINGWOMAN

Wesley

Saturday morning is now for working out instead of asking out. That's fine. It's totally fine. It's a rest day since we played last night, but cardio's cool on rest days. So, I hit the gym with Max and Asher, who give me hell from the StairMasters about me saying yes to Christian. If they only knew the whole of it. But I'm not telling them, now or ever.

"Maybe, I dunno, you should offer a room to the coach's daughter next?" Asher suggests, so fucking helpfully, as we're leaving the gym on Fillmore Street.

"Don't forget the owner's sister too," Max puts in.

"Mock me for being nice. That's a real good look," I say to the two of them as we head up the block, bustling with people pushing strollers and carrying coffee and more babies.

"You're so sweet, Wesley," Asher taunts.

"We must protect you at all costs," Max adds with faux

admiration.

After I check that no one's watching us, I hold my hands out wide, then flip them both double birds. "With friends like you…"

"Friends? Who said we were friends?" Max tilts his head, adopting a confused look.

"News to me," Asher says with an innocent shrug.

"And on that note, I'm outta here." I give them a wave and they do the same back, then I take off at a rapid clip. Why walk when I can run? I pop in my earbuds, blasting The Last Shadow Puppets as I near my favorite coffee shop, Doctor Insomnia's. Does Josie like coffee? Should I grab her one? I bet she likes lattes.

I'm turning toward the chalkboard sign by the door, tendrils of purple steam rising above a chalk drawing of a coffee cup in the same color, when I decide against it. That's a boyfriend move—not a roomie one.

As I cruise up the street, I get a little lost in the music, but when I turn onto Jackson Street, a strange mix of both dread and excitement builds in my gut. It gets stronger as I near my home.

I don't like this feeling.

Trouble is, I don't know how to behave around Josie. Yesterday, when I offered to help Christian, I figured it'd be a "ships passing in the night" kind of deal with his sister. She'd do her thing; I'd do the captain a solid. My parents always taught me to "help out whenever you can." True, when it comes to my dad with me, he *over helps*. But Mom had a good sense of balance and still does, so my offer wasn't so much sucking up as second nature. I wish I could call her and ask her what to do next in this situation since she's good with people, but she's been traveling across Asia with her husband. He's from Vietnam, so they're doing a connect-with-the-roots type of tour, and I don't need to bug her.

Too bad that give-a-hand instinct now has me living with my one-night stand who I wanted to date but can't. The whole situation gives new meaning to the word awkward.

When I reach my home, I bound up the steps, bracing myself for—I don't even know what I'm walking into.

I barely know Josie.

Plus, she wasn't awake when I got up. No idea if she's an ogre in the mornings or an angel. If she bounces around in pink workout pants doing pilates and planks, or shuffles bleary-eyed in jammies and fuzzy socks. Maybe she'll be wandering around post-shower, a towel cinched around her tits, her wet hair sleek down her back.

I pray it's not the latter, even though I fucking wish it were the latter. Which sums up my life right now.

But when I unlock the door and head inside, my home is eerily quiet. Well, her brother *did* say she kept to herself. He knows her better than I do.

I toe off my sneakers at the door, drag a hand through my sweaty hair, and head for the kitchen to grab a glass of water. After I pour a cup and down it greedily, I turn around, spotting an album on the counter, resting against the blender my dad got me.

It's a record I've been wanting. Plus, there's a folded-over sheet of paper with my name on the front. My heart gallops for a beat or two. Weird. Must just be the post-run adrenaline. Yeah, that has to be it.

I flip open the sheet of light blue paper. And I stand corrected. It's two sheets of paper. This girl loves writing notes with pen and paper. It's long as fuck, but I'm determined, and glad, too, she took the time to put it on two pages.

Dear Wesley,

Something you should know about me is this—when I go to bed after nine-thirty, I turn into a monster. Think Medusa, Grendel, Pennywise the Clown. And then I say things like "this room is the first thing that's gone right all week."

I'm sorry!

That was so insensitive of me to say. Clearly this room is not the first thing that's been good about this week.

Anyway, I'm the worst! My only excuse is the late bedtime.

The room is amazing, and so are you for helping me out yet again. I know nothing about the "Good Neighbors Band" but the guy who runs the record shop on Hayes Street (who incidentally looks like he runs a record shop, what with the shoulder-length hair, leather bracelets, wiry arms, and goatee) said if you like Ben Rogers you'll probably like the Good Neighbors Band. I hope you don't have it already!

Anyway, here it is. A thank you gift. The cactus doesn't count because it's a prick.

P.S. Since we're roomies now and this stuff is probably useful, here are five things you should know about me.

1. I love mornings!

2. I am not as neat as you but I promise I will be neater because your neatness is inspiring.

3. I love to explore, and I plan to learn everything possible about San Francisco over the next three months.

4. See 3—I like to learn. It's basically my entire personality.

5. I also am in a committed relationship with baking. But should I keep tempting food out of the house? I don't mind not baking for the next three months! I am very adaptable. Which is sort of a sixth thing about me.

Josie

After I take my time reading it, making sure I didn't miss any words, I set it down on the counter, rubbing my sternum because it feels a little funny. A little fizzy.

No one leaves me letters. *Ever.* In one week, I've received two from her. It's kind of...adorably old-fashioned. I bet she likes *Bridgerton* too. Probably old standards like Sinatra and Ella Fitzgerald as well. I pick up the album, my lips curving up in appreciation of the gift but mostly the gesture.

Something bothers me about the letter though. The time frame. She's only here for three months. There's an expiration date to her presence. But that's for the best. Really, it is.

I head to the living room to put the record on when the front door swings open.

"Good morning! I picked up fruit," Josie says, holding

a canvas bag, her chestnut hair back in a high ponytail, her jeans painted to the curves of her ass. "You said you had meal plans, and I know you don't need someone to cook, and I definitely don't want you to break your plan, but I figured fruit is always allowed, right?"

"Pretty sure," I say evenly since I don't want to let on how much I like that she bought me fruit. Or how hard it is to look away from her pink, glossy lips.

"Cool. So, maybe I can pay rent in fruit," she says, so damn hopeful. She's making such an effort to contribute that maybe I shouldn't be so rigid.

"You can pay rent in fruit," I say, acquiescing.

She pumps a fist. "Yes!"

"But you're not going to pay rent in cleaning, or cooking, or anything like that. You're a roommate—not a maid. Also, good morning."

"Thank you," she says with genuine gratitude, and acceptance, too, that rent isn't up for negotiation.

She walks toward the living room. She's wearing a sky blue top that slopes off one shoulder—a very tantalizing shoulder I want to kiss, lick, and bite. She stops in her tracks as her gaze lands on my feet. I'm just in socks now. She kicks off her sneakers next to the table with Prick the Cactus on it, then continues into my home, offering an apologetic glance my way. "Oh, I see you got the album."

"I did," I say, sliding the LP out of the cover. "You really didn't have to."

"I felt bad about last night," she says, frowning. "What I said. And the way you left the room."

What does she mean? I rack my brain trying to figure it out. "No idea what you're talking about."

She's peering at me through those cute glasses,

looking flummoxed momentarily. She takes a breath, then says, "Well, you left in such a rush. You just took off."

I flash back to last night in her room. She hugged me for a good long time. I caught the scent of her hair. Vanilla. Then the scent of her skin—cinnamon. My brain short-circuited, then sent me back in time when she pressed her face against my chest.

Oh.

Ohhh.

Shit. She thinks I was mad at her when I hightailed it out of her room. That couldn't be further from the truth. "That's not why I left," I say curtly.

"Okay," she says, but clearly she's still confused.

I could alleviate that confusion. Really, I could. But I'm not sure telling her I wanted to fuck her last night would fix this problem. Instead, I turn around and put the album on the turntable, taking my time setting the needle on the groove. As the first track fills the room, she heads into the kitchen to set the canvas bag on the counter.

She takes apples, pears, figs, and grapes from the canvas bag with intense concentration that's not needed for the task, but maybe it is needed to deal with a dickish roomie.

But what am I supposed to say? *You have no idea how hard it was NOT to fuck my hand to thoughts of you last night like I've done several nights prior? Also, your lips are incredible.*

Instead, I head into the kitchen to help her. I grab the grapes. "I can wash these."

"Thanks. I don't know where the colander is anyway."

I need to do better. "Let me show you where everything is."

She smiles at me again. "You don't mind?"

What kind of monster would I be if I did mind? And

who's treated her so poorly as to mind about something like that? "No. Of course not."

I spend the next twenty minutes properly showing her around the kitchen, and washing the grapes. Then I give her a better tour of the living room, the guest bathroom, the gym, and the garage. I don't show her my room, because what's the point? She's not going to come upstairs ever. I'm not that strong.

When we're back in the kitchen, I say, "So that's that."

"Thanks again," she says, cheery.

But it's like she's trying extra hard to be nice. Maybe because I was a dick. Maybe because I'm still behaving like one. I lean against the counter, and try a new tactic. "Who's Grendel?"

Her blue eyes sparkle as she says, "The monster in *Beowulf*."

Yeah, maybe it's for the best I never dropped off that scarf with my note. There's no way we'd work out—a guy who hates reading and a girl who's obsessed with it. No dating app is matching the librarian with the dude with dyslexia. "Pretty sure that was in my do-not-read pile in high school," I say, with a deliberately easygoing shrug.

"Confession: I think it's in everyone's do-not-read pile."

That's a minor relief—that she didn't like *Beowulf*. Did anyone? "But I like Pennywise," I say, then quickly add, "From the movie. Well, I don't like him. But mad respect for his villainy."

"Definitely."

"Also, I don't think you're a monster. Like you said in your letter." I scratch my jaw, hunting for a suitable explanation for my behavior. "Listen, last night when I left your room, it wasn't over what you said. I was just...adjusting."

She takes a few seconds, seeming to consider that. "I'm sorry. Am I...cramping your style, living here?"

Ah, fuck. We are not at all in sync. On anything. "No, not like that, Josie."

With big, guileless eyes, she says, "I'll look for another place. It shouldn't be a problem. I'm sure I can find something in a few days. I'm very resourceful."

That is not happening. No way. Failure is not an option. "No."

"No?"

I place more emphasis on the word: *"No.* You're staying here. Your brother wanted you in a safe neighborhood. But guess what? I do too."

She blinks, like that comment surprises her. "But I don't want to put you out or make things weird." Then, like an idea just landed in that big brain of hers, she says, "We can make rules for that too. Like what happens if you want to bring a girl over."

She offers it like she'd be my matchmaker now. Maybe my wingwoman. Like she's going to want to flop down on the couch next to me when I return from a date, rip open a bag of popcorn, and say, "So how did it go? Do you like her?"

And everything—every single thing—about that image is all wrong. Especially the flip side of it. What if she wants to do the same thing after she goes out with a dude? I grimace. But then, I try to do the right thing as I say, "Or if you do."

It comes out like there are stones in my throat.

She shakes her head. "I won't."

I cross my arms. "I won't either."

It's a face-off. For a too-long beat, we stand here in the kitchen, waiting for the puck to drop. Problem is I'm unsure what we're even fighting about. "Josie, it's all good. I'm happy to have you here. And you are definitely, absolutely not going to look for another place to live," I say, then lock my eyes with hers. "Got that?"

Her pink glossy lips twitch in a smile. "You're *still* bossy."

That's what she said to me the night we spent together. And just like that, some of my tension melts away. "Yes. I am."

She breathes out a big sigh. "Okay, then." She hesitates. "But I'm truly fine with us making rules. For anything. It'll make this whole roomie thing easier. And I just want us to...get along."

"Me too," I say, but the thought of making rules for when we want to screw other people makes me clench my fists. "But let's deal with that rules thing another time."

Speaking of time, I check the clock. "Hey, I need to meet up with my dad while he's in town," I say, then a terrible thought lands in my head. Frieda. What if she's there at lunch? What if she brings up *the woman in the T-shirt?* I don't want to deal with that with my dad. Don't want to tell him I have a roomie now. Don't want to hear how other people are distracting. Still, since Josie and I are trying to be honest, there's something she should know from that night. "Frieda from the art gallery is his girlfriend."

Josie's face goes pale, her voice strangled as she asks, "Frieda the Witch?"

"Unfortunately," I say with a laugh. I tilt my head, considering this woman who landed in my life with her words, and her gifts of fruit and song, and her belly button piercing, and her letters, and her clever mouth and her bright attitude. "Do you have a nickname for every-one? The Prick, Frieda the Witch, etcetera."

"Yes. I do," she says and before I can ask if she's given me one—though I probably shouldn't ask that, she adds in a worried voice, "Are they coming over?"

I scoff. "God no. He'd critique my walls and my choice to *not* buy art. I already got an earful the other day. Through my sister. Apparently, Frieda told my dad and my sister about the *woman in the T-shirt*."

I figure that'll ease the tension more. Make Josie laugh. But instead she looks like she's just seen a monster for real. She's covered her face with her fingers.

"What's wrong, Josie?"

When she drops her hand, she looks like she's bitten something sour. "I went to the gallery on Thursday night to get your last name."

If I were on the ice, I'd skate into the boards in shock. "You did?" There's no way she said that. No way she did that. There's no way she was doing the same thing I was doing. Amped up, I take a step toward her, like I'm going to close the distance between us, pin her against the wall and devour her.

Which would be a very bad idea.

And yet it has a hold on me.

She nods. "I did."

I'm this close to breaking our first roomie rule till she says, "I went there to thank you. For helping me the other night. So if she brings it up, that's what happened. I wanted to thank you. With...a cactus."

She spins on her heels and takes off for her room like I did last night—leaving me with more questions than before.

* * *

"And when you do the late-night workout, it can improve your performance," Dad says as he spears his fork into his salmon dish.

We're at his favorite seafood place by the Marina, and he's eating the same thing I ordered—seared salmon with asparagus, a little lemon on the side. I used to think this was ordering solidarity. But I'm pretty sure he eats like this when I'm not around too. The dude is made of iron and discipline.

"Yup," I say since that's what Domingo said already— the guy my dad hired who I worked with all summer.

"It's nothing that different from what you do during your regular workouts. Dead lifts, weighted push-ups, side planks..." he drones on. It's not that I disagree with Dad or Domingo. I'd just rather discuss something else during lunch. "Sports science shows the benefits of this. It's a productive time to keep up your strength," Dad adds.

After I finish my bite, I say, "And that means I'll be less likely to come up short in a race to the puck."

He beams. "Exactly, Wesley."

I knew that was what he wanted to hear.

His smile lasts, a rare one on his otherwise stoic face.

I've been told I look like him. Strong jawline, straight nose, same brown eyes. His hair is shorter though and speckled with gray. He's got the whole George Clooney vibe working for him. I guess that's why he's done so well with the ladies since he and my mom split when I was younger.

He chats more about the post-game workout plan, and I nod and listen as I finish my lunch. "I can send that all to you over email," he says. "You should read it too."

I grind my teeth, but then say, "I'll listen to it, Dad."

He knows that's what I do. He hired tutors for me when I was younger. He helped me get a handle on *my issue.* "Good plan."

When we leave, he says, "Listen, Frieda mentioned *this woman.*"

I groan. Seriously. I do not want to discuss Josie with Dad. Well, I would if he wanted to discuss it like a normal dad. "Yeah?"

"Are you seeing her?"

"Nope."

He nods, pleased. "Just making sure you're not distracted."

I snort-laugh. He's got me scheduled every second the Sea Dogs don't. "How could I be?"

He tilts his head in question.

"I don't have time to get distracted," I say lightly, trying, always trying to lighten the mood.

It fails though, since he says, "That's the right mindset."

When he says goodbye and I walk home, I'm entirely too distracted by thoughts of what my roomie's up to.

Figuring I should be civil to her, like she's been to me, I send her a text.

Wesley: Do you like Bridgerton?

15

JUST THE TIP

Josie

Maeve flips through the shelf of memoirs at An Open Book as I finish telling my friends my tale of woe. Fable is here too. She's the lead designer for the San Francisco Renegades and a friend of ours as well.

"And you didn't recognize him at all the night you met him?" Fable asks, but it doesn't come out as an accusation —more a legit question.

"I'm not into sports. I mean, they're fine. I don't hate them. But I don't know rosters. If any pro athlete but my brother was walking through this store I wouldn't recognize them," I say. "Would you recognize all the football players?"

"Yes, but I love the game," Fable says, as she tucks a strand of her red hair behind her ear and sets down the book she's been checking out. Freckles dot her fair skin.

"I'd recognize Asher Callahan," Maeve puts in.

I roll my eyes. "That doesn't count. He's your brother's friend!"

"I'm just saying. I would," Maeve adds.

I toss my hands up. "You two are not helpful. You're supposed to be on my side. Hockey players are not that recognizable."

Fable gives me that point. "Fine, that's true." Then she snickers. "Still, it's funny that Wesley Bryant is kind of known around town for being this hot tamale and you banged him without having a clue who he is."

"And now you're living with him," Maeve adds with a snort, her wild golden hair falling in her face as she doubles over.

"You two!" I say, exasperated. "I called this meeting today for you to help me deal with living with him. To give me tips."

Fable's lips go ruler straight as she says, "Like can you have...wait for it...just the tip?"

Maeve points at her, nodding. "That's totally acceptable. That won't violate any rules."

"You should definitely play 'just the tip' with him," Fable adds, with a *so helpful* smile.

My face flames hot. Why am I cursed with being easily embarrassed and also overly sexed? As if I haven't been thinking about Wesley like that already. "Shh," I say as an elderly woman walks past, a small child tugging her hand along.

"The other tip is this—just sit on a bucket of ice for the next three months," Maeve offers. "Freeze out your vagina."

"Or buy stock in toys," Fable adds with her signature confidence, and I can't get a word in edgewise with these two.

"Speaking of, have you figured out *that* issue?" Fable asks with mock concern.

Maeve parks an elbow on the shelves, her face going serious as she echoes, "Yeah, have you?"

"How I'm going to masturbate with him around?" I whisper, incredulous that they're really asking that.

"Yes. That's a real problem. Will you? Won't you?" Maeve asks with a straight face.

I am a beet. But I hold my chin up high and answer them: "When he's out of town for games I will. So there."

After they buy their books, and I make note of ones I'll borrow from the library, we leave. On the way down the block, my phone pings with a message from my roomie, asking me if I like *Bridgerton*.

I don't show it to my evil friends as we walk to a coffee shop. I reply quietly with: *Is that a trick question?*

Then I tuck the device away, only to be met by the Cheshire cat grin on Maeve. "That smile means he's texted."

I groan. "I can't have any secrets with you."

Giving in, I show them the text. Since I'm a glutton for punishment I tell them what happened this morning when I confessed to Wesley why I'd seen Frieda. "I couldn't very well tell him I wanted to track him down to see if he was up for hanging out again. He made it perfectly clear it was a one-night stand."

"And so did you," Fable points out as we reach Doctor Insomnia's.

She's right. But just because I *actually* wanted more doesn't mean we can have it. "Look. It's fine. It's for the best if we try to be nice to each other. To get along."

Maeve grabs the door and yanks it open. "Yes, Josie.

You should text him back because it's nice. Not because you still want to ride his dick."

"You're not making this easier," I say.

"I know, and I have no regrets," she says.

"Speaking of no regrets, let's talk about the list," I say, as my stomach dips thinking about item number two. Maybe I've been avoiding it. No, there is no maybe about it. I've definitely been avoiding the second item Aunt Greta left for me. Because it's about overcoming a fear.

Once we grab our lattes and seats, we shift gears to the list of the Top Ten Things I Never Regretted. "Question," I begin, with a hopeful smile. "Do you think it's possible I could get a pass on number two?"

Maeve stares me down sternly. "Josie."

Fable clucks her tongue. "Pretty sure that's a violation of the rules of Bucket Lists from Relatives."

I groan. "It's just...so not me."

Maeve pats my hand. "I know. But you didn't think number one was either. And Greta knew you well."

She's too right. I set my face on the table and groan some more, like a wounded beast. "Why do bucket lists have rules?"

It's asked of the universe.

Of course they don't have rules. I know that. But when the person who loved you most gives you one, you probably shouldn't skip a turn.

"And I thought the first one was hard," I mutter.

Maeve smirks.

Fable's eyes twinkle. "Well, wasn't it?"

I roll my eyes. "Very, very hard."

I sigh, lift my face, then brainstorm a plan for number two.

* * *

That afternoon, I take off to see Christian, Liv, the twins, and my mom, who's here in town now, helping out.

My brother and his wife are in another room in their palace of a house, napping. Mom spends the whole time parked on the living room couch, holding the babies and talking about the babies—what they eat, what they weigh, what they'll need, and how they've slept. I get it. They're her first grandkids. I'm not really bothered that she hasn't asked about my job—which is the reason I'm here in San Francisco.

She shifts gears, asking if I want something to eat. "We ordered pad thai with chicken for lunch. There are plenty of leftovers," she says, then catches herself. "Except... you're still vegetarian?"

Like it's the same as my pony phase. My *Sweet Valley High* phase. "I still am," I say.

"They have some carrots," she offers.

I shake my head. "I'm good, Mom."

A few minutes later, she finally says, "How is the library?" It's asked with clear interest, so I tell her the full truth.

"I love it already," I say. "I just do."

"Tell me everything," she says, and I give her the highlights, including Raccoon, which delights her.

"I'm so happy, Jay. And you know Greta would be happy too."

She would. She truly would. Sometimes I feel like Greta's all mine, but my mom lost a sister too, far too early. Then, since she knows it exists even though she hasn't seen the list, I draw a quiet breath and say, "I started it. The list Greta gave me."

Her eyes widen. "Oh. You did?"

"Yes, I finally did," I say.

"That's wonderful." She pauses, swallows, perhaps collecting her emotions too, then says, "Does it make you feel closer to her?"

Well, the one-night stand made me feel closer to my roomie. But I don't tell her that. I just nod. "It does."

"Good. I'm glad."

"Me too."

Later, when I say goodbye and head out with my map on my phone and a plan to check out the Painted Ladies, I think back to some of my fondest memories with my aunt. Days spent wandering the library she took me to in her town. Afternoons getting lost in the stacks. Early evenings back at her little cottage, eating tomato soup and grilled cheese and playing Monopoly while my parents took my brother to one hockey thing or another.

"How do you do it? How do you take me for everything I'm worth in Monopoly?" she'd ask when she'd land on Park Place and I'd ask her to fork over so much rent.

I'd just smile and say, "I'm good at following the rules."

"The rules aren't why you win. The strategy is," she'd say with a twinkle in her eye like she was sharing a secret. A secret just for me. "And you've got that, baby."

Baby. I was always baby. But it was said like *baby* was a Broadway star. That's how I felt with her—like the star.

I picture the list, tucked safely away inside a blank book in my canvas bag back in my room.

As I walk past the Victorians in pretty shades of yellow, lavender, and mint, I check the time. It's late afternoon on a Saturday. What does Wesley do on Saturday nights? Will it be weird for me to punch in the passcode on the door, wander in and say, "Hey, what are you up to on a Saturday night?"

I haven't had a roommate since my freshman year of college, and we were totally out of sync. Staying with Maeve was different. Besties don't have boundaries that can't be crossed. My stomach flip-flops with worry. I don't want to encroach on his space any more than I already have.

But that's what books and book nooks are for. That's what I'll do—escape into a book.

With that resolved, I walk up and down the blocks around Alamo Square, getting to know my new temporary home and settling into a plan for the evening. I'll make a cheese sandwich, slice an apple, and return to my room to enjoy the spine-tingling thriller about a suburban mom who becomes convinced her neighbors across the street are murderers.

* * *

But that settled feeling disappears when I head up the steps to Wesley's place. Returning this morning from my fruit and grocery errand was different. It was daylight. It's dusk now and nighttime is, well, its own mood.

Maybe I should call first? What if he just got out of the shower and is slinging on a towel? My chest goes hot. I stop mid-stairs, grabbing the railing. *Not a helpful thought, girl.*

I take a beat to let that tempting image subside, then reach the door, poised to tap in the code. But I can't shake the feeling that I'm an interloper. With a wince, I knock instead, offering a cheery, "Knock, knock."

I listen for noise. It's quiet. Then peer into the slim, rectangular window right next to the front door. Nothing.

I start to punch in the code when my breath catches.

Oh god.

This is not a drill. Repeat after me. This is not a drill. Wesley's in gray sweats and nothing else.

The man is shirtless, and I'm just dead.

16

A LITTLE NOSEY

Josie

I'm gawking. I really need to stop. I do my best to pick up my jaw right as he swings open the door, tilting his head.

"Um, you don't have to knock," he says.

I don't have to stare either but I'm doing that too. That carved chest. The smattering of dark hair across his ripped pecs. The ladder of his abs, with muscles stacked on top of muscles. I can't stop cataloging all the spots on the map of his body. That blue bruise I traced lightly last Sunday on the side of his stomach is gone now, but there's a fresh one on his right bicep.

And then there's the scar on his wrist. White and faded—a marker. Yeah, it's definitely not from a bike. "It's from a skate," I say, entering the conversation *in medias res*.

His brow knits as he motions for me to come inside. "What do you mean?" He asks it like I'm the weirdo he regrets inviting to live with him.

Because I am. I try to collect my thoughts. "The scar. On your right wrist. It's from a skate blade, right?"

He gives a small smile of resignation. Then a nod. One that says he didn't want to tell me he played hockey the night I met him. "Happened my first season."

I toe off my canvas sneakers as he shuts the door. "What happened? Did it hurt?"

"I got stitches and returned to the game to get an assist."

I roll my eyes but in admiration of his mettle. "Such a hockey player move."

He just shrugs. "It was the only thing to do." He tips his forehead to my chin. "Also, pot, kettle. You got back on your bike after you cut your chin."

My heart rate spikes. He remembers every detail. "I did." I pause then get out my conversational backhoe and fill in the rest of the story. "I was chasing my brother. So I had to get back on my bike. I was determined to stay on. But I'm not athletic. Like, whatsoever. I tried soccer once, and I stood in the corner of the field wondering if Katniss was going to save Peeta or not."

"She did. *A lot*."

"She really did," I say. "And even if I got back on the bike, I'm really *not athletic*."

"You're tougher than you think." He gestures to the kitchen. "I'm making some food. Do you want something?"

"Sure. I can make my own stuff though. I don't need to take your food."

"I'm offering," Wesley says, and I follow him through the house, walking through the living room where the TV screen is paused on a hockey game to the kitchen. He's set up quite the spread on a beautiful blond-wood charcuterie board with a pretty array of grapes, broccoli spears, daikon radishes, nuts, blackberries, and olives.

"Wow. You're a charcuterist," I say.

"I took a class," he explains.

"There are classes on charcuterie boards?"

"Josie, there are classes on everything," he says dryly, a little playfully, and the tone makes me feel like *maybe* we can figure out this whole "living together" thing without every second being awkward.

But also, his comment about classes makes me think about the second item on the list. A kernel of dread swirls in my gut, but I ignore it as I survey the offerings. I half want to tease him about the lack of cheese, but his comment from last night about meal plans tells me not to. "Your teacher would be very impressed. Looks good, but I don't want to take your food."

He sighs. "Josie, I'm offering."

Shit. I'm handling this badly. I meet his gaze. I can tell he's trying to navigate this whole situation. I'm trying too but failing, so I blurt out a confession: "I haven't had a roommate since college, and I'm pretty sure both of them hated me from day one."

He scoffs. "Why would anyone hate you?"

"Because I asked them to raise their beds," I say, then quickly explain. "We all had different move-in dates. They moved in the day before me into a freshman triple with three elevated beds. When I moved in both of theirs were already lowered and their bureaus and things were spread out. When I asked them to elevate their dorm beds so we could all have enough room to put desks and stuff under our respective beds, they both refused. One told me she was afraid of ceilings. The other said there'd be no room for her things then."

He sneers. "So they hated you in response to their self-ishness?"

"Yes," I say.

"That makes no sense. Also, why didn't you tell them that that was bullshit?"

I flash back to my freshman year, to how uncomfortable the living situation was after that. To how selfish they were. To how I dreaded returning to my dorm room every afternoon when I was through with classes. "I didn't want to make the situation worse," I admit.

"I'm not like your freshman roommates."

"I know but I really don't know how to do this. I don't want to get in your way," I say, choosing patent honesty.

He pauses, seeming to consider that. "I get it. And I don't want to get in your way either."

"But it's your house," I say, then flap a hand toward his bare chest. "Clearly you're used to walking around half-naked."

He looks down at his chest like he's just realized he's not wearing a shirt. When he lifts his face, he offers me a wry smile. "Maybe I was doing it in solidarity. Of your half-naked attire."

"By all means then, please stage a march in support," I say.

The corner of his lips twitches. "If I have to."

"I insist," I say.

For a hot second, his smile turns a little dangerous, but then it's like he thinks the better of it and points to the stairs, resigned. "I'll put a shirt on."

I want to tell him *please don't*. But instead I let him bound up the steps. While he's gone I pour a glass of water, and do my best to think unsexy thoughts as I drink.

When he returns, he's wearing a blue Sea Dogs shirt. He slides the charcuterie board toward me. "Eat," he says.

"Can I at least contribute an apple?" I offer.

"You are really determined, aren't you?"

"Yes," I say, lifting my chin. "Just like I was determined to make the best of my freshman year situation."

"I promise I am nothing like your asshole college roomies," he says, then wiggles a brow and shifts the broccoli, revealing a slither of red underneath. "Also, I did use your apples. Cosmic Crisps are fucking elite."

"Dude! I know," I say, then grab an apple slice and crunch into it. When I finish chewing, I grab another and point it at him, then gesture to the spread. "Is this on your meal plan?"

He brings a finger to his lips. "Shh."

"Scofflaw," I say in mock surprise.

But he just smiles. "Actually, it is. Under 'acceptable snacks.'"

"So you work out, you eat clean, you watch hockey. I'm sensing a theme," I tease.

His smile burns off, and his face goes stony for a minute. "I like other things besides hockey." It's said a little defensively.

I backpedal quickly with a bright, "Of course you do."

"It's just...the job keeps me busy."

I've really put my foot in my mouth. "I totally get it."

Dragging a hand through his hair, he sighs. "Sorry. Sore spot. You would have no way of knowing that."

I feel a little better that he's said that, but I'm still somewhat unsteady. "I'm sorry too," I say, then shrug helplessly. "I just...I'm not sure how to do this roomie thing."

"Honestly? I feel the same. I've never lived with anyone since my freshman year either."

"So we're in the same boat," I say, even though I'm mentally filing away the detail that he's never had a live-in girlfriend. Is he noting my romantic backstory too? That I haven't lived with a man?

Get over yourself. Of course he's not.

"But we'll figure it out, okay?" he adds.

"Okay," I say, focusing on food, and navigating our first night together sharing a meal in the house. I turn to the fridge to grab some cheese slices and make a sandwich.

"So...baking?" I ask, returning to my question from earlier today as I slice some bread.

"The ice cream was an exception. I have pretty good willpower in general, so I don't mind you baking."

And staying power, I think, remembering his stamina in bed. "But do you have the willpower to resist a cupcake?"

"Depends on how tempting it is," he says.

I shouldn't tempt him. Really, I shouldn't. But as we eat dinner, standing at the counter, two very different people, I start to think about another item on the list and wonder if he might wind up helping me with that one too.

Number Three: Make a friend who's nothing like you. You learn the most from them.

As we finish, he says, "By the way, whatever happened with your freshman year roommates? You made the most of it since that's what you do, right?"

I smile, a little evilly. "Actually, I plotted with some other friends and arranged for a room transfer. I traded with a girl who snored. Loudly."

He whistles in admiration. "Remind me not to cross you."

We manage the roomie thing easily enough. I'm out all day at work most days and one or two nights a week as well since we're open at night, and Wesley works most nights. When he is home in the evenings, I try to wander around local bookstores or check out museums not to avoid him, but to be polite. I don't want to cramp his style. When we do see each other at home, I give him space, and he does the same for me.

But mostly, I don't run into him since we're on such different schedules and he's busy with practice, workouts, and home games most of the first week. By the time the weekend rolls around, he takes off for a stretch of away games for several days.

I have the place to myself after work on Sunday, so I cook and bake, including lavender chocolate chip cookies that I bring to the library and they're gone in seconds. At night I also read and research the city.

One evening, as I'm on the bus home checking out an online course catalog, my phone pings with a new text—this one from Everly.

> Everly: How's it going? Settling into the city? Living with a hockey player? Don't trip over any hockey sticks!

The text sends a little zing of happiness through me. I like that she meant what she said the night I met her when she offered survival tactics. I reply right away.

> Josie: No tripping yet. So no two-minute penalties either.

> Everly: Damn! You know the sport! Impressed.

> Josie: It's hockey by osmosis with me, I swear.

> Everly: Whatever it is, it worked. Do you need anything? I'm an excellent tour guide.

Oh, that's tempting. I slide my teeth across my lower lip, considering. On the one hand, I want to say yes. I'm eager to make new friends. But is that greedy? I have Maeve and Fable. On the other hand, friendship isn't a thing to be stingy with.

> Josie: I love exploring. Also, if you have any recs for grocery stores that don't charge eight dollars for bread that'd be great. I'm totally not pointing fingers at the PLETHORA of bougie gourmet markets near where I now live. 🙂

> Everly: I got you, babe! Will send some recs. And we'll go check out the Marina or Russian Hill soon!

We chat some more then make plans to visit the Marina neighborhood. It's gorgeous there in the fall, she tells me.

When the bus arrives at my stop, I walk the few blocks to Wesley's place, then go into the silent home since he's not there again. These nights alone feel like ones when I was younger. When I used to babysit for the Murrays down the street. Once the kids were asleep, I'd wander through their home at night, curious about everything. The books on their shelves. The games on their coffee table. The food in their fridge. That's how I feel at Wesley's place as I check out a few party games on the table—Cards Against Humanity-type stuff, as well as video games, mostly involving zombies. His record collection is extensive, and I hardly know any of the bands' names. But I'm not a music person. There aren't any books, but maybe he's a digital guy.

The fridge is full of nutrients. That's what he eats—food with a purpose.

I try not to be too nosey. I'm a guest after all, so I don't open drawers I shouldn't, or paw through shelves. And I don't go upstairs. Still, my cat-like curiosity keeps rearing its head every time I pass the staircase.

On Thursday night, I stop and stare, my mind spinning in new directions. Is there a dungeon up there in his room? A sex swing? Would I like a sex swing? My chest warms. Maybe I would. Does he have a bed with those straps on it for tying up playmates? Now, my chest tingles.

I've read too many books. But even so, wouldn't that be something, if he had a room full of accouterments? He did seem like the tying-her-up type. A delicious chill runs through my bones at the thought.

But he also seems like the bend-you-over-the-kitchen-counter-and-fuck-you-hard-after-work type.

A sharp, hot blast of pleasure rushes through me.

Once again, I retreat to my room under the stairs and picture our one and only night together. But even though he's in Detroit or St. Louis or who even knows, I'm quiet as I come.

I bite back my moans. I can't shake the idea that this isn't my place and that somehow, someone could be listening.

Or really, that he could.

And that he'd know I was lying when I said I went to Frieda's to give him a thank you gift.

On Friday night, I'm exhausted from an energizing week at the library, helping patrons. I also came up with an idea for a digital initiative to help enhance the reader's experience, and Thalia gave it the go-ahead so it's been consuming my mind. Wesley told me he's not going to be home till late, so after I clean up my dinner so the kitchen is spick-and-span—I am Super Roomie—I settle into the couch, take out my blank book and my list, then flip through the course catalog from the Community Academy, checking out class offerings, wishing I could skip number two but knowing I can't. I need to find just the right class for the item about overcoming a fear.

But it's almost nine and a yawn overcomes me. I stretch then head to my room, grab some jammies, and take a quick shower before bed. I rub five different kinds of lotions and potions into my face, starting with under-eye cream, then serum, then night cream.

When I look dewy as fuck, I'm satisfied. I loop my brown hair into a bun with a scrunchie, slide my glasses back on, and return to the living room, stopping when I reach it, startled.

Wesley's sitting on the couch. I gulp. I had no idea he'd be home now. He said late Friday night. Is nine-thirty late for him?

"I didn't realize you'd be here," I say, feeling...caught. But why?

"I live here," he says, with a sly smile.

"I know. I just..."

"Flight was early."

He's still wearing his travel clothes, and they're too sexy. I hope the league never changes its suit rule ever, since he looks so damn good in charcoal slacks and a blue dress shirt, with a couple buttons undone. They show off that silver chain on his chest. I want to tug on it with my teeth.

As he leans back against the couch cushions, legs spread, eyes gleaming, he holds a tumbler of something. Scotch? Whiskey? Does he even drink either of those? I don't have a clue, but he holds that glass like a man who commands a room.

I'm not sure what to say next, but the air feels charged. Crackling. Especially when his gaze locks with mine, and he says, "I see I was number one on your list."

17

THE NOT NOT EXCUSE

Wesley

Maybe I should feel terrible. After all, Josie's standing frozen in place on the other side of the coffee table, dressed in white fuzzy socks with purple polka dots on them and cute matching PJs, and her eyes like a rabbit's.

But I'm too intrigued to feel bad. "I'm at the top, and I'm the only item crossed out," I continue, then take my time swallowing a sip of the scotch I poured. "Seems you've got a lot left to do."

This list is too fascinating to let go of. I've never met someone with a list of...dreams. Adventures. Personal challenges. Josie isn't like anyone I know, and I'm a little hung up on the way she's chasing a certain kind of life.

"I do," she says tentatively, but then her lip curls. "You really looked at my list?"

"I didn't *not* look." Should I feel bad? I don't. This list is like a gold mine of Josie.

"You're using the *not not* excuse?" She's confused, and maybe hurt.

Okay, I feel a little bad now. I set down the tumbler on a coaster on the coffee table. "I sat down with a drink and it was there."

"It was there?" she asks it with familiar emotion etched in her features. She's embarrassed, like she was the night I met her, especially as she repeats, "It was there?"

Well, shit. I scratch my jaw. But I don't understand why she's this upset. Why anyone would be this upset. The list isn't super personal. It's not sexual. It's an inspiration list. A bucket list. "It's not bad, Josie. The list is actually kind of...cool."

She swallows and looks away. Slivers of moonlight stream through the window, dancing across her ivory skin as she seems to *think*. "It's just...it's personal," she says softly.

Lesson I just learned—just because a list isn't sexual doesn't mean it's not private. "You're right. I shouldn't have looked."

She rolls her lips together, lets out a big breath, then meets my gaze, straightening her shoulders. "It's okay. I shouldn't have left it there," she says, then she shakes her head, like she's letting go of her emotions. "And it's fine. It's okay you saw it. Some of my friends know about it, like Maeve and Fable. They know bits and pieces, but I haven't shown it to them. My mom knows I've started it now, but that's all. None of them know everything that's on it. No one does."

She doesn't have to say *except you* for me to understand what she means. "I won't tell anyone," I say.

"I know," she says, but she sounds kind of sad, and I feel fucking worse.

"I promise. You can trust me. You know that, right?"

"I do. You caught me off-guard, and I don't always do well with surprises. That's all."

That's quite an honest admission. "I'll be more careful," I say, genuinely contrite now over the whole thing. And yet, I'm still a little obsessed with it. "For what it's worth, I think it's pretty cool. This list. I think you're brave."

She scoffs, then comes around to the couch at last, bends for the paper, and folds it back up along well-worn crease lines, holding it close. I feel a little chastened, perhaps rightfully so. I push to my feet. "Sorry again. I'll leave you alone."

A hand comes out, grabs my biceps. "It's taken me two years to start it," she admits quietly.

A beginning. A truce.

I sit back down. "Yeah?"

She sits too, taking her hair down and sliding the scrunchie onto her wrist. It's like she's unlocked. "My aunt gave it to me before she died. She'd been sick for a year. A really hard year." She takes a beat, to collect her thoughts I suspect. "But she wanted me to have fond memories of her. Of us. She wanted to leave me with something. So she wrote me this list so I'd have…" She stops again, her voice breaking. "This piece of her when she was gone."

My heart lurches toward her. "I'm sorry for your loss."

"Thank you," she says, then meets my gaze, her blue eyes pools of emotions. "That's why I was so happy when you had the scarf. It's hers, and she gave it to me."

"I'm glad I found it," I say, and not only for the reason I'd originally wanted it. But because it means something to her. Something important. "And I apologize again for looking at your list."

She shakes her head. "It's okay. I would have done the same. I didn't want you to think I wrote it myself, and it always takes me a minute to say she's gone. You know?"

No one I'm that close to has died, so I don't truly know. "I understand," I say since that feels true enough.

Fiddling with the scrunchie, she says, "It's taken me a while to start it because..." She stops, eyes welling. "I'm not that good at getting out of my comfort zone. I'm...a creature of habit." She meets my face, shrugs a little hopelessly. "I'm not the daring girl. I'm not the bold one. I'm the girl who escapes into books."

My heart clenches for her. For the way she sees herself. For how she believes she's not adventurous. "I don't buy that. You're the girl who walked half-naked through the city to get back into her apartment rather than waiting till her friend came home," I remind her.

She gives a small shake of her head. "But it's taken me two years because...I research everything. I've researched all these items on the list. I've never had a one-night stand. I'd only been with one guy. Before you," she quickly adds, and this intel should not delight me as much as it does. Yet it's so fucking delightful. "I mean, I even looked up how to have a safe one-night stand."

Yep, called it with her being adorably old-fashioned. "And everything about you makes perfect sense now."

That earns me a small laugh. "I did! I read articles on what to talk about, how to discuss STDs, and consent. Where to have one."

"Well, you nailed it—your first one-night stand."

"And you nailed me," she says, and now I'm picturing bending her over the bed, sliding home, feeling her tighten around me. Hearing her ask for what she wanted.

"And that is on my list of things I don't regret," I say, since we're being honest.

"Me too," she says, then pauses before she turns more serious. "With the list though, I put it off so long, and then it was easier to start it when I moved here."

"Why now?"

She sighs. Swallows. Inhales. "I missed her so much when she died. It was hard to..." She purses her lips, fighting off tears. "Move on."

My heart aches for her. I want to wrap her in my arms and kiss her hair. "Maybe it's not true that you're not the bold one. Maybe you were just holding on to someone you loved."

With a small smile of admission, she rubs her palms on her thighs, blowing out a breath. "I felt like she understood me better than anyone else. I guess that's why I didn't do it. Maybe also because I was getting my master's degree and school and all that."

"Maybe you weren't ready. Not being ready doesn't mean you're not bold," I say.

"But some of the list terrifies me. Well, not the item My *O* Supplier checked off."

It takes me a few seconds before I realize what she's done. Given me a nickname. "That's what you call me?"

"It's true," she says.

"It's seriously fucking true," I say, wishing, wishing so damn much that I could make it true again. Even though that'd be a big mistake. I force myself to think about the rest of the list.

Then, about walking into my home a half hour ago, pouring a scotch, sitting down to chill on the couch and play a video game, and seeing it there.

Too tantalizing to look away from.

The promise of new horizons, new potential, new possibilities.

The list is like a blueprint for becoming...your happiest self. It's a list that cries out—*do me now.*

Several minutes ago I was thrilled to be on it, masculine pride and all driving me on. Now, there's a new feeling taking root inside me.

There's a possibility that the Top Ten Things I Never Regretted would be good for both of us. Sounds, too, like that's what she needs—a partner in taking chances.

Excited by this possibility, I sit up straighter and jump headfirst into the waters. "Can I do it with you?"

She flinches, taken aback. "You want to do it?"

"I do."

"Why?"

"I'm already part of it," I say, and I feel connected to it. But I feel like it's what I've been missing too. "But it's also..." I stop, take a deep, fueling breath, and then say something hard. "You know what you said the other week about me being hockey, hockey, hockey?"

She winces. "Yes?"

"You're not wrong. I am. It's hard not to be. It's why things didn't work out with my ex, Anna. She said I didn't like anything besides hockey."

Josie shakes her head adamantly. "That's not what I meant when I said that. I was impressed with your discipline. That's all."

"I know," I say gently. "I know you didn't mean it the same way. She wanted me to be someone I'm not—someone who discusses theoretical issues at dinner parties. Who reads long-ass articles that go on for days. Who debates philosophical issues."

Josie shudders.

"Exactly. I don't want to talk about some man named Immanuel Kant," I say. "But it still made me think—I don't always have fun outside of my job. And I'd like to. I'd like to do something that has nothing to do with hockey. Someday my life won't be hockey, hockey, hockey."

"That won't happen for a while. You're twenty-seven."

"And yet, you never know." I tilt my head to the side. "So, what do you say?"

For the first time since she walked into the living room tonight, her smile spreads. "You really want to do this?" she asks, not uncertain but like she wants to be one hundred percent sure I'm on board.

"I do." Then I shrug, a little cocky, pointing to the item about making a new friend. "And anyway, I'm number one and number three, so you'd regret not doing the rest of the list with me."

She taps her chin playfully, seeming to consider my offer, then looks back down to the paper, her eyes landing on the third thing. "So we're friends now? The jock and the nerd?"

"We are. How's that for our roomie rule?"

She sticks out a hand and I take it, shaking on this new friendship rule. Too bad I still want to tug her onto my lap, pull her close so she's straddling my thighs, then hold her face, run a hand down her throat, and trace the outline of those pretty lips.

But there's too much at stake. This living situation. The team. And now, *her*.

This woman who's on the cusp of something. Who's changing. Learning how to be a bolder version of herself. Maybe I'd like to be another version of me too. The version that isn't defined by the one thing I've been good at, the *only* thing I've ever been told I could do well.

She takes the paper and unfolds it, then grabs a pen, and hands it to me. "Well, new friend, why don't you cross off number three?"

I uncap it, then make a long strike through that item—*Make a friend who's nothing like you. You learn the most from them.*

I set down the pen, then say, "Time for the next one." I read number two out loud. *"Overcome a fear (take a class you can't prepare for, baby! Psst—improv class time!)"*

She groans. "Why does anyone take improv class?"

"To think on their feet better."

"It sounds dreadful."

"Why?"

"I need to be able to prepare for things. Research them. Prep. There is no prep in improv. Ergo—it is my personal hell."

"And yet we're doing it. We're going through hell and coming out on the other side. When is it?" I smile, loving this little bit of intel I've gathered about her. "I'm sure you've researched the next and best class in town."

"I have. And it's Thursday night."

"And why does it sound dreadful?"

"See the list—*overcome a fear*. Your roommate has a fear of public speaking. When I teach classes at the library, I have to speak to groups of people, of course. But I can plan those out. I have materials and curriculum and information at my fingertips. But without information I'm free falling. I hate acting. And I am not good on my feet."

I smile, then drape an arm around her shoulders. "Well, I am good at all those things. So I've got you."

I might want more, but this will have to be enough.

18

A BRAND NEW BRUISE

Wesley

Two solid weeks does not a season make. But it's a better way to start than the alternative. Still, I put our 5-2 start out of my mind when I hit the ice two nights later. I always put our record, the past, and other games out of my head when it's game time. Years of working on mental fitness—thanks, Dad; no really, I do appreciate his insistence on mental prep—have honed me. When I'm on the ice, I'm all about the present.

Like now.

As I skate across the ice with the puck, racing behind the net in the third period, I'm determined to break this annoying fucking tie. The arena's alive with the thunderous beat of the crowd, their cheers and roars fueling every move as I narrow in on the prize.

Trouble is this bruiser of a Seattle defenseman has been up in my grill all night. As I fight like hell to hold on to the little black disc, Number Seventy-Eight looms in front of me, a giant clad in red and black, blocking my path to the goal.

But Asher's free, so I slip the puck to him seconds before their defender slams into me, then I slam into the boards. Goddamn, that hurts. Pain shoots along the side of my abs, a sharp burn. Gritting my teeth from the impact, I crumple to the ice, tangled up with the other player for a few seconds.

The crowd chants *fight, fight, fight,* but this moment is nothing. These moments happen in every game when you crash into each other. I get to my knees and push myself back up, and a few seconds later, I'm right back in the zone next to Hugo, who's blocking. This time Alexei, our center on the second line, passes the puck to me.

I slap it right toward the goalie's open legs. But Seattle's not our toughest foe for nothing. Their big goalie blocks it.

Frustrated, I skate to the bench, hopping over the boards for a line change, then grabbing some water. I'm next to Christian, who taps his stick to mine. "We'll get it next time," he says.

"We fucking will."

After his shift, I'm back out there as the seconds tick down on the game clock. Adrenaline courses through my veins as Seattle goes on the attack fast and hard across the blue line, two of their guys flicking the puck back and forth, barreling toward Max at the net.

But when Seattle's winger flings it toward our goalie's shoulder, aiming to send it whizzing past him, Max blocks it easily with a glove. Our defender gets the rebound, sending it to Alexei, who spins around, flying the other way.

I don't want to go into overtime. I really don't. I stick by

Alexei. Their big defender is all over me again, but I'm not in the mood. I'm faster, and I'm open when Alexei sends it my way.

And wouldn't you know? Asher is ready. I slip it to Asher like a goddamn pickpocket. Then, he's shooting it and the puck smacks against the crossbar and ricochets into the net...yes, fuck yes!

I smack gloves with my buddy. There's one minute left and all we have to do is hold on. Sixty seconds later, the arena is playing our victory song—"Tick Tick Boom" by Sage the Gemini—and I swear my shoulders loosen a little, the knot in the pit of my stomach unwinds.

Then, I relax a little more. Max, Asher, Hugo and I head off the ice and into the tunnel.

"Dude, we should call you Poker Face. That's your new nickname," Max says to me.

I tap his stick, earning the name by hiding a smile. "Works for me."

"Poker Face," Asher repeats, like he's trying it on for size.

"But you're the man," I say to the golden boy, since he's been having a helluva start to the season.

The dude flashes me a winning smile as Hugo seconds the praise. "I'd say stop showing us all up, but never stop," the teddy-bear defenseman says.

"That's the goal," Asher replies as we reach the corridor, where Everly's waiting as she usually is post-game. She's holding a tablet against her team-blue blouse, and she's ready for negotiations with that professional slicked back hair. Some of her requests will be easy. Others, not so much. She's smiling, but she's always smiling post-game. It's her superpower, I'm sure, come rain or shine.

"Asher. Wesley," she says, in her upbeat tone. "Will you two rock stars talk to the press tonight?"

"Of course," I say.

"Always," Asher seconds. He is not shy. The camera loves him, and he loves the camera.

"Hugo, I won't bug you tonight, because you were a sweetheart to talk to that sports podcaster earlier in the week. I can't even begin to tell you how happy the GM was about that," she says, and I've got a feeling she's heaping on the thanks both because she means it and as a way to needle Max.

"Anytime," Hugo says.

After Everly takes a quick—and likely soldiering breath—she turns to Max, amping up the wattage on her grin. It's part of their dance. They do this tango every time. "Max, are you up for it? That was a great game tonight."

As he rips off his helmet, our goalie flashes her a smile that's dripping with irony. "Aww, thanks for asking, but I have a bingo thing to get to."

It's a game, the excuses he makes to avoid the press.

"I'd be happy to charter you a helicopter to make it on time after you chat with The Sports Network," she says with a tilt of her head. "Would that help? You can talk to the media and still be at your bingo thing with minutes to spare."

He stops, seems to give it some thought, then asks, "Will there be strawberries and champagne on the helicopter?"

I roll my eyes, right in tandem with Asher. This is a new level of theater.

"If that's what it takes," she offers brightly, going toe-to-toe with the grumpy goalie.

He taps his helmet against his padded thigh. "Let me

get back to you. Your generous offer does not go unnoticed."

I can tell she's biting back a *fuck you, Lambert* even as she says, "Can't wait to hear." Then, with genuine gratitude, she says to Asher and me, "And I appreciate your help, guys."

"Anytime," Asher says, speaking for both of us.

When we turn into the locker room, Max says, "What's it like being the nice guys?"

"Let me see if my agent wrote a new sponsorship deal and I'll let you know," I say dryly.

"I'll check my bank account too," Asher says.

Max huffs, then trudges ahead to his stall and I go to mine—where Christian's waiting for me.

"I told you we'd get it next time," he says.

"You did, Winters," I say, but out of nowhere, a flash of tension rushes through me. That's weird. I don't usually feel tense post-game. Usually this is when I start to unwind. But I keep the focus on the ice as I undo my skates. "And nice goal earlier," I say since Christian scored the first point.

"Thanks."

"How are the kiddos?"

"Perfect," he says, a proud dad, then clucks his tongue. That sounds ominous. "Listen, how's everything with Jay?"

It takes me a beat to align Jay with Josie. But when I do, I try not to think of her list, or their aunt who passed away, or the fact that I know things about her that her brother doesn't.

Besides, well, the obvious thing that's a secret between Josie and me.

I don't want to misstep with him so I'm careful

forming an answer. "She's cool," I say, figuring that sounds low-key.

"Yeah? Everything going okay? No problems?"

It's not like I'd go telling on her to her brother if we were having problems. But it's easy to tell the truth. "Everything is super chill. We get along and give each other space," I say.

That's accurate-ish.

No, it's not. Space is not having dinner in the kitchen, hanging out on the couch, and planning to go to an improv class together as part of her get-out-of-her-comfort-zone bucket list.

"Awesome," he says, offering a fist for knocking. I knock back as he adds, "Really appreciate you helping out, Bryant. You're my eyes so I don't have to worry about her."

I bristle. She's a grown woman. She doesn't need a babysitter.

He seems to be waiting for me to say something, but it's not like I'm going to tell him all the details of her life like what she's eating, and when she leaves, and if she did her dishes this morning. "It's all good."

He sighs, contentedly. "My kiddos are good, my wife is good, we won the game. And my little sister is fine. I guess my work here tonight is done." He stands and surveys the post-game scene, then shoots one last look my way. "You still doing those post-game workouts?"

"Yeah."

"I'll join you when you're done in the media room."

This is when I really need a poker face because I did not expect that response. "Cool," I say evenly, and after I talk briefly to the press, I take off for the weight room.

Here, I definitely don't have to fight off teammates for

use of the equipment. It's only the team captain and me, moving through push-ups and bench presses, shooting the breeze about the game, the guys on the other team, and who we're playing next.

When we're done, he says, "If you ever need anything, Bryant, you let me know. I'll help you out. Like a mentor thing."

Oh, shit. He did not just offer that. Please tell me he did not offer that. I feel like a liar, and I haven't even touched his sister since before I knew who she was. "Appreciate it," I say, since that's not really an RSVP, even though the captain definitely offered to take me under his wing.

On the way back to the locker room, we pass Coach. He gives a crisp hello without cracking a smile. "Good game, guys. See you at morning skate?"

Christian nods. "I'll be there."

I'll be there too, and it feels even more important now than it ever has, and I'm not sure why. But I tell him I'll see him there.

After I'm showered and changed, I head home, my muscles tired as I drive. Once I'm in the garage, I walk quietly, then stop mid-step before I open the interior door to the house.

This is still new—this moment. So far, I've only come home once post-game with Josie in the house. She did say she goes to bed at nine-thirty, so I'm quieter than usual, slipping out of my shoes, then carrying them up the steps. Don't want to wake her. She gets up way earlier than I do.

The home is silent in that slightly eerie, slightly creaky nighttime kind of way. After I set my shoes down by the door, I head to the kitchen in the dark, my stomach growling.

I'm dead quiet here, too, and I grab an acai bowl from the fridge and—

Berries. There's a carton of raspberries sitting next to it, with *Property of Wesley* written on top, like it's in an office kitchen or similar. Seems she's still paying me in fruit. I can't say no.

I grab the bowl and the fruit while listening to my new tunes playlist, my earbuds in as I eat, getting lost in the beats of Frank Ocean and GIVĒON.

A soft light flickers on nearby around midnight. I hit stop on the playlist and peer down the hall. The bathroom light's on—the one by her bedroom under the staircase.

She's awake and my heart stupidly speeds up.

Get a grip. The woman is up to fucking pee. Not to see you.

I admonish myself for wanting a *hello*, or a *good game*, or a *how's it going*. I try to focus on the lyrics, listening for every word when the light shifts again, and I hit stop on the music once more as she wanders into the kitchen.

She's wearing a cami with her pajama shorts, and I can't stand how ridiculously hot that whole look is. Her glasses are on, but her hair is down, and my mind unhelpfully shifts to its own playlist, playing the refrain to My Morning Jacket's "Librarian," and the bit about the title character taking off her glasses and letting down her hair.

"Nice assist," she says.

I flinch in surprise as I take out my earbuds. She can't have just said that. Really, she can't. She's not into sports. She's definitely not into her brother's sport. "You watched it?" I ask, incredulous and grateful all at once that she gave me a reason not to think about her new anthem.

"Maybe." It's stretched out, a little coy. Her smile lifts.

"Did I watch it or did I watch the highlights? What do you think?"

She's flirting. She's fucking flirting, and I'm not sure I can resist it.

I consider her question, then roll the dice. "I think you watched it."

She shrugs playfully, and it's chased by a slide of her teeth along her bottom lip. A thoroughly distracting move.

"I wonder," she says, teasing me more with the possibility of her watching me play. A possibility that is lighting me up, that has electricity crackling under my skin. "By the way, do you have a new bruise from when you hit the boards?"

I grin. I guessed right. She watched me play. And this excites me. Because that is not roomie behavior. That's the behavior of a girl who maybe wanted another night with me too.

I pluck at my shirt as I meet her midnight gaze. "You want to check?"

Her blue eyes flicker with heat as I up the ante. She matched me, then she raises me saying, "If you want to unbutton that shirt."

Briefly, I think of Christian, my impromptu workout partner, my *mentor*. But thoughts of him evaporate as his sister's eyes roam up and down my torso. What is with her tonight? I don't know, but I'm not about to stop whatever this is. So I unbutton the shirt, letting it fall open so she can see my bare chest.

She steps closer, studying me through those glasses. Checking me out for a good, long time. "Yeah, you have a new bruise."

"Shame," I say, then lick my lips. "I know how much you hate those."

She doesn't answer right away. Just keeps her gaze locked on me as the air sizzles. Then sparks. "So much," she says, then yawns. "Good night, Bryant."

"Good night."

She leaves and I watch her till the door to her bedroom closes, wishing I could leave this kitchen, march to her room, and knock hard on that white door.

Then tell her everything I want to do to her.

But I force myself to replay tonight. The moment on the bench. The moment in the locker room. The moment in the weight room. My team captain's not in charge of his sister. He doesn't get to make decisions about what she does or who she sees.

But I'm in charge of me, and I should not do a damn thing to create a single ripple effect across the team. I finish my acai bowl, go upstairs, and get in bed.

Counting down the clock till Thursday night.

19

YES, AND…

Josie

"I spent my lunch break reading up some more on improv classes. The kind of prompts they might give, how to approach them," I say as I walk to the theater with Wesley a few days later, on Thursday night. I'm trying, I swear, I'm trying not to trudge there. But the pit of dread in my stomach is turning into a gaping maw the closer we get to the old theater in the heart of the Mission District where the Bay Area Banter Brigade hosts classes and shows.

"Of course you did," Wesley says, his lips curving up. We turn the corner, passing a huge graffiti mural of animals riding bikes. It looks like something Maeve would paint, and she has painted similar works of art in other sections of the city. But even that can't distract me from my dread.

It's skyrocketing now that we're a block away from the gates of my personal hell. "I even checked out a couple resources at the library on the history of improv, and I read some articles on the best improv teaching techniques," I continue, narrowing in on all the data I'm storing in my head. If I can keep my focus on the homework I did, I'll be fine. Just fine.

Wesley chuckles under his breath.

"What's that for?"

"You. Doing research on improv," he says, smirking now as he looks my way with more amusement than his light brown eyes should legally be allowed to hold.

But this is not amusing. Improv is not funny. "How else would I know what to expect in a class?"

He stops outside a convenience store peddling fruits and flowers in a display out front with a sign advertising Mexican baked goods inside. "Let me guess what they'll say." He taps his chin, then holds out a hand, like he's an emcee, saying *take it away*. "You're a team of astronauts who have just crash-landed on an uncharted planet inhabited by sentient alien beings who communicate through interpretive dance...and go!"

I shudder. "No! No one said anything about doing interpretive dance. We are not doing interpretive dance."

Tilting his head, Wesley arches a brow. "We might be."

I frown, then stab his chest. "Take it back. Take that horrid idea back right now."

He grabs my hand and curls his bigger one around it. "Josie, you might have to do interpretive dance." He lets go of my hand, then tips his forehead. "But I'll be right there with you."

Nope. I dig in. My feet are concrete. I refuse to move. I cross my arms. "I'm not doing it. I am never doing interpretive dance. Greta will understand." I raise my face heavenward and say to the starlit sky, "Love you, Greta. But you know that's a hard pass, right?" I listen for her answer, hoping it'll come in the sound of a throaty-voiced laugh, then return my focus to Wesley. "She said she gets it. A hard pass is a hard pass."

"Did she say that, Josie?"

"No," I grumble, but I don't look away from him. It's October in San Francisco so it's strangely warm out—but that's typical for this month, I've learned. And I don't mind the weather because Wesley's in a trim burgundy T-shirt that stretches across his pecs, and shows off those steel arms and the ink that climbs down his fair skin. I catch snippets of his sunburst, all of his music notes, and a view of the line drawing of the dog. The notes make sense —he loves music. I want to know about the sunburst and the dog. Briefly, I picture the bruise under his shirt too. The one I was so tempted to touch the other night in the dark of the kitchen.

But that night feels like it was years ago, especially since I may never escape this moment.

Greta was not wrong when she said *overcome a fear.*

"I bet there's a way around it." Then, it hits me like a baby grand piano crash-landing on a cartoon character. "How did I miss this? My specialty is digital literacy and information, so I should have thought of this sooner. We'll do an online class. Asynchronous learning. It'll be perfect. Has there ever been a better solution in the history of the world?"

He sighs, adding an eye roll, too, as he advances toward me. "Just know this—I have no choice now."

Before I realize what he's doing, Wesley hoists me up and tosses me over his shoulder. In the middle of the side-walk. As evening crowds stream by. "Wesley!"

He doesn't let go, even as I pound my fists against his back while he carries me fireman-style to the little theater.

"If I die of embarrassment you'd better say nice things about me at my funeral," I grumble.

"Don't threaten me with a good time," he says, too amused.

"It's official. I'm dead. I am dead from improv and you," I say, and he carries me into the theater, finally putting me down at the back row. I turn around and take it in.

It's a packed class.

Kill. Me. Now.

* * *

"Welcome to improv for adults."

The teacher strides across the front of the small theater as a welcoming smile spreads across her plum-colored lips. If I walked into her cottage, I'm sure she'd offer me tea, complete with a honey stirrer, then listen to all my heartache in front of her warm, crackling fireplace.

And still, I am annoyingly terrified. My chest is tight as I settle into the hard metal chairs placed in a circle around the room. My skin is clammy. My heart beats in my ears.

I wish I weren't afraid.

I wish I were fearless.

I wish I were bold.

"You might be here because someone told you you're funny," she says, and a couple of the guys in class chuckle. Dude-bros. There are dude-bros here. I want to find a tunnel to another universe.

"Or maybe you're here because you need to give

presentations at work and your boss sent you to class to prep."

A few men and women in business-y attire nod.

She stops, then looks our way. "Or possibly because you're on a date with someone, and this is a fun new activity."

Who would do this on a date? I'm literally sweating. I only want to sweat if I'm in bed and Wesley's fucking me so hard he's grunting and I'm begging.

And that is not a helpful thought. Nope. Not helpful at all.

As she talks more about what to expect, I sit up straighter, smooth a hand over my jeans, draw a quiet breath.

Wesley shifts closer, his shoulder brushing mine. His touch is reassuring and tingly all at once. He leans in more, moving toward my ear, his scruffy jaw touching my cheek as he whispers, "We can go."

It's said so thoughtfully, with so much tenderness. "Yeah?" I whisper back, a knot of relief untying in my chest.

"It's okay to say no, even if it's on the list," he says, and I sit with that permission for several seconds—seconds that soothe some of my nerves. That settle my worries.

This is a make-believe class for adults. The worst that'll happen is I'll be bad at it, and we'll laugh. I lean into him, my head brushing his now, my hair touching his. "I'm staying."

Wesley sets a big hand on my thigh, and squeezes.

It's distracting, and maybe that's what I need as the teacher paces across the room, saying, "Some of you might be scared. You might feel uncomfortable, you might hate this, but try to remember this is just for fun. And it's okay to be silly. In fact, I guarantee it'll feel silly." She stops, surveys the class in the theater. "And this is not a try-out for the next Taylor Tomlinson comedy troupe," she says, and I love her for citing a female comic. "You don't need to be Iliza or Ali."

I officially love her for all time.

"You're here to collaborate. Not to audition," she adds, then sweeps her gaze across the whole class, not singling anyone out as she says, "And it's okay to be afraid."

My throat tightens with emotions as I flash back to the time I had to give a speech in my debate class in high school. I'd researched the hell out of the topic, but no amount of research could truly prepare me for the questions portion from the rest of the class. I'd been nervous for the whole week leading up to it. Would I draw a blank? Trip on my words? Would I sound foolish? That morning, I debated with myself – was I too sick to go to school? I was fine, of course. Just nervous.

But then Greta arrived, unexpected, and I answered the door as my father made coffee. She stood there, wild red hair tumbling free, her black flowery scarf tossed casually around her neck since it was always chilly in Maine.

"I didn't know you were coming," I said as I stood in the doorway.

"It's a good surprise, I hope?"

"Definitely."

She bent closer, her voice only for me as she said, "I know you're nervous but it's okay to be afraid. It's okay, too, if you're not perfect on stage. And even if you're not, you're going to do just fine. And you're going to tell me all about it when I see you this weekend." Then she pressed a little charm into my hand. A silver book, like the kind that goes on a necklace. "Here you go. A reminder that it's okay to be afraid. You'll get through it."

She was right. I did get through it. I didn't fall in love with public speaking. But I survived it. Thanks to those encouraging words from her.

I shake off the fond memory but hold tight to the meaning—*it's okay to be afraid.*

Since I suppose I do want to do better at all the things I can't prepare for. That's why I'm here. To learn, to grow, to try.

I repeat that mantra till the clammy feeling fades right as the teacher claps her hands, drawing our attention back to her. "Let's begin. I want all of you to stand up, grab a partner, and get into pairs. Or work with a partner if you came with one. We'll start with a simple exercise to warm up. It's called 'Yes, And...' This exercise is all about embracing the ideas of your partner and building upon them, no matter how silly or absurd the suggestion may be."

Curious murmurs ripple through the crowd as she explains the concept a little further. She points to a woman in khaki slacks and a white button-down, then to the man in a polo shirt next to her. "Would you like to start?"

"Sure," the woman says, with some trepidation in her voice.

It's okay to be afraid.

I try to send that message to her.

"Great! Don't worry about sounding perfect. You can be absurd or silly. Goofy or serious. Let's start. You're two suburban neighbors competing for the title of 'Yard of the Month.'"

My brain kicks into high gear as I invent scenarios. *Just try to beat my flowers, buddy.*

They head to the stage. The man starts off saying his garden with its gurgling fountain is better. She says her flowers grow the tallest. They keep going, layering onto the scenarios to the point where they're pretending they're splashing in the fountain with flowers, and I'm wishing for an interpretive dance when it's my turn.

A little later, the teacher calls us up. *It's okay to be afraid.*

With mischief in her smile, she steps closer to the stage, the chime of her ankle bracelet floating through the theater. "You're two strangers who keep running into each other on the bustling streets of the city. Each time you meet, you start to realize there might be a deeper connection between you."

Can she read my mind? That was...exactly what I needed.

I look to my scene partner. Wesley gives me a reassuring smile, his eyes sparkling with encouragement. I return the smile, feeling a surge of courage at his side.

"I didn't see you there," Wesley begins in a playful tone.

Okay, that's a softball. Nice and simple. What's my *yes, and*? I imagine reading this scene in a book. What would the next line be?

I raise an eyebrow, playing it with some sass. "Well, maybe if you watched where you were going, we wouldn't keep bumping into each other."

"Then my days would be less interesting. Wouldn't yours?" he asks, and it's a simple question. But it's also a lifeline—a chance for me to build on what he's asking.

"Or perhaps you're just following me around the city for some unknown reason."

He's right here with me, offering me another easy response. "Or maybe for a known reason. Like I wanted to see you."

The next words tumble out of my mouth, saucily too. "You have a funny way of showing it. You could try, I don't know, saying what you want."

Wesley lifts an appreciative brow, then says dryly, "Ice cream. The answer is always ice cream."

A quiet gasp escapes me as he takes us back to our first night together. "Maybe you should get some now. I hear there are ice cream shops all over the city."

He nods in the direction of an imaginary shop in the distance. "Like that one right by a hotel."

A rush of heat blasts through me. *This man*. He turns me on and helps me out at the same time.

"Sounds like a plan," I say, then impulsively, I take his hand and lead him to the imaginary bustling city street and toward the invisible shop and hotel.

The teacher claps, along with the class, then calls up the next pair. As we sit down, my heart still beating in my throat, I say, a little exhilarated, "We did it."

"We did," he says, then we watch the others till it's our turn again a little later.

Once more, we head to the stage, and this time I feel a lot less afraid.

"You're two lovers meeting for a clandestine tryst," the teacher says, and I wait for more but that's it.

It's like she knows what we want. My face flames, but I ignore the heat in my cheeks.

"You're here," Wesley murmurs, his voice barely above

a whisper, his eyes drinking in every detail of me. My face isn't the only part of me that's hot.

This time, I don't pretend I'm in a story. This time, I'm just me.

"I couldn't stay away," I say, my voice husky with emotion.

The air crackles with unspoken words and unfulfilled longing. Wesley brushes his fingers against my cheek. "I've missed you," he confesses softly.

Is this improv or a fantasy?

My skin tingles everywhere. "I've missed you too," I whisper.

I hope this *yes, and* never ends.

"Then maybe we should make the most of this moment," Wesley suggests, his voice filled with a mix of desire and hope.

"And how do you propose we do that?"

His gaze darkens with a hint of mischief. "You could come over," he suggests.

The implication. Dear god, the implication.

My knees weaken. My bones melt. I have no *yes, and.* I only have one thing to say. "Yes, please!"

The class laughs, and the teacher fans her face. "Well done! I had a feeling you two would be naturals with these prompts."

Wesley looks away, so I can't catch his reaction. But as I return to my seat I keep wondering—if it was that obvious to the teacher that we'd be naturals at romantic longing, will it be harder rather than easier to be friends?

* * *

The answer starts to come when class ends, and as we walk out, Wesley declares, "We're taking a pic."

I feel like a superhero. No, a dragon slayer. I'm marching through the land, having vanquished the foe of my fear. "A victory shot," I declare.

Outside the theater, he reaches for his phone, clicks on the camera, and drapes an arm around me, drawing me closer.

Then, he curls that big hand a little tighter around me. A rush of tingles spread down my back. *From that.*

That's my answer—it'll be harder.

20

DOUBLE CHECKMARK

Wesley

She deserves a prize, and there's only one thing to get my bold librarian who faced down the beast of her fear and slayed it.

An hour or so later, I hold out the door to An Open Book on Fillmore Street. It's close to my house, but beyond that I can't tell anyone much about it. I don't hang out here.

But Josie lights up as she walks through the entrance, passing a sign for the Page Turners Book Club. "If I'd known I was getting a book as a prize, I'd have been a little less dramatic before class."

"My bad," I say dryly. "I should have told you."

"It's okay. I forgive you." She beelines for the thrillers. That's not what I'd expected. I'd have pegged her for something...sweeter. I join her as she flips through a book with a dark window on the cover. "I'm into thrillers this month," she explains before I can ask. "Since it's October. Halloween and all. Next month it'll be lit fic. The month after, romance. I'm an omnivore when it comes to books." She snaps up a paperback called *The Woman in the Hotel.* "What about you? Can I get you one too?"

For a guy who's quick on his feet, you'd think I'd have anticipated this moment. But nope. Didn't cross my mind she'd want to get me a reward gift as well. "Nah, I'm good," I say, keeping my answer light and easy, hoping she doesn't ask more questions.

But no such luck.

"I don't mind. I have the money," she says. Ah, hell, she thinks it's a finance thing, like when I refused her rent offer. "I pay my landlord in a couple pieces of fruit a week, so I've got extra."

"I'm all good," I say, and just so she doesn't try to buy me something, because she would—the fruit is the evidence—I add, "I prefer to read digitally."

That's a lie, but it's one that must make perfect sense to a reader like her since she says, "Oh, sure. I get that."

But as we head to the counter, I picture her sneak attacking me with a gift later, in the form of an e-book delivered to an e-reader I don't have. I'd be a jerk if I let her do that. For now though, I try to ignore this guilty feeling though as I buy her the book, then nod toward the café. "Want a cup for surviving item number two? Or is it too late for you?"

"It's way past my bedtime, but I will still take that victory cup, thank you very much," she says, lifting her chin, proud and rightfully so.

After we order and sit with our coffees, I say, "You should know I wrote your eulogy during the yard of the month bit."

"You did?"

"You demanded it," I say, then take a drink.

She sweeps out an arm. "I want to hear it."

After the other night when I unbuttoned my shirt for her in the kitchen, and after this evening when we flirted on stage, I don't hold back. I lean back in the chair, then, like I'm speaking before a crowd, I say, "She died flirting with a sexy stranger."

"Not a bad way to go."

"Fucking the sexy stranger would be better," I say, before I can think the better of it.

She blinks, her lips parting, and I love that look. Love her response even more when she says, "Yes, it would be a preferable way to go."

For a moment, the air between us is charged, sparking with possibilities. Her blue eyes darken, flames flickering in them.

But the flame gutters out because of those damn roomie rules. Because we're not going there. Because flirting during improv is one thing. Doing it in real life is another. Best to steer this ship elsewhere. "What changed for you? On stage? You seemed pretty good at improv in the end," I continue. "I'm curious."

"I thought about my aunt. She once said—when I was heading into a debate class in high school—that it was okay to be afraid. That memory sort of boomeranged back to me tonight. Like a reminder that it's okay to sit with discomfort."

I chew on that, thinking of how I'm sitting with the discomfort over her wanting to buy me a book. "Good advice. I probably feel that more than I'd admit."

"Discomfort or fear?"

"Both, if I'm being honest."

"What are you afraid of?"

I turn the cup, sitting with my discomfort over what I'm not telling her about myself. I can at least start with answering her honestly. "Not being able to play hockey. Not being able to play it well. Life without hockey. I want a life besides it, but I also want a long life with it."

"It's a paradox," she says, nodding thoughtfully. "But that also makes sense why you're so disciplined about it— so you can play for a long time." She pauses, tilts her head. "You're not afraid of public speaking at all though. Is it because of media training and stuff?"

I picture her list. The item we worked on tonight. The item wasn't *go to improv*. It was *overcome a fear*. She overcame one this evening. I ought to do the same. I dig down and face that fear head-on—sharing parts of myself. "No. I *chose* to be good at it from an early age. Because I hated it at first."

Questions flicker across her blue irises.

This isn't my fondest memory, but I share it anyway. "In second grade, when a teacher called on me to read something out loud to the class, I hated every second of it so much. I felt really stupid, because I could barely... read."

Her eyes widen, but she says nothing—just waits patiently for me to go on.

"Later, when I finally could, and we had to read out loud in class, I would count the number of kids in front of me so that I could take a guess at what I'd have to read. I'd spend the whole time reading that over and over so I wouldn't mix up the words. When it was my turn, I wasn't truly reading it—I'd have memorized it. But eventually, I had to get over my hatred of speaking in front of people, so I worked on it. Since speaking in public is easier for me than writing or reading is."

I don't offer this intel to most people. Not because I'm ashamed, but because it's no one's business. But Josie's shared herself with me. She's earned this knowledge. So I finish with: "I have dyslexia."

Her brow knits, then her eyes flicker with...interest. That's not what I'd expected to see in them. I'd figured sympathy would cross her gaze. Instead, I see genuine care, and curiosity. "I had no idea. But thanks for telling me," she says.

And that's that. She doesn't ask how to fix me. She doesn't say she's sorry. She doesn't give me a look like I'm too different from her. I scratch my jaw, feeling a little unburdened but also still uncomfortable. So I bite off the rest of the truth. "Actually, I hate reading," I say, and wow, that's freeing. "I don't want you to buy me a book. I *can* read. I learned how. I just think it's...well, let's just say I feel about reading the way you feel about improv."

"It's Satan's work?" she asks with a wry smile.

"It really fucking is to me."

She nods thoughtfully, clearly taking the time to absorb that comparison, then she winces. "Did the notes I left bother you?"

I shake my head. "Nah, your handwriting is like Comic Sans MS. It's awesome."

She laughs, bright and happy. "I always knew that was the best font."

"It is. That's just facts." Then, I tell her something else that I've held back. "I like your notes."

"You do?" She sounds delighted.

"They're a window into you," I add.

"You sure you didn't hate reading them? I can leave you voicemail messages in the future."

I appreciate the offer, but it's not necessary. "Voicemail is fine, but I don't want you to stop leaving notes because you think I don't like it. I definitely didn't hate reading them." But that's only a slice of the truth. I decide to take it a step further and give her all of it. "Actually, they're kind of my favorite thing to read."

Her smile blooms like a sunflower as she takes another drink of her coffee. When she sets it down, she says, "Be careful what you wish for then."

I lean back in the chair, cross my arms. "Have at it, *Jay*. Let's see those *five things you should know about me* start to pile up."

"Oh, it's on, Bryant. It is on." She pauses, her eyes curious again, then she asks, "Can I ask a question?"

"Sure."

"Why is public speaking easier?"

That's a good question. One I've thought about a lot. "I prefer speaking to writing—a whole helluva lot—so I made the effort to be good at it. And my dad hired like a million tutors, and got me all sorts of assistive technology, like text-to-speech and even this pen that scans documents and reads it to you. He got me *everything*."

"And that helped?"

At the time, it was so much work. Exhausting work learning new ways to, well, learn. But I'm grateful for how over-involved he was. He gave me the tools I needed. He had the right toolbox. "It did. I like the text-to-speech more than the pen. But yeah, I learned how to work with my dyslexia." Then I pause. "But it's not something I tell a lot of people. Like the team and stuff. It doesn't affect my ability to do my job."

"That makes a lot of sense."

But that's not all there is to it. There are other reasons. *In for a penny, in for a pound.* "I also don't want people to see me differently," I say, serving up that raw truth. "Or to think I can't do something or handle something because of a learning disability. Like, what if Everly thinks I can't prep for a media interview for some reason, or Coach thinks I'd have trouble reviewing plays? I *can* do those things." Then I give an easy shrug. "But honestly, I don't have the kind of job where reading is really a big issue, so I guess I'm lucky."

"I get that. And we don't owe every part of ourselves to the world. You don't have to share it with anyone you don't want to share it with."

She's quiet for a beat, and I can see the cogs turning in her mind. It's coming. I know it's coming. Anna tried this tactic with me, and I need to cut it off at the knees or it'll piss me off. "You're not going to tell me to listen to audiobooks, are you?" I ask it defensively. I *feel* it defensively.

Laughing, she shakes her head. "No. I'm not. I don't think you told me this so I could give you book recs. You told me because you wanted to share."

"I did. I want you to know me," I say, as my chest floods with a new emotion—something warm, something soft. Josie understands me and that's rare. It's not magic though. It's not fate. It's not even chemistry. It's effort—she takes the time to listen, and puts in the work to understand. But I like to think I understand her a little more each day too. "You're going to research the fuck out of this, aren't you?" I ask, teasing her.

She gives me a look like I've nailed it. "You know me so well."

Because she's let me in, and that's rare too. I want to treat it like the gift that it is.

On the way home, she pulls a tube of lipstick from her little bag and slides it across her lips as I drive along our block. I steal a glance at her as she presses them together. They're pink and shiny now, and I'm fucking aroused.

Great. Just great.

When I pull into the garage, I make up some excuse about checking a group chat with the guys. "I'll be inside in a second," I say.

She goes ahead, and when my dick settles down a minute later, I follow. She's on the couch already, waving the list. It's not like I want to be anywhere else but near her, so I join her. She grabs one of her pens and crosses off item number two, but only half of it. "We both did this tonight," she says, giving me the pen so I can finish the strike-through.

"We did," I say, seconding her as I draw the rest of the line.

Together, we look at the list of ten items with three completed so far.

1. ~~Have a one-night stand with a sexy stranger.~~
2. ~~Overcome a fear (take a class you can't prepare for, baby! Psst — improv class time!)~~
3. ~~Make a friend who's nothing like you. You learn the most from them.~~

When I give the pen back to her, she taps the fourth thing on the list. "Are you ready for number four?"

I shudder at the thought. It's a simple item, but a terrifying one too. I draw a soldiering breath. "I'd better be."

"We can do it next weekend. You have a game tomorrow and also on Sunday, so I'm guessing next weekend is better. Sunday morning?"

A surge of happiness floods me from this detail—she knows my game schedule. But then, I try not to read too much into it. We live together. It's just good sense to know your roomie's sked. Strategic too.

"Next Sunday works," I say.

"Good. We can plan this week."

"Of course," I say, amused at how thoroughly she does homework for everything in her life.

She caps the pen, looks at the clock on the wall with a wistful gaze, then says, "I should go to bed. I have an early meeting then I'm working late at the library tomorrow."

She pushes up from the couch, but pauses, like she wants to say something else. Or maybe *do* something else. "Wesley," she begins in a voice full of promise.

My chest seizes with a feral sort of want. A hunger rises inside me, climbing up my body. "Yes?" I ask hoarsely.

"I never showed you the video of the pigeons."

A laugh bursts from me. "Do you want to show me pigeon porn?"

"It's worth your while," she says, a teasing lilt to her tone.

I pat the couch and she returns, sinking back down onto the gray cushion. This time, she's a couple inches closer to me. This time, I catch her scent—the fading notes of cinnamon, twined with vanilla. Her hair, I think.

The combo scrambles my brain, and it takes every ounce of my willpower not to tug on her hair, dip my face to her neck, inhale her.

Especially when she leans closer, clicks on the folder on her phone, and scoots another inch nearer. We dip our heads toward the screen, but I'm acutely aware of how close she is as she shows me a video of birds banging.

"It's...not what I expected," I say when it's over. But then again, she's not either.

"I know, right?" Then she pulls back to meet my eyes once more in the near dark. "You're not either."

And tonight, I decide that's a good thing. "Same to you," I say, then narrow in on her glasses. They're a little smudged. Probably from the day. She doesn't need me to do this, but I do it anyway. "Your glasses," I say, then reach carefully for them. "They're dirty."

"Oh," she says, raising her chin toward me, a subtle way of giving me permission. Carefully, I hold the delicate arms and slide them off her face.

Her breath hitches. She swallows noticeably as I bring them to my mouth, and blow on them. Lifting the hem of my shirt, I gently rub the lenses, cleaning them. Her gaze drifts down to my stomach, visible now.

Did I do that on purpose? Maybe. She likes to look, and I like the attention. *A lot.*

I take a good long time cleaning her glasses. When I'm done, she shudders in a breath. Then holds in another one as I glide them slowly, carefully back on her face.

We stay like that, inches apart in the almost dark, neither of us moving for several stretched-out seconds.

Till she says, "Thanks. They're all better now."

"Good."

This time, she leaves, heading off to her room under

the staircase while I go the other way, trying not to think of her as I get ready for bed.

No such luck. She's exactly what I think of after I shut the door, change, and slide between the sheets. She's precisely what's on my mind as I turn off the lights and deal with all this lust for my roomie that's starting to feel like a little more than lust.

21

SHIRTLESS DRIVER

Wesley

How can one person make so much noise? It's like a pack of howler monkeys have barged into my home. Are they ripping cabinet doors off hinges? Swinging from the chandelier in the living room?

Rubbing my eyes, I squint at the clock. It's not even seven-thirty. No one should be up at this hour.

As sunlight streams horrifically bright through the bedroom window, I grab a pillow and yank it over my head. I'll just go back to sleep in three, two...

"FUCK!"

The scream doesn't just ring through the home. It echoes through the halls of time, reverberating back to the Stone Age.

I jump out of bed and fly down the stairs as the next round of the soul-rending *fuck, fuck, fuck* chorus continues from the kitchen. I skid along the tiled floor where Josie's hopping on one foot, gingerly clutching the other.

"I'm okay, I'm okay, I'm okay," she says, but she's clearly not okay, since she's breathing out frantically and grasping her bare foot. There's a puck on the floor, along with her canvas bag, where a tube of lipstick has escaped, along with some sunscreen and a glasses case. Ah, shit. I think I know what happened.

"Did you stub your toe on that puck?" I ask, advancing toward her like she's a thrashing animal.

"Yes. No. I mean, it fell on me," she bites out, and it's like she's trying to hold in all the pain. But no one on the planet can hold in the abject misery of a jammed toe.

"Let me see," I say.

She peels her hand off the toe. It's bleeding a little, just along the nail. Still, it's all my fault.

Grabbing her hips, I lift her onto the counter, then reach for a clean towel and press it to her toe. Carefully, I hold the towel in place as my brave woman fights off some rebel tears. "Just another few seconds, then I'll get you some ice."

She nods, and I hold her toe, rubbing her other leg. She's wearing a flowy skirt today with a white fitted T-shirt. If I'd known librarians looked like her I might have spent more time in the stacks. I check one more time. "No more blood," I say.

"Good," she says quietly.

I scoop her up into my arms, and carry her through the kitchen to the living room. She doesn't protest. She just groans, still in obvious pain as she wraps her arms around my neck, clinging to me. I tighten my hold on her, so she feels safe. Yeah. That's the only reason. "You need ice and a Band-Aid," I tell her, shifting into triage mode.

"I need to go to work. I have a meeting."

"It's gonna swell if you don't ice it."

"I'm going to lose my job if I'm late, and the bus comes in fifteen minutes and I already woke up after my alarm."

When I reach the couch, I set her down gently, sliding my arms out from under her. "Ten minutes of ice, Josie," I say in a tone that brooks no argument. I hightail it to the bathroom upstairs, taking the steps two at a time, and grab a Band-Aid, hydrogen peroxide and Neosporin, and a couple washcloths. Back downstairs, I snag an ice-pack from the freezer.

Briefly I set everything down and slide her glasses case, sunscreen, and that lipstick I'm obsessed with back into her bag, then I pick up the puck—a signed one I left here last night before we went to improv so I wouldn't forget to drop it off at the animal rescue this morning for a fan who volunteers there—and set it on the counter. She must have put her bag on top of the puck this morning, then it fell off when she grabbed her bag. Just a guess, but it seems logical.

Supplies in hand, I return to Josie, putting the first-aid items on the table. "Lie back on the couch. Let me clean it up."

She complies, then offers me her foot.

I pour some hydrogen peroxide onto a corner of the towel and clean the cut as she bravely rolls her lips together, keeping in her whimpers. With that done, I gently apply some Neosporin. I wrap the Band-Aid around the little toe. A tiny sound escapes her lips.

"Good job," I say, then rub my hand along her exposed calf as I reach for the ice. "It's going to be cold," I warn.

"I had no idea," she says dryly, and that's my Josie. Sassy as fuck.

I press the pack to her toe, and she grits out a long, "Ohhh god."

"This is my fault," I say.

"It's the puck's fault. But also mine since I grabbed my bag off the counter to get my lipstick at the same time that I was trying to open the fridge for a yogurt, since I was running late. The puck fell off the counter and landed right on my foot," she says as I keep the ice pressed to her little pink toe.

My gaze stays there, studying her feet. I'm not a foot guy, but her toenails are all polished an aqua green. The big toe sports a decal of...Alexis from *Schitt's Creek*. I scan the other toe. David. "These are cute," I say.

"Thanks," she says through gritted teeth. "At least it wasn't David the puck killed."

"Thank god for small miracles," I say.

She draws a big, shuddery breath, then closes her eyes. It's clear this hurt, which I get. "Did you know swearing mitigates the pain of a stubbed toe?" she asks.

That's so her to say that. I clasp the towel firmly, the cold seeping into my hand. "Let me guess. You researched that?"

"Not for me. For a patron."

"A patron wanted to know that?"

"He was British. He stubbed his toe on the Oxford English Dictionary. Which he'd left on the floor by his carrel. And he cursed up a storm of buggers, bollocks, and bloodies. This was back in grad school. I worked at the school library, and I learned swearing actually is a natural pain-reliever."

"I guess that explains why hockey players curse all the time."

A faint smile settles on her mouth. She must be feeling a little better.

"Let me see if I've got this right," I begin, relaxing a

little now that she seems to be okay. "In your first few weeks here, you've been attacked by a couch spring, a cactus, and a hockey puck?"

"Yes! Why can't I be attacked by, I dunno, a lifetime supply of free chocolate? Or too many orgasms to count?"

"I could help you with the last one," I say, then shrug. "Hypothetically."

"I know you could. Hypothetically. My *O* Supplier."

Funny, how a while ago I was sure she didn't want another night with me. Now, I'm pretty sure she might have.

Which is good, in a way. But also bad, because it just makes everything a little bit harder. A little bit more tempting. Temptation's like discomfort though. I'm learning to sit with it.

She's quiet for a little longer as we stay here, my hand on her foot. With my free hand, I rub her other leg, sliding it up and down her shin, soothing her.

At least, that's what I tell myself I'm doing as my palm slides over her soft skin. What if I let my hand glide a little higher, past her knee, underneath her skirt? Would she part those thighs ever so slightly? Would my fingers brush a damp panel of lace, lace that I'd want to push to the side, slip past, tear off?

She takes a deep breath, then opens her eyes. "I'm oka —" But the word cuts off as she stares at me quizzically. "Wesley?"

"Yes?"

Her eyes roam up and down me. "What exactly are you wearing?"

I glance down for the first time, noticing my clothes. Or lack thereof. "I believe these are called boxer briefs."

"You've been in boxer briefs this whole time? I must really be in pain if I haven't noticed," she says. Then she stares a little longer, and I think about where all the odd socks go and what kind of toothbrush I should buy next as I will my dick not to impersonate a flagpole. "You sleep in just boxer briefs?"

"I do."

"And you flew down the stairs in boxer briefs?"

"I did."

"And again, I didn't notice till just now?"

I smirk. "Evidently."

Sighing, she wiggles her toe. "I must be better since I'm noticing my surroundings." She pushes up. "Thanks. I should go finish my makeup and catch my bus."

I reach for her hand to help her up. "No."

"No what?"

"You should finish your makeup and meet me in the garage. I'll give you a ride."

She grins ever so hopefully. "In your boxer briefs?"

"You wish."

"Well, yeah."

I head upstairs to brush my teeth and change. But I don't change too much. Sometimes you just have to give a woman what she wants.

I come downstairs in a pair of running shorts and a workout tank. I sail past the fridge and grab her a yogurt, a spoon, and a cloth napkin. When we get to the car and I turn it on, I hand her the food. "Breakfast is served."

Then I flash her a cocky grin as I take off the shirt and back out of the garage.

Her eyes pop. "Drive me every day."

"Maybe I will," I say.

Then I amend it to *definitely* when she takes out her lipstick and slicks some on. It's like she knows what it does to me.

* * *

That night, I return home from an exhausting hockey game, where a puck didn't attack me but the boards did when I slammed into them during the third period. We lost, but I'm done replaying what went wrong. I did that already in the weight room when the game ended, with Christian. As we did push-ups and dead lifts, he went over a few key moments, like when the Phoenix team's star player kept getting the puck, and how we need to keep guys like that on the outside and away from the middle of the ice. Christian was serious about this mentorship thing.

But I need to put the captain and the loss out of my head, and I'm pretty good at that—at moving on, and taking what I need from a game and leaving the rest behind. I head up the steps from the garage, my shoulders sore, my thighs screaming.

Except when I get to the kitchen, I forget all that. There's a note from Josie on the counter. I'm a junkie. An addict. I can't get enough. I grab it, unfolding it in record time, needing my hit.

Dear Wesley,

You knew this was coming, right? Of course you knew. Once you said you didn't mind my notes, you really only had yourself to blame. I am a note monster unleashed!

And fine, since you never wrote back to my first note and told me five things I should know about you, I decided to write my own damn list of fun facts about my roommate.

Here goes. Five things I've learned about you.

1. You were a stripper in a past life.

2. You clearly moonlight as an EMT in this life. (That was hot—the way you showed up with first-aid supplies.)

3. You will be a singer in your next life. (You know all the lyrics to songs. I hear you singing when you're wearing headphones.)

4. You will never beat the zombies in your video game. Never, ever. (Sorry, you can't be good at every-thing! The universe gave you elite hockey skills and teeny, tiny video game talent.)

5. You are still the most generous person I've ever known. Thank you for the ride to work. Thank you so very much.

Your friend, Josie

P.S. I'll send you some ideas for number four! And next Sunday morning is perfect since it's right before you leave for your road trip.

When I set it down, my skin is hot and my bones are buzzing. From the words, from her knowing the specifics of my schedule, from everything. Without thinking twice, I leave the kitchen, crossing the hallway to her bedroom door, lifting my hand to rap my knuckles on the wood.

But before I make contact, I force myself to stop.

Frozen in place, a statue of desire, I stay like that, picturing her in her room. Then, flashing back to an hour ago with her brother. He's not in charge of my decisions, but what would he think if less than a month into living with his sister, I banged down her door to strip her naked and give her more orgasms than she could count?

More importantly, what would I think of me?

That's not what a good friend does.

Not what a good roomie does.

Taking a deep, centering breath, I find the will to walk away.

As I'm returning to the kitchen, my phone pings with a message. It's late, so I grab it right away, sliding open the screen.

My pulse spikes when I see Josie's name. Is she awake? Did she know I was *this* close to breaking down the door to her bedroom?

I swallow roughly and open the text. It's a voicemail. And I'm both psyched and touched. I hit play.

"Hi! I'm probably asleep. I scheduled this voicemail to send at eleven-thirty. You probably have ibuprofen, but I left you two next to the toaster anyway. You should take them after that game. Also, I got you something for next Sunday morning. It's by the toaster too." There's a pause, then I hear footsteps on the recording and I picture her walking around the house while she left this. "Good night...Wes."

Hardly anyone calls me Wes. But the girl who likes nicknames does now. I don't even know why, but I love the way it sounds on her lips.

I head straight to the toaster. I ignore the pills, grabbing the canvas bag instead and reaching inside it. After feeling some kind of fabric, I pull it out, then laugh when I shake open the gift.

It's an apron with lipstick marks all over it.

I'm so fucked.

22

IT'S A THING

Josie

Thalia was right. The Great Grimaldi is worth it. A week later, on Friday afternoon, I work with the former magician to help digitize his stage shows from the eighties full of close-up magic. By the time we've worked through a few VHS tapes, I'm convinced I can turn a glass of water into a deck of cards.

"Does sharing this with me violate a magician's code or something?" I ask him.

"Not if you don't tell a soul," he says, then brings his finger to his mouth. He still sports an old school magician's mustache and an air of elegant mystery.

"I'll protect your secrets," I say.

"Very good," he says, then whips his cape around him and vanishes. Okay, he doesn't vanish. But he's just like a character in a fantasy novel so I like to think he does.

As soon as I join Thalia at the reference desk, she tips her chin toward a group of teenagers spread out at a table in the study room. "Save me. There are some high school students working on a research project on the use of artificial intelligence in healthcare, and they have no clue where to go besides social media," she says, adopting a *this is making me batty* smile. "Please help before I melt into a puddle of dismay?"

Way to speak to my soul. Plus, this is why they have me. Why the foundation made this grant.

"On it," I say and if I can impart any wisdom in this lifetime, it's that there are many, many better resources than social media. I help the group of teens find reputable resources online, and I barely even look at the clock.

Fine, I check it a *few* times. I'm looking forward to shopping with Everly after work today, more than I usually look forward to grocery shopping. I took her up on her grocery store offer—we're going to hit her favorite hidden gem store in the city. I can get supplies for my project with Wes, and I kind of can't wait to tackle the fourth item on my list. Maybe because I like baking? Or possibly because I like our blossoming friendship? Spending time with him makes me feel...seen. I haven't felt that often. Not growing up at least, so it's a little thrilling.

His messages are too. We've been trading recipe ideas all week for number four, even when he flew to Vancouver for a quick away game a few days ago. He returned yesterday though.

As the day winds down, a new message lands on my phone from him, and seeing his name makes my pulse spike. Since it's quiet at the desk, I read his text right away, feeling a little bubbly.

Wesley: Take that back. What you said last week about my video game skills. I've been killing it today.

Josie: Really? You got shot forty-two times by the undead in the abandoned warehouse the second you started the game last night.

Wesley: That was an improvement!

Josie: All I can say is don't quit your day job.

Wesley: Damn, woman. Way to hit a man when he's down.

Josie: Need a Band-Aid for your wounded ego?

Wesley: Evidently. Will you put it on me?

Josie: If I can find one big enough.

Wesley: If I'm ever roasted, remind me that you should be the emcee.

Josie: I hate roasts but deeply appreciate the compliment.

Wesley: Agree. Roasts are evil. Like, you're my friends, and you want to tell me why I'm awful?

Josie: And make fun of me in public?

Wesley: But pranks on teammates are another story.

Josie: That is such a guy thing to say.

Wesley: I am a guy.

Josie: I know, Wes. I know.

Wesley: BTW, you're the only one who calls me Wes.

Josie: And...?

Wesley: Don't stop.

Josie: I won't...Wes.

I almost feel like I could text him all afternoon, but there's a patron heading toward the desk, so I slip my phone back in my skirt pocket and return to work.

* * *

When the day ends, I tell Thalia I'll see her tomorrow since I offered to take a Saturday shift for Eddie in research so he could go to his husband's mini-golf tournament. Then I leave, passing the fire station where the guys are washing their truck—again. And doing it shirtless again. I smile again. They wave back, then I catch a bus to a small store in Russian Hill. Everly's waiting at the door, wearing tailored slacks and a pretty blouse but dressed down with Converse sneakers.

"You look like a cocktail of business and casual," I say, admiring her outfit.

"I like you. I think I'll keep you around," she says.

The part of me—that part of everyone that wants to be liked—does a little jig. "Good. I'm very keepable."

She gestures to the entrance, waggling her phone. "Fair warning. I'm a little into coupons."

"Me too," I say, and we're clearly new besties as we head inside. She's another thing I like about San Francisco. I'll miss her when the job ends in three months. Actually, it ends in two months now, but I try not to think about the end date too much. This was always going to be a short-term gig, and there'll be other jobs when I get back home. Besides, there's plenty to keep me busy while I'm here.

Like the list. With a basket on my arm, I pick up supplies for number four—*eat dessert for breakfast from time to time*—with a little more vim and vigor than I usually employ when I'm picking up supplies.

"You look like you have something fun planned. What are you baking?" Everly asks as I grab cinnamon from the spice aisle with an eager hand.

Should I tell her? It's not a state secret. "A cinnamon sugar puff pastry. Wes and I are making it," I add. Nothing wrong with sharing that. We're roomies and all.

But that nugget seems to catch her attention more than I'd expect, maybe since I called him Wes. She tilts her head. "You guys are baking together now?"

Is it weird to cook with your roomie these days? "Of course," I say, fighting to stay nonchalant. "Sometimes we cook together."

And I leave him handwritten letters, and he drives me to work, and I give him ibuprofen, and he buys me books, and we're working through my aunt's bucket list for me in our free time. That's all totally normal, right?

"I guess that answers my next question—how it is living with one of the Sea Dogs," she asks, a pleased smile shifting her lips. "Sounds like you two get along."

"We get along great," I chirp out, feeling like a liar even though we do get along well. But I know I'm covering something else up. And it's not the burgeoning friendship. It's the reason I can't wait till Sunday. It's the flutter in my chest. The tingle sliding down my spine. The ache I feel when I'm near him.

"I'm so glad there's no weirdness, like sharing a bathroom," Everly says as we leave the spice aisle.

"We each have our own," I say quickly, trying to breeze through this uncomfortable conversation. I know she's not intending it to be uncomfortable. But it is since I'm keeping a secret from my brother, and in turn, *her*.

"And he's not parading around in a towel?"

I wish he were. "No," I say, but it comes out strangled because I would love if Wes did that. He drove me to work again on Monday. And a third time today. Shirtless both times. So thoughtful.

"I didn't think he would," Everly says as we reach the self-checkout. "But you know how they make it seem in the movies. The burly athlete walking around in nothing."

Flames lick my chest over that image. "He never does that," I say, and mercifully the conversation ends when two registers free up. We separate, giving me and my lies of omission some breathing room.

After Everly and I both pay and pack our reusable bags, we head to the exit, then to Everly's car parked by the curb.

Once we're inside, she drives me home, chatting the whole way. She's upbeat and friendly, but she still surprises me when she says, "I've been taking pole-dancing classes, and they're so fun. I had a friend who always wanted to do them." Briefly my mind latches onto those words—*had a friend*. But quickly, she moves past that, asking, "Would you ever want to go?"

Pole and me? Sounds like I'd get another scar on my

chin. Or my eyes. Or my vagina. "I'm not coordinated at all."

"I'm not either. But it's so fun," she says as she pulls up at Wes's home. "If you ever want to try it out, let me know. It's a great workout, and...I'd love to do it with friends."

Her voice seems to wobble a bit there at the end, and I can tell this matters to her.

"I promise I'll think about it," I say, meaning I'll look into every single aspect of it since I get the sense she really wants me to go.

But there's no time to look into it now, since I have to leave in ten minutes.

I don't even see Wes when I unpack the items for our Sunday morning baking session, plus a few extra apples for him as my "rent" for the week. But I'm not surprised I miss my roomie since he mentioned he was going to a Sea Dogs yoga class and then heading out for a bite to eat with some teammates. I'll be busy too. My brother's taking Liv for a quick dinner and I offered to babysit since the babies' nurse is off tonight.

When I arrive at my brother's home, he lets me in but immediately Liv hustles me away and tells me everything I need to know about newborns.

It's an ocean's worth of information, and my head is swimming. By the time she's done fifty thousand hours later, I don't know how Christian and Liv are going to have a moment left for their date. "I've got this. Now go," I say, shooing them to the door.

"Call me if you need anything at all," she says.

"I will," I say, but I probably won't call her. I want to show them I can do this. I owe it to them. The least I can do is help out with the one-month-old twins, after all my brother's done for me. Christian found me a place to live rent-free, after all.

That's another reason I shouldn't think inappropriate thoughts about my landlord. I don't need a complication in my life. There's no way I'd land another place to live like Wesley's ever again.

As they head to the door, Christian turns back and, like he just remembered to ask, says, "How's the bodyguard? Is he looking out for you?"

I'm twenty-six. I don't need looking out for. But Christian sees me as his kid sister rather than a grown woman. Considering I came to him in tears four weeks ago, begging for help, I suppose I haven't given him a reason to see me any other way.

"He's a great roommate," I say as an answer, and I'm ready to rattle off all the ways we help each other to show that it's a give and take with Wesley and me.

Maybe to show *me* that it's a give and take.

But even after I rack my brain, I've got nothing. What are a few pieces of fruit every now and then when you have a meal planner dropping food off every day? Do I help Wesley at all? Is this whole roommate thing a one-way street, fueled by Wesley's boundless generosity and my unlimited needs?

My stomach churns in worry as I add up our accounts. Wesley's made a practice of saving me from the second I met him—the plus-one to get into the gallery, the clothes to get out of my half-birthday suit, the cozy room under the stairs to give me a roof over my head. The list of his kindness doesn't stop there. He volunteered to go to improv with me. He bought me a book. He drove me to work when I jammed my toe and then even when I didn't.

My gut sinks. What do I do for him? Tease him about

video game skills? Leave him ibuprofen? That's nothing. A dark cloud moves over my head and I frown, so lost in my own gray thoughts that I barely register Christian's response, only keying in when he says, "He can be a great hockey player too."

That knocks me back into sharp focus. "*Can be*?"

Does Christian think Wesley's not good enough? I'm ready to fire off all the reasons why Wesley's an excellent player. How dare my brother think otherwise?!

"Yeah. He's good—so good I think he could be on the first line real soon," Christian says, with obvious pride in his tone. "So good I think he could be one of the great ones. That dude busts his ass in every game."

Oh. It wasn't a dig. It was a compliment—*one of the great ones* is huge.

Stand down, Josie.

"That's awesome," I say, pleased that my accomplished brother is impressed by my roommate.

"He's gonna go far," Christian says, and I'm glad. But his praise is another reminder why I really should stop imagining romantic possibilities with Wesley. My brother depends on my roommate for every game. Wesley made it clear, too, he doesn't want to take a chance at damaging a work relationship or hurting the team chemistry. "There is no one more disciplined than Bryant," Christian adds. "Did you know he works out after every game?"

Did you know I want to lick all those muscles he works? "I had no idea," I say with a big cover-up smile as Liv pats my brother's arm, like *enough, sweetie.*

"Babe, I'm pretty sure your sister doesn't want to hear about how many reps you two do at night."

"*You two do?*" I repeat, confused.

Christian nods vigorously. "Dude inspired me. I started doing these post-game workouts with him."

Great. Now, they're workout partners. I *really* need to give Wesley some space. His career is on the rise. He probably doesn't have the time to be my list sidekick. But he's too kind to say otherwise.

Liv rolls her eyes at her husband. "Why don't you tell Josie about his stats too? Let's go, babe," she says, then to me, she adds, "you're the best, Jay. Seriously. I appreciate you coming by tonight."

"Anytime," I say.

They take off, and Christian's remarks hang over me for reasons he can't know. But for the next hour, I don't wallow in my worries or think about number four on the list. I can't think about a thing but diapers and bottles and crying newborns and pacifiers and how to hold two tiny humans at once. It's literally the longest hour of my life, and by the time my brother and his wife return, I'm ready to collapse into my bed.

But seeing my brother with his arm wrapped around his wife, and her shoulders lighter from the date, fills my cup. They needed this, and I'm glad I was able to help.

Even though I am so not a baby person.

When I finally make it home to a quiet house, I'm sure I'll crash right away on my bed. Instead, my mind fast forwards to Sunday morning. To my plans with Wes. I wince when I finally realize why I've been watching the clock all day—it feels like I'm counting down to a *date* with him. I've been *letting* it feel that way. I've been bathing in that feeling, sinking into the warm water of foolish romantic hopes.

But it's not a date. It can't be one. And the more I act like it could be, the more I could hurt him. He's on the cusp of greatness while I'm only a girl trying to get out of her comfort zone.

Fact is, I've been trying to get out of that zone for a while. It's been two long years since Greta reached for my hand one rainy day in her little bungalow in our small town in Maine, more tired and frail than she'd ever been before, the days left for her on earth inevitably shrinking, and said, "My sweet girl, I'm going to give you something that I desperately want you to have."

"More time with you?" I croaked out, tears leaking down my face.

She smiled sadly, shaking her head, then said, "If only I could." She squeezed my hand as hard as she could, which wasn't hard at all, then pointed to a blank book on her nightstand. "This is for you. So you don't spend too much time thinking about me."

"That won't happen," I said.

"But maybe it should."

Then, she handed me a sheet of paper that was on top of the book. A beautiful, handwritten list of the Top Ten Things I Never Regretted, and she said, "Think about doing it, baby. Sooner rather than later."

It was like she knew I'd drag my feet. She was right.

I stalled out. I didn't do it. I didn't even try. I let it sit in the blank book, undone, untackled. Unseen for most of two years.

I could blame the grief. I could blame my master's degree. But the blame is all mine—I'm the kind of person who takes her time before she does something.

I started the list without Wesley, and truly, I should finish it on my own. That's the point, after all. I know how to do things solo. I know how to be invisible. I spent most of my life that way, except for when I was with my aunt.

I swallow past the uncomfortable knot in my throat then breathe out hard, past the residual pain of missing. A pain that's lessened over time but hasn't fully abated.

Once the emotions subside enough, I peel myself off the mattress, trudge to the bathroom, and wash my face. When I'm makeup free, I rub in vitamin C serum and night cream till my face is shiny.

I look in the mirror. Square my shoulders. Smile. *There*. I can do this alone, just like I read books alone. Study alone.

I return to my room and take out the list once more, unfolding it. In the quiet of the house, I stare at the fourth item once again—*eat dessert for breakfast*. I can't ask him to join me. Wesley is Mister Discipline. True, he had ice cream the night we met. But now that I've seen his meal plan and witnessed the way he treats his body like a temple, I can't ask him to break his rules again. Besides, the list was supposed to help *me* get out of my comfort zone.

Wesley doesn't need to change. I do.

I draw a deep breath and leave him a voice memo rather than writing a letter. "Hey! I was thinking about the list. You don't have to do this. Any of this. Especially number four. It's not fair for me to ask you. You don't need to wake up early or anything. I can totally do it alone! Also, you really should let me pay rent, and if you don't, I'm going to have to donate the money to your favorite animal rescue or something. Just watch me!" And so I don't sound ungrateful, I add in a brighter, cheerier voice: "But seriously. Thank you for everything you've done so far."

I hit send.

That's a start. I can do more though. Just to show him I

appreciate all he's done, I get on my laptop and I hunt for tips on Wesley's zombie video game. I dive into Reddit. I hunt through forums. I rappel through all sorts of tips on how to improve his gameplay. When I'm done, I send him a list of tips in bullet-point form on how to play better.

There.

It's a small thing, but at least it's a thing I've done for him—not the other way around.

23

TELL ME TO STOP

Josie

In the morning, I wake up to a handwritten note under the door.

> You're wrong.
>   Wes

A sob climbs up my throat, rising higher. I don't even know why I'm on the verge of tears again. But maybe it's the simplicity of his response.

Or the clarity.

Possibly, it's the way he makes me feel okay about all my messy thoughts and chaotic emotions. The way he distills them into something clear. I want to say thank you in person. But it's game day, and I don't want to disturb his routine. He'll have morning skate, then he'll nap, then he'll go back to the rink for warmups, and then it's game time.

Good thing I know how to be quiet.

I'm a veritable cat as I get ready for my own workday. I zip up a black pencil skirt with a cherry print on it, toss on a red twinset sweater, then twist my hair into a bun, sliding a hairpin along the side to hold it in place. I slide on my glasses, then pull on pink fuzzy socks so I don't make a sound as I move around the house to do my makeup and gather my things. I don't even head into the kitchen to eat. The sound of the fridge opening might wake him. I'll grab a bagel or a bar on the way to work, and I'll send him a voice note once I go.

With my makeup done and my lashes long, I pad back into my bedroom, grab my bag and a pair of black flats, and carry them to the door.

But as I'm reaching for the knob, the sound of footsteps pounding down the stairs grows louder. My pulse surges annoyingly. My heart slams frustratingly. I don't move. I'm still—a woman on the cusp.

"Where are you going?" he calls out, coming closer.

"I have to work today," I say to the door. I feel so foolish now, for the note, for all the feelings, and for, well, being so very me.

He comes closer. When he's inches away, I close my eyes, inhaling his scent. He must have showered when he came home last night. He still smells soapy clean but a little sleepy too. If I turn around, will he be shirtless again? With his ink on display? The music notes, the sunbursts, the dog...

The thought is too tempting.

That's not why I turn around though. I turn because

he came downstairs. I turn because he showed up. I turn because...I want to.

He's wearing a gray T-shirt and basketball shorts. His hair is a wild mess—like my heart.

But his eyes laser in on me with a ferocious intensity. "Why did you say all that? In your voice memo."

It's direct. Zero words minced.

I hold my head up high and speak from the heart. "Because you have done so much for me. And I don't want to feel like all I do is take."

He hauls in a long breath then sets his arm behind me on the door. My eyes drift up to his biceps, so close to me, to a vein pulsing along the iron muscles. To the way he's leaning into me. And to the ink on his body. I've never asked him about his tattoos. I wanted to the first night but it felt too personal. Maybe soon, I will.

"You don't see what I see," he says. But the scales are tipped so heavily in his favor, and he has to see it. He must feel it.

"You give me rides, and you give me a home, and you carried me to the couch and took care of my foot. And you offered to do the list with me. And you helped me into the improv class when I couldn't bring myself to do it. I just don't do..." I can't even finish and say *enough for you*.

He shakes his head, eyes hard, and it's the first time I've seen them that way. Jaw ticking. Brow tight. "Who told you you're not good enough?"

That wasn't what I expected. "What do you mean?"

"Who said that what you do for someone else isn't worthwhile?" It's stern, powerful.

I don't have an answer to that so I shrug, since I'm still knocked off-kilter by him. He lifts his other hand and gently runs it along my neck.

It feels so good. I melt into it.

"Josie," he says, his voice firm and passionate. But like an admonishment too.

"I don't know, Wes," I say, answering him at last, my voice a raw scrape.

"Just know it's not fucking true."

His words are a balm. Emotions rise in my chest yet again. I roll my lips together to seal in all these feelings. But it's hard to keep a cap on them when my heart is so soft for him. "Wes, I just want to be helpful," I say.

He doesn't answer right away. He stares intensely, touches me tenderly. Then he takes his time before he says, "My whole life is hockey. My whole life is this sport. Do you have any idea what it means to me to have fun?"

"You went out with your friends last night," I point out.

"I know. And they're fun. But I mean...separate from hockey. Separate from work." His jaw tightens. He clenches his teeth, then he grits out, "You're not the only one getting something out of this friendship, okay?"

He sounds almost angry.

That's so unlike him.

He's not an angry person. But maybe it's more like coiled restraint.

"Yeah?" I ask softly.

His eyes hold mine. "You're definitely not the only one." He runs his fingertips down my jawline and I shudder, then close my eyes. I don't want to go to work. I want to stay here with him touching me by the door, preventing me from leaving by the tractor beam of this...dangerous desire.

Last night, I swore I'd give him space.

I swore I'd let him focus on becoming one of the great ones. I want to do that. I truly do. And yet, when he slides that hand along my neck down to my throat, I can barely remember a moment in my life before this one.

"I want to do this list," he says, husky, determined. "I want it too. I need it too. You have to believe me."

I swallow past the heat that's building inside me. The sensations racing through me. The want that has me in a chokehold. "I do," I say.

He lifts a dubious brow. "You sure?"

"I'm sure," I say, then emphatically, I add, "I believe you."

He drags his palm along my throat, his thumb pressing lightly against the hollow of it as he says, "Don't underestimate ibuprofen. Or the thoughtfulness of the fruit. Or watching me play." He runs the pad in a half-circle along my heated skin. "Or video game tips." He breathes out hard, then shoots me a lopsided smile. "Fuck, I love those tips. Do you know I play video games to unwind? It relaxes me before games. And after games."

I had no idea, but this info delights me. "I didn't know that."

"I kind of get lost in video games, and now you've helped me play them better," he says, and he's sharing this so easily while touching me so seductively, while talking to me as a friend.

I feel so reassured and unmoored all at once.

His hand roams back up me so that his fingers brush one side of my jaw, his thumb the other. After a long, lingering beat, he takes a breath then says, in the most vulnerable voice, "There's...some promo material Everly sent me. A PDF. For an upcoming event we're doing in Las Vegas. It's kind of long. I had the computer read it to me, but I want to make sure I didn't miss anything."

My heart clutches. I get it. What he's saying. What I

can do for him. "Can I read it for you too? As a backup." It comes out more eager than I'd expected. But I'm giddy for the chance.

He nods. "I'll send it to you."

"Want me to do it now?" I ask breathily, eager to help.

He shakes his head, smiling softly. "You should go to work," he says. "We can go over it tomorrow. I leave around noon for our road trip. We can do it after we have dessert for breakfast." He's still staring at me with his eyes blazing. "Unless you're backing out of number four?"

It's hardly a question. It's more...a challenge.

My chest floods with warmth as I shake my head. "I'm not." But that's hardly enough, so I add, "Thank you. I needed that."

"I had a feeling," he says, then his tongue darts out, catching the corner of his mouth.

I watch the tip, my body going up in flames.

His smile is downright wicked as he says, "About what you said last night. I appreciate you looking out for me, but just because I follow a regimen doesn't mean I'm rigid."

"I'm learning that about you," I admit quietly, grateful he flew down the stairs and came to me.

"Good." He's silent for a moment, his mouth tight, then he adds, "I don't always let people see me."

I hear him, and I hear the subtext too—*he's letting me in*. "They see you as easygoing and a hard worker."

"Yes," he admits.

"But there's so much more to you than that."

He just shrugs, but it's an admission of sorts. Impulsively, I rise up on tiptoes, clasp his face, and run my thumb along his scruff-lined jaw.

I'm giving something to him—touch. Just like he gave to me.

My thumb traces his jawline. I'm slow and lingering. And even though the clock is ticking, I watch him, savoring every detail. The way his eyes close slowly, how his lashes brush against his face, how a slight tremble seems to run down his body.

But before I let go, he grips my wrist, turns his face to it, and opens those heat-filled eyes, holding my gaze. He brushes the gentlest kiss to my wrist.

I gasp.

It's a whisper of a kiss, and yet it's everything. He leaves another, taking his time pressing his lips to my forearm, then one more, and his tongue flicks against my flesh. And finally, he gives a deeper, open-mouthed caress of a kiss from my elbow all the way down to my palm.

Chills erupt down my spine. I can't breathe. I can't move. I am undone.

He drops my hand. "You should go," he says firmly, his tone making it clear I need to leave for me and also for him. Because if I stay, the kiss won't end.

With a reluctant nod, I tear myself away, open the door, and race down the steps, feeling like tomorrow isn't a date.

It's something else entirely.

Something I can't even name. But something I want desperately down to my very bones.

* * *

It's not a date. It's the next step in this unusual friendship. Still, makeup is always a good idea. In the morning I put on a cute sundress with pockets, twist my hair into an artful messy bun, slide on some mascara, and, of course, my signature lipstick. I tuck the tube into my pocket and head to the kitchen to do some prep, like preheating the oven and prepping the pastry strips. Fifteen minutes later, footsteps echo on the stairs.

My heart sprints. I touch up my lipstick—I hate dry lips—then set the tube down on the counter as Wes strolls into the kitchen at eight a.m.

"I'm never up this early," he says, yawning as he scrubs a hand across his scruffy jaw. He's wearing gray sweats and a blue T-shirt that hugs his pecs and reveals those steely biceps I want to curl my hands around. But I won't. We're here for...dessert. That's all.

"It'll be worth it," I say, tying my apron tighter. It's covered in tiny illustrations of cake.

"It better be, woman," he says, then waggles his phone at me. "Okay if I play music?"

"Not a record?" I ask.

"I have a playlist I like. Some new tunes."

"Do it," I say, and he sets it on the counter into a phone holder, then sends the music to his speakers. It's something upbeat and not too screechy. A folksy guy voice, full of longing. I think it's that Ben Rogers he's been listening to lately, and I like it. Wesley grabs the apron with lipstick marks all over it and ties it on.

"You wear that well," I say.

He tugs at the bib, giving me a pointed look. "Another thing you did for me."

I roll my eyes. "Please."

He grabs my hand, shakes his head. "Nope. You did do this, and I like it."

There's that tone again. Commanding. Certain. Like

he was in bed. But like he is in the kitchen, the car, and the street when he wants to drive home a point.

"Well, I figured we should make a—" I cut myself off before I say *date of it*, course correcting to, "Some *fun* of it. Eating dessert for breakfast is one of the simplest things on the list."

"Sometimes the simple things are the best things," he says, sounding like a saying on a kitchen towel, but a true one nonetheless.

"I've been thinking about this item. Why it's on there. Maybe because it's easy. But also because it was something my aunt and I used to do together," I say, opening up and sharing more of my time with her. To remember her. To celebrate the days we spent together.

"Maybe she wanted you to keep doing it." He stops, then adds, "With a friend."

"Maybe? Most of the other things are new," I say as we mix together sugar and spices in a small bowl. "But this one?" I gesture with the wooden spoon to the bowls on the black counter. "This was our thing. We made cakes and pies. Cupcakes and cinnamon rolls. We made chocolate croissants, which is dessert just masquerading as a breakfast food."

Wesley goes thoughtful. Humming even.

"What's that for?"

He shrugs. "Crazy idea. But maybe she knew all along —somehow, some way—that you were going to do this list with another person. So maybe number four was never meant to be a solo thing. Maybe none of it was."

My chest glows at the thought. My whole body feels warm, like I'm looking at the past through rose-colored glasses but it's a past that earned those glasses, a past that deserves the fond filter. "You might be right," I say.

"I'm definitely right," he says, with a cocky smile I want to kiss off.

And even though we came temptingly close yesterday, we're not going to today. This is friendship. He's said as much before.

But when Wes slides in closer to me, his shoulder bumping mine, there's nothing easy about this moment. There's nothing simple about how much I want him to shove the ingredients off the counter and kiss me ruthlessly.

We mix for another minute until he moves to the other side of the counter to brush melted butter along the pastry strips I prepped earlier. "You remember how much I wanted the ice cream the night we met?"

That night flashes before me in technicolor and fire. "I remember."

"So when you think I'm all disciplined, just remember I like to...bend the rules," he says, and those words slide down my spine like a brush of his fingers. The innuendo curls through me too, settling between my thighs, a fresh new ache.

"I'm learning that about you," I say as I layer the cinnamon sugar mixture on top of the butter.

"And you like it?" he retorts.

Reasonable question. I tug at my apron. That oven is warmer than I'd thought. "You think so?"

"Sure do. I think you like getting me to break," he muses.

My throat is dry as I try to make the treat—try but fail because I can't focus. "Why do you say that?"

His gaze drifts down to his apron. "The apron."

"How exactly is the apron getting you to break?"

He's quiet for a while. For several seconds, maybe

more. Clearly contemplating. He breathes out hard, his forehead pinched. I watch him, searching for the answer as to why he thinks the apron is my way of getting him to break.

Then, he lets out a long-held breath and shrugs, *fuck it* style. "Because you know I can't stop thinking about this," he says, gesturing to the lipstick marks all over him.

"You think it was a subliminal message?"

"I do."

Was it? I'd thought it was funny when I bought it, considering how he's always looking at my lips. But maybe that was my mind playing tricks on me. Maybe deep down I knew it wasn't intended as a joke.

But rather as an invitation.

To kiss me again.

And I hope—I truly hope—he's RVSPing as he crosses to the counter, picks up the rose-gold tube behind me, and then comes closer. My chest squeezes, and heat floods every cell in my body. He's holding the tube in front of me, and I can't stop staring at the lipstick, at his hand, at his eyes. At the blaze in them.

"Wes," I say, desperate.

He groans. "Yeah?"

"I didn't go to the gallery to get your name to thank you," I confess, and his beautiful brown eyes flicker with wild hope as he waits for me to finish. "I went to get your last name. So I could see you again."

His smile takes its time turning wicked. Turning satisfied. "I had your scarf all ready to take to your friend's apartment. Along with a note to ask you on another date."

The double confession is like fireworks lighting up the kitchen. Sparks rush through me from head to toe, chased by a *whoosh* of desire. The thrill of reciprocation. I back up another inch so I'm against the counter. After he sets down the lipstick, he grabs my hips and lifts me up on the counter. Stands between my thighs. Spreads them open with his hips. "This is a very bad idea," he says, like he's fighting with himself.

But I'm not on his side. I'm already on the other side of this battle. "Or a good idea," I offer in a flirty whisper.

"Tell me to stop," he mutters as he unties my apron, as the song slows to a moodier beat, as if in tandem with us.

I slide a palm up his chest. "Don't stop."

"Tell me no." It's almost a plea.

I shake my head, smiling, inviting. "I'm saying yes."

With a sigh of acceptance, he reaches behind me for the lipstick. Lifts the tube and says, "Then maybe we can just bend the rules."

24

A LITTLE LIPSTICK, PLEASE

Wesley

This is playing with fire on so many levels. Sure, she's my teammate's sister, but more importantly? In a few short weeks, she's become my friend. A good one, at that. Most of all, she's my goddamn roommate.

Giving in to this lust is such a risk. It's a massive complication. We'll be sharing this kitchen, this living room, this home through the end of the year. Every second I see her in my house could be uncomfortable.

And yet, I don't stop.

I go.

I gather up the hem of her peach sundress in one hand, my other hand holding the lipstick tube. "This gives me an idea," I muse as I push up the fabric, revealing more of her lovely thighs.

"A very bad one?" she asks, turning my words right back on me.

I lean in closer. "A very good one."

Her bright blue eyes flash with excitement. With filthy hope. "Well, don't leave a girl hanging."

That's my Josie—full of sass and fire. My bold, funny, daring one-night stand. The woman I couldn't get enough of. The woman I was desperate to see again.

Right now, I try to think of her that way rather than as the woman who's inextricably wrapped up in my life.

Letting go of the cotton material, I sweep a hand behind her, pushing ingredients, the cutting board, and the bowls, farther away on the counter, making room. Then, I return to her, sliding my palm down her bare thigh, savoring the way she trembles as I touch her. When I reach her ankle, my gaze shifts to her toes. She fixed the aqua polish on the little pinky, and this detail makes my heart squeeze. It's so very Josie.

In fact, it's so very her, I'd better not think too hard on it or it'll do dangerous things to my heart. Instead, I hike up her foot, setting the arch of it on the edge of the counter so her legs widen.

A sharp breath crosses her lips. I groan. Those lips. Dear god, those pretty pink lips. I ache to kiss her—with a sharp pang that's so insistent, it's borderline impossible to deny.

But if I kiss her again, I'll get lost in her. It's best to play. Have fun. Bend the rules. Not break them. That's my plan—and it's a plan that I've been formulating ever since I set eyes on that rose-gold lipstick tube.

I travel my hand back up her leg, goose bumps rising on her soft skin as I coast my palm over her. When I skim that hand along her thigh, she shudders, arching her back, lifting up her tits.

My mind goes hazy. My skin burns hot. Her reactions thrill me to the marrow. I'm so tempted to kiss her. But I focus on my impromptu plan. I push up the skirt to her waist, revealing her panties. They're white cotton with pink polka dots, and—"You're soaked, baby."

She meets my eyes with a naughty smile of her own. "News flash: you kind of turn me on."

I smile, feeling ten feet tall. "Kind of?"

She purses her lips then shudders out a breath. "Find out if it's more than kind of."

With a smirk, I waggle the lipstick tube, then lower it between her thighs.

Her eyes widen to moons. "Are you...?"

"Going to use this on you? You bet I fucking am."

She draws a deep breath. "Then bend the rules."

Yeah, she does know me so well. Knows exactly what I'm doing. I'm using a loophole. Technically, I'm not touching her. The tube is. I slide it over the fabric covering her clit. She parts her lips in the most gorgeous O. Then she breathes out a small but feral, "Oh god."

She's so aroused. So ready.

And I am so determined to get her off. The top of the tube is angled, so I rub it around her clit, then down the damp panel of her panties. Her eyes flutter closed and she grips the counter. Her fingers claw at the edge as she holds on while I stroke her. Circle her. Caress her.

She has no reservations, and it's beautiful to watch. Josie is so free in bed, and I'm in awe. She leans her head back, and I don't even think she realizes she's still wearing her glasses. Or maybe she does and doesn't care. She lifts her chest. Her tits are heaving, her body arching, her foot curling over the edge of the counter.

She is shameless, and it's so unbelievably hot.

My bones are on fire, and I'm going to let them burn.

Mesmerized, I slide the metallic tube slowly, tantalizingly over the white wet fabric, then I zero in on her clit.

She's moaning and panting, giving in to the way we're playing. "Feels so good," she mutters.

"You need it badly, don't you?" I say, fighting to keep control, focusing on her pleasure only.

Getting her off is all I'll allow myself.

Correction: Getting her off like *this*. This is...like cheating on a diet. Skipping the bench press at the gym. Eating one cookie. It won't ruin me. This extreme focus on her will simply release the tension between us. A valve loosened—that's all.

With that squarely in mind, I tease her clit through the soaked fabric. Her noises grow deliciously louder. Soft murmurs. Hungry whimpers. A breathy cry. Her thighs are spread. Her cheeks are flushed. Her hair is falling out of her bun. It's the perfect picture of this forbidden moment. But then she lets go of the counter, and I tense all over. I want her to touch me so badly, but if she touches me I'm so fucked. My control—frayed to a thread already—will snap.

She doesn't reach for me though. With eyes closed, she squeezes her breast. My brain goes haywire, nerves firing, mind popping. As she fondles herself, she parts her lips and whispers, "Wes."

For a split second I gaze down at her gorgeous mouth, then give all the way in, "Fuck it."

I let go of her thigh, cover her throat with my palm, and yank her toward me.

My mouth crashes down on hers. I kiss her wildly as I stroke her with the lipstick tube. I devour her sweet cinnamon mouth as I rub the lipstick faster. I suck on her tongue. I bite her lip. I consume her.

She snakes a hand down, grabbing mine, breaking the kiss, and muttering, "Fingers. Or cock. *Please.*"

I am not strong enough to withstand this demand.

I am not disciplined enough to resist.

I am just unable to stop.

I toss the lipstick somewhere on the counter, but before I can even get my fingers inside her soaked panties she's grabbing my hand, guiding it over her, showing me how she likes it, and fuck, if that's not the hottest thing ever.

This woman is using my hand to get herself off, covering her fingers with mine.

She knows what she needs and she takes it from me, working herself over with just my middle finger, covered by hers.

"I fuck myself to you every night," she whispers, and I nearly explode.

She gasps, then freezes in place. The world goes still and savagely hot. It sparks, crackling like wildfire as she calls out my name, coming on the counter mere seconds later.

It's the sexiest thing I've ever seen, and it eats me alive.

As she's panting, she lifts her mouth to me, an offering. Like I could resist her anymore. I grab her face and kiss her hard, ruthlessly. Tug her against me. Own that gorgeous mouth.

She wraps her legs around my waist, tugging me closer. Then breaking the kiss to say, "You'd better let me objectify your cock now."

It takes me a beat to reconnect her words to the night we met—when she wanted to suck me off and I stopped her so I could eat her sweet, perfect pussy instead.

I have no regrets from back then. But I know I'd regret

stopping this. One glance at the oven clock tells me there's not nearly enough time for the things I want to do to her in bed. My flight leaves in a few hours. But there's time for more rule-breaking. There is absolutely fucking time.

After I remove my apron, I scoop my hands around her ass and lift her off the counter. "Get down on your knees. Take my dick out. And suck me off like you do when I picture your mouth every goddamn night."

"Finally," she teases as she drops down to her knees and tugs at my sweats.

I'm so turned on, so aroused I feel like a hedonist taking the pleasure of her mouth as she pushes down my briefs. When my cock springs free, she slides her teeth across her bottom lip, like she approves of my dick.

"Will that work for you?" I ask playfully.

She smiles. "Your dick will do."

"I want to fuck the innuendo right out of your mouth," I growl.

"Then do it." With mischief in her eyes, she says, "After all, you wanted to have fun besides hockey. Here's your chance."

A laugh bursts from me. A fucking laugh as a prelude to a blow job. Who even is this woman in my kitchen on her knees, about to lick the head of my dick? But the second her pink tongue teases the tip, questions fall out of my head, along with thoughts and reason.

I'm nothing but a livewire as my roommate twirls her tongue along the tip, treating me like a piece of candy, humming as she goes.

"You look fucking incredible," I murmur.

That catches her attention. Josie stops. "Hold on," she says, and like she just remembered she's wearing them, she darts up a hand, removes her glasses, and sets them on the counter. She returns to my aching dick in seconds. While she draws me back into the warmth of her mouth, she reaches up and undoes her hair from the messy bun. It falls in wild, just-been-fucked waves over her shoulders.

I'm toast. "You're my sexy librarian," I say, then I push in, "taking off your glasses." I thread a hand through those lush chestnut locks as she parts her lips wider. "Letting down your hair."

She murmurs something against my dick. I'm not sure what, but it sounds like *for you*.

That's all I need to hear. I curl both hands around her head. She grips my thigh with her right hand while she curls the left around the base of my cock. She's pumping me and sucking me, and I'm sizzling everywhere. Crackling in my cells. My bones vibrate with hot, urgent need like they do every damn night when I'm alone in my bed. "I picture this," I mutter, beginning my confession.

She looks up at me with wide eyes, asking for more of the story.

"At night. I get off to you."

With a throaty *yessss*, she urges me to thrust deeper.

"Bet you want to see that," I say, remembering how she stared wantonly at me fisting my cock the night we met.

She nods.

"You have no idea how many times I've wished you'd come up the stairs," I say, needy, hungry.

She groans. Keeps going. Me too. I'm pumping and confessing. "I listen for your footsteps as I fuck my hand. I picture you turning the corner into my room." A spark jolts through me. My thighs quake. "I see you in the doorway."

Heat builds as I thrust between those gorgeous lips. "I

tell you to ride me," I say, then all the bliss crashes into me at once—a punishing, ruthless wave.

"Coming," I warn, and there's no stopping this orgasm. It's got me in its grip and she holds on, her fingers circling my dick, her mouth clamping down as I spill. She swallows my release.

I grunt and groan, enjoying every single second of fucking my roommate's mouth.

She sucks me dry with a satisfied sound. Seconds later, she pops off, wiping her wet lips with the back of her hand. Her grin is both devilish and angelic as she licks her lips, then nods to the counter and the cinnamon pastries. "We really should put those in the oven."

* * *

Somehow, it's not awkward as we finish baking the cinnamon treats, stopping a couple times to take pictures like we did outside the theater. It's almost like we slide right back into the friendship zone—the one we've been living in for the last month or so. The roomie rule, so to speak. "A record of the list," she says as she snaps each pic. "And I like records of things."

"Such a librarian," I tease.

"You can take the girl out of the library. You can't take the library out of the girl."

While the goodies are baking, she reads the promo material in the kitchen as I finish packing my bag. When I return to the kitchen, I lift my nose and inhale the sweet, doughy scent. It almost smells as good as her.

"You're like a dog," she says with fondness. "And I mean that with great affection."

"I like dogs," I say. "So I'll take it as a compliment."

"I keep meaning to ask about the dog tattoo on your wrist."

I look down at it, running a finger along the inked silhouette. "I always wanted to adopt one. My dad said it would never fit my *lifestyle* as a hockey player."

She frowns. "That sucks. But I kind of get it."

"Yeah, me too," I say. "Guess I showed him. I got a permanent one."

She laughs. "You sure did." She offers me a baked good, then recaps the important parts of the promo with the Las Vegas team, the Sabers. The first game we're playing on this road trip is against them, and we're taking part in the team's recycling initiative. As I take a bite of the cinnamon sugar puff pastry, she reviews the details Everly sent over on the recycling bins the Sea Dogs and the Sabers are delivering together tomorrow morning around town.

"This is good," I say, with a foodgasm-esque moan after a bite.

"The pastry?" she asks, lifting her phone to take another picture.

"Yeah, but also you reviewing the details." My brain appreciates hers so much.

She lowers her phone and sets it down with a pleased smile. "Good. Also, it's cool that you're doing this—the team and you. We have some green-centric initiatives coming up at the library. Makes me think of another item on the list."

"Volunteer. Number six," I say, skipping over number five, since she's brought up the subject of number six.

"We'll have to figure out what that would be. You sure you're up for it? It's probably not just a one-time thing."

That's one of the many things I like about challenge

number six. "Yeah, I am," I say, but we shouldn't linger on all those things right now with the clock ticking closer to my flight. I nod toward her room, where she keeps the folded sheet of paper. "We need to cross off *eat dessert for breakfast* though."

"We do. We're forty percent of the way through," she calls out as she hustles to her room.

"You can math," I say dryly.

But not only *is* she right, that benchmark also *feels* right, given how long she's been here in San Francisco and the time she still has left in the city. Given what's still to come on the list too. There's plenty of time to finish it though. No rush.

Seconds later, she returns with the paper and a pen. She hands them both to me. "It was easy for me. You cross it off. I'm proud of you."

Laughing, I shake my head. "For eating?"

"Yes! Do it."

Unfolding the list carefully, I spread the paper out on a freshly cleaned section of the counter. This piece of paper feels like an artifact, a precious heirloom that should be treated with care.

I lift the pen but don't cross the item off right away. I consider the list again, the reason she has it, the love behind it. The gift her aunt gave her—a way not just to remember her, but to move on, to keep on living.

"Maybe she wanted to give you a road map for life without her—a good life," I add for emphasis, looking at Josie and reaching for a strand of fallen hair, tucking it behind her ear. "For the way to move on. By giving you the way through."

She takes a big breath, nodding, perhaps considering that, then meets my eyes. Hers are shining faintly, but a hint of a smile forms on her lips. "Maybe she was," Josie says thoughtfully. "And maybe she wanted me to have fun too."

"Did you? Have fun?" But I don't want it to sound like I'm fishing for sex compliments. I try to backpedal with, "Baking I mean."

She rolls her eyes as she roams a hand up my arm, curling it around the sunburst that starts on my biceps and climbs over my shoulder. "Baking was so much fun," she says dryly.

"So much fucking fun," I say, getting her completely.

"Now, cross it off, Wes."

I turn my focus back to the list.

1. ~~Have a one-night stand with a sexy stranger.~~
2. ~~Overcome a fear (take a class you can't prepare for, baby! Psst—improv class time!)~~
3. ~~Make a friend who's nothing like you. You learn the most from them.~~
4. *Eat dessert for breakfast.*

I cross off the fourth one. And the thing is—I feel a little like a scofflaw. A lot like a rule-breaker. And it's seriously fun. After I put down the pen, I hold up the flaky treat, dusted in sugar and spice, take another bite, then chew. When I'm done, I sigh the most satisfied sigh. "And I don't feel guilty."

"That's good too."

But I feel a little guilty about touching her. Especially because I don't want to stop even though I know I should.

Setting down the pastry, I reach for her. "Josie," I say, my tone serious as I cup her shoulders.

With a rueful smile, she nods. "I know. We shouldn't do that again."

"We really shouldn't," I say, hating myself for saying it but knowing I have to.

But an hour later after we've cleaned up, I'm at the door, saying goodbye, and all the *shouldn'ts* can't stop me from hauling her close and kissing her hard—a kiss I want her to feel for the rest of the day.

No. I amend that. I want her to feel it the entire time I'm gone. And that is a problem I don't know how to fix.

She hands me a huge Tupperware container full of dessert for breakfast. "For the team."

I take it. "Thank you."

"And good luck in New York," she says, since our road trip ends there, against my former team. "Your first time playing them since you were traded?"

Damn. How does she keep doing this? Knowing the little bits of intel and what they might mean. My heart slams harder against my chest. All these little details make it impossible not to feel...all the things. "Yeah, it is."

"You'd better kick their ass then," she says.

"I plan to," I say, then take one more kiss and go, knowing I'm not going to stop thinking about her at all while we're apart.

Maybe that's the real problem.

25

A FUCKING PAGE-TURNER

Wesley

Note to self: Never bring baked goods on the team plane again. I've gotten nothing but grief since I cracked open the container and passed it around. And there are no signs of stopping.

"We're gonna call you Muffin Man now," Asher decides after he polishes off a treat in record time. We've barely reached our cruising altitude and he's wiping crumbs off his mitts.

I point out the obvious even though it's pointless. "That isn't a muffin."

Asher waves a hand dismissively. "It's either that or we call you Dough Master."

"Somehow, that's worse," I say.

"Didn't he make everything though? The Muffin Man?" Max barks in question from across the aisle as he waves his pastry around, then takes a bite.

"Who knows? Who cares?" Asher asks, with a satisfied

smile, clapping my shoulder. "You should seriously consider opening a shop. These are fuck-all better than the way you played last night."

Yup, this is the hell they give me. "I scored a goal, you dickhead."

"My bad. It was one less than the number I scored. So I'd forgotten," he says, the cocky fucker.

"Do you need a separate jet for your ego, Callahan?"

This remark comes from Chase, who's a row behind us, sitting with Ryker, one of our top defenders.

"Not a bad idea," Ryker grumbles.

"Come to think of it, I wouldn't mind that at all," Asher says, offering a smug smile.

Ryker leans forward from his seat so he's locking eyes with the guys in our row—Asher and me, and Max across the aisle. "You know there's an urban legend that the Muffin Man was a murderer?"

"The fuck?" Asher asks.

"Supposedly, he went around London murdering children, using muffins as a lure," Ryker says, in the same tone he'd tell you where to get a great taco. Nothing fazes the dude.

Asher's face goes ashen. "That's horrifying."

"This is why I don't read nursery rhymes to my little daughter," Hugo calls out from his row behind us. "I read her sports news instead."

"Some might say that's scarier. Also nursery rhymes are supposed to be scary. It's literally their purpose," a female voice chimes in from a row or two in front of us. It's Everly, weighing in.

"Hey Ev, is it true that Max was chirping nursery rhymes at reporters? And that's how he scared them all off?"

Max stretches across the aisle and knocks Asher upside the head. "If you played on the other team..."

Asher flashes his golden-boy grin. "But I'm on *your* team. You lucky bastard."

Max shakes his head, then waves his pastry in my direction. "Here's what I want to know, Muffin Man. Do you have an apron?"

Yes, and the team captain's sister gave it to me. And I like the way she stared wantonly at me when I wore it. I especially like that she was sending me a subtle message with it. And I fucking love that the illustrations on it inspired a new use for lipstick.

"Remind me to never bake for the team again," I say, mostly so I don't linger too long on thoughts of Josie.

Everly's still popped up in her seat, twisted around, and her eyes connect with mine. "Sounds like the cinnamon puff pastries came out great though?"

I tilt my head. "You knew what I was making?"

"I shopped with Josie. Took her to my favorite grocery store in the city."

A warmth spreads in my chest from this knowledge, which is a stupid reaction. Of course Josie shopped for the supplies; of course she bought the ingredients. I know all this. She told me she wanted to, and she said she wouldn't let me pay. And yet I still find it adorable, the idea of her shopping for the baking we did this morning.

So adorable it's making my heart flip annoyingly in my chest. What a pointless reaction. "Cool," I say to Everly, just to say something.

"You made these with our teammate's sister?" Asher asks with genuine curiosity.

"Yeah. She is my roomie," I add. Is it weird to bake with your roommate? Am I wearing a sign that says I've got it bad for her? Or worse—one that says I nearly fucked her today?

I picture Josie spreading her legs for me on the counter a few hours ago. Josie getting down on her knees after we baked.

I smirk over my little secret. Baking is foreplay. I close my eyes to sleep even though it's a short hop over to Vegas. "Enjoy the treats," I say. "My roomie can fucking bake better than you clowns play hockey."

But as I drift off, I'm hoping Christian didn't hear me.

* * *

When we land in Vegas, it's time to focus on work. *Only work.* I grab my bag and head off the plane, mentally reviewing the plays we've been prepping for this stretch of games. On the tarmac, Christian catches up to me, clapping my shoulder. "Those were good."

I guess the treats made it all the way around the team. "Glad you liked them."

"You and Josie made them?"

Is this front page news? "Yes."

"That was nice of you," he says, like I did it to entertain her. "She was always into that—baking. No idea how she got into it since the rest of us never did."

Seriously? He doesn't know? "Her aunt," I say, then correct my response to: "Your aunt."

Christian's expression is blank for a long beat, then recognition must dawn. "Right. That makes sense."

How well does he even know his sister? Josie told me she was in a committed relationship with baking the morning after she moved in, and then she shared recently that she used to bake with Greta all the time. I've only known her for a month or so, but this is part of the Josie file. But I give Christian the benefit of the doubt. He's got not one but two newborns at home.

"Yeah, it's one of her things," I add evenly so I don't let on in my voice that it's another thing about his sister that I like. That list of things is *long.*

He smiles. "I told you she'd be a good roomie. Quiet, reads all the time, likes to bake. Thanks again, man."

I get what he's doing. Truly, I do. He's still selling me on this living arrangement. Understandable. He asked the team to pitch in when his family was in a bind. I offered. He wants to make sure I'm still good with it.

Little does he know I'm so good with it. So damn good with it I'm annoyed she's leaving in less than two months. Josie and I have barely talked about the end of her time in San Francisco. But now that we're nearly half done with her list, I'm thinking more about the expiration date of her stay. I'm wishing her job wasn't short-term. I'm wishing for a lot of things.

Like a lot less complications.

But as Christian peels ahead of me to chat with Chase and Ryker, doing his captain duties of catching up with everyone, I study him for a beat longer. I admire the guy. He's had a hell of a career. He's shared some great tips since I've been with the team.

Trouble is, I'm not so convinced anymore why he thinks he has a say in who his sister dates or sleeps with. Or if his opinion—if it's even real or mere bravado— matters to me. Sure, I understand team chemistry. Truly I do. Of course it's important. And yeah, I get that dates and romance can go awry, and you don't want bad blood between teammates if that happens.

But I don't tell Natalie who to go out with. I'm not sure Christian should be telling anyone either.

* * *

That night at the hotel when I'm alone in my room, I reach out to my sister.

> Wesley: What would you say if I told you who to date or not date?

Ten seconds later, my phone rings. When I pick up, Natalie is cackling—a long laugh that lasts forever. "That's funny, Wesley. That's really funny."

And that's illuminating in its own way. "Glad I amused you."

"Who is she? And on a scale of one to besotted, how far gone are you?"

I scoff as I flop down on the king-size bed in the room. "I'm not far gone."

"Why are you asking the question then? You never asked questions like this when you were with Anna."

True. But my relationship with Anna wasn't fraught with complications. It wasn't full of reasons why we were a bad idea—although Anna and I were a bad idea in the end because we didn't gel. "That was different."

"So what is it about this new relationship that's making you ask the question?" she asks, then, as the sounds of the city play in the background, she says, "Sit,

Frosty." She must be out walking her dog and stopping on a corner.

I drag a hand through my hair and sink down into the pillow. "It's not a relationship."

"Is it with the girl in the T-shirt?"

I am see-through. "Yes, but she's my roommate."

Natalie lets out a low whistle. "Oh, that hurts."

"Tell me about it."

We shoot the breeze a little longer, and she tells me about Frosty's day. She adopted him recently from Little Friends and has been treating him like a prince. "Today, he went to the dog camp with the indoor pool and spent most of the day fetching tennis balls," she says.

"So, he's only a little bit spoiled?" I ask.

"He's exactly as spoiled as he should be."

"Tell him I'll see him soon."

"I will pass on the message."

When we hang up, I stare at my phone. Weighing what's next. Debating with myself. On the one hand, I shouldn't act like I'm in a relationship with her. Especially since—I'm fucking not.

On the other hand, I want to text her. And lately, want wins.

> **Wesley:** The cinnamon thingies were a hit, and the guys gave me hell.

> **Josie:** Because?

> **Wesley:** Because they're dicks.

> **Josie:** Prank them!

> **Wesley:** Not a bad idea. You prankster.

Josie: Do that one where you cut the bottom of their laces, so they can't tell at first.

Wesley: You know hockey pranks?

Josie: Um, yes.

I don't ask why. It's obvious. Her brother. And the more I get to know Josie, the less I want to make my relationship with her about him. He's hardly the reason I need to resist her. I need to resist her because I live with her. And because she's leaving. I shift to another topic altogether.

She's told me about the cat at her library and sometimes sends me pics.

Wesley: How's Raccoon?

Josie: He spends a lot of time licking his balls.

She's so blunt sometimes it kills me.

Wesley: I'll probably regret asking, but where in the library does he lick his balls?

Josie: On a big yellow chair in the children's section. He has zero shame. And, since he's neutered, zero balls.

Wesley: But so much hope.

* * *

The Vegas Sabers are sluggish the next night. But we are sluggish-er. It's a slow game. Hardly anyone crashes into the boards. Or slams into each other. I'm not an enforcer so it's fine by me, but we need something to liven up this game since we deserve to lose.

During the second intermission, Christian is fired up. In the visitor's locker room, he's all business as he says: "We can do better. We came here to win and we're all skating like it's a fucking stroll in the park and we're hungover. Get out there and show some grit."

It's embarrassing, the acknowledgement of how we're playing. But a swift kick in the uniform pants with a sharp blade is what we need. When we hit the ice for the final period, we're chasing the puck ferociously. Making plays ruthlessly. And eking out a win on enemy ice. An hour later, we're soaring out of the city of sin, its glittery lights and bright billboards fading in the midnight sky as we fly toward the East Coast.

The plane is quiet, as night flights often are. There's no trash talk at this hour, so I take out my phone to listen to some music, but before I click on an R&B playlist that helps me sleep, I find a note from my roomie.

Josie: Nice turnaround.

I smile stupidly against the dark window so no one can see how I look right now. The glass is cool, but I'm warm everywhere. I don't want to talk about me with Josie. Not with my teammates around. And honestly, not that much in general. I want to talk about her.

> Wesley: It was. But what are you up to?
> Also, it's late. Go to bed.

> Josie: That's where I am.

> Josie: Here's your proof of bed.

She sends a picture of the lower half of the bed. Her legs are clearly under the covers. A paperback sits on the white blanket. Zooming in, I read the title. *Someone Else's Ring.*

> Wesley: New book. Does this mean you've
> finished the thriller? The Woman in the
> Hotel?

> Josie: I did, and the thrill was thrilling.

> Wesley: How's this one?

> Josie: It reads like you fuck.

Forget warm. I'm red-hot under the collar of my dress shirt, remembering the words she wrote on hotel stationery more than a month ago. *He fucked like a page-turner you didn't want to put down.*

Is it just me or is Josie getting...naughtier? Bolder? More brazen? Pretty sure it's not just me—it's her, turning up the heat.

I'm feeling the burn in the dark of the quiet jet, streaking across the sky. Here, it's like no man's land, free of consequences, devoid of risk. A place where we can flirt because of the miles between us. So I tap out a reply.

Wesley: Bet I still "read" like that.

Josie: You'd keep me up all night?

Wesley: Like a page-turner, Josie. Like a fucking page-turner.

26

THE SAME SPACE PROBLEM

Josie

I have reached peak librarian awesomeness. I am officially better than an algorithm, and Amazon has nothing on me as I update our *Your Next Five Reads* list with fresh recommendations.

It's an extra thing I wanted to do, and so far, the digital initiative has been a success. It's a new service I've set up during the last few weeks—something we've been promoting on the branch's website since then. Patrons submit their favorite books and top authors, telling us what they liked, and then add what they might be in the mood to read next.

We—usually me—write back within a few hours with five recommendations of books, either paperback, digital, or audio, and explain why we think they'll like them.

It's a mood reader's dream, and I review the final one I worked on today, checking each rec. Yep, these look good. Feeling like a smarty-pants in the best of ways, I hit the send button when a flurry of papers flies my way.

I jerk my gaze away from the computer screen.

Of course.

A giant Siamese has landed on the counter, sending pages soaring as he gives zero fucks. I grab the papers, sorting them as Raccoon stretches his humongous body across the keyboard, belly up and carefree.

"You bad boy. You knocked everything off the counter," I say, chiding him, but he doesn't respond to criticism, being a cat and all.

Thalia's at the other end of the desk here on the second floor. "It's no use," she says, popping up from her chair to wander my way. "He's above it all."

"Clearly," I say, looking down at the creature relaxing shamelessly on the keyboard. "He's trying to lure me now with his big sexy routine."

"Ah, I see you've learned his trick."

"Yes! He does this long, languid stretch where he offers his sleek belly, ostensibly for petting. But if you touch him there on the very belly he's offering, he will strike."

"He's a touch-me-and-die cat," she says nonchalantly, scratching Raccoon's chin, the one acceptable zone on this cat for petting. "So sweet."

"And yet I'll miss him," I say, then wince, wishing I could take those vulnerable words back. I shouldn't be putting sad vibes out in the air. I wasn't hired for this temporary job to talk to my boss about how much I'll miss this place when I finish the contract in seven weeks, but who's counting?

Thalia gives me a sympathetic look. "This place is addictive," she says.

But that's all. She doesn't add *hey, how about I pry open*

our budget and hire you for a permanent gig? You're the city's
most awesome new digital specialist librarian.

"It is," I say brightly.

"Drinks this week with the crew? We're doing Thursday night this time," she says, shifting to another topic all together. "And we're going to add trivia this week."

"Book trivia?" There is nothing worse than librarians trying to best each other with book knowledge. It's like a battle royale of the nerds, and no piece of information is left un-hurled at your rival.

"Please," she scoffs. "We do pop culture. Sports. Music. That sort of thing, so it's more challenging. We need it to be hard."

"I'm in. Librarians like it hard after all," I add, then realize the full weight of the innuendo in the statement.

Thalia sees it too, tilting her head in approval, then tapping her wine-colored nails against the counter. "That ought to be on a sticker, girl," she says, then heads off in a swish of flowy magenta skirt and jingly bracelets.

Come to think of it, that's not a bad idea. Maybe I could become a sticker queen and stay in San Francisco on the riches I'll amass as I peddle a line of cheeky librarian sayings.

Meet me in the stacks.

Let's do it on the reference desk.

Dewey Decimal to me all night long.

I have a free minute so I google the price of cute stickers, then the best fonts for stickers, then where to sell stickers. But soon enough, I sigh, vanquished already by practical matters. There's just not a big enough market for naughty librarian stickers.

I take off my glasses for a second to pinch the bridge

of my nose, since studies show ideas flow faster when you pinch your nose. Oh! I've got it! What if I can win another grant from The Violet Delia Foundation for Library Digital Empowerment? Thalia would probably say nice things about me to the non-profit. Maybe they'd crack open the coffers and fund this position for longer? I could look for other grants too, but most grants in my field fund professional development for librarians, not their salaries. This is a rare one. But if I can prove I'm a unicorn...

I'm also a workhorse though. I've been scanning the job listings regularly in San Francisco—old habits die hard, and when I was finishing grad school I was glued to the job listings. While I haven't found any openings yet, I can widen the search beyond the city maybe. Like San Jose, or Oakland, or Marin County. I can apply to anything within a fifty-mile radius, even though I don't have a car. But I'll deal with that issue later. I'm aces at applications. Not only did I apply to sixteen colleges (accepted at thirteen), I submitted my résumé for more than one hundred fifty jobs before I landed this one.

I have an endless well of application energy, and I will put it to good use tonight in the job hunt. Because I want to stay here. Close to this lovely city. And my brother...and Maeve and Fable and Everly.

As I leave that evening, heading onto the streets of the Upper Haight to catch my bus, I text Wes to tell him what happened today. Well, not my "blanket the Bay Area with my CV" idea. That would definitely seem clingy. *Like, hey, you life-hacked a lipstick tube into a sex toy to get me off on the counter. Clearly you want me to stay in town, don't you?* Nope. I'll keep those plans to myself. Instead, I tap out another note.

. . .

Josie: It's a wonder I still have a job.
Today at work I said the following out loud
to my boss: "Librarians like it hard."

As I'm getting off the bus twenty minutes later, his reply
lands.

Wesley: Can confirm.

I laugh and blush all at once.

* * *

The idea takes a hold of me though—the stick-around-
town one. That evening, after I whip up some carrot
bacon, I spend an hour crunching on my veggie food
while I write a bang-up cover letter to The Violet Delia
Foundation for Library Digital Empowerment, letting
them know what I've accomplished so far and what else I
hope to achieve. I send it off, then hunt for library grants,
just in case there are any I might have missed. I search for
more grants on the way to work the next day too. But I
only unearth a few I'd really qualify for—or really that
this library, or any others in the city, would qualify for to
keep me on. But I check the job boards for open positions
as well. I'm ready to pounce on any.

Spoiler alert: there aren't any for—*gulp*—entry-level librarians.

Sigh. Sometimes starting out just sucks.

But there's plenty of time. I've got seven weeks left in this job. I'll keep at it. In the meantime, I order some stickers for fun.

On Thursday at work, the digitization center is quiet after I teach one of the digital literacy classes, but my brain isn't. Maybe *meet me in the stacks* isn't such a bad idea. Not for a sticker though. For something else. I take some notes, and work on some ideas all day, then I'm out for blood at trivia night.

News flash: our team wins, and Thalia lifts her beer in a victory toast. "You're hereby required to play on my team for the rest of the year."

I smile even though I don't feel it as much inside. It's nice to be wanted, but wanting won't get me to stay.

The next day after work, I take off for a girls' night out with Maeve and Fable. I invited Everly, but of course she's traveling with the team and they don't return till Saturday night so she can't join us.

When I meet up with my friends by Patricia's Green in Hayes Valley, a cute little park and playground, I'm giddy to share my news. Is it news though? Nothing has actually happened, but still after hugs and hellos, I spill the beans: "I'm looking into a grant extension and searching for a job to see if I can stay."

With her wild, blonde-streaked hair framing her pale face, Maeve gazes heavenward to the starlit November sky, pressing her palms together. "My prayers are answered. She'll be here, goddess. She'll be here."

"First, I love that you pray to the goddess," I say.

"Who else would she pray to?" Fable asks dryly.

"Exactly. And second," I say, frowning, as reality kicks me in the ass again, "it's a long shot. But I'm trying."

Fable squeezes my arm. "That's how you start. Maybe there will be something perfect for you."

Librarian jobs aren't easy to come by, and they don't pay gobs. I know librarians a few years older than I am who work a couple part-time library jobs in the hopes of landing a full-time one with benefits. But you never know.

"We'll see what happens," I say, and since I don't love hogging the attention, I make a shooing gesture to Hayes Street. "Let's start."

We're doing a photo scavenger hunt together. Rather than competing against each other, though, we're working in tandem. If we check off all the items in two hours, we'll get cake. This is the kind of team-building activity that calls my name.

I click on the list on my notes app since I planned it. I'm kind of the friend group social director. I start the clock.

"First one. Mirror selfie in a fancy bathroom," I say, then swivel around, tapping my chin as I scan the surroundings, catching the facade of a sleek, modern building a few blocks away. "How about The Resort hotel? That place is five stars."

Maeve nudges me. "Which you know since you were there."

I smile smugly, a fond filthy memory sashaying past me of the night Wes and I spent in that hotel. The way he manhandled me in bed, giving me exactly what I'd learned that night I craved—a man to toss me around and eat me out.

"And it was quite a night," I say with a throaty rumble. "I've given this hotel five out of five for...being a wingwoman."

"My boss owns that hotel," Fable puts in, so nonchalant as we walk through the evening crowd on Hayes Street toward The Resort.

"Ma'am, excuse me," Maeve says, whipping her gaze to Fable. "*My boss owns that?* I'm gonna need details."

"*He* owns it. Not *me*. But this shouldn't be a surprise since I do work for"—Fable stops and lowers her voice to a conspiratorial whisper—"a billionaire."

Color me intrigued. "Tell me more about this billionaire boss. Is he hot? Ripped? Does he want to bend you over the desk?"

Fable swats my arm. "I'm dating someone. Steven, you know," she says a little primly, mentioning the bartender she started seeing a few months ago. "So the answer is no."

"No, your boss is not hot because you're dating someone else?" I ask with a doubtful arch of an eyebrow. "That doesn't add up."

Maeve pffts. "Oh, he's hot all right. I've seen pics of Wilder Blaine," she says, mentioning Fable's boss, who owns the city's Renegades football team and some hotels, as well as some green energy businesses. "Pretty sure he's San Francisco's most eligible billionaire. And sexiest. The man is rough-around-the-edges hot in a tailored suit."

"Well, tell me more, Maeve," I tease.

"I'm just saying. Fable needs to open her eyes."

As we reach the chichi hotel, Fable relents a bit with, "Yes, empirically, Wilder Blaine is good-looking, but I can't think of him that way since he's my boss. Also, hello! I'm seeing someone."

"You're not denying your boss is hot," I add, because it's fun to rile her up.

"Speak of the devil," Maeve whispers out of the corner of her mouth as we walk into the lobby, its mirrored walls reflecting the opulent chandeliers above. "Her hot-ass billionaire boss is walking our way at twelve o'clock."

As if we've summoned him, a tall, dark-haired man with a chiseled jaw, ink on his knuckles, and an intensity in his eyes strides across the hotel lobby. When he spots Fable, something flickers in his gaze. It's more than recognition. It's awareness. Interest maybe?

He stops at my redhead friend. "Evening, Fable. How's everything? Are you staying here tonight? I can comp you a room."

I swear he looks at her more like he wants to take her to a room than gift her one.

"We're doing a photo scavenger hunt," Fable says, then quickly introduces us to the man. When she's done, he nods our way. "If you need anything, let me know."

Then he heads off, a faint hint of expensive cologne trailing behind the mogul of a man.

"Someone has a crush on you," Maeve mutters under her breath.

"Shut up. He does not," Fable admonishes.

I clear my throat. "Hate to break it to you, but that man has 'secret crush' written all over him."

"Does not," she says.

I hold up my hands in surrender. "Fine. I will back down but I reserve the right to say *I told you so* someday."

Maeve nods in solidarity. "Double I told you so."

Fable rolls her eyes, but spins around. "Focus on the prize. We have a two-hour cake countdown."

We get to work. *Fast.*

We march past the elegantly arranged bouquets of dahlias in the hallway off the lobby, their petals shimmering in the soft glow of the lighting, then head into the fancy ladies' room. In front of the mirror, we give our best pouty faces as we snap a mirror selfie. After that, we're onto the next stop. "Take a picture by a statue," I read off from the notes.

Maeve screws up the corner of her lips, eyes narrowed. It doesn't take long though. "Ooh! The giant coffee cup sculpture at Yerba Buena Gardens," she says, then rattles off details. "It's part of a temporary art installation. A public art initiative. Ask me how I know." She wiggles her fingers, urging us to ask.

"How do you know?" Fable says, taking the bait.

"Because I'm obsessed with public art. I want someone to commission me to paint another giant installation. Could be coffee cup murals. Anywhere in the city," she says wistfully. "Or anything, for that matter." But then she seems to shake it off. "We'll have to get there quickly though. So we can get in the cup. The cops aren't usually there till late."

I stop, digging my heels in. "What? Cops show up?"

"Yes, but mostly after ten."

I shake my head. "Nope. Pick another statue."

"So there's no *do illegal things* on your top ten list?" Fable asks wryly.

"Not at all," I say, and maybe I'm a Goody Two-shoes but it'll keep us all out of jail, and I fear Maeve could find jail easily on her own.

"Fine. We'll pose *on* it, not *in* it," Maeve says with an aggrieved huff.

We catch a bus to Yerba Buena Gardens, a multi-block square that includes a playground, lawn, bowling alley, skating rink, and theaters. As the bus rolls down Union Street, Maeve cocks her head my way. "Hey. I just thought of something—is this on your list somewhere?"

"Taking a bus with my girlies?"

"No, doing a photo scavenger hunt. Or taking pics like this?"

I blink, awareness hitting me sharp and fast. Actually...it is. Number five—*Take photos of your fun times.*

Why hadn't I thought this girls' night out activity qualified for the list? A photo scavenger is precisely number five. But it never occurred to me. How did I miss something so obvious? It's a little embarrassing, frankly.

Because you want to do the list with Wesley.

And I've been doing this item with him without realizing it either. I flash back to the pictures Wes and I have taken so far—the photo outside the Bay Area Banter Brigade's theater, then the pictures on Sunday as we baked and ate. "A record of the list," I'd said in the kitchen, somehow completely oblivious to the fact that we'd already been doing number five.

We've done it so well we could even check it off. We've been snapping pics as we go.

But that's not why I'm embarrassed I missed this girls' night out as a possible number five. My stomach churns because the list feels like it belongs solely to Wes and me. The list is something I do with him. It's dating him without the label of dating. Saying that out loud, though, is like cracking open my chest.

Maeve nudges me, asking, "So, is it?"

Shoot. I haven't even answered her.

"Would something like this qualify?" Fable asks too.

That's a reasonable question—"have fun with friends" *feels* like a list item. But I also want to have fun with my roomie, so I do something I don't love. I shake my head. "Bond with friends isn't," I say, pasting on a grin as I spin a tall tale.

Fable narrows her brow, maybe thinking I've missed the point when she adds, "I think she meant this whole thing—pics and all."

"Not really," I say, doubling down on the lie, flicking a strand of my hair off my shoulder, like that proves I'm not making things up.

Fable arches a brow. "You lie."

I flinch. "I don't."

"You do. I bet *this* is on there," she says.

My heart slams hard against my rib cage. I feel... caught. "It's not," I say as she grabs at my shoulder bag, like she can find the list in it. The list's at home though.

As the bus curves past Market Street, Maeve leans forward in the blue plastic chair to stare slack-jawed at me, wagging a finger my way. "This *is* on the list. Somehow. And you don't want this to count."

She says it playfully, but like she's delighting in busting me.

Shame climbs my throat, combined with foolishness. I misled my friends. I roll my lips, then blow out a breath. "Fine, fine. You're right. Taking photos of fun times is on it. This counts, okay? I missed it, and I felt stupid."

But Maeve doesn't back down. "That's not what's going on." She stares at me longer, studying me, like she can find the answer in my expression. She must find it, since she says, "Oh my god! I know what's going on. You're doing this with Wesley, aren't you?"

I drop my face into my hands, groaning. But when the bus rumbles to a stop at Yerba Buena Gardens with a mechanical growl, I let go and look her in the eyes. "Yes," I admit, and there's a momentary reprieve as we trot down the steps. Once we head into the gardens, I revisit the topic with a genuine apology. I don't want to be the friend who fibs. "I'm sorry, guys."

Maeve grabs my arm, tugging me to a nearby bench. "Josie. You don't have to apologize."

Fable gives me a soft smile, exonerating me too. "Yeah, it's not apology level. We get it. But why didn't you tell us what's going on?"

That's the bigger issue. I've been keeping something from them. Something important. That I'm spending more and more time with my roomie. That I'm developing feelings for him—feelings I shouldn't act on. Correction: shouldn't act on *again*. "Yes, but it's stupid. He's my roomie, and I'm leaving, and he works with my brother, and it's all just annoying," I say with a frustrated huff.

Maeve sets her head on my shoulder, sighing sympathetically. "I'd have been surprised if you weren't falling in like with him. You liked him that first night. Now you've gotten to know a man who's been nothing but generous since the first time you met him," she says, her voice stripped of its usual sass and teasing. She's straightforward, and I love it. "Maybe it was all supposed to happen."

I take a moment to consider her view of fate. Since I landed in town, Wes and I have been in each other's orbits. We can't stop circling each other. "Maybe there's an inevitability to us," I admit.

"Sometimes two people are just meant to be in the same...place," Maeve says, her artist soul shining through.

I noodle on that for a beat, drawing in a breath of cool November air. I've read enough stories to bet on that little thing called fate to bring people together who need each other. "That might be true in some ways," I acknowledge. "Wes and I seem to understand each other in the way that we both want and need. But on the other hand, we're not going to be in the same place for very long. And the fact that we literally live in the same place right now is a problem." I look from Maeve to Fable and back, shrugging helplessly. "What if something happens and then...I don't want it, or he doesn't want it? We're stuck together, and that would be weird." Uncomfortable too. My back aches in a reminder of The Kid, waiting to torture me on Maeve's couch if I need a new place to stay. "I really like living there."

We're all quiet for a beat. Humming. Sighing. Thinking.

"You really don't think a romance or relationship can go anywhere?" Fable asks, clearly needing to make sure we've turned over every stone.

"It's hard to imagine it will. There's a lot in the way. It's so hard finding a job and a place, and even if those aligned..." I don't finish the thought because I don't have more to say. Wes and I are complicated. Besides, I want to focus on my friends. "But thanks for listening. I needed it."

Maeve shoots Fable a look. Fable shoots one right back at her, like an unspoken language. With a nod, Maeve squeezes my thigh, then says, "You should take pics with him. For the list. This is a fun girls' night out. That's all."

My heart swells with love for them, for this gesture, for their understanding. "I love you two. So much," I say, then I wrap an arm around Fable, another around Maeve, and hug them close. "This should be on every list. Tell your friends you love them."

Maeve's eyes glisten, and she swipes at her cheek. Fable rolls her lips together, holding in obvious emotions. But not for long. "Love you," Maeve says softly, and Fable echoes her with, "Love you too."

I check the clock on our hunt. One hour down. One to go.

Fifty-nine minutes later, we finish with a photo of a group hug with a random dog, a human pyramid of the three of us, and a photobomb in the ferry terminal before we head to a cake shop for our reward.

I'll miss them, too, if I can't find a way to stay. I'll miss them so much.

27

A THOUSAND DIRTY WORDS

Josie

I shouldn't do this. I really shouldn't. And yet that night, when I'm home in Wesley's place, wandering through the living room, my footsteps echoing as I enter the kitchen, I stop and snap a picture.

Of the kitchen counter. We agreed not to "do that" again. But a photo's not breaking a rule. That's what I tell myself as I hit send on a text.

> Josie: Does this count for number five?
> Take pictures of fun times?

It's late in New York, a little past midnight, so I don't expect to hear from him. But as I leave the bathroom after applying my lotions and potions, a reply blinks up at me.

. . .

> Wesley: Well, there were definitely fun times there.

A smile takes me hostage, along with my reason and good sense. As I walk to the bedroom in the dimly lit home, I dictate another text.

> Josie: I went to The Resort with my friends for a girls' night out. I thought about the last time I was there.

> Wesley: Yeah? What about it?

They say text has no tone, but his sounds intrigued.

> Josie: I thought about when you said "What are you into?" Nobody has ever asked me that before. No one.

> Wesley: Their loss. My gain. Since you knew exactly what you wanted. I can still hear you saying it.

A delicious chill slides down my spine as I wander into

my room, shedding my sweatshirt, a little intoxicated already by this exchange.

> Josie: What did I say?

I haven't forgotten what I said. I doubt he has either. I just want to hear him say it. Or write it.

> Wesley: You said the hottest words ever.

My breath halts. A ribbon of heat unfurls inside me. He's lit a match. Then he drops it on some kindling, setting the blaze with his next message.

> Wesley: And I quote: "Can you bend me over the bed and fuck me hard?"

> Josie: And you understood the assignment.

I float to the bed in a sex trance, remembering that night, but boomeranging to the other morning, too, here in the house. That first night with him, he was my sexy stranger. The second time, he was my hot-as-hell friend.

Wesley: What would you say now? If I
asked you what you're into?

My lungs are hot. My bones are lava. I sit on the bed, my
entire body aching for him. I close my eyes. Picturing.
Then I sink down onto the pillows and respond.

Josie: Your hands on me. Your mouth
exploring my skin. Your dirty words
whispered in my ear.

Wesley: Where do you want my hands?

I drag a hand down my chest then back up, touching the
valley of my breasts, my skin tingling as I trace the path I
want him to touch. I sigh greedily, a precursor to the moan
building in my chest, then write back. *My neck. My throat.
My back. When you push me down. When you tug me close.
When you put me in position.*

Except I don't send that. A picture is worth a thousand
words. Instead, I angle the phone's camera with my left
hand, then push down my tank top so the tops of my
breasts are exposed. Holding the phone, I take a picture of
my hand spread across my tits, inching toward the hollow
of my throat.

After I check it, I hit send. Feeling bold, I stretch
against the pillow, my neck long, my hand curling around
it gently. Another pic. Before I can stop I take off my shirt,
flip to my stomach. Resting the phone against the pillow

as a stand, I set a timer and strike a pose of me in a bra and jeans, my hand pressing on my back.

I send it.

Thirty seconds later, my phone pings.

> Wesley: You. Are. Killing. Me.

I grin, giddy on his lust, craving more of it. I write another text. *Don't die before you fuck me again.*

But, smiling wickedly, I rethink it. Erasing that. Writing something new. Short, to the point.

> Josie: Your turn.

I've never sexted before. I've never sent naughty pictures. I've never received them either. But when my phone buzzes, the throb between my thighs builds. A low, hot pressure spreads in my belly. I click it open.

"Oh my god," I say, all breath and fire.

It's a shot of him from the chest down, taken with a view of the naked ladder of his abs. They're covered by his muscular forearm, his wrist, and his hand, shoving his boxer briefs down. I can't see anything. There's no peen in the pic. But it's clear what he's doing. The idea of him gripping his cock right now is too much to bear.

I dictate a reply.

> Josie: Gonna need a sec with this.

> Wesley: Yeah, me fucking too.

Then, I take that second and turn it into a minute or two as I shove my fingers down my panties and imagine Wes taking matters into his own hands across the country.

In a hotel room in New York City, there's a tall, strapping, six-foot-three hockey stud with inked arms, ripped abs, and talented hands, fisting his cock.

To me.

I am a volcano. And soon, I erupt.

I try to catch my breath, but I'm still panting, still a little electric everywhere as I reply.

> Josie: Was that number five? Take pictures of fun times? :)

Wesley sends a picture of his face with a cocky satisfied smile. It makes my chest ache. I wish it were this weekend. I wish he were here. And I know we shouldn't do this. But I did it anyway. I guess I was in a *fuck it* kind of mood.

I hop out of bed, grab a few things, then take one more picture. A photo of the list, updated.

1. ~~Have a one-night stand with a sexy stranger.~~
2. ~~Overcome a fear (take a class you can't prepare for, baby! Psst — improv class time!)~~
3. ~~Make a friend who's nothing like you. You learn the most from them.~~
4. ~~Eat dessert for breakfast.~~
5. ~~Take pictures of your fun times. (It's okay to stop and snap a pic! That doesn't mean you're not living in the moment. It means you're giving yourself a beautiful memory for later.)~~

We're halfway done, and it feels like time is running out.

28

TAKE IT OFF

Wesley

I'm addicted to these pictures. I'm practically climbing out of my skin on Saturday morning when I wake up in the team hotel, flicking through them again, staring at them, enjoying them.

I think about them at breakfast with my teammates.

I think about them as we check out of the hotel.

I think about them on the way to the New York arena for a Saturday afternoon game.

But that's the problem. I can't have a woman on my mind when I'm playing, especially against my former team. I want to do well against everyone, but I especially want New York to miss me hard.

I liked it here in the city. Liked the fans. Liked the camaraderie. Tried not to take it personally when they traded me last season. I had the stats. Had the skills. Had the ability to play well here. Am I pissed they let me go? Hard to be when I'm playing even better in San Francisco.

Their loss—my gain.

Still, I want to show them it's their loss. That'll take my mind off those goddamn pictures too. When we reach their arena, I laser in on hockey, only hockey.

New York wins the face-off and charges down the ice ferociously, their center hell-bent on scoring early. He slams the puck toward Max, and like it's invisible, the black disc flies right past our goalie. Well, shit.

The lamp lights in the first fifteen seconds. That won't do. That won't do at all.

Maybe I'm having a delayed reaction to the trade, but fuck them for not needing me. Screw them for casting me off. I'm not letting my new team lose to my old team.

When the line changes, I hop over the boards, single-minded in my pursuit of one thing and one thing only—a win. Whatever it takes.

Maybe I'm a little hungrier since it hasn't been the greatest series of away games. It's a rare week when we play four games. We've played two since our win in Vegas and lost both. I'd really like to salvage this trip and return to San Francisco evened up on this road trip.

As we're jostling in the corners, I get knocked into the boards. They get the puck, and New York rushes ahead toward center ice. I'm flying there seconds later. But Alexei snags the puck from their forward, then passes it back to me as I spin around. I've got it, and I skate toward their net as fast as I can. But the toughest defenseman on the New York team—a big, mean guy named Karlsson—strips me of the puck when I'm *this* close to the net.

"Fuck," I mutter.

He flashes a dickhead smile. "Looks like you missed us. Can't say the same."

I know this drill. I was on the same side of it when I played with him. Guy is mouthy. And yet, I'm letting it get to me since I'm clenching my jaw as I hop off the ice.

My annoyance skyrockets, though, in the second period when Karlsson's blocking my every move, knocking me into the boards, chirping at me with real winners like "Guess you went soft on the West Coast" and "We traded you just before you started sucking."

He's always been such an asshole, but I vastly preferred it when he was an asshole to *others.*

Irritation pours through my veins, but I do my best to ignore it. A few minutes later, after Asher flips the puck to me, I try to get a shot on goal, and I'm this close, I swear I'm this close. But Karlsson barrels toward me and I rush the play, colliding with their goalie instead of slipping a puck past him.

Fuck me.

I grit my teeth, knowing it's coming—a two-minute penalty for goaltender interference. I hit the box and stew.

Should I have tried to avoid contact? Yes. You can't take a shot while messing with the goalie's ability to defend the net.

And yet I did. Because of a former teammate's trash talk throwing me off.

The New York fans are chanting power play, but the guys on my side hold them off. Thank fuck I didn't make it worse for my team. When I'm out of the box, I try to shove whatever residual emotions I didn't think I'd have far, far away.

Like to the South Pole far.

Once I'm back on the bench a few minutes later,

Coach McBride comes over and gives me a chin nod. "Put that out of your mind, Bryant. Got that?"

It's said gruffly but without judgment. Like he understands but needs me to move the hell on. Fair enough.

"Yes, sir," I say, then narrow all my focus to the game.

When I'm back on the ice and get a shot on goal again, I refuse to mess it up this time. Hard and aggressively, I send the puck flying till it lodges in the twine, taking no prisoners.

Yes!

That ties it up, and in the third period, Chase scores to seal a messy win. It's exhausting, but that's hockey for you. The best part is when I leave the arena, heading toward the team bus, and my phone buzzes with a text.

> Josie: Fuck Karlsson.

A smile has me in its grip. Immediately, I'm picturing Josie at our next game, parked in a seat on center ice, cheering me on and heckling the other team. That thought revs my engine—her ferocity. I would love to play with her in the house.

> Wesley: We need to get you in the stands at the next game.

Ideally in my jersey. But I don't add that.

. . .

Josie: I'll wear my good luck scarf.

A burst of hot adrenaline rushes through my veins. I don't even need to ask why she's calling it her good luck scarf. I'm betting it's because she wore it the night she met me. By the time we're crossing the tarmac to the team jet a little later, the thrill of victory hasn't totally worn off—nor has the buzz from Josie's texts.

"Did you get a feeling that Karlsson has bad blood with Bryant?" Max drawls as we head down the aisle, claiming our usual seats.

Asher shakes his head sympathetically as I shoulder my way into his row, across from Max.

"Did you date his mom?" he asks. "Steal his girlfriend? Put Whiny Bastard as the name on the back of his jersey one night, and he didn't notice?"

I smile evilly. "Should have done that one," I say, then I scratch my jaw as I settle into the seat. I really can't let the assholes of the world get me down. "But I did beat him at poker every single time. Dude has zero strategy."

"And you, man—you're all fucking strategy," Max says with a proud nod.

"You are and we appreciate it," Asher adds, just as earnest.

It's a rare moment among these guys when we aren't giving each other hell. When we're abundantly honest, and I'll take that, along with the bruises from all the hits I took tonight.

"Thanks, man," I say, to the both of them.

"Speaking of, we should play," Max says, then takes out a deck from his bag and shuffles. Before Texas Hold'em starts, though, my phone pings with a message.

I'm itchy to check it. What if it's Josie again? My hand moves to my pocket, but I stop myself. I should just play cards. It's risky to open a message now. Then again, my texts don't automatically show pics. Max isn't done dealing...

Screw it. I'm too amped up on the dizzying possibility of a note from her, so I click on my texts lightning fast, but groan in disappointment.

"It's my..." I cut myself off before I say Dad to my friends, saying agent instead. He reps Alexei, too, and plenty of other pro hockey players. Best if I try to think of him as my agent.

"Go ahead," Max says, getting it.

I shake my head. "I'll catch him in between hands."

But I fold easily—maybe I'm distracted by what I know is coming from him. Criticism. When they're upping the ante on the hand, I return to his text, and yup, I'm right.

> Dad: Nice goal, but you've got to play cleaner. Haven't seen a goaltender penalty on you in years.

No shit, Dad. It was practically Karlsson's fault, but that's not an excuse.

Wesley: Yeah, I know, but being back in
New York and all...

Only, the second I hit send I know that won't fly with him, and he calls me on it.

Dad: What does that have to do with it?

My stomach churns. My teammates get it. My dad probably never will. Trouble is, he's also...right. I don't usually let that shit get to me. I was sloppy. That's why Coach told me to move on. Different approach, and I like Coach's better. I blow out a breath and suck it up.

Wesley: Good point. You're right. Thanks
for the reminder.

Dad: Happy to help! Let's get together for
lunch when you're back in town. We also
still need to find some art for your walls.
Tomorrow?

I stifle a groan. I just want to...do nothing tomorrow.

Wesley: I'll hit you up then.

I do ignore the phone this time as I play a few hands with my teammates, feeling understood with them. With how they saw the interaction with Karlsson. Who cares if my dad and I don't see eye to eye? At least my teammates do. We play for an hour, and Max and Asher take all my money. Coach strolls by at one point and Asher tips his chin at the guy in charge, saying, "Coach, you want to get in on it? Bryant is an easy target tonight."

He stops, peers at Asher, and gives him a stern, serious look. "But I'm not. You still sure you want me in?"

Asher gulps, blanching. "No, sir."

We play a few more hands till the game peters out, and I waggle my earbuds. "Gonna chill," I say, then I turn to the window.

But chilling doesn't come easily. As we slide into that time on the flight when everyone goes into their own worlds, I can't quite get into my playlist of new tunes. I'm antsy, revved up.

My phone is burning a hole in my pocket. My mind is flooding with those images of Josie from last night. My body is crackling as we cross the country, flying closer to home.

I haven't seen her since last Sunday. It's been nearly a week. I thought about her more than I'd expected while I was out of town. I'm still thinking of her. I'm not sure that's going to stop.

I'm not sure I want it to stop.

I click open the messages, sliding my thumb over the screen, weighing my choices. I'll be in the same space as her very, *very* soon. What's that going to be like? But I know what I want it to be like. If one *fuck Karlsson* text thrills me this much, I'm pretty sure I made my choice. I send her a text with no guilt, no second-guessing.

> Wesley: Can't get those photos out of my mind.

It's Saturday night. No idea what she's up to. But she responds in ten minutes.

> Josie: Maybe this will help get them out of your mind.

My phone says an image is loading. My pulse roars. Excitement pings through my every cell. Furtively, I scan the plane. It's dark and quiet, but I angle the phone even more, so no one can see it. I'm not the first guy on my team who's angled his phone. I won't be the last.

My mouth waters as I click it open. I push my fist against my mouth and bite my knuckle so I don't groan in pleasure.

The shot is artful and dripping with desire all at once. It's like a slice of life and a moment of lust somehow combined. Looks like she's on the back deck of my house, with a glass of wine sitting on the wooden table at the edge of the shot. There's a charcuterie board on the table too, with some grapes and fruit on it. But that's not where my gaze goes. The forefront of the shot is her hand on the side of her chest, looped around a black lacy bra strap. She's tugging it slightly away from her skin—skin I want to lick and kiss.

Is that...new? The bra?

No idea, but the possibility that she bought a new piece of lingerie turns me into a furnace. I can't hold back.

> Wesley: Is that new?

> Josie: The charcuterie board? No, it's yours, Wes.

Even though she sent a text, I can hear my name said on her mouth. Can feel the vibration of the letters as she says them in a tease. All I want is to speed up time.

> Wesley: Don't take it off yet.

Too bad I have two fucking hours left.

Two hours to think.

Two hours to consider.

Two hours to debate.

* * *

But really, was there ever any debate at all? Or, to put it more accurately, I spent the last six weeks debating. The debate is over now.

When we land, I'm off the plane before anyone else. Turning on my car in no time, racing home through the streets of San Francisco at a record pace, then pulling into the garage and getting out of my car right as the garage door closes behind me.

I don't waste a second.

I leave my duffel on the floor and head up the stairs, not even bothering to toe off my shoes.

If she's asleep, I want her to hear me. I want her to wake up. I want to make it worth her while.

I scan the living room. No sign of Josie. I walk into the kitchen. It's quiet and clean. I stop at the sink, quickly wash my hands, then I march to her bedroom, ready to rip down the door. But it's wide open and when I peer inside, she's not there.

I need to see her right now.

I stride to the back deck, a man on a mission. At the glass door, my heart stops, stutters. She's curled up in a deck chair, a blanket around her, reading a book under the soft floodlights, the glass of wine empty, her gaze steady on the e-reader.

The heat lamp is on. I slide open the door.

She looks up, parts her lips, roams her eyes up and down me. "Hey, you."

I'm wearing a suit, no tie. She takes me in for a beat, but before she can say another word, I close the distance to her. Lean in. Set a hand on the back of the chair next to her face. Hold her heated gaze.

"Now," I say. "Take it off, now."

29

I GET NO RESPECT

Josie

I've lived in my head for so long. I've studied the world down to the last detail, arming myself with information and insight for any situation. But there's no book to prepare me for this experience.

For his demand.

But I don't need one, it turns out. My body knows what it wants when Wes tells me to strip for him.

On the back deck, with a cocktail of heat lamp and cool November air kissing my skin, I drop the blanket, set down my e-reader on the table, and reach for the zipper of my maroon hoodie, like I'm mesmerized by his order. Eager to follow it. I don't need to research how to undress for your sexy roomie that you're a little caught up with.

I just...do.

I tug down the zipper.

The sound of each metal tooth sliding open unlocks me more. When my sweatshirt opens, I let the material fall to the seat of the chair, my chest rising and falling with an anticipation that's gripping me.

Wes still has one hand pressed to the back of my chair. Like that, his gaze strays up and down my torso, then lands on my face. There's an *I'm waiting* look flashing in his sinful eyes. "Almost," he says in a command.

Sweet, hot tension curls through me. My breath comes fast and urgent as I reach for my bra straps and slide them down my arms, letting them fall to the crooks of my elbows. I bring my hands to my tits, taking my time, pushing the cups down but only a little. "Like this?" I ask, my voice pitching up in playful curiosity.

"Close," he rasps out.

With my head tilted, I lower the lace a little more, exposing the top of one nipple—a tease. "How's this?"

Wes swallows roughly, a rumble escaping his lips. "All the way, Josie." It's a demand now.

I slide my teeth along my lower lip, savoring his reaction, then rewarding him as I push the cups down, freeing my tits. "Is this what you had in mind?"

"Yes. Fucking yes." It's full of filthy approval as he reaches out with his free hand, plucking at the fabric of my lacy bra. "I ask again. Is this new?"

I didn't reply to him before. I wanted to play. He clearly needs the answer now, so I give it to him. "Yes."

His breath is hot. Shaky. He lets go of the chair back and drags his hand through his hair, like he's steadying himself. The moonlight coasts across his handsome face, lighting him up for a few potent seconds. His stare is serious. But there are no questions in his eyes. No uncertainty on his face.

This is a man who must have come through the door determined to fuck me tonight. That knowledge sends a blast of heat to my core. Then another rush comes when his hands cover my breasts, and he kneads them. He's not at all gentle.

"Oh god," I gasp.

He rolls my right nipple with his thumb, then the other. Then both at the same time, and I'm nearly flying out of the chair as pleasure twists in me. He squeezes my tits, nice and rough.

"I'm into this," I gasp out.

"That makes two of us," he says dryly. With a carnal groan, he drops one hand so he can drag a thumb along my jawline. Holding my face in his hand, he pulls me closer, then gently slides off my glasses, handing them to me.

I set them carefully on the table.

Then he crushes my mouth with his.

The kiss is deep. His tongue urges me open, and I part my lips for him. He kisses like he plays hockey—he goes all out. His teeth are hard against my lips. His tongue is insistent. His hold is powerful. The kiss is downright dizzying and soon, my mind is fuzzy, full of static, like a machine going offline.

And I want so much more.

My hands snake up around his neck, and I try to pull him closer to me in the chair. He lets go of my mouth, drops to his knees in his tailored suit pants, and blazes a trail of open-mouthed kisses down my throat, then traveling to my collarbone. Biting me.

I yelp, because it was unexpected. Because I've never been bitten. And I like it.

He dips his face to my breasts next, tugging one nipple into his mouth and biting again too.

I cry out as a sharp, delicious pain tinged with plea-sure ricochets through me.

Wes looks up, grinning wickedly. So damn pleased. He goes for seconds, kissing up my throat again, this time running his finger along my bottom lip, pressing it into my mouth.

I moan as I suck on his finger. I wriggle, getting more turned on. I had no idea this would feel so...filthy and free. He pushes in another. I swirl my tongue along both, sucking more. They taste clean, like he stopped to wash his hands before he came to me, and this thoughtful gesture makes me wetter. This attention to detail turns me on.

I suck harder, squirming in the chair as his other hand ropes into my hair. He curls some strands around his fist. And tugs.

A breath staggers from me. He lets go, looking down at me, a wry grin forming on his handsome face. "I think I know what you're into."

They're my favorite words, and he knows it. "What am I into?" The question comes out as desperate as I feel.

With a crook in his lips, he drops a hand between my thighs and squeezes me through my jeans. Roughly. Like he's grabbing my pussy. Is that supposed to be hot? From a guy you like, I guess it is. Because the temperature in me shoots higher.

I like being manhandled by Wes. I like his size, his big hands, his rawness. He's a bedroom explorer, taking me down an unmarked trail, cutting down branches for me as we go.

He slides a thumb under my chin, his dark eyes locking with mine as he says, "I think you want to be fucked by someone who's not gentle. By someone who's not polite. By someone who's figured out that smart girls like dirty sex."

That's a sticker the world needs. "Yes," I gasp. "This one does."

"Then let's break that roomie rule so I can fuck you dirty."

This is not a drill. This is my wild, wicked life. "Yes. Now. Thanks," I say, grabbing my glasses and putting them back on.

He laughs, then reaches for my hoodie from the chair, offering a hand next. I take his as he tugs me to a stand. I pull my bra up so I'm not walking around tits free, since that's awkward. Wes moves behind me as I go, setting his hands on my waist, kissing my shoulders while I walk through the sliding glass door into the home.

He stops and shuts the door, but doesn't relent in his kisses. He's kissing the back of my neck as he locks it, then as we walk down the hall.

I keep shuddering.

Trembling.

Moaning.

I stop in the hallway, setting a hand on the wall. "Wes, I can't focus when you kiss me."

"Good. Don't focus."

"But we'll never get to my bed."

That stops him. He spins me around, making me face him. He's silent for a second, then says in a softer voice, "Come upstairs. Come to my bed."

I blink at the unexpected vulnerability in his tone. "You've never invited me upstairs."

"That was deliberate."

"Why? Is it messy? I've never gone."

"I know you haven't."

"How do you know? Do you have cameras?"

He laughs, shaking his head. "No. I trust you."

"Good. I wanted to respect your privacy."

His lips curve up as he travels a hand over my bare arm, leaving goose bumps in his wake. "About that…"

"About respect?" I ask to clarify.

"Yes. You need to know why I didn't invite you up."

"Okay," I ask, but I'm not nervous. I'm…aroused. This is getting good.

"Because all I've wanted since you moved in is to get you in my bed, Josie." He slides his hand into my hair, gathers some strands and tugs me closer, like my hair's a leash. It's hotter than I would have thought. "And to fuck you like I don't respect you."

A rush of heat whooshes down my body, settles in my core in a needy ache. "Take me upstairs and fuck me like that right now."

Adventurous Josie is in the house.

30

HORNY GUSTO

Wesley

The second I open the door, I want to haul her against me and kiss her ruthlessly, but Josie's a processor. She'll want to see things.

I turn on the light. She drinks in the room as I set down her hoodie on a chair.

It's not like my bedroom is some inner sanctum of man secrets. I don't have a hunting knife hanging over the bed, or a collection of *Star Wars* bobblehead dolls I'm afraid to let anyone see.

In fact, there's not much to it.

It's just a big room I really like to sleep in, but I try to look at it through her eyes. She'll try to read me in the decor, because that's what she does.

I scrub a hand over the back of my neck, tensing briefly. Didn't think of this before, but I hope she doesn't figure I'm a player since this room gives off that vibe. It's so sleek and monochrome that it screams *playboy cool* when that's not who I am. The wooden flooring is polished. The walls are white and minimalistic, with hardly anything hanging on them—just a couple black-and-white beauty shots of San Francisco. I asked the decorator to make it feel like I was part of this city, this team, these fans. But I didn't choose the pics. Or hang them.

On the far wall, a massive king-size bed takes center stage, its silver metal frame glinting under the light. The bed is covered in pristine white linen. Plush gray pillows are scattered by the headboard.

There's one picture framed on the nightstand.

I wince, hoping she doesn't think this means I don't like roots. I'm just not into decorating. But I hadn't thought how it might look to someone else. "You're the first woman to see it," I say, scratching my jaw.

Josie turns to me, a smile shifting her pretty lips. "Lucky me." She sounds enchanted.

Well then. I guess that's all it takes to show her I'm not a player—the truth trumps the decor. I smile back at her. "Guess it's a little like a hotel room. Pretty sure you like those."

"I do. They make me feel a little...like I'm getting out of my comfort zone."

A wave of heat rolls down my spine. That's what she wants. To mix things up. Break up the routine. She came to the right guy.

But before I can strip her naked and do unholy things to her, she zeroes in on the framed picture, beelining toward it on the nightstand. She stops, stares at it, then turns to me, like she's busting me. "You have a picture of a dog."

It's a shot of a black-and-white Collie mix catching a frisbee. "Yeah, that's Frosty. My sister's dog. She adopted him a year ago. He's a senior—that's why she calls him Frosty."

She blinks. "Your sister's dog? You have a framed photo of your sister's dog?"

"He's cute," I say easily, but maybe defensively.

Shaking her head, Josie advances toward me. "Shut up. Nothing makes me want to lose my clothes faster than that."

Holy shit. This is my lucky night. "Good because you're about to," I say, then jerk her against me so she feels the length tenting my pants. I kiss her hard, unhooking her bra this time, then shoving her jeans down. She steps out of them. "Last night," I begin, kissing the hinge of her jaw, "over text. You said no one had asked you what you're into."

"Right," she says, breathless as I coast my mouth along her chin.

"Tell me what else you like. Tell me what you watch." I stop, meet her gaze, give a tug to a handful of her chestnut hair. "Besides pigeon porn."

She laughs, but then asks carefully, "Really?"

"Fuck yes." It's decisive. I want her to know I mean it completely.

She nibbles on the corner of her lips, then breathes out, like she needs courage. I curl my hands around her hips. "You're not going to scare me off," I say, since I sense she needs some reassurance that it's okay to crack open her box of turn-ons. I will treat them with care, and, probably, horny gusto.

"I've never told anyone."

That only makes me want to know more. "Tell me," I say, a demand, but I hope she can hear the vulnerability in my voice. I want to be the man she shares her dirty wishes with. I'm not interested in foisting my likes onto her. "It turns me on to give you everything you want," I add, so she's clear—I'm game to give her all her filthy fantasies.

There's a pause, then she says, "If you insist."

I grind my dick against her so she gets the message. "I do. I fucking do."

With a *here goes nothing* shrug, she says, "There's this site I like. It caters to women. And I find myself watching videos that have these types of scenes."

Then she tells me the scenes, the things, the wishes.

I am blown away. The night I met her our chemistry sparked. But I had no way of knowing she was so perfectly dirty.

"You want all that?" I ask.

She nods eagerly. "I do."

"Good. Undress me," I say, and that's not technically on her list, but it's a necessary start.

She reaches for the top button on my shirt, then makes quick work of undoing it, pushing it off me. Then, her eager fingers work open my belt, the button, then the zipper. In no time, my pants are off, and I'm down to boxer briefs. I grab a fistful of her hair and jerk her close, planting a rough, bruising kiss to her mouth. Hooking my thumb into her panties, I shove them down.

She steps out of them and stands before me, naked and glorious, wearing only her black-and-white glasses. "Disrespect me, Wes," she says.

"Get on your back, spread your legs wide, and show me how wet you are," I tell her, using her road map.

A breath stutters across her lips as she complies, lying down, spreading those thighs, then gliding a hand between her thighs. I grab my shirt from the floor, carrying it as I walk toward her, watching her the whole time. "This is what you did in your room the last few nights, like a dirty girl?"

She strokes faster. "Yes."

"You sure you didn't come up here? Get on my bed? Play with yourself right fucking here?"

She gasps. "I'm sure."

I tilt my head like I just don't believe her. "You didn't go into my closet, flick through my clothes, put on one of my shirts, then sit on the edge of my bed, and stroke that sweet cunt as you sniffed me on my shirt?" I toss her the shirt.

She grabs it. "I didn't. I followed your rules." She slides her arms into the sleeves.

And my dick is a skyscraper.

Holy fuck. That is the sexiest image ever in the world. Josie, in my white dress shirt that smells like me. Spreading her thighs, twirling a strand of hair, her glasses on. She turns her face to the collar and inhales.

I burn. The equator has nothing on me right now.

I shed my boxer briefs and her lips widen into an O. She strokes her pussy faster as she stares savagely at my dick. I grab my aching cock, give it a tug. The tip of her tongue flicks across her bottom lip as she watches me touch myself.

"My girl is hungry for my cock, isn't she?"

"I am," she says.

I give it a rough jerk, so she can imagine easily how I fuck my fist to her. She arches as I tug. "Slide two fingers between your thighs," I tell her as I let go and climb up on the bed.

She obeys.

"Part those lips for me," I say as I move between her knees.

With her fingers in a V, she spreads her pussy lips, showing me how aroused she is.

My dick jumps, eager to meet her again. I give it another pump. "You're fucking soaked," I say in admiration.

"You're fucking hard," she counters.

I love her sass. Just fucking love it. I let go of my dick and drop my face between her thighs. I suck on her clit mercilessly. The gust of breath tells me she's surprised. I suck harder, kissing her sweetness, lapping it up. She squirms against my face. One more deep, hot kiss. Then I stop, pull back, and coast my hand between her thighs, spreading all that wetness around some more.

Then, I lift my hand, the fingers wet from her. "You want this, Josie?"

"You know I do," she says. My girl really likes her dirty videos.

I give her what she wants—I slap her pussy.

For a second, I hold my breath. Hoping she likes it. Wanting her to like it. Wanting her reality to match her research. The moment suspends, full of filthy desire as her blue eyes register shock. Then it's like a pulse moves through her, a vibration. She murmurs something incoherently, then whispers clearly, "Again."

Guess she likes it.

I lean in, kiss her sweet lips, then pull back, lifting my hand a second time before giving her a light slap once more. This time I use three of my fingers, right against her diamond of a clit.

It's a quick smack, then I soothe it with a caress, spreading all that wetness around. I stare for a long breath at her pussy. She's glistening. "Fuck, you look good like this, Josie baby."

"I'd look better on my hands and knees," she taunts as she takes off her glasses, setting them next to Frosty's pic.

I groan, then flip her over, pushing up the shirt to the middle of her lovely back, lifting her ass, spreading those pale, pretty cheeks.

For a heady moment, I let myself enjoy the view of her like this—long, lean and, turned on. Lifting the shirt more, I move down her back, licking a path from her neck to the top of her ass, taking a beat to enjoy the flavor of her skin, that cinnamon scent that drove me wild the night I met her.

That drives me even wilder now.

I press a kiss to the top of her ass, and she shivers under me. Murmuring against her skin, I lay another soft kiss to her skin, then I'm not soft at all when I rope my arm around her, sliding my hand down, pushing one finger into her pussy, then two.

She bucks. "Oh my god," she says, her breath halting. Her body knows what it wants though. She starts to fuck back on my fingers. I crook them, kissing the top of the small of her back as I fuck her ruthlessly with my fingers. Like she wants.

Two, then three. A hot, possessive kiss. A deep, greedy finger fuck. Then, I smack her ass with my free hand till she says, "Wes, fuck me please, now."

I ease out my fingers. "You want my cock?"

"I do."

"Say it," I demand.

"Fill me with your cock."

"Beg for it," I encourage her.

"Please, fill me with your big dick," she begs.

"That's my dirty girl," I say, then I let go so I can sit back on my heels. After reaching for a condom, I cover my dick, then get on my knees behind her, angling her up. "Look at you. So fucking wet you're dripping," I say, then I smack the head of my cock against her clit. She moans, a keening sound, carnal and inviting.

I do it again till she's writhing, pushing her body back, asking for more and more.

I give it to her, slapping the tip against her clit till I'm raw nerve endings and she's nothing but a chorus of *please, please, please.*

I angle up her cheeks, giving me more room to slide my cock into the warm, welcoming home of her pussy. The second, the very second I'm sliding in, my mind snaps. Wires fry. Circuits blow. This is so damn good. The heat, the friction, the tightness.

The way she wants me.

The way I want her.

The way she's asked for it. She's perfect for me. Here, in my white dress shirt, on her hands and knees, she cranes her neck back to watch me as I fuck her deep.

"Like the view?" I ask dryly as I sink into her.

"I do," she moans.

"How about this?" I ease out, leaving her empty, making her beg for *more.*

I slam back in, and we set a pace like that—a little relentless, a lot hungry as she swivels her hips, taking me deeper.

The room fills with grunts and groans, then a demand from Josie. "Smack my ass again."

My dick gets even harder. Feels like granite now as I lift a palm and smack.

She cries out.

I soothe the red mark with my hand—a gentle caress that doesn't last too long. I lift it again.

"Harder," she begs.

I smack her, and she yells an *oh god* but clenches around my cock at the same time. She's so tight and wet and eager, and now she's fucking back onto me with ruthless abandon as she chases her pleasure. I thrust deep inside, then ease out, making her wait till I slap that cheek with my hand, leaving a beautiful red mark.

She's panting, moaning, and seemingly lost to the moment. It's perfect. So perfect, how my wild girl gives herself to me. As I fuck her, my hand travels up the smooth flesh of her back then into her hair. I curl a fist around her chestnut strands as I cover her with my body. "You like it like this, baby?"

"I do," she says, then my other hand slips between her thighs and finds her eager clit, and I pinch it.

Her scream is the stuff of my filthy dreams. It's erotic and carnal and all mine.

I pinch again, then caress her clit. Josie's back is arching, her tits are swinging, and her face is twisted. "I want to come," she whispers in a needy plea.

"I know you do, baby," I say, then I repeat the motions —fuck, pinch, soothe. I rinse, lather, repeat till she's bowing her back and chanting *yes, yes, yes*.

Only thing left for me to do is not break her rhythm. I fuck her hard as she curls her fingers into the sheets, clawing at them. Her whole body tenses beautifully, gripping my cock as she comes with a groan that lasts forever and not nearly long enough.

Her arms slide out from under her. She lets her face fall to the mattress, but her ass is still high up in the air. So hot it's almost all I need. It occurs to me that I could finish like this. It'd be so damn easy to fuck her for thirty more seconds till I tense and spill. But I want more.

I want to look at her. I want to see her. I want to experience her. All at once, it hits me—I don't just want hard, rough, dirty sex with her.

I pull out. "Josie. I gotta see your face," I say, desperation coloring my tone.

"Yeah?"

"I do," I say urgently, then I loop an arm around her waist and shift her to her back. She lifts her arms above her head, stretching out languidly, an invitation to take her tenderly. The shirt is open. She pulls up her knees, giving me room. Beautiful and aroused.

My heart catches in my chest, stops, then speeds up again. "You're stunning in my shirt," I tell her as I slide in.

"Does it make you feel possessive?"

"Yes. You look so fucking hot in my clothes," I say, filling her all the way, then pulling back. "Want to see you in my jersey."

"That so, Number Sixteen?"

The image is too much. I shudder, lust shooting down my back in punishing waves.

"Want it so badly," I say, then I slow the pace, take my time easing in, out. Pushing up, bracing myself, watching those blue eyes sparkle beneath me. "Want you so much. Want you more every day. More than the night I met you."

"Same," she whispers, the playfulness slinking off.

We turn quiet, the sex slower, the mood more tender.

She wraps her arms around my neck, then loops her ankles around my ass. I follow her lead, slow-fucking her for a few mind-bending minutes. It feels like the room is spinning, or maybe it's my heart in my chest that's spinning out.

"You're fucking me like you respect me now," she says, her throat catching. The sound goes straight to my chest, squeezing it.

"Is that a problem?" *Say no. Say fucking no.*

She shakes her head. "I like this too."

"Good. Same here, baby."

I move in her till she's panting again, then I rise up to my knees, grab her hips, and drive in deep, rubbing her clit with my fingers till she's shuddering and grasping at the sheets.

But she doesn't seem to want to hold on to the covers. Instead, she reaches for me—grabbing at my hair as she comes again.

It's so sexy I can't stand it, and pleasure barrels into me, blurring out the night, the city, the whole damn world.

My thighs shake and my body tenses.

I come so hard, my mind blanks out for a long minute or more.

When it comes back online, I'm sure we broke our roomie rule, but sure, too, we're on a collision course to smash others. Maybe ones we didn't even set. Unwritten rules like *don't fall for your roommate.*

Though I'm pretty sure I broke that one a while ago.

The rest is just details.

31

NO GHOST HERE

Josie

The Internet can prepare you for a lot of things—orbit-shattering orgasms among them. But can it truly prepare you for the back-to-earth moments after the O? Like when you need to, well, clean up? It's all so terribly awkward once the penis slips out.

"Excuse me," I say a minute later, then hop out of bed and dart into the en suite bathroom as quickly as I can, leaving Wes to dispose of the condom.

I straighten up, pee, wash my hands, and re-emerge into his bedroom. Wesley must have ditched the protection quickly. He's now lying on top of the covers, arms parked behind his head, skin sweat-slicked, looking entirely too sexy and sated.

The moment's still weird though.

Because...do I go home?

As in, downstairs?

Do I stay here?

No research prepared me for this truth of modern sex —banging your hot-as-hell roomie is great until you have to figure out who's kicking who out of bed.

My stomach flips with fresh nerves as I take tentative steps in my birthday suit into the bedroom. But I stop near the doorway, the entrance to the stairs just beyond.

"Sooooo," I begin.

Translation: what's next?

Wes rolls his eyes. "Get the hell over here, Winters," he says, patting the bed.

My body throws a parade, confetti and ticker tape raining down inside me. Feeling wanted, I hustle my naked booty back to bed and flop next to him. I grab my glasses and slide them back on.

He props himself on his side, parks his head in his hand. "Were you going to sneak out?" He sounds playful as he calls me on it.

"Is it sneaking out if I live here too?" I counter, even though I'm still uncertain. How do you go from having great sex to not knowing what to do next? Why didn't I do my homework on that?

"Yes, it's sneaking out, so don't do it," he says.

"Still so bossy," I say, but I think I love his bossy side. It settles me. Makes me feel comforted. My chest is warm, and my cells are a little fizzy.

He tugs me closer, buries his nose in my hair. "The hotel pillow smelled like cinnamon that morning when you were gone. Your lotion, right?"

My heart sprints. He remembered what I told him at the ice cream shop the night we met. "Yes. Good memory."

"I was hoping you were going to still be there. At the hotel in the morning," he murmurs, sounding lost in time as he absently strokes my hair while revisiting our first night together.

I feel lost in time too, but in this heady moment. "I was hoping you'd find me," I say, admitting something I hadn't fully processed that morning. Something I didn't truly realize till I bought a cactus to get his last name.

"I'd thought it might be a clue. A line in your letter."

"Which line?"

There's no hesitation as he says: *"Maybe I'll see you around the city. It's big, but it's small too. You never know..."*

"You memorized it?" Each word lands with space between them.

"I did," he says easily, like that's all there is to it. But it's a big deal for anyone to memorize three lines. Only, I don't make too huge a thing of it. I hold on to this nugget for safekeeping in a drawer full of special memories.

"Maybe it was a clue. I think I was hoping I'd see you again," I say, admitting that now too.

"Then I found your scarf, Cinderella," he says, recounting more of that morning as he nuzzles my hair again. "I had it all packed up to return to you the morning after our first game. I'd even written you a letter, asking you out."

My heart is a pinwheel, fluttering in a spring breeze. "You told me you wrote me a letter too." He said as much the morning we baked. "Do you still have it?"

"I do."

"I want the letter," I say, impulsively. "No one has ever asked me out in a letter."

His smile is smug as he rustles around in the bed, reaching for the nightstand drawer, then he slides it open. He removes a sheet of paper and hands it to me.

My heart is beating loudly in my ears as I open it. Then wildly in my throat as I read.

Hey Josie,

You left this behind, and I'm honestly glad you did. I'm returning it since it's yours. But also because I'd really like to see you again. Can I show you around San Francisco sometime soon?

Wesley Bryant

It's so simple and so perfect. I clutch it to my chest, closing my eyes, my cells flooding with sunshine. His lips sweep over my shoulder once more. "Guess it was just a matter of timing," he murmurs against my skin.

Timing.

That's always been the challenge for us. I open my eyes and meet his—they're full of longing and want. "Our timing hasn't always been right, has it?"

He shakes his head, his tone sad as he says, "No, it hasn't."

And it still isn't. Timing is the reason I'll have to move home far too soon.

And I don't want to push anything now. I don't want to define this. But I do want—I'm just realizing it this very second—more of him. I'm scared to ask for it though. Scared to figure out what this new thing with us is. What if this moment is just pillow talk?

"Hey. What's going on?" Wes asks.

If I went to improv, I can do this. *It's okay to be afraid.* "I like you. A lot," I say.

He laughs, smiles, and then covers my mouth with a kiss before he says, "It's sooo mutual." He reaches for my hand and slides his fingers through mine. "Was that hard to say?"

"I had one serious boyfriend in college and then after college we dated too," I say, then quickly backpedal. "I'm not suggesting this...or that we're having a...or anything. But just that a lot of this is...new to me. I haven't been with anyone in a while."

He understands what I haven't said out loud, since he nods, then says, "I haven't been with anyone in a while. Not since New York. I dated a woman there. Anna," he says, and I remember what he said about her—that she said he didn't like anything but hockey. She was the one who wanted him to debate philosophical issues with her.

He drops another kiss to my shoulder. "It's different with you, Josie."

The world halts, slowing to this moment, to that admission, to the thing every person longs to hear—that we're special to someone else.

I touch his cheek, tracing a line along his jaw. "It's different with you too."

I don't entirely know what that means or where we're going or what we're doing. But I'm sure tonight isn't a one-time thing.

I settle into the crook of his arm, then run my fingers over the ink covering his right arm. "I think I've figured them out. Your tattoos."

"Decipher me, then."

I trace the dog. "You're into dogs. You want one. So the dog is like a goal."

"Yes."

I run a finger along the music notes. "The music is

your love for songs and lyrics. It's your present—but also your purest interest."

"You're too observant," he says, sounding ridiculously pleased.

"And then you have these sunbursts," I say, traveling along the thick black lines that curve and bend near his shoulder. "What are they for?"

"Passion, desire, bravery," he says simply.

I sit with that for a minute, considering the meaning behind them. "Who you want to be? In your job and in life?"

Wesley's gaze catches mine, and he holds it for a long, potent moment. His eyes are dark brown pools, and it feels like the air is shimmering between us. "You know me," he says easily, but that can't have been easy to say.

"I think I do," I whisper.

"You do." He cups my face and presses a gentle kiss to my lips. "Stay the night."

I had a feeling he was going to say that. But I needed to hear it.

I curl up next to him, terribly unsure of what will happen in the morning—but incredibly okay with the uncertainty.

His eyes flutter closed as he coasts a finger along the scar on my chin, then kisses it before he falls fast asleep.

32

MONSTER-SIZE

Wesley

I wake up to a note from my dad blinking at me on my phone.

> Dad: What's the verdict? Lunch today? We can go to a new bowl place by the Marina. And I've been thinking, if Frieda's artwork isn't your style, I can take you shopping for…something else for the walls. Before your session with Domingo this afternoon

.

As I drag a hand through my bedhead hair, I snort a laugh —the dude is relentless, but I guess I did say I'd connect with him today.

Josie rustles. Shit, I didn't want to wake her. She turns to me, eyes fluttering open, question marks in them.

I waggle the phone. "It's my dad. I *think* he acknowledged that Frieda's art is horrifying. But of course it's wrapped around reminders of what he wants me to do today."

"Sounds like a new version of a sandwich compliment —a sandwich admission," she says sleepily, then stretches.

Damn, she looks good in my bed, her hair fanning out on the pillow, her cheeks flush.

"That's him for you," I say, debating whether to reply to my dad right now or not.

"You and he have a complicated relationship," she says, an observation rather than a question.

"We do. He's intense. A little controlling," I say in an obvious understatement. But she's seen the fridge, she knows my schedule, and she's aware I work out after games, too, and that Dad hired a personal coach for me as well. "He wants the best for me though. Always has."

"That probably makes it even more complicated," she says, with a sympathetic smile.

"Yeah. It really does. He's a great agent though. The deals he's landed for me have been top-notch. Both with the teams and endorsements."

"Maybe because you're a great player."

I glance over at her, all soft and morning sexy. "Maybe," I say absently, then what the fuck? Why the hell am I talking about my agent-slash-dad while I'm in bed with this woman? I toss the phone on the nightstand, far away, then slink a hand around her stomach. "Play hooky with me today."

"What?" She asks it like she's never heard of the concept.

I pinch her side. "Did you ever skip class?"

Her jaw drops. She swats my chest. "Wesley Bryant!"

I laugh. "Is that a no?"

She narrows her brow at me, all stern. Librarian stern, come to think of it. And I don't mind. "Of course I never skipped a class. Why would I?"

"To have fun," I counter with a smirk.

She lifts her chin primly. "Class is fun."

This woman. She's the total opposite of me, yet that doesn't seem to matter. I drop a kiss to her nose. "You're such a hot nerd."

Narrowing her eyes, she growls at me. "And you're such a sensitive jock. So there."

"Then you should understand why I need to play hooky with you. It will help my sensitive side," I say, laying it on thick.

She rolls her eyes. "Right. Sure." She takes a beat. "Also, I don't have work today, so there's no hooky to play."

"But I bet you were going to do errands, or read a book, or research something. So play hooky from that." I refuse to give up.

She winces. "I signed up for a walking tour of the Marina this morning. With a local city guides group."

Damn. That means she's taking off soon, even though I'm intrigued. "That sounds like fun actually."

"See? This is why I don't play hooky. Because other things are fun."

"When is it? The tour?"

She peers at the digital clock on my nightstand. "In an hour and a half."

I could offer to tag along, but the thing is...I'd rather have her to myself. I go in for the kill. I nuzzle her neck, grazing my mouth along her skin up to her ear. "I bet I can convince you to skip it."

With a hitch in her breath, she asks, "How would you convince me?"

Another kiss. Then, a flick of my tongue against her ear while my hand coasts down her stomach. "Let me fuck you again and then take you out for that second date instead."

She stops squirming. Something I can't quite read flickers in her blue eyes. A question perhaps? She parts her lips, like she's going to ask me something after all. But she must think the better of it since she says, "Let me brush my teeth first."

"I'll do the same."

A minute later, our minty-fresh mouths meet and I pull her on top of me, kissing her as the morning light streams through the windows, running my palms along her sun-kissed skin. As she melts into my touch, I slide a hand up her breasts, over her chest to her neck.

She loves when I touch her there. I don't press too hard. But I do curl my palm around her throat gently and hold her close as I cover her mouth with mine.

It's the kind of slow, sultry kiss that has her moaning, arching, asking. Then, I fuck my roommate, and I don't think once about the things or the people I'm avoiding.

Why would I? I've convinced my roomie to go on that long-awaited second date with me.

This is winning.

* * *

An hour or so later, I do write back, telling my dad I'm hanging with a friend today, but I won't miss my training session with Domingo this afternoon. It's one thing to skip lunch with Dad; it's another to blow off a trainer. That's just rude.

But I do feel a little rebellious—in a good way, and in a necessary way too—as I send that note. Maybe that's why I never confirmed lunch plans with him last night. Maybe I knew on some level I was going to have other plans for today. Plans with her.

I tuck the phone in my jeans pocket and head down the hall with Josie. When we reach the foyer, that inquisitive look from earlier returns to her face—the one that says she wants to ask something. Or maybe she's working her way up to it.

"Wes," she begins, as I grab the car keys from the table.

"Yes?"

But she shakes her head, walking toward the stairs to the garage. "It's nothing."

Nope. It's not nothing. It's never nothing. "Josie," I say, my tone firm. I'm not worried, but I do want to know what's on her mind. "What's going on?"

She stops in her tracks before she goes down the stairs. She turns around, resolute now. "You said this was a date. Right?"

A knot of tension forms in my gut. I'd thought it was crystal clear I was asking her out. "Well, yeah."

"But..." She lifts her hand, waves it toward the home. "What about the roomie rule?"

"We broke that, didn't we?" I ask wryly, but it doesn't quite land as a joke because she's not only referring to sex. We both know this thing with us isn't just about what happens between the sheets. I clear my throat, giving her the gravity she deserves. "Are you asking what it means that I'm taking my roommate on a date?"

She shrugs, smiling, looking uncomfortable. "What do we do in public? Like if someone sees? You're not exactly *nobody.*"

Oh. I hadn't thought about that. It barely occurs to me, though it probably should. I do get recognized from time to time. I am a public figure. And roomies or not, I'm still working with her brother, but I don't think either one of us wants to deal with whatever that means now. Heaving a sigh, I think this through. "I'm not sure I know the right answer. For now, maybe it's best if we"—I stop and gesture from her to me—"keep this between us?"

She freezes.

And I've said the exact wrong thing. I'd better fix it, stat. I step closer, reach for her hand. "I don't mean a dirty secret like an affair. I just mean let's keep it between us...as we figure it out."

Only I don't know what we're figuring out. She's leaving and I'm staying, and we live together. I don't know if she'd even want more than a simple arrangement if we didn't have those obstacles between us. Just because I'm developing feelings for her—*liar, you already possess monster feelings*—doesn't mean she's on the same page I am.

I don't want to pressure her though. "What if we don't rush defining this," I suggest, even though I want to define it, I want to stake a claim on her, and I want to tell the whole damn city I'm dating the most incredible woman I've ever met.

Yeah, monster fucking feelings that I have to tamp down for now.

She tucks a strand of chestnut hair behind her ear, seemingly satisfied. "That works. Especially since I have no idea how he'll react." The fact that she doesn't say her brother's name tells me she's a little worried. "Also, I don't feel like a dirty secret," she says, curling a fist around my shirt. "But you should keep fucking me dirty in secret."

Her eyes twinkle with mischief, and I close the short distance between us, grab her ass, and give her a rough kiss. "It's a deal."

That settled, we head down the stairs to the garage, where I open the car door for her. She slides into the front seat, and I head to the driver's side.

Finally, a month and a half later, I'm getting the second date I wanted. I pull out onto the street and slow to a stop at the red light. I steal a glance at her.

Fuck the rules.

I lean across the console, grab her jaw, and kiss her. Maybe to prove a point. That I'll do this soon. Then, I take her for our second date at last.

Though it hardly feels like a second one.

* * *

Route 101 Diner is not a roadside diner like the name implies. More like a waterside one since it sits inside the Ferry Building on The Embarcadero, overlooking the glittering bay. A vintage neon sign beckons us, giving the place a mid-century feel. The walls inside are decorated with black-and-white photos from the 101, the highway that runs along the California coast, overlooking the ocean.

We settle into a booth that comes equipped with a

mini jukebox. I nod to it. "You can pick show tunes. Or pop. Or Taylor," I say.

"You're assuming that's what I like," she counters.

I laugh. "Josie, I've heard you singing in the shower."

"Touché," she says, then opens the menu.

After we order—veggie burger and fries for her, chicken sandwich and salad for me, which isn't entirely cheating on my meal plan; it's just bending it—I say, "This is where I was going to take you if I'd given you that scarf and the letter."

"But you wouldn't have been able to use that *you can pick show tunes* line," she teases. "You didn't know that then."

Scoffing, I eye her up and down. "I'd have guessed. You give off that vibe."

She stares me down, but she's smiling. "Why's that?"

Is it weird if I say because she likes makeup? Because she's got a girlie side to her? Because she wears fake lashes? At least I think they're fake. Never seen anyone with lashes that long for real. But I like Josie with makeup and without makeup.

I find a different path to an answer. "Probably because of the way you were with your friend that night. You seemed close. Made me think you were a girl's girl."

"I am," she says, her shoulders straightening. "Good guess."

I tip my chin toward her. "So tell me more about you. What do you do for a living?"

"Are you recreating the second date we never had?" Her smile touches down straight in my chest, stirring my heart.

"Yes."

"I'm in town working at a library. And it's turned out to be an incredible job."

"Yeah?" Even though we talk about her job often, I'm still dying to know all the details about it.

"My boss is smart, and sarcastic, and my colleagues are fun. We played trivia the other night and I destroyed them. It was very satisfying."

"Winning can be like that," I say. "Have you always wanted to be a librarian?"

She nods enthusiastically. "Pretty much. But especially once I learned what it entailed. Maintaining records, finding information, and helping people connect with books of all kinds. It's been a dream job my whole life."

I get that completely. "Same thing for me—with hockey." But I don't want to focus on me. "So this job you have now—is it a dream job?"

Her smile is somehow both excited and wistful. "Yes, except it's temporary, but it's amazing. My boss has given me a lot of autonomy. I started this new thing called *Your Next Five Reads*, and it's going really well," she says, then tells me more about an online recommendation service she's started.

"That does sound pretty cool," I say, but something doesn't add up. "You're doing all these great things. Why does it end? Why is it a temp gig?"

Is it too obvious I don't want it to reach the finish line of us?

Sadness flashes briefly in her eyes, but then she seems to blink it off. "It's fine," she says, her tone cheery and bright. "It was never supposed to be more than temporary. The library landed a special grant for its digitization center from a non-profit that was founded a couple years ago. It's pretty unusual, but the library was able to use that funding to hire a digital specialist for a few months. It's just a contract post."

What happens in January? Where do you go? Will you miss me?

Those questions form on my tongue, but I swallow them down. Now's not the time to talk about the new year. There might never be a good time to talk about it. Her situation is different from mine. Hell, she lost her short-term rental mere days after moving to the city. And heck, I may own my own place but I know as well as anybody that the cost of living in this city isn't exactly free. I can't be a pushy dick about where she'll live or go while she's sorting out her life. She's here for now, and that has to be good enough for me.

"They're lucky to have you," I say. "If you were my librarian growing up, maybe I'd have liked books more."

She shoots me a challenging look. "So, let's play this out. A young Wesley Bryant comes to my library and crushes on *librarian me?* That's not weird at all."

"Hey now. This is a college fantasy. In it, I'm eighteen, it's my freshman year, and I find you in the stacks at school. Your hair's up in a bun. You're wearing a black skirt, a tight white blouse, and black heels. You're shelving a book. But you can't reach the tallest shelf, even though you're stretching, and your skirt's riding up."

She leans back in the booth, crossing her arms and staring at me pointedly, her eyes dancing. "Tell me you watch librarian porn without telling me you watch librarian porn."

"Don't need to watch it," I say, then tap my skull. "My brain makes it right here free of charge. Has for the last month and a half."

She dips her face, hiding a smile at the clear compliment before she says, "Then what happens next in your librarian fantasy?"

I lean closer, parking my elbows on the Formica, locking eyes with her as I drop my voice to an even raspier tone. "I slide the book in for you. You lick your lips as you watch it go right in. It fits perfectly. You thank me, then I ask if you can help me find a good one...to open up."

"And what do you say?"

"I say I'd like to find a good one on Ten Things a Man Can Do to Please the Woman He's a Little Obsessed With."

Her cheeks go pink. "Sounds like you've already read it."

I shake my head. "No, I haven't finished it. It's something I want to read every night. It keeps me up late."

She rolls her lips together like she's holding in a gasp, then whispers, "You should keep reading."

"I will," I say, feeling like at least we've figured out that much. Whatever this thing between us is, it's not ending.

* * *

The next morning, when I'm coming down the stairs early to drive Josie to work, she's standing in the kitchen wearing a black skirt, a white shirt, and heels. Her hair's twisted in a bun, with a few strands coming loose. Her lips are glossy and pink.

"I hate to be the one to tell you this..." I say when I reach the kitchen.

"Hate what?"

"That you're going to be late for work."

She glances at the clock on the microwave. "Wes, I can't be late." She sounds sad.

I look her up and down in her perfect outfit down to the heels and of course her glasses. She's my librarian fantasy. "You're right. You can't be," I say, then I loop an arm around her waist and tug her against me.

She bites the corner of her lips but then shakes her head. "I mean it."

"I know you do, baby," I say, dropping my face to the crook of her neck and pressing a soft, barely there kiss to her skin. "But..."

"But what?" she asks breathily.

"Did you know that clock on the microwave is five minutes fast?"

She gasps. "Wes!"

I pull back. "Got five minutes?"

"That's not much time," she says.

I slide a strand of hair behind her ear, running the pad of my finger along the shell. "I'll have to be very, very focused."

But before I can spin her around and lift her onto the counter, she grabs my hand and pulls me into the living room. Then she shoves my chest, pushing me down onto the couch.

Taunting her is officially my best idea ever as she hikes up her skirt to her thighs and drops to her knees.

Fuck me.

In no time, she's tugged down my shorts and my briefs and is flicking her tongue against the head of my cock. She sucks the crown just past those gorgeous pink lips, and I shudder out a harsh breath. "Fuck, Josie," I mutter.

With a goddess grin, she drops my dick, takes down her bun, and says, "You've got less than five minutes to make my lipstick messy. Better get to work, stud."

It. Is. On.

I grab her head, rope my hands through her lush hair, and guide her back onto my hard dick. She slides her palms up my thighs while she takes me deep with barely a second thought.

Like she's showing off, she sucks hard, voraciously, all while keeping her eyes on me.

I curl my hands tighter around her skull as her lips stretch wide, inviting me to fuck her throat. A few pumps and I'm shaking. Groaning. Hell, I'm lifting my hips off the couch and fucking her invitation of a mouth.

My balls tighten. My thighs shake. My chest is overheating. Pleasure crackles in my whole body as I thrust past those lush lips till she coughs.

"You okay?" I ask as I pull out.

She lifts a stern brow. "Two minutes, Wes. You want to talk or you want to come?"

I close my eyes, smiling like a lust-struck fool. *This woman.* I shut my mouth and fuck hers till an orgasm marches through my body, slamming into me as I warn, "Coming."

And she sucks me dry.

My vision is still blurry when she rises, adjusts her skirt, and says, "Be right back."

When I look down though, there's a pair of panties on my lap. And they're soaked. I'm going to need to make her come many, many times tonight to thank her for that five-minute drill.

* * *

A few minutes later, we get in the car with just enough time to take her to her little library. Time always seems to be running out with us, and the next six weeks will go by so much faster than I want them to. Once we're on our way to the Upper Haight, I return to the thing that brought us together in the first place.

"We should figure out number six soon. Volunteer," I say, reminding her of her aunt's top ten list.

Along the way, we toss out ideas and maybe plans to pick one this weekend, and by the time we near the library we've narrowed it down to a few options. But when I pull up after passing the fire station, she gestures casually to the guys outside milling around the fire truck. "That reminds me. The Friends of the Library Association is having a pancake fundraiser at our library in partnership with the fire station this weekend. We'll have to do our volunteering after."

I glance back at the station. It's teeming with guys who look like they belong on a fireman calendar. I grit my teeth, then breathe out hard. I breathe out fire. "With firemen?"

"Yes, that's who usually works at a fire station," she says dryly.

I stare back at the scene in front of the firehouse. Yeah, there's easily a dozen firemen, the type that everyone crushes on. "I'll pitch in at your fundraiser. That can be our number six."

"But don't you have morning skate? And a nap schedule to adhere to?" she asks, but she's not being mean —just the woman who knows me so well.

"I do," I reply, because she's right. The fundraiser starts early though. "But I can serve pancakes, and still make it to the rink for morning skate, then hit the hay."

"A regular superman," Josie muses. "You'll really help?"

One of the firemen seems to linger on my car—or more specifically, the woman inside it.

I growl. "Yeah. I'll absolutely be there."

Since no way am I letting the firemen snag a chance to hit on my sexy librarian.

She's mine. Well, for another six weeks she damn well is, and fuck anyone who tries to take her.

33

IF YOU GIVE A PIG A PANCAKE

Josie

At work on Friday morning, I bite into a brownie, and it's so sinfully good, I moan shamelessly. Eddie chews his and whimpers loudly. Thalia devours hers and groans for days. "Dolores can never leave us," she says of the dark chocolate treat, courtesy of the children's librarian.

Someday maybe they'll feel that way about me. But I keep that thought to myself, focusing on my colleague's baking prowess instead. "I swear, I'm going to find a way to get her brownie recipe from her."

"Good luck, sister. I've been trying for years," Eddie says, shaking his bald head.

"I can see why," I say as we finish off our brownies before the vultures from circulation can descend on them. When we're done, I head to the digital center on the second floor. Thalia catches up with me on the staircase. "Question for you, Josie. Do you think you could do a display for us at the fundraiser tomorrow? Of *Your Next Five Reads* recommendations?"

Did she just say a display? Like a display of books? I'm salivating. "Yes. For different combos of books?" It comes out like I'm on helium.

"Yes, maybe three or four sets total. Different genres for a table by the pancakes? To get the word out about the online recs you've been doing."

"Yes," I say. Possibly I sound louder than I do when Wesley makes me come.

That's something he's done every night this week. If I'd known having regular sex with your roommate was going to be so fun I'd have started it sooner.

"That would be great," Thalia says, and I'm doubly excited for tomorrow—both to make a display and to spend more time with Wes.

I'm not so excited about my inbox though. I haven't heard a word from the non-profit that sent me here. I've already gotten two rejections for grants. They were long shots, but still, it stings. Then, I found a job opening in Marin County earlier this week and submitted my application in mere seconds, only to be shot down the next day.

Talk about disheartening.

I try to remind myself that there's time. Maybe I need to tell Thalia that I'd love to stay. What if she could help? What if she knows someone? I haven't said a word yet because I wanted to prove I could do a good job first. Best not to come in hot in your first several weeks on a job and say *hey, boss, can I stay*?

But she's also not a mind reader, so she'll only know I want to stay if I tell her.

Before I go to the center and she goes to the reference desk, I stop next to a display of romance novels that'll keep you up all night, swallow some courage, and say, "There's something I wanted to talk to you about."

Her eyes turn serious, and she stops walking too. "Sure. What is it?"

I hope I don't sound as nervous as I feel. For someone who likes to escape into books rather than sales pitches, this is so hard. I try to keep my tone calm and upbeat though. "I love the work I do here. I think I've done a good job. And if there's any way I could stay on, I wanted to let you know I'd say yes in a heartbeat."

"You have done a great job," she says, but her smile is of the let-you-down variety. "The budget's tight though. We're all feeling it citywide. But you know I'll give you an excellent reference for anywhere."

My stomach sinks, but nope. That won't do. *Chin up.* It'd be a fairy-tale ending if she waved her magic wand and said, "Oh you want a job? I have one! Take it."

A good reference is a critical step in my Stay Here plan.

"And I will keep my eyes open, too, for any jobs in the city. Would that help?"

Immensely. "I'd be so grateful," I say.

She crosses her fingers. "Let's get you a full-time gig here."

I start the workday glad I told her after all. Maybe I'll find the guts to tell Wes soon too.

* * *

Early the next day, I put the job hunt out of my mind since it's time for the fundraiser. Budgets are definitely tight if we need pancakes to lure patrons. But then again, that's how it's always been in my field.

I'm scurrying around the home, grabbing my bag and phone for the fundraiser, when I spot a package on the porch. It must have arrived late last night. I swing open the door and grab it, squealing a little when I see the return address.

It's the stickers I ordered last week. I shut the door and rip open the compostable envelope, then rush to the kitchen where Wes is downing a cup of coffee. I hold it up for him, proud of myself for making these. I dip a hand in and take out a purple sticker, showing him the saying. "Look!"

"Librarians definitely like it hard," he says, reading it with a glint in his eyes.

"I made them for fun. But I also wanted you to have one." I offer him a sticker. It's a little thing, that's all, but I hope he likes it and its irreverence.

After Wes sets down the mug, he takes the sticker, unpeels the back, and smacks it on his gray T-shirt. "Perfect for today."

That's bold. "You're going to wear it to the pancake breakfast?"

"You bet I am," he says, and that's Wes for you—fearless.

He whirls around, reaches into a cupboard, and takes out a pretty pink gift bag with a black bow on it. "For the game."

He already got center ice tickets for me for the game this evening, as well as for Fable and Maeve. I was so excited he thought of my friends too that I thanked him on my knees.

"Wear this tonight," he says in a simple command, so bossy and confident. Like there's no chance I'd even think to say *no*. He thrusts the bag at me.

Pretty sure I know what it is, but I'm still giddy when I yank out a number sixteen jersey. "Wes," I say softly, touched.

It's such a romantic gesture—a jersey that says I'm there for him.

But then a dark cloud descends over me. Will everyone know? What will my brother think? Will he put two and two together if he sees me in Wes's number this evening? Fine, it's truly none of Christian's business what I do and who I do it with, and while I worry more about when the next George R.R. Martin book might release than what my brother thinks of my sex life, I still understand the complexity of the situation. Wes works with him. It's a depend-on-every-man kind of job. And Wes and I agreed to keep this thing between us quiet as we *figure it out*.

I'm not sure it's time yet to tell Christian anything. Or if we're even required to say anything. But at the same time, it's also polite to give him a heads-up.

When? Not rink-side at a game, that's for sure.

I'm about to ask if this shirt will give it away to the team what we're up to but a glance at the clock tells me now's not the time to tackle that issue. Besides, so what if Christian sees me in Wesley's jersey? Wes isn't only my roommate—he's my friend. It makes sense I'd wear my friend's number to a game. Perfect sense. Case closed. I clutch it to my chest. "I can't wait to wear it."

Wes downs the rest of his coffee and sets the mug in the sink. "Wear it today too."

There's that demanding tone again. The one he uses when he tells me to spread my legs, suck his cock, and fuck myself with a toy in front of him.

"To the pancake breakfast?" I ask, more breathily than

the question demands. But that's how I feel with Wes. A little light-headed all the time.

"Yes." He seems dead set on this. A little fiery too. His eyes are darker than usual. I'm getting dangerously turned on as he says, "Put it on, Josie."

The command in his voice sends a wicked thrill through me, straight to my core. I whip off my top and change in front of him, sliding his jersey over my cami. It's big and baggy.

"Fuck, you look hot," he says in a dirty rumble.

I suspect he'll be thinking about taking it off me the whole time I wear it since there's nothing friendly about the way he's looking at me.

* * *

I'm in front of the library, finishing up the romance display—putting the new Hazel Valentine next to a TJ Hardman, since I would definitely recommend those two together—as Wes sets out recyclable plates.

"Should I read this one?" a masculine voice asks.

I turn toward a strapping fireman with a thick beard. He's just strolled over to the display, and he's pointing to the Hazel Valentine book.

"If you like banter, spice, clever plots, and happily-ever-afters," I say with a smile.

The man holds my gaze for a beat, his gray eyes twinkling with...possibility, I think. "All of the above," he says, then adds, "I'll have to check it out." He looks around the breakfast area, full of tables and serving trays, then back to me, a smile forming. "I'm Tom. I'd love to get some more recs from you. Maybe after work some time?"

Did this nice fireman just ask me out? Before I can

even process my surprise, a throat clears. Out of nowhere Wes is right by my side, wrapping an arm around me.

"She has a whole display of them right here. Those are her recs." His arm bands tighter around my waist, curling over my hip. "You don't have to get them from her after work since she's busy."

Someone is staking his claim.

Tom holds up his hands in surrender. "Sorry, man."

"It's all good," Wes says, in a tone laced with *don't let that happen again.*

Tom nods at me with an apologetic smile, then walks away.

I turn to Wes, arching a brow at his boyfriend behavior. Color me intrigued. "Are you marking me?"

He's unrepentant with his "yes."

I furrow my brow. "He was only asking for book recs."

"And maybe he legit wanted them. But he also wanted you. And you don't have any idea how sexy you are. How often men check you out. You have no clue."

"And it's your job to ward them off?" I'm not annoyed. I am curious though.

He nods. "Yes. It is. It's that simple."

Yeah, boyfriend behavior.

And the low pull in my belly tells me I like it.

After a squeeze of my hip, Wes returns to serving pancakes next to me as several families pass through.

Eddie's on my other side, and when there's a lull in the action, he nudges me. "Is something up with you and Number Sixteen? Mister Hockey has been staring at you this whole freaking morning like he wants to have *you* on his pancakes."

A tingle coasts down my spine, but a kernel of worry

rolls along it too. "We're...friends," I say, because that's true enough.

Eddie sketches air quotes. "Yes, *friends*. Did you know my hubs and I were friends at one point as well?"

"Then you understand," I say, avoiding the topic with an *oh so innocent* smile.

"I understand," he says, then lets his gaze drift to Wes. "I understand everything."

"Oh, shut up," I say softly.

He pats my shoulder reassuringly. "Don't worry. I got you, girl."

And I believe that about Eddie. But I also can't help but wonder about this possessive side of Wesley. Is it going to be a problem tonight? If Wes is this obvious here, will he be able to hide it when I go to the game? Will his teammates figure us out? Will people talk? And, most of all, will that hurt him?

I better prepare thoroughly for the game. Maybe I can figure out how to interact with him so it's not obvious I spend every night in his bedroom. I know! I'll devise a list of do's and don'ts.

Like, do cheer subtly and don't maul him in the corridor post-game. Like, do say hi to everyone, and don't flash my sports bra at Number Sixteen.

Yes, that's a plan.

But I'm pulled from those thoughts when a family with young kids marches up to the breakfast line, and a young girl with her towhead hair in pigtails holds out a plate and says, "Pancakes, please."

"Of course. And did you know if you give a pig a pancake..." I begin as I serve her a flapjack from my tray.

"She'll want some syrup to go with it," the girl says

with a bright smile, finishing the next line in the popular kids' book *If You Give a Pig a Pancake*.

She turns to Wesley with big expectant eyes. He looks down at her plate, and I figure he'll give her another pancake. "You'll give her some of your favorite maple syrup," he says, surprising me.

He's reciting a line in a children's book? Who is this man?

The towhead does a little jig. "She'll probably get all sticky!" That's the next line.

Unable to contain her pig and pancake glee, the young blonde kid recites the next several lines in the kids' book till her dad says, "All right, Ellie. Let's leave the nice librarians alone."

Nice librarians, I mouth to Wes.

"Thank you, Mister Librarian," Ellie says to Wes, then to me, "And Miss Librarian. I read that book karaoke style."

That catches my attention. I don't hear that often but I know exactly what she means. That's an assistive technology the library offers in the kids' section. The words light up on the screen, like karaoke highlights, as the book's read to you. It helps readers follow along, and helps those who learn in different ways.

The night he told me he had dyslexia, Wesley mentioned he'd used tech like this as a kid. Right now, his face lights up—it's a look I've never seen before. A sort of pure delight. "Dude. Me too," he says to her, then offers a fist for knocking.

Ellie stands on tiptoes and knocks fists with him. "I read them *all* like that. With my app and my headphones."

He leans closer, like he's telling her a secret. "My dad made me read like that."

"Mine too! Did you read them all that way? The moose and the dog and the mouse?" she says, rattling off the characters in the other books in the series.

My heart is so full I don't even know what to do with it. The way it's beating. The way I'm smiling. I steal a glance at Ellie's dad. He's looking down at her with pride in his eyes.

Wes nods. "Every last moose and muffin," he says with a sigh, but it's not an annoyed one. It's more a sigh of solidarity—a *been there, done that* sound.

"Same!" Ellie gazes longingly at her plate of pancakes. "But I'm hungry so I should go eat. If you find any more books, let me know, Mister Librarian." She's about to leave when her brow knits and she adds, "But you might be a firefighter." Then she looks to me. "And you might be a firefighter too. Whatever you are, thank you!"

She skips off to eat, and I turn to Wes, too delighted to even know where to start—the way he talked to her, or the way she talked to him. But I bet he won't want me to home in on the tools he used as a kid, so I say, "She thinks you're a librarian."

"And that you're a firefighter. Too bad Halloween's passed. We could have dressed up like that...or maybe next year."

Those last two words echo in my mind—*next year*. Is he imagining a future costume party with me? Or is that just what you say? No idea, so I stay focused on the present and that moment. "Also, I think you made her day," I say.

He shrugs like it was nothing. But it wasn't nothing. That was a real connection, and I want him to know that. Sometimes I think he demands perfection of himself, even when it comes to reading. He might not like it, but just letting a kid know that he learned the same way she did is a very big deal. "It's great when a kid can meet an adult who learns and reads like they do."

He gives me that generous smile that hits me straight in the chest like it did the night we met. It's the kind that makes me think he wants to kiss me instead of talk. Which is fine by me, because it's also an acknowledgment that he did make her day.

"Glad I was here then," he says as bells jangle nearby, a sign that Thalia's headed in our direction. "And honestly, maybe my dad made me, but damn, that was a good series. Personally, I'd recommend *If You Give a Dog a Donut*. It's underrated, but might be the best of the bunch...Maybe add it to *Your Next Five Reads* book recs, and in all formats."

Thalia arrives at the table, giving Wes an approving look. "Actually, that's not a bad idea. The first ones in that series are always checked out. We should promote the next ones, Josie."

"I'll take care of it," I say, beaming as I picture the display already. I can show the hardbacks but also put up a placard with info on where to download a free text-to-speech app as well as the audiobooks. And as a bonus, maybe all this effort I'm putting into the recs will make Thalia's reference for me stand out even more.

Thalia smiles at Wes, then sticks out a hand. "I'm Thalia. Nice to meet you."

"Nice to meet you too," he says, shaking. "I'm Wesley."

"Oh, I know who you are. And I'd appreciate it if you'd destroy Colorado tonight. I hate their team so much," she says with a growl that reveals some serious vitriol for his opponent.

"Me too," Wesley says. "So, count on that."

She gives a crisp nod—my boss, who's evidently a hardcore hockey fan—then heads off while Wesley turns from me to serve another family.

I'm a little amazed by this man and his hidden talents. But perhaps more awestruck at my matchstick reaction that came out of nowhere. At my unexpected desire to protect him.

But as I watch him, his ease with people, his charm, I realize my reaction didn't truly come out of nowhere. It was born from the last month and a half of getting to know him.

* * *

Later, after we've cleaned up, we head to the car. "We can mark off number six now," I say.

Wes shakes his head, *sad boy* face in effect. "No, we can't."

"Why? That was volunteer work for you and me." I'm confused. Why wouldn't we cross it off?

He sighs deeply, and once we're alone in the car, he runs a hand down my leg. "Doesn't count. I said yes because I was feeling jealous and possessive."

My reaction is slow—a blink, then a long stare. Before Tom even arrived at the book display, Mister Hockey was jealous of the attention I *might* have received from the firemen? "You showed up today because you were *pre-jealous*?" I'm secretly fizzy from this revelation as we leave, pulling into traffic.

"And justifiably so," he says, owning it. "But we still need to work on the list."

It's a good reminder that we have a project to focus on. Wes is around for a few more days, then he travels again for a stretch of games. Time will run out if we're not care-ful, and we won't get to finish the list.

"What if we volunteer at a dog rescue for the next month? Seems we should do the volunteer part more than once anyway. So it should be a month-long thing," he says as he drives along a hilly city street.

A warm, hazy sensation spreads in my chest. A month feels like it means something. It feels like a part of *figuring this out*. Like it's somehow something that connects us even more to each other.

Settle down—you're living together for at least another month. That's all it means.

"We should," I say, keeping my voice even so I don't read something that isn't there at all in the *let's do it for a month* idea. "And a dog rescue feels right. For both of us," I say, trying to ignore the flutters in my chest. Then I notice the sticker curling at the edges of his shirt. "Did you wear this sticker, too, to stake a claim on me?"

He nods, proud and certain. "I did."

Funny—there's something I want to stake a claim on. Something I've been imagining since I moved in with him.

Maybe it's something I can do after the game. And just like that, I have a plan for tonight—what to do during the game, and what to do after.

34

THE GLEAM AND THE GLOW

Josie

As I get ready for the game, I can hear Greta's voice loud and clear. *There's only one thing to do with a baggy shirt. Belt it, baby.*

I tighten a peach crocheted belt around my waist as I peer in the mirror. Yep, it's a shirt dress now, and this belt's shade looks good with the royal blue of the Sea Dogs jersey that lands right above my knees. I'm wearing dark gray leggings under the jersey.

Seriously, why don't hockey teams make jerseys for regular-size people? Fine, they don't have regular-size people playing the sport. And this is one of Wes's actual jerseys, not simply the kind I could pick up in the team shop. But Christian will never know that. Since, well, the team shop sells all sorts of sizes. Christian also won't know for another reason. My brother doesn't pay close attention to my clothes—nor should he when he's playing hockey.

Still, my nerves rattle around as I look in the mirror, checking out the outfit. I look like a hockey girl. It'll be obvious to everyone I am. Including my brother. And I feel weird not telling him, given the way he's helped me out.

As I'm tugging open a drawer to find something else to wear, the doorbell chimes. That'd be Maeve, since she's meeting me here. I race to the front door and let her in.

"Hello, tiger," she says approvingly, eyeing me up and down.

Yeah, that's bad. "The whole outfit screams *I'm fucking the forward*, doesn't it?"

"No. It's not the outfit that says that," she says, blunt and direct.

My stomach pitches like a pirate ship at an amusement park. "Then what gives the secret sex life of this librarian away?"

She smiles wickedly. "Your eyes. They have that well-fucked look."

"Eyes do not get a well-fucked look."

She parks her hands on my shoulders and spins me around so I'm facing the mirror by the front door. "They do. See?"

I peer more closely but come up empty. "I don't know what you're talking about."

"It's a gleam. The gleam of *getting some*," she says knowingly, staring back at me in the glass. "And damn, I am jealous. You got the glow on your skin and the gleam in your eyes."

I laugh, and my worry slinks away for now. Maeve just has that carefree effect on people. I'm not going to stress about my clothes or my brother. "We all deserve a glow and a gleam, don't we?"

"That should be the name of a new skin-care line."

"And you should do the artwork for it," I say.

"God, your brain is hot," she says.

I grab a jacket and my bag, and because sometimes I like to take a little extra piece of Greta with me, and tonight feels like the start of something new, I grab the book charm necklace she gave me way back when and slip the jewelry on so it hangs under the jersey—a little symbol of me next to a little piece of Wes. We head to the rink.

Fable's meeting us there. So is Everly since she offered to give us a behind-the-scenes tour beforehand. When we hop off the bus and head up the steps to the arena, Fable's outside the media entrance wearing a Renegades sweat-shirt with the team's logo in rhinestones. "Gotta represent the football team," she says.

"More like represent your own awesome design," I add since she made this fun sweatshirt.

"Thanks, babe," she says, proud of her creation and rightfully so.

Everly's with her, and she waves a hello at Maeve and me. She's dressed in black wide-leg slacks and a dark gray blouse that looks satin-y. Her blonde hair is shiny and slicked back in a high ponytail. "Hey, you," she says, her eyes straying up and down me. "Don't you look adorable in your sassy little Sea Dogs dress."

I give a little curtsy. "Apparently I'm known for makeshift couture."

Maeve nods. "She sure is. Did you know she was wearing one the night she met—" Maeve slaps her hand to her mouth.

Everly laughs, dropping a hand on Maeve's shoulder

as we walk past the early arriving crowds. "You mean Wesley, right?" she asks in a low voice, just for us.

Shaking her head, Maeve mimes zipping her lips as we reach security. After we all pass through the security checkpoint, Everly says to me, "It's okay. I always had a feeling you and Wesley had known each other before I introduced you. And honestly, I thought you liked each other."

It doesn't even occur to me to lie to her. Nor do I want to. "We met the night I arrived in town. We had no idea who the other was, had a great time together, and then it turned out...he was my new roomie. Just don't tell my brother."

Everly gives me a genuine smile. "I would never. And listen, don't you feel like you have to tell him either. Only tell him when it's right for you and Wesley. Take your time if you need to, okay?"

That's the best advice I've heard on this topic ever.

Fable points toward Everly. "I like her," Fable says.

"I can be wise," Everly says.

"I think you're right. And I needed to hear that," I say. It's a weight and a worry off my shoulders.

Everly shows us around the arena, stopping at a long wall of foliage outside a range of fancy concession stands. "Since sports teams have such a high carbon footprint and we want to offset it as much as we can with foliage."

"It's gorgeous," Maeve remarks, admiring the emerald leaves growing along the wall.

"So gorgeous," a deep, playful voice calls out from behind us.

It's a voice I don't recognize, but when I spin around, a tall, broad man with golden-streaked brown hair and a toothpaste smile is striding toward us. He's wearing a well-tailored sky-blue suit, the kind athletes wear on game night.

Wait. I know who that is. But so does Maeve, evidently.

She gives a little wave to Asher Callahan. "So glad you enjoy the gorgeous foliage too, Ash," she says, then makes a shooing gesture. "Also, hello? Don't you need to, I dunno, suit up for the game?"

He smacks his forehead. "My bad. I almost forgot I have to score some goals to impress..." His sharp eyes linger on Maeve for a long beat before he adds, "my friend."

"Go, go, go," she says, still sending him away.

When he heads off to the locker room presumably, we're all staring at Maeve—who's watching Asher walk off. And is there something sparking in her hazel eyes? Dare I say it? "Maeve, do you have a gleam and a glow?"

Whipping her gaze to me, Maeve crinkles her brow like that's crazy. "Please. We've been friends forever. And he's besties with my brother."

Fable purses her lips. "Asher's your friend, and your brother's best friend? That's like a double dose of gleam and glow."

"I'd say," Everly puts in.

"Excuse me! We were talking about your G&G," Maeve says, pointing to me and maybe, possibly, deflecting from the talk of Asher.

"Actually we were talking about foliage before someone called you gorgeous," I correct, because facts matter.

But Maeve just scoffs. "Show us the rest of the arena, please," she says to Everly in the most businesslike voice ever.

"As you wish," Everly says, and while we walk, I glance down at Everly's footwear—heels.

I flash back to the night we went grocery shopping and her comment about pole dancing. Then to my whole reason for having a list in the first place—to get out of my comfort zone. No reason I shouldn't offer my friends as tributes too. "Hey, Ev, what if we all took that pole-dancing class with you?"

Everly's eyes brighten. "You'd all want to?"

Yes, I just threw Maeve and Fable into the fire without asking. But I know my girls. Maeve is already nodding a big *yes, please* and Fable shrugs happily then says she's in.

"I guess we have our next girls' night out," I say, as warmth spreads in my chest. But it's bittersweet, too, since these girls' nights out will end in the new year if I can't find a grant or a job.

* * *

Before the puck drops, a loud, ominous voice booms through the rink, telling a tale of the Sea Dogs rising from the depths of the ocean, while electric blue and iridescent orange light displays of the logo and mascot play on the ice. Videos of the athletes fly by on the jumbotron.

When the announcer warbles the starting lineup at the end of the light show, I cheer for the goalie and the five other guys as they rush out of the tunnel and hit the ice, including the one whose last name I share—Christian Winters. But it's not till Number Sixteen jumps over the boards a few minutes into the game that I cheer the loudest.

It's a sound ripped from the depths of my heart—loud,

exhilarating, ravenous. I'm not sure I can cheer any other way for Wesley.

Especially when he looks my way with a very public, private smile.

The game is raucous, with players jostling for the puck in the corners then slamming against each other as they fight even harder for it. Wes plays fast and aggressive but never dirty. Just sneaky, finding the puck and stripping it from his opponents.

But even so, neither team scores during the first period.

During the second period, the coach must have mixed up the lines, since Wes is out there with Christian a couple times, and they pass the puck back and forth as they fly up and down the ice.

"C'mon," I shout, like my sheer will can force a goal. Then, the noise amps up to an electric level as Wes slings it back to my brother, who smacks it right past the goalie's outstretched glove.

"Yes!" I shout, jumping to my feet and hugging my friends, like we all did it.

When we let go, I catch sight of us on the jumbotron, embracing each other to celebrate a goal scored by my brother and my secret boyfriend.

I like this secret. No, I'm falling hard for this secret.

* * *

After a decisive 4-1 win, the three of us meet Everly in the corridor, since she told us to come here post-game. She's ushering the players out of the media room, and I tense briefly.

Will it be obvious after all? Will my brother figure us out before we figure us out?

When Christian emerges from the pressroom, sweaty and elated, he beams my way. "You're here, Jay-bird! Bryant told me you were coming," he says, then wraps me in a gross hug.

"Eww. You smell."

"Like victory," he says, then Wes comes out next, looking insanely hot in his sweat in a way my brother does not.

His brown eyes are practically burning off my clothes. I feel singed from the heat of his stare.

Christian looks down at my outfit quizzically. "You're wearing a Bryant jersey," he says, but it's toneless—an observation.

My pulse quickens.

I could say he's my roomie. I could say he's my friend. Instead, I lift my chin and say, "Yes, I am."

That's all. I don't need to explain anything more tonight, no matter how Wes looks at me.

Everly pipes up, "Christian, can we get a picture of you two for social? It'd be great to have our captain and his sister. Hockey's a family-friendly sport, after all."

"Course," he says, then drapes an arm around me.

As she shoots, Wesley watches, a knowing smirk on his handsome face. When Everly lowers the camera, she says to both players, "Thanks again. I've got everything."

After the guys head into the locker room, my phone pings with a text.

> Wesley: Wait for me by the players' entrance. I want to take you home and show you how much I appreciate the way you cheered so fucking hard for me.

I shiver as I read it. I look up, turning to Everly, grateful for her deflection. "You're a savvy PR woman."

"That is true," she says, then takes off while Fable and Maeve read the room, hugging me goodbye.

"You're going to get gleamed so good tonight," Maeve whispers.

Yes. I am.

Since I have a plan.

35

YOU LIKE TO WATCH

Josie

I'm waiting at the foot of the staircase, wearing only his jersey and a pair of white cotton panties. Music beats low from upstairs, something sultry with a lot of bass.

The lights are dim in the home, setting the mood.

The scene is set, but before I take the first step upstairs, I bring a hand to my chest. My heart is beating so fast. I try to catch my breath. I've imagined this so many times.

He's taunted me with this scenario since the first night we were together when he said in the hotel: "Bet you'd watch me if you saw me jerking it to you."

Yes, I would.

Tonight, I will.

I take the first step. The stair creaks—the soundtrack to desire. I ascend, my pulse spiking with every move. When I reach the top, the music grows louder. That's Wesley for you—always having a playlist for everything. I turn down the short hallway and pad across the hard-wood floor, heading toward the sliver of moonlight refracting through the doorway. An invitation. I step past it, then stop. A sound of pure desire crawls up my throat.

He's stretched out on his bed, his big body sprawled in all his naked post-game glory. Bulging biceps, carved abs, thick thighs—and that gorgeous dick. He's stroking it. But not with too much intention. Not like he's about to burst. Like he's just started. Like he's weighing it.

His curled palm slides down to the base, then back up. My body clenches. He coasts his fist over the head, pushing out a drop. My mouth waters. I want that drop so badly on my tongue. His eyes are closed. His lips are parted. His chest, rising and falling. He's pretending he doesn't know I'm here. I'm pretending we're not yet together.

Then I hear a noise that lights me up. A rasp rumbling its way up his chest. It's the sound of an American muscle car hurtling down a road. With a groan, he grips his cock harder and I stare wantonly, like a voyeur.

He shuttles his fist along his length, the rhythm picking up, the pace increasing, his grunts growing louder. Then, low and guttural as he murmurs a strangled, "Josie."

I gasp. My legs are shaking, and my panties are soaked. I am outrageously wet.

To watch him get off in front of me is better than any porn I've ever seen. The man I want is touching himself while thinking of me.

Pleasure pools low in my belly, and I could honestly probably come from watching him. Like a dream orgasm, the kind that crashes over you in your sleep.

On an upstroke, his eyes float open. He blinks, locks

his gaze to mine like a sniper. Doesn't say a word. Takes a long, lazy stroke, pointing his cock my way. Like he's saying he's caught me. "You like to watch?"

I nod, unsure if I can even speak at this moment. My throat is dry with desire.

He stops his strokes though. I whimper.

"You want to keep watching?"

I find words this time, needing them, I sense, for the show to go on. "Yes. Please."

Crooking his fingers, he beckons for me to come closer. I cross the room, climb up, and kneel on the foot of the bed.

"Ready?" he asks.

"So ready."

He grips his cock again. I stare hungrily. He jerks harder. "Ever watched me before?" It's borderline confrontational. A man cross-examining me.

I shake my head no, then confess, "I've only imagined it."

"How do you want me to finish? In my hand? On your tits?" The questions are aggressive too, spiking my arousal as he goes on. "In your mouth? On your back?"

This part wasn't scripted, but the image of him spilling his release on my body and rubbing it into me with his palm has me gasping and crying out. "My back, please. All over me."

"Bet your sweet little pussy is soaked," he observes, pumping his cock harder as I stare, mesmerized.

"It is," I say, desperate for relief.

"Bet it's fucking dripping down your thighs."

My core throbs. "Feels that way."

He tips his chin carelessly at me. "Show me. Take those panties off."

I remove them quickly, but before I can drop them on the bed he reaches out a hand, asking for them. I give them to him without a clue what he's going to do next. He turns them inside out and grips his cock with the damp panel of my cotton panties.

My mind short-circuits. The sight of him spreading my wetness along his dick has me moaning uncontrollably.

I didn't know that was something I desired until this very moment—him pleasuring himself with my wet panties. It's so dirty, and it turns me on beyond belief.

"So much better," he says in a haze, stroking faster with the fabric till he stops abruptly. "You know what would be even better?"

I'm lost in a sex trance and can only shake my head.

"If you sat on my face right now."

Dropping the panties, he reaches for me, then grabs my hips. Quickly, I take off my glasses before he pulls me down onto his face. He's not gentle—he's hungry and horny as he French kisses my pussy. But I'm wearing a long jersey that's covering the view of his face, so I grab the hem, and loop it through the neck like a halter top tied off, exposing my belly.

The look in his eyes is feral. "Now fuck my face."

I start moving, thrusting against him as he eagerly drinks me up. The sounds we're making are ridiculous—loud, wet slurps from him and high-pitched moans from me, harmonizing with the slap of the headboard against the wall.

We find a pace, and then he lifts a hand and smacks my ass. The sting radiates straight to my clit.

"Do it again," I urge him.

He rewards me with a slap on the other cheek.

My body responds with a flood of pleasure, and I cry out as I come hard on his face. When I return to reality, he gently lifts me off him then slowly guides me down his body so my pussy rubs against his chest, his stomach, his groin, leaving a wet trail in my wake.

"I need you on my cock so fucking badly," he says breathlessly.

That's where I want to be. "I'm on birth control. I've been tested too. Negative."

He nods savagely. "Me too. Negative."

That's all there is to it. I sink down on his beautiful dick, savoring the feel of him bare as he fills me easily. Stretches me.

I ride him like an expert horsewoman, hot and sweaty and wild in our post-game victory fuck. His breath comes fast, urgent. "I want you to keep coming upstairs. I want you to keep finding me. Want you every single fucking night," he says.

"I'll be here," I gasp, and it seems like we're promising more than sex.

He rises up so we're face-to-face. He runs a hand up my back and around to the ends of my hair, tugging my mouth closer to his. This kiss is messy. A stop-and-start kind of kiss, chased with a new desperation. His lips slide to the corner of my mouth and he nips me there, then groans, pulling back while still fucking up into me.

His eyes are wide, dark, and full of filthy promise as he lets go of my hair, then coasts that hand around to my front, across my chest, and up my throat.

I gasp, stretching my neck for him. His thumb and fingers clasp the sides of my throat, but his palm never comes down too hard on me. He's gripping me without choking me, and I feel...taken.

"I love that," I murmur.

"I fucking love it too. All of this. Just fucking love it."

I've never heard him like this. So urgent. So raw. His tone ignites me, and so does his body. His movements turn jerky. As his breathing staggers, he lets go of my throat while I shove a hand between my thighs and rub my clit until my body spirals once again and the world blurs. I come again, sharp, hot, and loud. I'm shaking and he's groaning.

He's got to be right there with me, but when I open my eyes, his jaw is ticking, his eyes full of restraint. "Hands and knees, baby," he says.

It takes me a second to realize what he's doing and why. But I ease off him and comply, getting on all fours. He moves behind me on his knees, then there's the sound of a quick jerk and hot liquid splashes on my lower back. He marks me with his come, then spreads it into me as I moan.

My reality is even better than my fantasy.

* * *

Later, after we've cleaned up and we're lying in bed together, Wesley pulls me close, kisses my hair. "I want to tell your brother that I'm with you. You good with that?"

With you.

It's so simple. So clear. There are no questions with those two words.

"Yes." If I say anything else, a sob of happiness might climb up my throat. Because I am so, so good with that.

I don't know how long we'll have, but however long it is, I want it to be on our terms.

36

NO BODY BAG

Wesley

On Monday morning, I grab another book from the shelf, adding it to the stack in my arms. "So that's what I'm going to do."

Max stares at me like I just told him I'm going to skate with my laces untied. "This is your big plan?"

"Yup," I say, resolute as I pass a stuffed frog chair in the children's section of An Open Book, having just told my two closest friends about my meeting with the captain in, oh, thirty minutes' time.

I'm incredibly calm though, and also determined. Like a play unfolding on the ice, I can see what I need to do and what I need to say to make this happen. The moves I have to make. The way I need to skate.

All that's left is the execution.

Max blows out a *better you than me* breath, "Then I have a question for you."

Before he can ask it though, Asher comes over and

drops a metric ton of copies of *Where the Wild Things Are* onto the pile in my arms.

Oof. It's getting heavier. "Dude. Can you not hold these?"

"Dude. Are you not strong enough?"

Fighting words. I hoist the books higher. "I can carry them all, dickhead."

"Language," Max chides. "You're in the children's section."

"No one's here yet," I point out since it's early and the store just opened.

"But you're a good guy, Bryant. Be one all the time, even in the kiddy section," Max deadpans, and he makes a fair point—one I'll use very shortly.

"Anyway, what was your question, Lambert?" I say to Max as I weave past a tiny castle filled with beanbags and head toward the front of the store. I already left a huge stack at the counter earlier.

"Can you record it for us? The whole interaction with Winters? I feel like it would be really great for team morale."

I roll my eyes while Asher jumps in, saying, "Not a bad idea. We might want to look at it when we review video." He pauses, like he's deep in thought, then holds his hands out wide. "How to handle the puck you didn't see coming."

I groan. "You did not actually make the world's worst pun."

Asher flashes me a grin. "I did."

We arrive at the counter where I buy several boxes of kid books, then wait as a man behind the counter gift wraps a small handful for me.

The woman who rang me up smiles. Her name is

Trina, and she's a fixture at Sea Dogs games. "So glad Ryker told you to shop here," she says with a smile.

"As if we'd shop anyplace else," Asher says.

"Except Once Upon a Good Time," she points out helpfully. "That's my romance-only bookstore. But I still work here from time to time too. I guess I'm just a 'why choose' girlie with bookstores," she says with a knowing smile. Trina's married to two of our teammates—Ryker and also Chase. It's unconventional, but it works for them.

"And I'll be sure to stop there when I need something new to read," Asher says.

"You read romance?" Max asks with a dubious arch of his brow.

"Don't you wish you knew?" Asher retorts.

Max grumbles, "Actually I don't need to know."

We thank Trina and leave. My friends do help carry boxes, though, since we have a big haul. My car's parked at the curb, so we set the boxes of books in the backseat, along with the stack of wrapped ones.

I take a breath then check my texts, confirming Christian's address. I messaged him this morning and said I need to stop by to chat with him before morning skate in an hour or so.

I give a tip of the hat to the guys. "Pick you up in thirty at Doctor Insomnia's?"

"Unless we need to pick you up in a body bag," Max deadpans.

"We'll get you a nice body bag, Bryant," Asher says.

No more Newman, no Muffin Man, and no Poker Face. I'll take just Bryant. "No body bag, thanks."

I say goodbye then hop in my car. Before I turn it on, I send Josie a text.

. . .

Wesley: I'm on my way.

Then I add a heart, because I know it'll make her happy.

Josie: Don't worry about me. I'm totally not glued to my phone waiting for an update while I'm worried to five million pieces about you.

But I'm not worried. When I first met Josie, my entire life was prescribed by what I do for a living. I'm not just a guy who plays hockey.

I'm a guy who has dessert for breakfast sometimes. Who knows how to sit with discomfort. Who cares about his friends and also his teammates.

And I'm a great teammate. Part of being a great teammate is communicating. Even when it's hard. Sometimes it's telling a guy you play with that he needs to cool off. Sometimes it's telling the goalie he'll have a better game next time. And sometimes it's telling the captain how you feel about his sister.

I send her one more text.

Wesley: And you don't have to worry about me. I've got this.

. . .

I drive to Christian's home on California Street, park, and grab the wrapped books.

I bound up the steps, take a deep fueling breath, and ring the bell. I wait but not impatiently. I'm simply ready. After twenty or so seconds, Christian comes to the door, swings it open, and says, "Hey."

It's friendly but also comes with a question baked in. That's understandable. No doubt he's curious as to why I wanted to meet with him.

I nod toward the inside of his house. "Can I come in?"

"Yeah, of course."

I head into the foyer, glancing down at his socked feet. I toe off my shoes. When in Rome and all...

I follow him into the living room that boasts a stunning view of the Golden Gate Bridge. He gestures to the couch.

I hand him the stack of wrapped books, then sit. "I realize I never got you a gift when you had your twins. These were my favorite books growing up. My parents read them to me over and over. It's a pretty good series."

"Thanks, man," he says with genuine appreciation as he tugs off the ribbon and rips open the wrapping paper, picking up the first one, a warm smile taking over. "If You Give a Mouse a Cookie."

He taps the cover approvingly, and that eases any remaining bit of tension in me.

I don't hem and haw. I don't search for the right moment. The right moment is now. I go for it like I do when I'm on the rink. "I have a question for you."

"Hit me."

I meet his blue-eyed gaze straight on, no bullshit. "You think I'm a good guy, right?"

His brow knits. Down the hall, an infant cries softly, and he holds up a finger. "Give me one second."

A couple minutes later, he's back, holding a baby, patting the kid's back, soothing him with a *there, there*.

It's sweet, this side of the captain I've never seen. The doting dad.

"He's probably hungry, but he might also fall back asleep on me."

"Is that Cooper or Caleb?"

"Cooper," Christian says with a *holy shit* grin, like he can't believe I remembered his kids' names. But his smile erases and he sits again, giving me a serious look. "You're a good guy."

Grateful, I move on to my next question. It's all part of the plan. "You think I'm a good teammate?" To make it easy, I add, "The kind of guy who has your back on the ice. The kind who would step in for you if you didn't want to talk to the press. Who would help you out in a pinch."

His forehead knits. He's not dumb. Maybe he's even putting this together. Hard to say. He gives a direct "yes."

There you go.

"Good. Because I'm crazy about your sister, and I wanted you to be aware of that."

He blinks. Furrows his brow. "You. Are?" It comes out a little strangled.

"One hundred percent."

I don't need to explain anything more. I've come to realize that just because I'm new to the team doesn't mean I owe him an explanation of the choices I make when I'm not playing hockey. Or the choices his sister makes. All I owe him is the courtesy of the truth.

But there is one thing I want to underline. "Just to be clear, I'm *not* asking you for permission to date her."

Christian swallows, pats his son's back, starts to say something, stops, then says, "Right. Right."

Like he's adjusting to this new world order. Aren't we all?

But with all that out in the open, maybe there is one more thing I need to say. Or really, it's something I want to say. To show him that I prioritize her. Because that's what a good teammate would do. "She was honestly worried about coming to you, Christian. Worried that you might freak out. Team rules and all." I sketch air quotes, then pause, letting that sink in before I say, "But I don't think you'd do that."

He gulps. Rearranges his face. "Right. Of course not. I wouldn't." It's a backpedal, but I get where he's coming from and why he's doing it, so I give him some grace.

"I didn't think you would," I say, even though I had no idea how he'd react. I'm just glad I don't play hockey with a douche.

"I wouldn't," he says.

"Good," I say, relieved to have this uncomfortable conversation done. Can't say it was easy. But it wasn't supposed to be. "I'll see you at morning skate in an hour?"

"Definitely. Always," he says.

As I push up to leave, I hear laughter, like bells. Then the sound of footsteps as a woman emerges, holding a small baby. Christian's wife, Liv. She gives her husband a look. "Please tell me you didn't pull that *don't touch my sister* routine?"

I smirk as she stares daggers at him.

Christian shakes his head several times. "Not really."

His wife turns to me, lasering her sharp stare my way. "Did he do that?"

And because I am a good teammate, I know how to

handle this moment too—by having my teammate's back. I smile and say, "We're all good."

Christian meets my face and mouths a relieved *thank you*.

Liv's eyes drift to the table, then sparkle. "Oh! I love these books. I can't wait to read them to the boys. Did you get these, Wesley?"

"I did."

"Thank you so much," she says, then turns to her husband. "I think the twins are hungry."

That's definitely my cue to go. I point toward the front door. "I can see myself out."

But before I leave, Christian clears his throat. "My sister...Josie...she's pretty cool. She's five years younger. And she spent so much time with my aunt while I was playing hockey that there were times when I didn't feel like I totally knew her. But that was because I was busy. Not because I didn't want to get to know her. She was also really, *really* good at taking care of herself." He pauses, his eyes thoughtful. "I get the sense, though, that you do know her." There's another pause—a weighty one. "And I appreciate that."

"Thank you."

He blows out a breath as he adjusts the fidgety baby in his arms. His tone shifts back to the commanding locker room voice I'm used to at the Sea Dogs arena. "And Bryant? Don't be afraid to use your top hand a little bit more when you take a wrist shot. It'll help with control."

Instantly, I can visualize holding the stick, lifting it, smacking the puck. As if I'm already practicing the move, I flick my wrist, picturing the path of the shot. Yeah, that does feel good. "I'll do that. I appreciate it."

I guess that's how team chemistry works.

A few minutes later, I'm waiting outside the coffee shop, feeling pretty fucking good as Max and Asher pile into my car, with expectant eyes. In the passenger seat, Max peers at my face, studying me intensely. "Hmm. Don't see any new bruises or scars."

"And you won't," I say.

From the backseat, Asher claps my shoulder with pride in his grip. "Look at you, man. Look at you."

I peer into the rearview mirror, doing just that. Yeah, I like what I see. I like it here in San Francisco with my team, my home, my life. There's only one thing I wish California had.

A permanent job for Josie.

For now, we drive to her library and bring several boxes of books to donate to the children's section, handing them off to Thalia. Then, I give her a box of a dozen headphones I bought too—I ordered them online for same-day delivery. "For anyone who wants to read with their ears but who doesn't have their own headphones."

"This is amazing," Thalia says warmly. "And I promise they will be flying off the shelves and put to aural use."

"Glad to hear," I say, and it's time to hustle over to morning skate, but it's also time to see my girl. Yet before I can head up the stairs to the second floor to find my sexy librarian, Josie's flying down them in her pencil skirt and blouse, flats slapping the tiles, hair twisted up. At the bottom of the steps, she's breathless as she says, "How did it go?"

Max points at me. "He has no bruises."

"That's good?" Josie asks, with a bright smile.

It's her place of work. So even though everything inside of me screams to haul her against me and kiss her senseless, I curl my hands around her waist and drop a chaste kiss to her forehead. "You're with me."

I can feel her smile against me as she whispers, "I am."

I tear myself away but not before the sound of clapping rips through the air, chased by a loud wolf whistle.

"Told you so, Josie." It's Eddie and he's on the stairwell, clapping, then turning to Thalia. "I was right, boss."

Josie's boss is smiling. "Yes, you were."

Josie blushes. "You did."

And I guess they don't mind a little show of affection, all these book lovers. So I give Josie a kiss on the cheek, savoring her cinnamon scent, then I go.

On the way to the rink I remind myself to make the most of the next five weeks. But here's what I want to know—does she really have to leave?

37

THE FIVE-WEEK PLAN

Wesley

The question vexes me as I head to the arena for morning skate, then home afterwards for a pre-game nap. Though I'm not sure I'd call it a nap. I doze for a couple minutes here and there, but mostly I stare at the ceiling, wondering.

I should feel lighter after talking to Christian. I should be fucking ecstatic. I got what I wanted. We *figured this out* in a little more than a week. She's not a secret. She's mine.

But...is she?

I want more, and I don't know if I can get it.

I know this—I have to try to put these wants out of my mind or they'll get in the way of my job. After I grab a prepared meal from the fridge and polish off some salmon, asparagus, and pasta, I head to the rink, trying to slough off these thoughts of the future.

Dark futures, indeed.

As I pull into my parking spot in the players' lot, my

phone trills with Eric Bryant Management flashing across the screen. I tense, but it's better if I take the call before the game. Dad's calling from his office, but he is my father. He'd never give me bad news before a game because it might mess up how I play. It's gotta be good news. "Hey, Dad."

"Hey, son. How's it going?"

"Great," I say, thinking of Josie this morning and how it felt to embrace her in public. Too bad that's not enough for me since I don't feel great right now. Not that I'd tell him. He doesn't want me to be distracted by romance. "What's up with you?"

"Tip for you for tonight's game. I've been studying the defense on LA, and there's a real weakness on their second line," he says, and as I get out of the car he dives into detail on what he's been seeing in tonight's opponent, then with the goalie in particular. "I think you have a great chance to play hard and aggressive and win. Your stats this season are great. I'm thinking we could even get an early renewal."

My heart rate spikes dangerously as I cross the lot. I never let myself think about contract stuff. I am compart-mentalized all the way. But now I'm thinking about it—about staying here for a long time. Maybe even with her. "Yeah?"

I sound more excited than I want to. I don't like to show too many emotions with him. He'd probably want me to regulate those too.

But my dad sounds excited as well. "All that work you've done—your discipline, your training, your condi-tioning—is paying off. I'll keep studying your opponents. We're going to make this happen." I'm at the players' entrance so I should go, but then he says, "And I've got interest in another endorsement deal. A health-food chain. Perfect, right?"

"It is," I say. And truly, it is. There's no sarcasm in my tone. I appreciate the hell out of what he does to make my future possible.

And ideally, not dark.

I say goodbye, but as I go inside, I'm not thinking of hockey or healthy food. I'm wishing it were easy for Josie to get these perks. To land the sort of work she loves as easily as a pro athlete does. Then, a traitorous thought crops up. An endorsement deal would more than cover her expenses. I could take care of her. I could make a future for us possible.

But I groan privately.

I can't buy her to stay. She wouldn't want that. And it's too soon. I'd really better not get distracted. Trouble is, I think about it too much as I get ready to play. When game time nears, I need some new mental tricks to stop thinking about what's next.

"Shake it off, buddy," I mutter as I lace up.

And I do my damnedest to do just that during the game.

* * *

That night we lose, and it sucks. My gameplay is weak. I miss shots. I miss passes. And I can't do a damn thing with the tips from my dad or the one from Christian. I'd be an idiot if I pretended I didn't know why.

I was in my head tonight.

When I get home, I've got to face this mess my brain is making.

Overcome a fear.

I did it the night at the bookstore when I told her about my dyslexia. I can tell her this one too—that I'm afraid we won't last when she leaves. And I want her to stay.

But once I'm upstairs, she's asleep already, and I can't bring myself to wake her up. Especially since she's in my bed.

Not hers.

And I fucking love that she came upstairs and made herself right at home where she belongs—*with me.*

My heart squeezes in my chest as I stare at her, her chestnut hair spilled out on a pillow, her black-and-white glasses on my nightstand, a library book next to them. That's my girl. I lean against the wall and rub my sternum, like I can ease the ache I feel when I look at her. But it won't go away.

When she shifts, I hold my breath, hoping she'll rouse. *Please wake up, baby.*

But she sighs softly, flips to her side, and slides deeper into slumber.

Enough.

I turn away, shed my clothes in the closet, then get ready for bed. When I slide under the covers, she stirs, blinking her eyes open. She smiles softly. "Rough game," she murmurs.

"Yeah." But not for the reasons she thinks. Rough because I was in my head too much. Rough because I was distracted. I'm never distracted. I try to shake it off since tomorrow we leave for a road trip.

But I can't let the thoughts go. They eat away at me all night, and in the morning too as she moves around downstairs, getting ready for work. I grab my travel bag and head to her room, where she's zipping up a skirt that I want to unzip.

Focus.

I set an arm against the doorframe, then say, "Hey."

She spins around, eyes soft. "Hey."

I don't mince words. "What if you stayed? Like got a job extension? Is that even an option?" I sound reckless, but I'm, evidently, okay with that.

She smiles faintly, giving me a glimmer of hope. "I've been wanting to tell you this for a while, but I've been trying for one."

Holy shit. She's on the same wavelength as I am. I feel like I'm made of sunshine. I feel like I could fucking dance, and I hate dancing. "You have? Why didn't you tell me?"

But I'm not mad. I'm elated.

"I didn't want to be presumptuous. Or seem clingy or anything," she says.

"*Presume. Cling,*" I command.

"I like it here. It'd be great to stay." But her upbeat expression falters a second later. "It's hard though," she says, her lips thinning, her gaze worried. "Thalia doesn't think they have the budget to keep me. But I applied for another grant with the foundation that paid for me to be here in the first place."

"You did?" I can't contain my excitement. Don't want to contain it.

"It's a long shot though, Wes," she says, playing the realist, before she shifts gears slightly. "I've been looking for jobs though. At other library branches. Even in Marin County and San Jose."

I feel ten-feet tall. This is the best news. "I'll drive you to work every day," I say.

"You can't do that," she says, laughing.

"Like hell I can't. Watch me. Just fucking watch me."

"I have to get a job first. And it's the end of the year so there are never as many postings. Budgets and all. And hiring slows in December. But I'm applying for everything."

She brightens at the end, giving me a ray of hope. And I'll cling to it. "But you're trying. That's what matters," I say, then I close the distance between us and kiss her goodbye.

For a few seconds I taste salt. Or maybe I'm preparing myself for more of these kisses in five weeks' time.

38

IN MY POLE ERA

Josie

One week turns into another one, then one more. When Wesley's in town, we volunteer at Little Friends Dog Rescue, transporting dogs to foster homes while they wait for adoptions. Wesley's car has two dog beds in the backseat. When he drives, he peeks in the rearview mirror and says things to the passengers like, "You're the best boy" and "Aren't you a good little cutie" and "You deserve all the treats in the world."

He might be at his happiest when he's buckling in rescue pups. It's a pure kind of joy, and it makes my heart sing to see it.

Other times, we do mundane office chores together. Like review applications for adoption. But we split those tasks, leaning into what each of us does best. I read and screen them, then he makes phone calls and vets prospective adopters for the rescue. Soon, we'll cross off number six officially, and then we'll do number seven—explore a new skill. We'd debated that one for a while, as I made a list of our options—candle-making, cocktail mixing, or pottery classes, while he suggested kayaking, a *foraging for food in the woods* workshop, and badminton.

"You made a list for a list," he'd said, laughing one night when I showed him my suggestions for number seven.

"I can't help it if the list is spawning," I said, but then surveyed his choices while tapping a pen against my chin. "Sorry, Wes. Kayaking is too cold, the outdoors is not my friend, and I'd get hit in the eye with a birdie."

"Let me get this right—you've vetoed all mine? Just like that?"

"I prefer to think of it like this—I'm letting you pick from my three very excellent choices."

He laughed. "Good thing I like you," he said, then leaned down and captured my mouth in a kiss before whispering, "And I'm picking cocktail mixing for *explore a new skill* so I can taste the flavors on these perfect lips."

"I guess number seven will be foreplay then too," I said.

But we haven't been able to do that yet since the next-cocktail mixing class that works out for both of us is next week, shortly before Christmas. It can wait since first Wes has to get through this punishing road trip he's on right now to Minnesota, Chicago and Calgary—*punishing* is right since they've lost two games so far. That sucks, especially since the coach has played him on the first line a few times. But Wesley hasn't talked much about the team or his performance, so I haven't pressed. He gets enough pressure from his dad about his performance and doesn't need it from me. I try to focus on us and making the most of our time together. Like when I make plans for number eight on the list. That's coming around the corner, but it's easy to fit that in when the mood strikes.

That might be the one I'm most looking forward to—dancing in the park.

It's so seemingly random, but so not. My aunt and I used to do that when I was a kid. She'd take me to the park for a picnic, and we'd run around the slides and jungle gym—the extent of my athletic skills was mastering the monkey bars. Then she'd declare it was time for *impromptu dance party*. And we danced our butts off in the park, using her iPod and corded headphones, always finishing with Bill Withers' "Lovely Day." It wasn't even her favorite song. She told me it was *my song*. Wes and I will probably tackle that next week, too, since he'll be in town.

While Wes is traveling, we text and sext as much as we can. One night in December, I start a new series of photos for him, showing off the shoes I tried on for Everly's class, before the Internet schooled me—you don't need to wear heels for your first pole-dancing class. Or your second. That's definitely for the best. They're seven-inch platforms and it's possible I might die in them. But they do look hot, so I took a pic at the thrift shop and now I'm sending it along.

> Josie: I'm in my pole era. Or I'm trying to be.

> Wesley: I'd like you to be in the wrap those shoes around your man's face era.

My man. Somehow, that's what he's become. Mine. Or really, mine for now.

> Josie: Why am I not surprised that's your first thought?

>> Wesley: Why would you think I'd think anything else when you send me a photo of you in hot shoes?

> Josie: Fair point. But where's my pic?

>> Wesley: You want to see my shoes? Whatever works for you. I'm on the plane right now, in a pair of suede loafers. (Cruelty-free suede, of course.)

> Josie: No! I want to see your face!

I want to add *I love your face* but I'm careful not to use the L word. I've been careful about the F word, too—F as in *falling*, like *falling for you*. But Wes is careful as well. He hasn't said either of those words either. I think I know why. Because of the other four-letter word.

Time.

There's not enough of it. There's never enough of it. It just keeps marching inexorably forward, and with it so do the days when I don't hear from The Violet Delia Foundation for Library Digital Empowerment, and when I get turned down from the few openings in the area, and when I don't find any new ones to apply for.

And when I want one more and more.

Especially when Wes sends me a picture of his face.

He's on the plane, resting his head against the window, giving an easy smile. His scruff is scruffier than usual, and his eyes are tired but brighter than when I've seen him on TV playing these last few games. My heart jumps. This is getting to be ridiculous. I'm falling too hard for him.

But the look in those eyes tells me he's falling too.

How utterly inconvenient. I don't think falling in love for the first time was on my aunt's list.

* * *

When I'm walking to work on a Tuesday morning, listening to a podcast about how to be unforgettable in your job search, an email lands that makes my breath halt. I stop short outside the fire station, my fingers tingling. I try to remember to breathe as I open this email with far too much hope flowing through my veins.

It's from the foundation.

Dear Josie,
We're writing to let you know we received your application and have reviewed it. Do you have time for an interview sometime this week?
All the best,
Violet

The head of the foundation herself? This is almost too good to be true. Maybe this means I'm getting that extension. Maybe I can stay on at my branch with this. I hit reply, sending them the times I'm available.

Then, I float into the library. Maybe this long shot isn't such a long one after all.

I walk toward the reference desk, past the trees decorated with ornaments of books, and smile at my co-workers.

"What's that look for?" Eddie asks.

I flutter my lashes. "I have an interview," I say, then tell them the details.

Eddie knocks fists with me, and Thalia gives an approving nod.

"Would either of you be willing to do a mock interview with me? To help me prep?"

Eddie taps his chin as if in deep thought. "Would you be willing to make those lavender chocolate-chip cookies again?"

"Done," I say.

"Then we'll help," he says, "Right, Thalia?"

"Of course we will. And until then, you've got some requests for *Your Next Five Reads*."

It's business as usual, and maybe that's what my life can be.

"I'm on it," I say, and I keep myself occupied until it's time for a mid-morning break. I pop into the bathroom, texting Wes the good news on the way. Once I swing open the door, I nearly jump. Raccoon's perched on the edge of the sink, licking the faucet.

"Raccoon. You hate being normal, don't you?" I head over and turn on the tap so he can drink from a light stream.

When he's done, a reply from Wes lights up my screen.

Wesley: Can we celebrate by skipping number eight?

Josie: Never!

Wesley: Also, fuck yes!

Josie: Well, it hasn't happened yet. It's only an interview.

Wesley: It's the first step.

* * *

That afternoon, my colleagues quiz me, and when I leave another email lands—I landed an interview at a library in Petaluma early next week too. It's about an hour away, but I don't even care. Everything feels possible.

* * *

That night, after I've finished all my prep for tomorrow's Zoom interview with the foundation, I'm hanging out on Maeve's couch before we meet up with Fable for a paint-and-sip class (which doesn't count toward learning a new skill because we all mostly know how to paint and we definitely know how to sip). I'm plucking pistachios from their shells while Maeve layers tiny ocean-colored mosaic tiles onto an old tequila bottle. That's for the lamps she's been selling at farmers' markets and night markets around the city.

"I was honestly worried I was going to need to call my mom, tuck my tail between my legs, and go home to Maine in January. Look for work from there," I say, but then once those words come out, I want to flick a pistachio shell at myself. "Actually, I might still have to do that. Of course that's what I'll have to do." A burst of panic curls inside me, rising higher. "What am I thinking? There's no guarantee I'm getting this grant. Or even a job here. I should be realistic and assume I won't and figure I'll go home and live with my parents while I look for work, like any other person my age these days. Plan for any contingency."

"You're right. You might not get the job you want," Maeve says with supreme focus while she glues in the final tile. Then she looks up. "But thinking positively harmed no one."

Her attitude doesn't entirely settle my new worries, but it does distract me. "Maeve, are you a closet optimist?"

"Maybe I am," she says, dusting one palm against the other. "Especially because I think we tell ourselves not to put our dreams out into the universe, like we're afraid they won't happen if we dare to whisper them. But that has nothing to do with whether they come true or not. Look at me—I sell lamps from old liquor bottles at the night market, and I told you eight months ago I wanted to do that."

I flash back to when I visited her in March, while I was on spring break. Maeve loves painting, but she also loves making art. We visited the market she wanted to get a spot at for the lamps, and she pointed to it, and said, *"I want that to be mine so badly."*

Then she did the work and landed the spot recently.

"And look at you now."

"Well, I'm still catering but I'm getting closer to my dreams. And honestly, I think it's because I say them out loud. There's this media company that creates videos to inspire change, and one of the things they did a couple years ago was build a massive custom megaphone. Like twenty-feet long, and they set it up in Union Square with a sign that said *Shout Your Dream to the World*, and they recorded videos of people doing it all day long. And it's beautiful," she says, then pops up on the couch, tracks down the video and shows it to me. In it, people of all shapes, sizes, ages, and colors shout through the megaphone to tell the city, and the world, what they long for. Love, a job that fulfills them, to live debt-free, to make art, to find the love of their life, to travel the world...everything feels possible after I watch it.

When it's done, Maeve says, "You should put your dreams out there."

That sounds well beyond my comfort zone. So I say yes.

* * *

The next day, I do the interview and it goes well. I'm prepared, engaged, and full of questions. So is Violet. That night, I gather Maeve, Fable, and Everly, and we head to the foot of the Golden Gate Bridge with a megaphone that Fable borrowed from the Renegades. It's not a twenty-foot custom megaphone, but it'll get the job done. Everly didn't travel with the team this week—one of the guys in the PR department did—so she joins us.

Fable waggles the megaphone. "Who volunteers as tribute?"

My bold outgoing Maeve grabs it first, then turns toward the Pacific Ocean where the waves crash against the rocky shores then stretch all the way to the edge of the inky night horizon.

"The ocean can carry our dreams," she says, then

squares her shoulders, brings the megaphone to her mouth, and shouts, "I want to make art that matters."

My heart swells, and I squeeze her arm in support.

She gives it to Fable, who takes a deep breath, then goes next, muttering *this is crazy, this is crazy, this is crazy.* Then she says, "I want to launch my own jewelry line."

The words echo across the sky and over the water, and I imagine the sea catching them in gratitude.

Everly's next, and a sadness crosses her eyes, but a steadiness too. A certainty. "I want to live my best life, especially for those who can't."

My heart clutches, and I flash back to what she said when we went grocery shopping. *Had a friend.* I drape an arm around her. While I'd never try to replace anyone, I hope I can be one of her friends in the present and into the future.

She hands it to me. "Your turn."

I take the red megaphone then look to the stars, thinking of my aunt and the list she gave me. I wasn't sure what it meant for a while. Was it a connection to her? Was it a pathway through grief? Was it rules to live by? I'm not sure I'll ever know, and I need to be okay with that. To navigate the world without her guidance, but with her love as a compass. Maybe that's what the list was all about.

I have a lot of dreams right now, but there's one dream I've had my whole entire life. I give it to the ocean with my voice. "I want to be happy."

It feels like it might be coming true. But not because I put it out there. Because I've been doing the work.

39

DANCE LESSONS

Josie

Dance practice might be the perfect time for me to ask Wes the next thing—would you want to try long-distance?

If I can't get a job in time—and really, the clock *is* ticking—would you want to try to stay together? I mean, it's not like I'm going to ask him if I can stay here and free-load while I look for work. That's not happening.

"Are we really doing this?" Wes asks, groaning on the couch the next night, slouching deeper into it. He returned home late last night from his road trip, but barely has a break since he has a game tomorrow evening. "I could play video games instead. That's kind of like dancing."

I laugh as I grab his hand, trying to tug him up. "Video games are not anything like dancing. How is it that you don't like dancing?"

"I'm bad at it."

I scoff. "Doubtful. You're an athlete."

"Yeah, and hockey is not ice dancing."

"It's not creating a charcuterie board either, and you still do that in your free time," I tease.

"Seriously. Dancing is like the opposite of hockey."

"You're an athlete. You know how to move your body."

"In bed and on the ice," he says, then pulls me onto his lap. "Speaking of the first one...maybe dancing is a euphemism for sex. See? We've already crossed it off ten million times."

He's picking up my fine art of exaggeration, but he's wrong here. I reach for the chain around his neck and fiddle with it. "You got sex from the list. The first one. And number eight is dance in the park. Pretty sure my aunt didn't want me to bang a dude in the park."

"I dunno. She sounds like she was pretty cool."

"She was. You tossed me over your shoulder and carried me into the improv theater. Don't make me do that to you now."

Begrudgingly, he lets me pull him up from the couch. I pat his firm chest, eager to move onto our practice. "But you know how you said *I got you* then? Well, I've got *you* now. I studied all the little foot drawings on a how-to-dance page."

"You did?" he asks, brow furrowed, then he shakes his head. "What am I saying? Of course you did. That's so on brand."

I head to his record player, put on a Frank Sinatra tune, then turn around. With a resigned sigh, Wes strides over to me. "I'm only doing this because it's you," he says.

"Good enough reason for me," I say, especially since it gives me the confidence that now might be the right time.

He loops his arms around my neck and as the old standard plays, we practice to dance in the park. "Soon, we'll cross off three more things," he says as he brings me closer. His tone is wistful. Maybe this is the time to bring it up.

"We will," I say, then offer hopefully, "but maybe we can start a new list." *Like when we're apart? Something that'll help keep us together.*

"Yeah, maybe."

Except...that's weirdly non-committal from him. Especially since he turns silent as we sway.

My radar beeps. I might be wrong. Maybe now isn't the best time to say *do you want to try long-distance if I can't find a job?*

My heart beats faster in worry as the silence extends, I should really try not to read into the silence. I try to just enjoy dance practice in the living room with him. But he's seemed a little off since he returned home. Three losses in a row will do that to you though. Maybe that's what his mood is about. What if he wants to talk?

"Hey. Is your dad pressuring you?" I ask, a subtle way of saying *is hockey stressing you out?*

He huffs out a breath. "Yes, always, but he's also pressuring me about coming to Christmas at Frieda's house in Sonoma. She's having some big party with her friends, and it sounds...like hell."

"Can you get out of it?"

"Easily. All I have to do is tell him I want to work out more, or do more yoga, or meet with the performance coach. Or get in some extra ice time," he says it flatly. Not like it's a clever way to avoid the visit, which it is. But more like he wishes he didn't have to devise an excuse. "Besides, we only have a couple days off anyway."

Did he sidestep the question about pressure? I think

he did. But the answer still came through loud and clear. "Do you usually spend the holidays with your dad?"

"Him or Mom. She's still traveling with her husband but I've gone to see her in Colorado a few times in the past. It's weird. Being an adult and going home for Christmas," he says and maybe Wes is just contemplative tonight.

"Mine are coming here for the holidays. To see Christian and Liv and the babies of course," I say, forgoing my plans for now since the time doesn't seem right. "But I know what you mean. I feel lost in time when I go home. I lived at my parents' house during the summers when I was getting my master's, and then right up until I moved out here. And I just felt like, am I a kid or an adult?" But maybe this is a way to broach the topic subtly? "I really don't want to go home if I don't get a job here."

That seems to snap his focus back to me. He gives me a steady look. "You'll get one."

Time is running out though. But I don't say that. I say nothing because I don't trust myself not to say how I feel.

"Will you go home?" he asks finally. "If you...don't get one?"

Why are you asking? Where do you want me to go? What should I do? I say none of that though. "I don't know. But maybe it'll be fine if I do. They hardly noticed me growing up. I got used to it. There are benefits to being the invisible child," I say, trying to lighten the mood.

I half expect him to say *I see you*, but he turns quiet again as the song ends.

"Are you thinking about how much you hate dancing?" I ask.

He drags a hand roughly through his hair. "No, just

thinking about the game tomorrow. Sorry. I'm not the best company tonight."

"It's okay." I let my arms fall from his shoulders and take his hand, leading him back to the couch again. "What's wrong?"

Another hard sigh. Another hand through his hair. "It's New York. We're playing them again, and that last game was rough. The last week has been rough. I want to do my best. I don't think I have been lately."

I hate that he's hurting. I hate that he's beating himself up. "You will," I say, squeezing his hand, but when his phone buzzes on the table, he tenses, peering at the screen.

His father's name flashes across it. He usually ignores his dad when we're together, but this time he grabs it. Reads. Replies. Then puts it down. "He's just telling me stuff about the game. He'll be there."

Oh. Nerves whip through me. "Should I not go?" Then another question swoops down. "Does he know about me?"

With a guilty look, Wes shakes his head. "No."

For the first time, I feel like we're out of step.

40

A TERRIBLE BOYFRIEND

Wesley

The crowd roars deep in the second period the next night, barking like dogs, the rallying cry for the Sea Dogs. But I block it out and focus on the thumping of my own pulse. Hell, it's all I want to hear. If I listen any harder, I'll hear that fucking voice of doubt again.

You don't belong on the first line.

I grit my teeth as I skate hard toward New York's goal, alongside Christian. But when Karlsson swarms him, trying to strip the puck, Christian flips it my way. I lunge for it, the stick connecting solidly. Since I've got an opening I slam it to the net. But instead of flying into the twine, the puck misses by inches.

Frustration boils inside me. It's not the first time it's happened tonight. I skate behind the net, and as I'm racing the other way, Karlsson catches up, getting too close. "First line pressure getting to you? It's hard when you suck, isn't it, Bryant?"

I want to kill him.

Instead, I skate furiously, the cold air stinging my cheeks as I try—I swear I try—to block out the doubts and frustrations echoing in my mind. I try not to look at center ice either. Don't want to get distracted. By Josie. By my dad. By my own damn expectations haunting me every second. I'm grateful for the line change, and I try to calm my emotions when I'm on the bench. But during the next line shift, I miss another shot at the net, the puck sailing wide, and I curse under my breath.

Karlsson's right there again, bumping into me, taunting. "I'd say better luck next time, but maybe better luck in the minors."

He smirks, and it takes everything I have not to drop my gloves and pummel the asshole.

His insults aren't even personal. It's just who he is. It's literally his job to talk trash, and it's mine to take it. When I hop over the boards at the end of the shift, I pull off my gloves and hurl them on the floor in front of me on the bench. And that's not like me either. I don't fling shit. Coach arches a brow, more serious than I've ever seen him.

Ah, hell.

He leans in and whispers something to the assistant coach.

My heart freezes.

This is bad.

This is really bad. And it's all my fault.

By the time the game ends, my team pulls off a win, no thanks to me. I contributed zilch to it. When I trudge through the tunnel, I don't even look to the stands to find Josie. Can't fucking face her. Can't stand failing like this in front of her.

When I reach the end of the tunnel, Coach is there in his suit and his game face. The snapshot of him would be titled *ominous*. "A word, Bryant."

A word is never good.

He pulls me aside into his office, then glances at the clock on the wall, like he has to be somewhere. "You're doing great, Bryant. But let's stick to the second line. You seemed more comfortable there."

My chest caves in. My stomach sinks to the bottom of the earth. I knew it was coming, but that doesn't make it hurt any less. "Yes, sir."

"We can talk more about it another time," he says. "I need to do an interview."

But what else is there to say? It's clear. When I leave his office, my dad is waiting for me in the corridor. I am not in the mood for him right now. Not at all.

"Let's grab a bite after you work out," he says.

Like I'd forget the post-game workout. Like I don't know what he wants to talk about either.

"Yep," I mutter.

I head to the locker room, grab my phone, and text Josie to tell her I can't introduce her to my dad tonight, and that I'll see her at home. I feel like such an ass. I stare at the message. I'm a terrible boyfriend. But I can't. I just can't. Just like I knew what Coach was up to, I know what's coming next from my dad. I brace myself for it as I strip off my uniform, shower, and change.

* * *

Dad asks if I want to go to Sticks and Stones, but that's a bar frequented by my teammates. Don't need to get reamed in front of everyone, especially on a busy Friday night in December when the place will be packed. I say no, and we opt for a Thai restaurant on Fillmore that's open late. I order the chicken with vegetables and a papaya salad. No less than ten seconds after the server leaves, Dad gives me his best *I'm concerned* face.

"You're distracted," he says, and his tone is kind, but I want to shove his words right back into his mouth. "You have been since that game against LA."

I know all too well which one he means. That was the day I talked to Christian and told him I was seeing his sister. But that night when I played, I was up in my head about Josie staying in town or not. She was all I thought about when I was on the ice, and that is *not* like me. I've learned mental discipline. I've cultivated it over the years. Hell, Dad's paid for me to train my body *and* my mind. I don't get distracted.

Ever.

But the more I think about the future with her, the worse I play. "I've just had a couple bad games this week," I grumble, then take a drink of my ice water.

Dad nods a few times, thoughtfully. "Which happens when your mind is elsewhere. Like when that girl Anna broke it off with you last year."

"That's not what happened," I snap.

He gives me a placating look. "Wesley. It kind of did. There was that game against Boston, then one against Montreal..."

Are you kidding me? He remembers when she dumped me and that I played for shit then? "Don't go there," I warn, since I can handle a lot of his advice. I can absorb a ton of his input. But I do *not* want his advice about romance.

He leans forward in the booth, his voice so calm, so

opposite mine. "But we need to figure this out. Like I've said, this is a critical year."

My jaw ticks. I've heard that a thousand times. "And yet, I still don't want to talk to you about women," I bite out, surprising myself for standing up to him. I'm so glad I didn't introduce him to Josie. He would never understand the way I feel for her.

He lifts his water, takes a drink, sets it down. Smiles. Perhaps he's heard me and we're moving on from the topic of romance. But he's not a lawyer for nothing. "Level with me. Is this because of your roommate?"

The fuck? How does he know? I never told him we were dating. "What are you talking about?" I ask with a sneer I can't hide.

"Wesley, it's not hard to figure out. I took a guess that you'd fallen for her," he says, then shrugs easily. "The evidence added up. Looks like I was right."

How smug can he possibly be? I grind my molars but I don't say anything, because I have nothing to say to him about my love life.

But he has plenty to say. "You need to work on your focus. Life is going to keep coming at you. Do you need a mental skills coach? A psychologist?"

All he wants to do is hire people to improve me. No wonder I felt like I was hockey, hockey, hockey when I met Josie. Because that's all he ever wanted me to be. That's all he ever sees me as—a hockey player.

But, a voice whispers meanly in my ear, stirring up all my old fears, *Maybe there's a reason. It's the only thing you're good at. Except...what if you're not good at it after all?*

"No," I say, answering him at last.

He tilts his head, seeming confused momentarily. "No what?"

"No, I don't want you to hire anyone. Okay? Coach already moved me back to the second line. It's done. Can we just eat in peace?"

"But what about the roommate situation?" The implication is loud and clear.

I clench my fists. Take another deep breath. Then one more. "I meant it. I do *not* want to talk to you about women."

He takes it on the chin with a resigned nod. "Fair enough."

I stick to my guns, shutting my mouth. But that means he drones on and on about hockey for the next thirty minutes, and I sit there and eat and take it.

When I leave, I both want to talk to Josie and run from Josie, and I hate feeling this twisted and torn.

Maybe I can get some sleep and sort it out in the morning. Curl up with her and fix it when the sun is up.

But when I get home, she's not in my bed, and that feels like a kick in the balls.

41

KIND OF A LOT

Josie

Wes said to presume a few weeks ago, but I can't presume tonight. I can't presume he wants me upstairs. I can't sleep either. That's the problem.

I never have trouble sleeping—never. But tonight, I'm in my own room for the first time in more than a month. The lights are out and I'm trying so hard to bring sweet dreams my way.

But as soon as I hear him return to the house and head up the steps, I know he's looking for me. I know he's disappointed. Even if I feel him pulling away from me, have felt it since we danced in the living room last night, I don't want to be another thing that hurts him. I want to help him like he helped me the night we met.

Besides, I've been trying to be brave. I've been trying to be bolder. I fling off the covers and push out of bed, pushing open the door right as he's stepping into the doorway.

I flinch in surprise, then back up. "Oh."

"Hey." That's it. A heavy syllable breathed into the night. He looks terrible. Devastated.

"What happened? Do you want to talk? Did your dad give you a hard time?"

He grits his teeth then breathes out hard. "Yeah. He said I'm distracted. Coach said as much, too, when he moved me to the second line."

"I'm sorry," I say, guilt lancing through me. This is my fault. Wes *is* distracted, and I know why. Still I have to try to make him feel better. "But that's where you started the season. It's not that bad, right? You know exactly what to do there, and you can keep working your way back."

But that's the exact wrong thing to say to an athlete. A step back isn't fine. He's wired for excellence, not acceptance.

"No, Josie. It's bad," he says in a hard voice, correcting me sternly.

I feel stupid all over again. "I'm sorry."

He frowns, apologies in his brown eyes now. "Shit, baby. I didn't mean to take it out on you." He reaches for my face and cups my cheek, and it feels so good as he strokes my jaw. But it feels awful at the same time because it's an *I'm sorry* gesture.

I'm sorry I'm about to hurt you.

"I'm a wreck right now," he says, his voice strained, full of potholes and self-loathing. "But it's not your fault."

Except...is it my fault? That's what I can't shake—the feeling that *I'm* to blame. "Do you think you're distracted? By me and us and my job search and by what's going to happen? Is it stressing you out? All the...unknown?" My chest aches horribly but I have to ask these questions.

He pauses for a long while. In that stretch of silence,

his face is honest, brutal even, with the truth in his eyes—the truth is yes. We are a distraction. I am stressing him out.

But Stoic Wes takes over and erases the emotions on his face. "No."

That's a lie.

He has another game coming up in two days. Then another after Christmas. They're important games, especially after the last few rough ones. I could ask him what happens next for us. I could mention the long-distance thing. I could say I want us to make this work. But what can I offer him right now that'll settle him? Nothing. I'm still in limbo. I don't know if I'm staying or leaving.

But I know this—I'm not the one trying to play professional hockey in front of twenty thousand people every other day, with media who breathe down my neck, fans who cheer and jeer me, and a father who gives me a hard time.

I do know what that's like though.

I was raised with it.

From the comfort of my books, I watched that world unfold as my parents focused on my superstar brother. Gave him every opportunity to succeed. They were right to channel their energy into him—look where he is now. At the top of his game. Growing up, he was the plant that required a lot of water.

Me? I'm the cactus after all.

My family barely notices what I do, and really, it's okay. I've always had books and friends. I've always done a good job taking care of myself and getting out of the way. My aunt taught me to cook, to bake, to learn, to read. Most of all, she taught me to be independent.

With a cold, stark certainty, I'm sure I have to do for Wesley what I did for my family growing up.

Get out of the way.

With a gentle smile, and I hope, a caring one, I reach for his forearm, rub my hand along the dog and music notes. "But what if you are too distracted by everything that's happening here? With me? I mean, I'm kind of a lot."

"Don't say that," he says, but it lacks his usual...vigor. His usual bossiness.

"I am," I insist. "The night you met me I was locked out and half-naked, and you saved me. The next time I lost my short-term rental, and you saved me. Then, you found my list and you offered to do it with me." Emotions climb up my throat, tightening it in a chokehold. But I try to push past the tears stinging the backs of my eyes. "I'm a lot. You've given me a lot. But you need to leave something for yourself."

His brow knits. "What are you talking about?"

I roll my lips together, fighting off the waterworks, then I dig down and say, "Would it be easier if I finish the list on my own and give you a little time to refocus?"

Time—it's the one thing we don't have.

But right now, that doesn't matter. It doesn't matter because Wes is quiet again, chewing on that, perhaps.

That's another sign I'm doing the right thing for him.

Wes is quick and passionate. He doesn't mull things over. He doesn't stew. For the first time ever, he's stuck.

The man is twisted in knots.

I have to give him this lifeline. I throw him some more rope. "You didn't want to dance in the park anyway, and that's okay," I say gently, kindly. "The list is a lot too. I could do it with my friends. I haven't done anything on it with them. Maybe I should."

He breathes in deeply, nodding the tiniest amount, absorbing that.

"And the cocktail-mixing class," I say, exonerating him more. I wave a hand. "Let's do it another time."

That's a futile promise, because we don't have time.

But he doesn't correct me so I continue, "Right now, you should focus on hockey."

He runs a hand down his face, closes his eyes, then breathes out. For a few seconds, I hope so damn hard he'll resist my overture. But when he opens his eyes, he grumbles, "You're probably right."

My heart breaks. But I try to keep it together.

What he doesn't say next is, *"Let me hold you all night. Come to bed with me. Or we'll figure it out together."*

Instead, he nods to my room and the bed I haven't slept in in weeks. "I should let you go to sleep."

What I hear is, *"I should let you go."*

42

THE STEP AROUND SKILL

Josie

I've spent the last few weeks reading every blog post, watching every video, and gobbling up every article I can find on what to expect in your first pole class.

But Everly also tells me to expect "cardio and fun."

I need the latter now more than ever as I tiptoe around the townhome on Sunday morning. I am quieter than I've ever been, and I use my morning person-ness to my advantage. I successfully avoided Wes yesterday by waking early and exploring the city, then hanging out with Eddie and his husband playing mini golf in the evening.

Today, it will be even easier to avoid Wes since he has a game.

Once again, I'm determined to escape before he wakes up. I'm dressed in leggings, a sports bra, a T-shirt, and a sweatshirt, and I've got knee pads and a water bottle in my canvas bag, right next to the blank book where I keep the list. I've even slipped my book charm necklace into a pocket in my bag. I have them both with me today. Maybe because I need to feel close to my aunt.

I walk quietly past the stairs, half expecting him to hear me, wholly wanting him to call out, "Let me drive you."

What a foolish wish. But he loved to drive me wherever I needed in the city. He's an acts-of-service guy through and through.

The house is painfully silent. The emptiness tunnels through me as I pad to the door, carefully lift the latch, then grab my sneakers and take off.

On the porch, I lace up my shoes quickly, ignoring the onslaught of feelings I don't want to feel. I manage to make it down the front steps before my throat hitches. Tears prick my eyes, but I suck in a breath. I'm wearing my fake lashes to pole classes so these tears can fuck off.

Down the street, I catch the bus and head to Russian Hill to a dance studio that Everly likes. But even though I've done my homework, no amount of prep can gird you to walk into a class when your heart is shattered, and you're pretending you're fine.

Everything hurts.

Everything reminds me of him.

Even *this.*

I would have shared the story of this class with him, told him about it, taken some pics. He would have eaten up every detail. But, I guess he can't have love and hockey, so I go in alone—but I'm not truly alone. Everly's a welcome sight.

She's dressed in a long-sleeved shirt, which surprises me, but maybe she doesn't sweat like me. She's stretching in front of the mirrored wall in the brightly lit studio, and she beams when she sees me. "You made it!"

"I don't back down," I say, even though I tried to wiggle out of improv.

But I soldiered on and did it. Come to think of it, I haven't backed out of anything on the list. And dammit, man in my life or not, I'm going to finish it. In fact, I don't need to go to a cocktail-mixing class for number seven—*explore a new skill*.

I'm living number seven right now. With my friends. The awareness hits me all at once, and I smile like a giddy fool, tugging on Everly's hand, pulling her to the cubbies in the corner of the studio as Maeve strides in. Fable couldn't make it—she had to do some Christmas shopping with her sister. "I have this list from my aunt. Like a bucket list. Top Ten Things I Never Regretted," I tell Everly.

Her eyes light up. "You do? That's seriously cool."

"And one of the items is *explore a new skill*." I motion for Maeve to join our huddle and gamely, she hustles over. "I was going to do number seven with Wes, but I want to do this one with you two. Can this be *explore a new skill* for my bucket list of no regrets?"

"As if you have to ask," Maeve says, then tilts her head, and I know what she's thinking—what changed with Wes and why now?

I swallow down more tears. "I'll tell you later."

For now, it's time to dance.

* * *

Ten minutes later, I'm walking around the pole. That's it. Walking. But as Kyla, the instructor, says, "It's harder to walk than you might think. You want to make space between the pole and your body, and then you can do the step around."

She explains that basic move, then asks Everly to demonstrate. In no time, my new friend's swinging around her pole like a goddess, all muscles and badass attitude, shiny ponytail swishing down her back.

"Now, let's try the step around," Kyla says to the rest of us.

Sounds easy and looks easy too. But when I try the basic move, gripping the pole with my right arm, then rising up on my toes so I can stretch out my left leg to the side, I'm not sure I can move around the pole without falling on my ass.

But then...so what if I fall? I stop thinking and I *do,* swinging around it.

And...I manage a quarter turn. Actually, that was more like an eighth of a turn, but I'm stupidly excited over this most minor accomplishment, and so is the teacher. "Great start," Kyla says to me with genuine enthusiasm.

Those words burrow into my aching, hollow heart.

Great start.

As Maeve attempts her step around like she's jumping off a cliff—since that's how Maeve lives life—I think of the list. Of the other night by the Golden Gate Bridge. Of my dreams. They don't have to be anchored to a man.

Just like that, I can see a new future. One I haven't planned for or prepped for or researched. But maybe that's part of me exploring new skills.

I don't mean this skill. I mean another one—I'm learning to leap.

43

A DAMN FINE BAGEL

Wesley

Funny how I never noticed the room under the staircase much before. I barely paid attention to it for the first several months I lived here.

Now it's all I see.

It taunts me. It lures me, and I have to fight the pull. I give her space. I avoid her. I stay upstairs when she's downstairs.

I don't know what to say or do when I see her. I guess this is why there's a roomie rule in the first place. Because it is complicated when you cross it.

When things go south—like they did two nights ago— you're still stuck together, walking uncomfortably around each other.

But a little while after she leaves on Sunday—I'm pretty sure she's going to that pole class with her friends, and I hate that she's not going to be sending me a picture —I get out of bed, get dressed, and head downstairs to make my way to morning skate. The problem is...that door.

To her room. It's halfway open.

I stop in the entrance to it, press my palm against the white wood of the door lightly, till it creaks open. I look inside. My chest aches at the signs of Josie.

The white sweatshirt I bought her the night we met is tossed on the bed. The black scarf she left behind hangs from the closet door. Pillows are arranged in a whole new way on the window seat.

I lift my nose in the air and draw a big inhale. I can smell the remnants of her cinnamon scent. On the bureau, there's a pad of blue paper, like the one she used to leave me notes on.

My chest hollows, and I press my fingers against my temple. I wish I had the courage to grab that paper and write her a note. But what would I even say?

I'm sorry?

I miss you?

I'm a mess?

That's all true, and she knows all that, so I tear myself away from her room, trudge to the kitchen, and yank open the fridge.

But it all looks so boring.

I flip my middle finger at the prepared food, then trudge down to the garage, peel out quickly, and stop at a nearby bagel shop for a pineapple smoothie and a toasted sesame bagel. That's a damn fine breakfast.

* * *

An hour later, I'm dead focused on the rink during morning skate, passing to Asher, Hugo, and Alexei.

Shooting on Max. Flicking the puck under a low bar, then racing behind the net and slapping the disc under it again and again. Practice makes perfect. Muscle memory. Discipline.

Midway through, Coach blows the whistle and calls me over.

"Bryant, why don't you get out there with Winters and Weston?"

He gestures to the other end of the rink. Naturally Christian is here, since he never misses practice. Chase is too. "But that's...first line," I point out so helpfully, like Coach doesn't know the intricacies of his lineup.

"I'm aware. You've got great chemistry with the second line. Chemistry doesn't come overnight on the hockey rink. You've got to get out there and work with them."

He points to me and I turn back around, flying toward the other two guys. I'm not sure what to make of this direction, but I am sure it's not my place to question it. I run the drills with Christian and Chase until we're done thirty minutes later.

In the locker room, Asher tips his chin toward me as he laces his shoes. "You want to grab some dinner after the game tonight?"

"Maybe," I say with a shrug.

He stares me down. "Dude, what's with you? You're not your usual self."

I could deny it. But instead I scratch my jaw, shrug, and say heavily, "Yeah. I know."

He seems to give that some thought, nodding a few times, but when we leave a couple minutes later, he claps me on the shoulder in the corridor. "Remember, it's a game. Just have fun. That's what you got to do at the end of the day."

Then he offers me a fist for knocking. Since you don't leave a teammate hanging, I knock back. Asher has the right attitude. He always has. He has an easy way about him and a carefree attitude, and it works. My stomach twists, and I don't normally put myself out there, but impulsively, I ask, "How do I do that?"

"Stop trying to be perfect. Just get out there and play."

It's good advice. Truly it is. After I go home and nap in the deathly quiet house where I miss Josie more by the hour, I return to the rink. I do my best to focus on just that.

Fun.

Hockey used to be fun once upon a time. Then it became work. Then it became pressure. Then it became performance. Then it became the relentless pursuit of perfection. But during the last few months, I've learned how to have fun again, thanks to Josie.

The woman I let go.

44

A GREAT START

Josie

Everly was right. Pole class is cardio, and I'm a sweat-soaked monster when we leave, but I don't care as we dart into a nearby café for lunch.

After we order, I clear my throat and return to the great start. "So I was thinking...I really do want to stay here, and I don't have a job. And it might take me a while to get one. But I've saved up in the last few months because I didn't have to pay rent."

Everly's expression is thoughtful while Maeve's is dead curious. Both wait for me to keep going though.

It's okay to sit with discomfort. It's okay to do the hard thing.

"And I want to stay here even if..." But my voice catches, and all my emotions well up into my throat.

"Oh, sweetie, what happened?" Everly says, rubbing my shoulder, like she's the big sister I don't have.

I fight off the onslaught of emotions and say through

tight lips, "I'm not sure it's going to work out with Wes. He's...blaming himself for his bad games."

Everly sighs. "Hockey players are the worst."

"I'm sorry, Josie," Maeve says. "Men sometimes suck."

"Yeah," I say with a sigh. "But I also didn't want to get in his way. I sort of offered to take a step back."

Maeve blinks, her brow furrowing. "What?"

I don't want to reveal too much of the private conversation the other night or expose Wesley's fears. I keep it simple, saying, "I was worried he was too distracted by me, so I asked if it would be helpful if I finished the list on my own and if we took a step back."

"And he agreed?" Everly asks, arching a brow.

"Yes, he did," I say.

"Hmm," she says, seeming to chew on that.

"What's that for?"

"It's great and all that you're being respectful. But it sounds like you're both being too respectful," she offers.

It's like a slap. But a friendly one, if a slap can be friendly. Still, I reel a bit and push back. "I'm not going to force him to stay with me when he's in a funk."

"I get it," she says, then leans closer, her eyes shrewd but her tone kind. "But maybe he needs you to fight for him."

I freeze. I hadn't thought of that before. Does Wesley need that from me? I'd thought I was doing the right thing, being respectful and all for his job. But did I back off when I should have forged forward?

"It's not *her* fault," Maeve points out, squeezing my shoulder protectively.

"I know that. Wesley probably knows that." Everly locks eyes with me, fixing me with a tough stare. "But only you know if you should fight for him."

"Or if he should fight for her," Maeve suggests.

Everly exhales for a long beat, then perhaps shifts some. "Maybe you both need to fight for each other."

Maybe we do. I nod, but I'm not entirely sure I'm ready yet. There's something else I need to do first—fight for myself.

Grabbing a napkin, I swipe it across the table to clean up any crumbs, then take the list out of my bag, spreading it out for my friends to see. "I might as well cross off number six. I've been doing it for the last few weeks, and I'll keep doing it."

I draw a line through *volunteer.* Then, I say to the women at the table, "Let's cross off number seven," I say, then add, "Together."

It feels right to do this without Wes. Just like I'll do the rest myself. Then, I'll be ready. After all, that's what number ten is all about. But I have to do number eight and nine first. And I have to do them alone.

I hand Maeve the pen. Maeve starts the strike-through, crossing out *explore.* Everly goes next, marking off *a new.* It's my turn, and I finish the line. I look down at the list that's nearly complete. From the one night stand, to overcoming a fear, to making a new friend. We've done so many other things too, like eating dessert for breakfast, taking pictures, volunteering, and now this one with my friends – exploring a new skill. There are only a few more left and I read eight and nine, though I know them by heart.

8. *Dance in the park*
9. *Celebrate your goodbyes.*

After folding the list up carefully, I put it back in the

bag, fighting off this tug in my chest, this pull toward Wesley. And I fight for myself a little more, a little harder. "Could I stay with one of you while I look for a job?"

"Of course," they both say in unison.

I don't even care about The Kid in Maeve's couch. But when Everly says she has a guest room, I'm so there.

Maybe I should even move out tomorrow after my job interview in Petaluma.

45

HE CAN LEARN

Wesley

When I hit the ice that night, Asher's advice repeats in my head like the chorus to your favorite song, an Arctic Monkeys tune or a Yungblud number. Something anthemic, a love song you can't get out of your head.

Have fun.

As I play hockey that night, I try to have a good time.

And a funny thing happens.

I do.

* * *

After the game, I'm in the weight room like usual. Not because I have to be, but because I want to. It might've been my dad's idea originally, but the fact is I like the way these post-game workouts make me feel—strong, resilient, ready. In my body and my mind.

As I'm doing dead lifts, Christian strides in.

"Hey," I say.

He gives me a chin nod and starts racking the bar on the bench press. "Been meaning to ask," he says, then clears his throat, "do you want to come over for Christmas? Josie and everyone will be there."

I stop midway, barbell in hands. Things I didn't have on my bingo card—a Christmas invite from the captain. As I finish the lift, I grunt out, "Um. I'm not sure."

He narrows his eyes, looking me up and down like I've given the wrong answer in class. "You broke it off with my sister?"

I blink. Am I that transparent? "No." But I say it defensively and frankly, in the shape of an obvious lie. "It's just...I've had some bad games, as you know, and she offered to give me space."

Christian stares at me for a long, shocked beat. "And you took it? You, the guy who came barreling into my house a few weeks ago, just took her offer for space?"

When he puts it like that...

"I did," I say, wincing, because I'm pretty sure that was the wrong answer again. I did the wrong thing. I fucked up big time.

He shakes his head in disgust. "Dude, I don't leave my wife when I have a bad game. You had a couple of bad games. Get your shit together."

It's said authoritatively. The captain in charge. And the captain is right. But what am I supposed to do to fix this— both the hockey and the romance?

I swallow past my discomfort and ask a hard question. It's one I've only ever asked of my dad before. "What do you do when you have a bad game?"

His expression is thoughtful, open as he says, "I talk to

a teammate, or I see the athletic trainer, or I speak with a coach. I ask for help." He sits on the bench and fixes me with a no-nonsense stare. "You could come to me."

He's right. My gut churns with regret. But the world only spins forward, so I step past my discomfort, and I do one of the hardest things I've ever done on the team. "Can you help me?"

Christian smiles. "I thought you'd never ask."

We chat for a good long time, and when I get home, I peer longingly down the hall, checking for a sliver of light from Josie's room.

But it's dark, so I go upstairs and dictate his advice on a note on my phone.

Then I visualize tomorrow morning when I can start over.

Around eight a.m., when I hear Josie moving around, I do the same. I fly out of bed, brush my teeth, and throw on shorts and a sweatshirt. I hustle downstairs. I'm dressed and ready to take her to work. At her fucking service.

I'm buoyed by Christian's advice—set short-term goals, not long-term ones; focus on the positive; and lean on your teammates—when I find her in the kitchen. She's gathering her things and wearing a black pencil skirt and a soft pink sweater. She looks like the polished, put-together, young librarian she is. I want to pull her close and run my fingers through her hair and tell her I'm an ass. But I focus on her needs first. "Can I give you a ride to work?"

She flashes me a soft smile and shakes her head. "I'm going to Petaluma."

That throws me for a loop. "You are?"

"Yes, I have a job interview. Thalia gave me the morning off so I could focus on it. And since it's kind of far."

Right, right. She mentioned the interview. I didn't realize it was today. *Because you've barely been talking to her, you dumbass.* "That's huge," I say, my heart racing five steps ahead, hoping this means she can stay, but do I even have the right to ask her that anymore? I need to fix things first.

"And I should really go because there are about three buses I have to catch. At least it's only two buses back to work though," she says before I can get another word in.

Nope. No way am I letting her catch a trio of buses on the way up alone. "I'll drive you. I want to. I can," I say, playing the bossy card.

She shakes her head. "Actually, I kind of want to do this on my own," she says, then gives me an apologetic smile. "I should go." She pauses, frowning, looking like she wants to say something more. After a beat, she exhales. "For what it's worth, I think you're too hard on yourself. I really do, and there are a ton of things I want to say." Her voice is laced with emotion, but her gaze strays to the clock on the wall even as her eyes shine. "I have to go."

But what do you have to say?

The desire to hear those *ton of things* claws at me, like a wild beast let loose in my chest, but I have to give her space.

She heads to the door and I watch her leave, strangely impressed by her gumption, and her guts.

I want to chase after her. I want to insist she lets me

drive her. But I flash back to what she said the other night —that she was *a lot*.

To how she felt I'd kept saving her, like I did on the first night, then less than a week later. I get it. Some things you have to do on your own. You have to save yourself.

She closes the door and leaves.

I wander aimlessly, a lost kid at the zoo. But a few minutes later, my phone rings. Maybe it's her. Maybe she's changed her mind. Maybe I can go pick her up on the corner at the bus stop.

I'm about to say all that when Natalie's name flashes on the screen. I answer it, a little defeated. "Hey. What's going on?"

"Listen. I need to know, are you going to Frieda's for Christmas?" That's where Dad is hosting this year—with his girlfriend.

I groan. "I tried to pretend that isn't happening."

"But it is happening. And Lila and I want to know if we should go."

That's her girlfriend. "You two should go," I say dryly.

"What we're trying to say is we want to go if you're there."

But I want to go to Christian's with Josie—if she'll have me. "I don't know if I will be."

"What's wrong, Wes?"

My sister's the one person who understands me completely, so I say, "I had a couple bad games. I was pretty distracted, and at first I thought it was because of Josie."

"Wes," she says kindly. "Do you think maybe the pressure isn't Josie, but Dad?"

I don't move. I don't say a word. I stand in the kitchen with a simple and obvious truth.

She was never the distraction.

"You're right," I say to my sister, then end the call, my mind spinning over this revelation.

I have to tell Josie right away. Trouble is, I won't be the complication in her life. Not today. Not when she's worked so hard to achieve her dreams.

But I can leave her a letter because I finally know what I want to say.

I head into her room, grab her notepad of blue paper, and bring it back to the kitchen. I write her a short letter and leave it on the counter. She'll find it when she comes home from work.

When I return the notepad to her room, I catch sight of the list sticking out of the blank book. I take one step toward it. Then another. It's a tractor beam pulling me closer. I'm so tempted to look. I reach out a hand, my fingers itching.

I'm dying to find out what she's crossed off without me.

But I stop, close my eyes, and shake it off. Then I open them and I tear myself away from her room, shutting the door.

I don't have to see the list to know she's crossed off more items. The question is—how many?

* * *

I take a yoga class, grab some lunch with the guys, and go to the animal rescue and volunteer. All day, I count off the hours till she comes home. Till I can apologize. Till she finds this letter, and I can talk to her and try to figure us out. But the day moves too slowly. The hands on the clock trudge by. I'm convinced her work will never end. Around four, I wander around the house. It's eerie and dark since it's late December. My footsteps creak on the floorboards, and I'm painfully aware that she's not here.

And I'm just...waiting.

What is wrong with me? In hockey, you don't wait. You *do*.

Spurred by a burst of adrenaline, I run upstairs, change into a nice shirt and jeans, and race to the garage. I can wait outside the library. Surprise her with a ride home. Be the guy who's leaning against his car, ready to pick up his woman and celebrate her successes.

I hightail it to the library with the letter in the passenger seat. I park in the tiny lot. But when five o'clock ticks by, she doesn't emerge from the main doors. With nerves strung tight, I march inside, looking for her and finding Thalia. "Hey, is Josie here?"

"She left early. She had some things to do," Thalia says, and I can't read a thing into her tone—if that's good or bad or if she even knows.

I race back outside to the lot, stabbing Josie's name on my phone. She doesn't answer. I pace, dragging a hand roughly through my hair. Where the hell did she go? Home is the obvious answer, so I hop back in the car and return to the house. But she's not there, and she's still not answering.

"Where are you?"

Then I remember—there's someone who might know.

I call Asher and ask him for Maeve's number. Then I ring Josie's friend immediately.

The first night I met Josie, she'd told me she'd turned on her location tracker for Maeve. Later, she told me that she never turned it off. "It amused us too much," she'd said.

When Maeve answers, I waste no time. "I need to see Josie now. She's not answering. Do you know where she is?"

Maeve laughs, clear and bright. "As a matter of fact, I do. She's at Dolores Park."

I drive so fast to number eight.

46

LOVELY NIGHT

Josie

This isn't weird at all.

That's what I tell myself as I walk into the park solo... to dance on a Monday night. Normally, I wouldn't go to any park at night, being a single female and not having a death wish and all.

But I picked tonight for a reason. Dolores Park is hosting its tree-lighting ceremony. The iconic palm trees on the edge of the park are proud statues, their trunks decorated with white and red lights blinking in spirals, their fronds decked out in flashing pinks, purples and blues.

Crowds fill the park, a motley crew of couples, friends, and young families heading toward a towering Christmas tree in the center of the space where a band plays on a gazebo stage and vendors peddle hot cocoa and candied pecans. Upbeat Christmas tunes in a rock beat reverberate from the stage. Something by Gwen Stefani, I think. A cover of one of her Christmas songs.

Nerves skitter up my spine, but I look around, getting my bearings. People are swaying by the stage, and kids are running in circles. Yup. This is the right time. I'll blend in and, besides, so what if I don't? So what if I stand out? It's fine if I look silly as I dance alone, rocking out to Bill Withers' "Lovely Day." Greta's non-favorite song.

My hand curls tight around my phone, my fingers circling by the playlist, at the ready. I clicked it open on my way over. Sure, I'm trying to be spontaneous at times, but you can't take all the prep out of a girl like me.

My phone's on Do Not Disturb. I didn't want to be distracted by checking my email for job news. I need to do number eight. I *want* to do number eight.

I settle into a corner fifty or so feet from the street, moving behind a pack of revelers wearing ugly sweaters and nipping sips from silver flasks. I'm wearing jeans and a sweatshirt since I changed after work. Didn't want to draw too much attention in full-on work interview garb.

Here goes.

With the park lit up at night, I turn on the song in my AirPods. This isn't what I planned with Wes. But after I dance alone, I can fight for him.

I can tell him he's wrong. That life is more than work. That he shouldn't focus on just hockey. That he should focus on how to be happy.

Ideally, with me.

So I shimmy my hips. I shake my booty. And I mouth the words to the song I've known by heart my whole, entire life. As I move to the familiar beat, a memory flashes before me. Days when I'd dance like this with Greta, carefree and joyful. She danced like she had no stress, and I learned to groove like that from her. The scarf she wore would blow in the breeze, the music would drum in our hearts, and the day would be lovely.

Now, as I sway, it doesn't just feel like I'm dancing in the park. It feels like I'm living with no regrets.

I get into the groove, blending in with the crowds until...

I jump.

My lungs explode with worry since someone has curled a hand around my shoulder.

I spin around, ready to slam a fist into their nose since that's what you do...when I'm standing in front of Wes.

He holds up his hands. "I come in peace," he says. At least, those are the words I read on his lips. I hit stop on the song then yank out my AirPods, my pulse rocketing to the stars in the night sky.

"Hi," he says.

"Hi," I say, my heart still sprinting.

"I came here to find you."

That's clear, but still, I say, "You did?"

"I went to the library to pick you up. You were gone. I went home. You weren't there. I called Maeve, and she told me you were here. I can't let you do this alone."

My skin is tingling, and hope bursts in every cell as he reaches into a pocket and hands me an old iPod. With a set of corded earphones, just like I told him Greta and I used once upon a time.

They're so old school and so right.

My heart swells. And I'm not even sure what to say except: "Let me start it over."

"Yeah. I'd like that, Josie."

When the song is cued up on the old iPod, I put one earbud in my ear then offer him the other. He takes it and then curls his hands around my hips, a white wire connecting us as he brings me close and we slow dance in the park.

He lifts a hand to my neck, threads fingers through my hair, looks me in the eyes, and smiles—that warm, generous grin that hooked me the night I met him.

That's like an arrow through me all over again.

We dance on a chilly December night as the park lights up, and the city celebrates around us.

I don't know what it means that he's here, but I try to live in the moment. And I love this moment.

We dance till the song ends. We remove our headphones, and he says, "I wrote a letter for you."

"You did?"

"As soon as you left. I wanted to give it to you when you got back from your interview but didn't want to ruin your day."

A prick of worry races down my spine. "Will it ruin it?"

"No. At least I hope not. But then, maybe...since you've pretty much ruined me," he says, and I gasp.

I roll my lips together so I don't shed happy tears before I even begin to read. He takes the letter from his pocket and hands it to me.

With eager fingers, I unfold it and read. My breath catches. Warmth cascades down my body. Wes is a man of few written words, but his words hit me in the center of my soul every time.

Dear Josie,

You said you thought you were a lot, but I'm a lot too. Why don't we be a lot together instead of apart?

Xoxo

Wes

When I look up from the letter, all my emotions climb up inside me, soaring through my body. My heart is beating so fast. "Wes," I say, just because it feels good to say his name again like he's precious to me—because he is.

He captures my face in his big hands. "For a while there I thought I was falling in love with you. But it's done. There's no more falling. I am so ridiculously in love with you, it's unreal. You're not a distraction. You put *me* first and did something huge for me by trying to give me space for my job and what I thought was going on. And I was so, so stupid to let you step away. I'm not going to do that again." He pauses and swallows, those warm brown eyes so vulnerable. "If you'll have me again."

I throw my arms around him. "I'm yours." I drop a quick kiss to his lips, then pull back. "And I love you so much it's kind of ridiculous too."

I don't know what tomorrow will bring. I don't know where I'm going at the start of the new year. But I know I'm with him, no matter what.

47

RIP IT OFF

Josie

We barely make it out of his car. The second he turns off the engine, he curls his hand around my sweatshirt and jerks me close. He covers my mouth with his and kisses me like he's gone mad. His fingers slide down my neck, his thumb tracing my collarbone, his mouth owning mine.

But my hip is pressing into the console, and that damn steering wheel is in the way, and there's a whole house full of surfaces for us to use. I wrench away, panting. "Inside."

He seems to blink off the fog of lust, then rasps out, "Now."

We barely make it up the stairs to the main level. His hands are on my hips the whole time and he's kissing the back of my neck. Tingles whoosh down my body with each step.

"Wes," I warn him. "I can't make it up the stairs if you do that."

"Good. Let's fuck on the stairs."

"And the crying and wailing I'd feel tomorrow in my back would go on my list of regrets."

He smacks my ass. "Move faster then, baby."

I hustle up the stairs and toe off my sneakers in record time. The second they're off and his are too, he hauls me back in his arms in the foyer. "Missed you so much."

"It was only three days."

"Too long," he mutters, sweeping his hungry lips along the column of my neck.

"Same here," I murmur, giving in to the way he touches me. How his lips move down my throat. How we're both breathing frantically. How we need each other so much.

I rope my arms around his neck. "Fuck me now."

He pulls back, a wicked grin spreading on his face. "Against the wall?"

"The wall, the couch, the floor—I don't care," I say, grabbing at his shirt, tugging on the material. I feel mad with hunger, feral even as I yank at his annoying buttons.

"Rip it off," he urges.

I feel wild as I tug hard on the next button, then the next, till one pops, then lands on the floor in a plink.

The sound sends a rush of heat between my thighs. I rip his shirt open the rest of the way, spreading my hands across his chest.

He shudders, closing his eyes for a few seconds, savoring my touch.

This thrills me—his reaction. The way he melts, too, when I touch him. How I light him up the way he does me.

I've never experienced a connection like this before. He wants what I have to give, and that's so rare and so wondrous.

And he wants it desperately. He jerks at the zipper of my jeans, then I grab at his. Soon my pants and underwear are on the floor, and he's carrying me to the couch. He sits, then unzips his jeans the rest of the way, freeing his cock.

My mouth waters. "I've missed you too," I say.

"Show me. Get on my dick and show me how much," he says, gripping the base of his cock and offering it to me.

"So bossy," I say as I straddle him and sink down. A tremble races through my whole body as I take him deep. "Oh god," I gasp.

"Fuck," he groans, letting his head fall back on the couch.

It's too much and never enough. It's hot and passionate. We're fast and frenzied. He thrusts up into me, and I grind down on him, and I can't get enough of this man.

This man who's shown up for me over and over again.

Who's come to my rescue so many times, then who let me help myself when I needed that most only so he could find me again tonight.

He's found me, and I don't ever want to lose him again.

His hands curl tight around my hips as he lifts his face and smashes his lips to mine. It's a sloppy kiss, full of so much passion as his fingers trace my jaw, and his tongue tangles with mine.

And we come back together.

It's needy and frantic, and when I come, he's right there after me, arms wrapped tight around me, lips whispering across mine, back where we belong.

* * *

A little later, after we straighten up and change, we're on the couch again. This time, though, we have a different mission. The list is spread out on the coffee table, like it was the night Wes discovered it.

"Your turn to check this off," I say, handing him a pen.

But he doesn't look away or turn toward the paper. His soulful brown eyes hold mine with reverence. "I really wanted to finish it with you."

Warmth floods my body. "We're almost done."

He takes the pen and slashes off number eight. Then he stares at the list, humming. Seems deep in thought.

"What is it?" I ask, eager to know what's on his mind.

"Do you think you've been doing number nine all along? Celebrating your goodbyes?"

My heart seizes, a tight fist. But then I breathe through it. The grief doesn't last long anymore. Just a pang here or there. A dull ache now and then. Mostly, I feel the love. I felt it tonight before Wes showed up, then it carried on with him, changing shape, changing size into a new kind of feeling.

I look down at the list. "Maybe we have. Maybe that's what this list was all about after all."

I take the pen from him and draw a line through number nine.

1. ~~Have a one-night stand with a sexy stranger.~~
2. ~~Overcome a fear (take a class you can't prepare for, baby! Psst — improv class time!)~~
3. ~~Make a friend who's nothing like you. You learn the most from them.~~
4. ~~Eat dessert for breakfast.~~

5. ~~Take pictures of your fun times. (It's okay to stop and snap a pic! That doesn't mean you're not living in the moment. It means you're giving yourself a beautiful memory for later.)~~

6. ~~Volunteer.~~

7. ~~Explore a new skill.~~

8. ~~Dance in the park.~~

9. ~~Celebrate your goodbyes.~~

There's still one more item on the list, but it feels like something I'll be doing for a long time, so I leave it. Some things are just unfinished and that's okay too.

Or maybe I'm not entirely ready to say goodbye to this list. But I don't have to let it go. Not really.

I can keep it with me for as long as I want to hold on to it.

48

BUT CAN I HAVE A LADDER?

Wesley

How am I supposed to choose? I stare at the cookie porn on Josie's tablet later that evening, unable to pick. "All of them," I say, salivating at the Christmas cookie images.

"Wes," she chides me, leaning on the kitchen counter, scrolling through recipes on her tablet. "You can't pick them all."

I drop a kiss to her neck. "Just like I want to fuck you in every way possible, I want all of these too."

She shivers, then shakes it off, all business again. "Pick three then. Will that be enough for you?" She glances at the kitchen clock. "I don't even know if we can get the ingredients in time."

"Of course we can," I say, then steal another kiss.

It's still Monday night but since Christmas is in two days, we need to get moving on this project. I tear myself away from kissing her to check out the tablet again, and I study the recipes.

"Do you need me to turn on the text-to-speech?" she asks.

I shake my head. "Nah. Recipes are easy enough. The way they're laid out and all. I love bullet points," I say, but then my mind whirs in another direction. "But you could always read me something dirty. I'd happily listen to that."

She gives me the flirtiest look ever, then says in a husky purr: "Add peanut butter, softened butter, granulated sugar, light brown sugar, and salt to the bowl of a stand mixer fitted with the paddle attachment or a large bowl if using a hand mixer. Beat on medium speed until creamed well."

And I can't pick right now. I yank off her leggings, lift her onto a stool, and help myself to her. After she comes on my face five minutes later, I stand, wipe my hand across my mouth and say, "Peanut Butter Blossoms." Then I add, "Also, shortbread, because you only live once, and snowball cookies."

After we clean up, we hightail it to the grocery store.

When we get home, we go for another round. What can I say? Gotta make up for those few days without her. After, when we're lying in bed, I address the big thing—the thing I've been wanting to say for a long time. I turn to Josie. Her skin is still glowing, and her lips are still bee-stung as she slides her glasses back on.

I didn't ask before. But I'm ready now. "Would you stay?"

A smile teases the corner of her lips. "What do you mean, Wes?" It's said teasingly—like she doesn't know what I mean, when she does.

I don't play games though. I don't beat around the bush. "Here. In San Francisco. With me," I say, strong and certain. "Look, I know you're going to get that job you interviewed for today. I have no doubts."

"It would be a great job," she says, sounding so hopeful. I love that she's not playing it cool. That she's allowed herself to *want*.

"Stay then. Whatever happens in January. If you turn down that job, stay. You can look for other jobs from here as easily as any place else. Stay." I say that beautiful word one more time.

She smiles like a little minx. "Well, I *was* going to move in with Everly."

My jaw comes unhinged. "What did you just say, woman?"

"We discussed it on Sunday. Before you got your act together."

I stab the pillow with my forefinger. "My act is together now. I want you here. And you can't pretend we're anything but excellent at living together."

"We are pretty good at it," she says playfully, still keeping me on my toes.

I kiss her shoulder, then layer a path of more kisses up to her ear, trying to convince her with my lips. But then, I have a better idea. A fail-safe way to get her to say yes. I stop the path of kisses, and meet her gaze. "We can even turn your room under the staircase into a library."

Her eyes sparkle. "Can I have a ladder in it?"

"You can have anything you want."

"Sold!"

* * *

In the morning, we do our favorite things.

Fuck.

Then, bake.

The kitchen is a mess of flour and chocolate and cookie dough, and a gorgeous, smart, feisty woman who somehow is willing to put up with me. That's the real holiday miracle. After she slides the last tray into the oven, then swipes her hands over the cake drawings on her apron, I haul her against me for another kiss.

"Mmm. You taste like sugar," I say.

"Then you must really like my lips."

"I love them," I murmur. "And you."

When I break the kiss, I scan the kitchen and the mess. There are measuring cups, bowls, and flour for miles. "This will take a while to clean up. Why don't you lie down with a good book and read and I'll clean?"

She arches a brow. "Are you even real?"

I smile like a cocky fucker. Yep. I know how to take care of my woman. "I am. And you deserve some time to read." But there's another reason at play. And since it's the season for being honest, I say, "And I need to call my dad."

She sets a hand on my shoulder. "You can do it."

She's right. I can. We talked about the things I need to say to him this morning while we were baking.

It's time. When she leaves the kitchen, I pop in my AirPods, grab a sponge, and gear up. Like when I'm about to hit the ice, I zone in on three things right now—focus, determination, and grit.

I call my dad, and he answers right away. "Hey, son. Good to hear from you. Merry Christmas Eve," he says.

"Merry Christmas Eve to you too," I say, and we make small talk about the holiday for a minute but after that I square my shoulders. "Listen..." I begin.

"Okay," he says with a touch of nerves in his voice.

"I appreciate everything you've done for me. My whole life. Getting me tutors and tools for dyslexia, and making sure I could handle my homework and get decent enough grades. And getting me to hockey practice, buying me equipment, and getting me the best coaches. I am beyond grateful."

"Good. You deserve all that. I'm hearing a but."

I draw a deep breath. "I'm canceling the meal plan, and the performance coach too. Domingo's a good guy, but I don't need him."

Dad's quiet for a long beat. That's rare. Then, he says with genuine curiosity, "Why? They're so good for you."

I wipe down more of the sugar on the counter to stay busy. "I eat balanced already. I just don't want to be obsessed with calories. Sometimes I eat cookies. Like, right now. I made Christmas cookies with my girlfriend."

"Your girlfriend? So you are with her?" It comes out a little like *I knew it*, but fact is, he did know it.

"Yep. And she's not a distraction. She's incredible. She's supportive and kind and funny, and she's taught me to have fun," I say, then I smile. Can't help it. Josie makes me feel that way—lighter, easier, more carefree. "Do you know what that's like? When you meet someone who makes you smile and laugh? It's better than shooting the winning goal."

He scoffs lightly. "Well, I'm glad you're happy but—"

"You're a good dad. But you're too involved as an agent. I'm not firing you, but I am telling you I need you to back off. The way you're over-involved is honestly a distraction. Just be my dad, and be my agent, but don't make me your project anymore, okay?"

He sighs. "I only want the best for you, son."

"And you've given me the best."

He sighs again, this time more heavily, but perhaps it's directed at himself. "I've overstepped," he says, plainly.

"You have. But it's nothing we can't fix. We can...start over."

"You think so?"

"I know so."

He pauses, and I know this isn't easy for him. Hell, it's not easy for me. But it is necessary. His voice is tinged with some regret when he says, "I've really only ever wanted the best for you. But I hear you. I've been pushy. And I'll try to back down."

"You can do it," I say encouragingly, like he'd say to me.

"You're right. I can do it." He hesitates, but only to shift gears. "Will you come to Christmas dinner?"

We're going to her brother's house earlier in the day, but dinner should work, so I say, "Yes, and I'm bringing my girlfriend. Tell Frieda she's the woman in the T-shirt, and she'd better be nicer to her than she was the night she met her."

I say goodbye and finish cleaning, feeling a whole lot lighter.

* * *

Christian chews approvingly on a peanut butter blossom. "These are even better than those cinnamon things you guys made the other month," he says, relaxing on his couch, the wreckage of Christmas morning gifts for two-and-half-month old twins scattered on the floor in front of the ten-foot-tall Douglas fir.

As the baby in his arms mouths on some pacifier shaped like a bear, Christian stuffs another cookie in his mouth. The fact that he eats sweets with no obvious guilt is another thing I admire about him.

I reach for one from the red-and-white-striped cookie tin and pop it in my mouth. Yup, it tastes like zero guilt.

When I finish it, I say, "You know what? You're right. We can bake."

"We're exceptionally good at following recipes," Josie says, from her spot next to me. Her parents are here too.

Christian nods toward his sister. "Are these Greta's recipes? I remember this one Christmas when the two of you made seven-layer brownies, and they were the best."

Josie beams. "Those were really good. Wes, we'll have to make those next."

"We will," I say.

Christian leans back on the couch, shifts the baby to his other arm. The last time Christian brought up baking, he could barely remember his sister liked to putter around in the kitchen. Now, he's remembering details and sharing them. It's a welcome shift.

From across the couch, Josie's mom meets my gaze. "Wesley, tell us more about you. What do you like to do for fun?"

Easiest question ever. I drape an arm around Josie, squeezing her shoulder. "Mostly I like to spend time with your daughter. That's what makes me happiest."

Josie's mom tilts her head, knitting her brow like she's trying to figure me out, then says, "I can't think of a better answer."

In the early afternoon, we make our way toward the door to head to Sonoma and see my dad. But before we go, Josie's mom pulls her aside. "There's something I have for you. A gift, if you will."

"What is it?" Josie asks.

"Come with me."

I watch as they head down the hall, wondering what this gift could be.

49

SALTY SWEET TEARS

Josie

This isn't ominous at all. My mom hardly ever pulls me aside. But she has this *mom* look on her face, like she wants to tell me something Very Important.

Tension winds through me as she leads me into the guest room where she's been staying, then shuts the door. The sound of it clicking freaks me out. Yes, she said she had a gift, but I can't escape this queasy feeling. "What is it, Mom? Are you sick? Is something going on?" All I can think is that she's next. I've lost someone I love already, and I don't want to go through that again.

She frowns sympathetically. "I didn't mean to scare you. I'm not sick. I'm great, and I have something for you. It's from..." She draws a breath—a fortifying one it seems. "My sister."

My pulse stops. I can barely breathe. "W-what do you mean?" I stammer out.

"When my sister wrote you the list, she gave something to me too. Before…" my mom says in careful bites, like this is hard for her. "That's why I kept asking you from time to time if you had started the list. Because she wanted you to have something when you finished it. I don't know if you've finished it but I have a feeling that you have." She pauses, like she can read list-finishing in my eyes. I'm not sure she can, or if she just figured two years was about right for me to make it through. "Am I right?"

I've finished nine items of the top ten. I still have number ten. But ten isn't something you finish. Ten is an everyday kind of thing. So I feel like I'm being honest to Greta's memory when I say, "Yes."

Also I want what my mother has *badly*.

She spins around, heads to her suitcase, and takes a letter from the inside pouch. She carries it in both hands like it's precious—something excavated from an archaeological dig that she must handle with great care. I stare at it. I can't look anywhere but at a simple cream envelope and then the letters on the front. The most familiar handwriting ever spells my name.

I want to snatch it, but I take it carefully and hold it tight to my chest. "Thank you."

* * *

The letter whispers to me the whole time I'm at Frieda's house. It taunts me, saying *I'm here*. But I focus on meeting Wesley's dad for the first time and Frieda for the third time. Even though we've of course already met, Wesley re-introduces me to her saying, "Like I said, this is my girl-friend." And Frieda is cordial to me for the first time ever. Wesley's father is friendly enough too, but I love Wesley's sister immediately. She welcomes me with open arms, and so does her girlfriend and their dog. But I think about the letter my mom gave me the whole time. I don't dare open it until I'm home and safe. Hours later, after we've driven back from Sonoma and pulled into the garage, I'm desperate to rip it open. I told Wes about it on the drive up and told him, too, that I was going to wait.

We go inside, take off our shoes, and head straight to the living room. I fish the letter out of my bag, and it's like I've slipped out of time, like I'm floating above my body as I stare at the envelope one more time.

It's not often that you get a letter from the next life.

"Do you want me to leave so you can read it alone?" he asks, his tone gentle.

I shake my head. "I want you to stay."

He squeezes my hand then lets go.

I close my eyes, breathing in the quiet stillness on Christmas night. When I open them, I slide my finger under the flap and read.

My darling Josie,

By now, you've finished the list. Knowing you, you've probably researched it thoroughly. Done your homework. Studied every single item. Am I right, baby? Or am I right?

Of course I'm right because I know you, and I hope after taking on this top ten list you know yourself a little better—the person I've been so lucky to know for your whole life. A woman who's funny, kind, bold, bright, caring. And maybe now, a little more daring.

You might be wondering why I left this list for you.

Was it a way for us to stay connected once I'm gone?
Is it a way for you to honor my memory?

Please.

It's none of those things.

I gave this to you because I've lived exactly the life I wanted. So much of that is because of the one thing I did that's at the top of my own list of no regrets— spending so much time with you.

You made me so very happy in this life, and, I'm sure, I'll carry that joy with me into the next one.

With so much love in all our lives,

Greta

I don't know how long I cry. But it's long enough to go through a whole box of tissues, to turn my face red and splotchy, to soak through Wes's shirt with my salty tears as he holds me and strokes my hair.

But they're happy tears. Or maybe they're the happiest. The kind that only come once you've made it through the sad moments and come out on the other side.

50

THAT SAID

Josie

The library's open the next day since lots of patrons like to hang out with books they can borrow during the holidays. As Wes drives me to work—he's seriously the best chauffeur with or without a shirt—my phone pings with an email. The envelope icon winks at me on the top of the screen.

A promise, full of hope. It's from the library in Petaluma. "This might be it," I say, then I tell him who it's from.

"Open it right now," he says as he pulls up in front of my little library and turns off the engine. I only have a few more days here.

I click on it, and it takes all of three seconds for my heart to sink.

It's the "that said" in the email.

It's one of those turns of phrases that means a rejection is coming. *We enjoyed the interview with you immensely*

*and you were one of our top candidates, but that said, we had
many exemplary candidates for the information specialist role.
We wish you the best in your job search.*

I hate that I want to cry.

"You'll get the next one," he says, reaching for my
hand and squeezing it.

I nod, then fight off the disappointment welling in my
chest and go inside. It's hard to focus on work, even
though I try. It's hard to focus on anything but the ticking
clock, especially when we gather for our last trivia night
after my shift—a farewell party for me.

"You've done wonders," Thalia says. "Perhaps something will come up in the future..."

"I hope," I reply, and I do, even though the odds don't
seem to be in my favor.

The next morning, I keep that focus on hope. In the
afternoon, my phone trills as I'm finishing up a display of
the best edge-of-your-seat romantic thrillers in audio.

The Violet Delia Foundation for Library Digital
Empowerment is calling. Thalia's walking past me, so I
wave it her way. "Look," I croak out, barely able to accept
the call.

"Answer it now," she says, sounding nearly as excited
as I am, but a lot more demanding.

They don't call you unless it's good news. That's the
first fact of interviewing. But I'm so nervous it takes me
two tries to actually take the call. "Hi, this is Josie."

"This is Violet Delia. It's good to hear your voice
again."

"It's great to hear yours," I say.

"I hope I haven't caught you at a bad time," she says.

Oh my god there's no bad time when you're calling. "I'm

available," I say, bright and upbeat and full of double meaning.

I hope she's picking up what I'm putting down. "Good, I hope you're available for this too. I want to make you an offer."

My dream job. I'm about to get my dream job.

I'm a pinball machine, whirring with a high score as she continues. "We love what you've done at the branch in the Upper Haight with the grant. The training that you've done, the work with the digitization center, and the efforts to educate patrons on media literacy are exactly why this foundation exists. And we want you to keep doing it."

My hand flies to my mouth. This is too much. This is too good to be true. This is everything.

"I would love to."

"I was hoping you'd say that. There's only one little stipulation."

I tense, then say with some trepidation, "What is it?"

"The job is in Boston."

51

THE AIRPORT GOODBYE

Wesley

"Boston?" I repeat, like saying the name of the city will change the situation.

"Boston," she says, in the corridor after my game that night. A game she came to. A game we won. A game I scored a goal in.

Then I skated over to the stands and blew her a kiss. Best night ever. Except, now it's not.

"Boston," I say again, this time heavily.

I'm too shocked to say anything more. This is the last thing I'd expected, but Josie is smiling. Like she has a trick up her sleeve. "Wes," she whispers.

"Yeah?"

"It's another three-month gig. It's only three months. I won't even be gone that long."

Oh.

Fuck yes!

I can breathe again. "Three months is nothing. Three months will pass in the blink of an eye."

"Right?" She sounds so excited.

"I'll be traveling and playing, and you'll be working."

"But not just in Boston, but a couple other libraries in New England—in Providence and Amherst too. They want me to do the job at a handful of branches. It's a dream job," she says, but I can hear the worry in her voice even though she's not asking my permission to take it.

She wants to know if I'll wait for her. Like I'd do anything else. I grab her hand. "You're taking it, right?"

"You'd do long-distance?"

"For three months? Baby, I'd do it for a year for you. Hell, I'd do it for as long as it took for you to come back. And I want you to get on that plane and know I'm waiting for you whenever you return. I promise."

She lets out a relieved breath, and I'm glad I could give her what she needs—certainty in us.

* * *

The first day of the new year, I put my money where my mouth is. I drive her to the airport, walk her to security, then tuck a strand of chestnut hair behind her ear. "We've got this."

She gives me the saddest smile that's chased with a tiny bit of hope. "It'll go by so fast."

We've made plans to talk every night, to text, to sext, to FaceTime. I'm going to see her as soon as I can too. We've worked out details for a quick overnight at the beginning of February. I won't have much time but I can squeeze it in between road trips. Then another few weeks later I'll fly her home to me for a weekend in early March. It'll be easy.

So easy.

It'll be almost the same as having her here.

Lies. Sweet little lies.

But I have to keep telling them to myself. What else can I do?

I press a tender kiss to her forehead, inhaling her cinnamon scent, letting it go to my head one more time. My chest aches. It hollows out, and I can't stand that she's leaving so soon after we've started. But I also know I'll wait for her to return for as long as I have to.

I brush my fingers down her cheek, along her jaw, and then lift her face so I can look into those gorgeous blue eyes. "I'm so in love with you. And I'm never going to let you forget it a single day that we're apart."

Her smile is bright now. "Be careful what you wish for. You're going to get so many letters."

"Bring it on." I kiss her one more time, a poignant goodbye kiss that has to carry us through.

When we break it, she waves sadly, then turns around and heads through security. I stay till she's on the other side, walking farther and farther away from me.

As I watch her go, I know with crystal clarity—I have to find a way to get her back.

52

HARD NIPS AND HARD DAYS

January 1

Dear Wesley,

I'm writing this on the plane! And in Comic Sans MS on my tablet. You can listen to it or read it.

By the way, did you know that real plane seats are tiny? You probably don't because you have those cushy, fabulous seats with so much room but I like to remind you now and then of how the rest of us live.

I'm keeping busy on the plane, trying not to miss you by writing and reviewing my notes for my first training session. It's—gasp—on Friday.

The best part? I'll be teaching some high school students about the different resources we have available for research. I'm a big fan of the Internet myself. My favorite things to research? Top Five Positions for Mind-Blowing Sex. Don't worry. I won't share those tips.

Here's a fun fact for you though—we've tried them all. But practice makes perfect, as they say. Maybe tonight when I get to the rental apartment I'll google how to ride your man's cock like a wild cowgirl.

Love,
    Your dirty girl, Josie

My very dirty girl,
    We should have a viewing party when you get to that rental. I'll be waiting.

Wes

* * *

January 13

Dear Wesley,

Trying to wipe the freshly fucked grin off my face as I head into my third week of work. You're as voracious with long-distance sex as you are in person. And as I walk into the library in the freezing cold of New England—seriously, this place is Antarctica levels, and I think my nipples are perma-hard here—I'm still thinking of the things you said last night, and the way you looked. Have I mentioned I love FaceTime? They should rename it FuckTime though.

Love,

Josie

Josie,

What did you say? I was thinking of your perma-hard nipples and my brain went offline.

Also, I'm about to get on that cushy plane for a road trip. It's to the East Coast, but the wrong part. The big toe of Florida. If I were any closer I'd sneak off and see you. Not just because of the nips though. Because I fucking miss you every day and as much as I love FuckTime, I want the real thing.

Love, Wes

* * *

January 21

Dear Wesley,

I have an intern! She's amazing. Her name is Penelope, she's a mom to a ten-year-old boy, and she went back to school at age thirty-two to get her master's degree. I adore her. She loves shoes, makeup, books, and her kid, though not in that order of course. We're working on the digitization initiatives together and yesterday, we nerded out over metadata and how to best organize a catalog. It was heaven!

Then, we went to a taco shop with her son (who loves hockey, but the Boston team), and I asked them to turn on your game, and I seriously went wild when my boyfriend scored a goal. Penelope said, "That's a boyfriend goal for you."

That felt sort of apropos. To the game and also to you.

Love, Josie

Josie,

Got back to the hotel room late and crashed hard. The thought of you watching my game is still the hottest thing ever—you better have worn my jersey. Only a few more weeks now till I can see you again. P.S. I called Thalia to see if she needed help at any more Friends of the Library fundraisers, so I'll be serving pancakes again next weekend.

Xo
  Wes

Dear Wesley,

And I love you even more for volunteering at the library. I will reward you with several extra blow jobs. Wait. That's a reward for me, too, given how much I love your dick.

Josie

.   .   .

Josie,

My dick loves you too, so it's a reward for both of us.

Wes

* * *

February 4

Dear Wesley,

I feel terrible doing this but my boss asked me to lead a seminar the day you were going to come visit. She needs me to fill in because the other librarian is sick. Flu season is the worst, but I'm sturdy, and I haven't so much as had a sniffle.

I'm sorry! I hate long-distance. I miss you. But I passed a record shop the other day, and I popped in and asked them what someone who likes Ben Rogers, the Good Neighbors Band, and The Last Shadow Puppets would like, and well, surprise! The record shop in Hayes Valley should have dropped it off for you. It's a consolation prize.

Josie

Josie,

I'm listening to this new Mini Mansions right now. I can't stop thinking of you. But that's every day.

Wes

* * *

February 14

Dear Wesley,

Six dozen pink roses! For the number of weeks left till I return to San Francisco! They're perfect.

Love, Josie

Josie,
So are the chocolates you sent from Elodie's. I had one. I'm savoring them.
P.S. It was great talking to you last night. I'm glad you're loving it there.

Wes

* * *

February 15

Dear Wesley,

I do love it. I really do. But I love you too. And I wish I could see you. I had a hard day today.

Your Josie

53

THE BRIGHT SPOT

Wesley

It's six in the evening, and we've beaten Philly in an afternoon game on their turf when I finish reading her letter. I'm heading out of the home team's arena to the Sea Dogs bus, but I've got five minutes before we go, so I duck down a quiet hall and dial her number, since she clearly needs to talk, and I want to be there.

"Why did you have a bad day?" I ask when she answers.

"Because everything went wrong," she says, frustration in her tone, but not like she's mad at the world. More like she's upset she couldn't fix everything. "The screen froze during my class, which wasn't the worst thing because I knew the material, but it was still challenging—I don't love improv, as you know. But I handled it. Then later, I was trying to help a patron digitize some home movies and the computer ate one of his movies and he yelled at me."

I growl at that asshat in Boston. "It's not your fault."

"I know. It was just a computer glitch, but he was angry and wanted to lash out. He'd been telling me he was getting a divorce and wanted to copy over these old movies before his wife took them. I figured he was going through something."

"It's no excuse to be mean," I say. "If I were there, I'd give him a piece of my mind."

I hear her smile as she says, "I know you would." She pauses, then soldiers on. "But it was one of those days where everything went wrong. Another guy was waiting to pick up a book and it was taking a while to find it so he oh-so-helpfully yelled at me that his taxes paid my salary. Our circulation software went down, and it was like one thing after another. But there was one bright spot."

"Yeah?" I say, eager to hear her good news.

"There was a woman in the library who's been living out of her car recently. And, she's trying to transition out of homelessness. Her name is Justine, and she was sniffling while working at one of the terminals, and people were looking at her. It's so hard because other patrons don't always want the unsheltered and those less fortunate there, but it's part of what we do. We serve the community and that includes everyone."

Her heart is so big. "I love that about the library and you. So tell me, what did you do?"

"I gave her some tissues and asked if she needed help on the computer."

Such a simple, practical way to help someone. "What did she need?"

"She was trying to apply for housing, and struggling with the application, so I sat down and worked with her for an hour. And she was telling me her story, and how she lost her home when she was laid off, but she had just gotten a job at a roadside diner so things are starting to look up for her a bit." Josie lets out a long breath, filled with obvious relief, and hope. "And I was glad I was there for her."

"You had the tools. It doesn't always happen, but when it does, it's great to be able to help someone in the exact way they need."

"Exactly." She takes a beat and sighs somewhat contentedly. "Thanks. I just needed to share. It was hard, but it was fine. The job is hard sometimes, just like yours. How was your game in Philly?"

"We won," I say.

"And you take the train to DC tonight?"

"Yep," I say, and the trip's too tight to squeeze in a visit, but then I start doing the math a second time.

* * *

A few hours later, I send her a text saying *I'm at your door,* then I knock on it. It's past her bedtime, but she must have her phone on since thirty seconds later, she's swinging open the door.

She's wearing fuzzy jammies with penguin illustrations on them, a white T-shirt that slopes off her shoulder, and her glasses. She's never been more beautiful as she blinks, parts her lips, then flings herself at me. "You're here? How the hell are you here?"

"You had a bad day," I say, as if the answer's obvious. Because really, it is. "I wanted to see if you needed another bright spot."

She tugs my sweater, pulling me inside her warm

apartment and out of the bitter cold night. "You're my bright spot."

I didn't grab the last flight out of Philly to Boston for sex, but I know, too, that what she needs right now is connection. So I gather her close, hold her face, and kiss her senseless. It's a kiss that says I'll do whatever it takes to make her days better, to show her she's special, to hang the moon for her.

Right now though, she doesn't want the moon and the stars. She wants me. Josie pulls me to the bed, and our clothes vanish in seconds, then I'm inside her. Everything is right in the world for a few delirious, mind-numbing moments as we come back together, limbs tangled, breath hot and fast, skin slick with sweat. Words like *miss you, need you,* and *love you* are traded as if their store is infinite.

I suppose it is with her.

After, she curls up against me. "I needed that."

"I could tell. I want to lift your spirits."

"Orgasms do that. But really it's you," she says, then she sighs heavily as she settles into the crook of my arm. "I love my job, Wes. Even on the bad days it's everything I want to do. But I miss you so much it hurts."

My chest hollows out, aching in a fresh, new way. I hate that she's hurting. That this is hard. It's hard for me too. It's painful not to see her like I did in San Francisco. At first, her letters seemed too happy. Too perfect. But she's human after all, and it's a strange relief to know she's struggling like I am. I wish I could do something about it. But she's doing all she can—applying for jobs in San Francisco that might start when she's done with this assignment.

All I can do is reassure her that I'm waiting, and wanting, and loving. "You'll be back soon," I say, and I try to remind myself that that's all that matters.

Especially since time keeps unwinding for us. Before the sun is even up, I'm out of there, catching a crack-of-dawn commercial flight to DC. Up in the air, I'm staring out the window, wishing we weren't so far away. But soon, she'll be back.

That's what I keep telling myself.

That's what I have to believe.

* * *

One day in mid-March, my phone rings as I'm heading to my empty bedroom for a pre-game nap. Josie's name flashes on the phone. Weird. She doesn't usually call me during her workday. It's two on the East Coast.

I answer right away. "Hey, baby. What's going on?"

"Hey!" She sounds cheery, but also...wary.

My chest tightens with worry. I cut to the chase. "What's wrong? You seem...off."

"I have good news and bad news." My gut sinks. I brace myself as she continues, "The foundation asked me to stay on. Permanently. Out here in Boston."

I stop and grab the wall as the floor buckles under me. Of course I knew something like this could happen. Of course it could happen to me, too, and I could be asked to move. But somehow I didn't think that her dream job could be across the country from me forever.

"What do you want to do?" I ask evenly.

She's quiet for a beat, pensive. "I really don't know."

I lean against the doorway, staring into the room under the staircase. And all at once, I know what's next for me. "When do they want you to decide?"

"Sometime next week."

That should be enough time.

54

MIC DROP

Wesley

Nothing is getting in my way tonight. Not the score, not the opponent—not a single thing.

The second I hop over the boards in the third period in the game, I'm lasered in on the puck more than ever. The score's tied. All night it's been a tight, tense game against the Las Vegas Sabers on our home ice. It's March, and every game matters.

This one especially.

I hunt for that puck like a sniper, chasing after it on the ice, jostling past Sabers defenders who want to take me down.

Not tonight, Sabers. Not tonight.

I'm single-minded, a man on a mission. Every time Asher or Alexei flip the puck to me, I narrow in on the goal, searching for a shot. I miss one, then another one's blocked. The game's locked up 1-1 when my shift's over.

I park myself on the bench, down some water, and

stare at the action like a horse with blinders on. Then I see it.

The way their goalie's got a tiny blind spot. If I can slap the puck in just a little more to the left...

When Coach tells the second line to get back out there, I jump over the boards so fast, hurtling into the action. Asher's on the puck right away, and I fly down the ice, adrenaline coursing through me as he races, the stick a blur of motion. But he's jammed up near the net, and he whips around, flicking the puck to me.

I narrow in on the blind spot, take aim, and fire.

It flies right past the goalie, landing beautifully in the net.

I punch the chilly air. My teammates clap my back. I imagine Josie cheering till she loses her voice at a taco shop with her librarian friend.

There are five more minutes to play and the game's not in the bag yet. But if we hold on, I've secured *my* goal for tonight.

* * *

The clock winds down with the Sabers trying but failing to score on Max, and the horn blares. "Tick Tick Boom" plays in the arena. The game-winning goal is mine, and as soon as I reach the end of the tunnel, I scan it for Everly.

She's waiting for us, polished and put together in a pantsuit. I march right up to her. "I want to take point tonight. Let me talk to the press."

She beams, then mimes making a checkmark. "Done."

Five minutes later, I'm in the media room, pads off, jersey on, surrounded by the press. Local reporters, hockey bloggers, the TV station, podcasters, and the national sports network that carries the game.

I've had media training. I know how to give the kind of bland answers that can never bite you in the ass. *Just happy to help the team. Everyone played hard tonight. Just doing my part.*

I've got those chestnuts ready, so when the first reporter asks about the game-winning goal, and how it positions us at this point in the season, I say into the mic, "I'm happy to help the team, but I don't actually want to talk about the game tonight."

A sports reporter in the front row tilts her head and lifts her phone higher, recording me. Everly arches a brow from her spot by the door.

I'm seated at a table on a riser, surrounded by a dozen members of the press. And I'm counting on them to do their part. To give me the help that I need.

But first I have to do my part.

"What do you want to talk about then?" the reporter in the front row asks.

I square my shoulders. "The fans," I begin.

And the faces of the reporters are mostly disappointed. They probably figure this is nothing they haven't heard before—*we have great fans, and yada, yada, and we do.*

"We have great fans," I begin. I practiced what to say at home. I recorded myself speaking into my phone. I worked the ideas over. I listened to the recordings again and again, and memorized what to say. Because I don't want to fuck up this chance. "We have the best fans. They show up for game after game." I wave my arm in the direction of the rink, which was packed for all three periods. It's been packed all season long. "They fill this place, and I know I speak for the entire Sea Dogs organization when I say we're seriously grateful for the way they support us." I pause, take a fueling breath, and march on. "And since you all support this city so well when it comes to games, I want to ask you to support the city in other areas too. I started volunteering at a local animal rescue—Little Friends—last fall. It's life-changing, helping them help animals find homes. And there are so many great opportunities to volunteer in this city. A homeless shelter. Beach cleanup. Giving rides to seniors." I take a breath. No one is stopping me. No one will. Because athletes are lucky— they have a platform afforded by uncommon talent. And sometimes you need to use it for good. And for your own good. Fortunately, they're one and the same right now. "Or, my personal favorite—the library. Do you know how underfunded most libraries are? I didn't know that for a while, but I've learned that in the past few months by volunteering at some of their pancake fundraisers." I pause, letting that sink in. "Yeah, libraries still have to resort to pancake fundraisers to make enough money for their services. Which is great on the one hand, because I love pancakes."

There's a collective murmur in the media room.

"But it's a shame, because the library has a lot of great services—and services that mean a lot to me personally because..." I pause, but only for a second or two, only because I've never said this out loud in public, and it's not because I'm ashamed. It's because there's never been a need. But there's a need now, so I offer up a part of myself so the public can see another side to this athlete. A more personal one. "I'm dyslexic. And libraries are doing amazing things to help *everyone* learn to read. They have some great initiatives going on, from offering audiobooks, to text-to-speech, to this really cool technology that reads a book to you like the sentences are words on a karaoke screen. But what they're also doing at this branch in the Upper Haight is something called *Your Next Five Reads*," I say and I'm on a roll. This is like flying down the ice on a breakaway. A clean open shot. "If you like George R.R. Martin, or *If You Give a Pig a Pancake*, or if you're into classics like *To Kill a Mockingbird*, or books by S.A. Cosby, Kristin Hannah, or Ana Huang, there are recs for everyone, whether you read with your eyes or ears, or have the computer read to you. And to support the city's library's initiatives, I'm going to donate a dozen headphones to every branch of the library in the city of San Francisco. The boxes should arrive tomorrow." I stop, give a smile, then lean into the mic. "If you've got a few extra bucks, maybe give it to one of these libraries. If not, go ask a librarian to suggest your next five reads. And thanks for coming tonight."

I walk out.

* * *

Two days later, I pull up to the little library on a Friday morning. Thalia emailed me late last night and begged me to stop by. I don't want to presume it's anything but chatting about the volunteer work I've been doing.

But I also want to presume everything.

I head inside and find her on the second floor. The second she sees me, she claps. Eddie does too.

I wave my hands for them to stop, meaning it. "Stop. Seriously."

But she shakes her head. "We've been inundated. Everyone's been inundated but especially this branch since Josie started *Your Next Five Reads* here. Everyone is writing in and asking for book recs."

"Thalia's inbox is horrifying," Eddie seconds, and he's smirking.

"Sorry, not sorry," I say dryly.

"Oh, you'd better not be sorry. I used the horror of my inbox to secure funding from the city. Have I mentioned donations have gone through the roof since Mister Hockey became Mister Library?"

Sunlight spreads in my chest, warming every inch of me. "Yeah?"

She nods. "And I've hired someone to manage it."

Shit. Fuck. No.

That wasn't the plan. That wasn't the point. I mean, that's great and all, but there's one person who should do that instead.

Before I can even sputter out, *"No, hire Josie. That was my plan,"* Thalia says, "Would you like to be the one to tell my new hire that she has a permanent job here?"

55

TOP FIVE LIST

Josie

I'm helping Justine find some reliable sources on how to make the leap from working at a diner to working at a fine-dining establishment when my phone buzzes with a text. Wesley's chime sound.

"One second," I say, then steal a glance at the text from my boyfriend. *Look at your email.*

All I want to do is click on my email, but I need to finish with Justine. Five minutes later, I peel myself away, slipping behind the desk next to Penelope to check my phone.

It's been lit up since Wesley's speech the other night—a speech that shocked me and brought me to gloriously happy tears. Proud tears. Patrons here heard about it. Our donations increased a little bit, and the Boston team donated headphones too, following Wes's lead.

My heart stutters as I read the first line.

Top Five Things For You To Do

1. Pick out your hottest librarian clothes.
2. Pack your bags.
3. Go to the airport.
4. Find a hockey player to collect your suitcase to take home.
5. Start your fully funded new job at the library near *your home.*

I gasp, shuddering out a shocked breath. My eyes widen, and I read it again and again.

"What's going on? Did you get a coupon for deals on shoes?" The question comes from Penelope.

"Better. It's from Wes. I got a job in San Francisco."

Penelope beams, then sweeps out an arm toward the door. "Go!"

* * *

Two weeks later, I shuffle off the plane in San Francisco as if I've drunk ten espressos. Every cell is buzzing. I'm amped up. I can't wait to race down the jetway, then fly along the concourse. But first, I have to get off this plane. It takes as long as the Pleistocene era, but eventually I make it to the jetway, and then...I run.

Past the gate, down the concourse, toward security, through the doors, and into Wes's arms on the other side.

He scoops me up in a koala hug. "You did it!"

"No, you did it." I kiss him again and again. "You did."

"Nope." Then he shrugs, and smiles. "Okay, we did."

The funding made it possible for Thalia to make my

old job a regular one, where I can manage the *Your Next Five Reads* and also the library's digital efforts, like I did before. I didn't want to leave the foundation in the lurch, but I didn't have to—Penelope is taking the permanent job they'd offered me in Boston.

With that behind us, and the future ahead of us, Wes takes me to the charming townhouse where I've laughed, cried, and loved. The second he pulls into the garage it feels just like that—home. I'm ready to race up the stairs and reconnect with him, but once we're in the foyer, he says, "Remember that promise I made you?"

"Which one?"

He reaches for my hand. "I'll show you."

He takes me to my old room under the stairs and swings the door open. I gasp. He's turned it into a library. Gleaming white walls are filled with shelves and books, fresh pillows line the window seat, and best of all—there's a ladder resting against the shelves.

I tug him close to me, against the ladder, and kiss the breath out of him.

He's always been the most generous person I've ever known, but to put himself out there like he did the other week? He's not just my boyfriend. He's the man I want to spend the rest of my life with.

But first things first. "Will you fuck me on this ladder? I feel like this belongs on a list somewhere after all."

"Our new list," he says, then fulfills a brand-new fantasy.

EPILOGUE: NUMBER TEN

Josie

As I settle into my new *old* job at the little library next to the fire station in the Upper Haight, I feel both like an explorer in San Francisco and like a regular.

When I first arrived here back in the fall, I connected instantly with the city. San Francisco is a vibrant tapestry of cultures and experiences. It's a little like a new book. You crack it open and discover a story on every page.

When our schedules align, Wes and I explore the city's neighborhoods, from the postcard charm of Chinatown to the edgier vibes of the Mission District. We go to book-stores, and we check out night markets, picking up some of Maeve's lamps to decorate our place.

It's not quite black and chrome now. It has a little more color.

Tonight, though, it's time for that cocktail-mixing class at last. We're taking it with our friends. We go to Sticks and Stones, a bar the guys on the team like.

We join Max and Asher at the sleek silver counter.

Miles is here too. He's a center on the team, and he's started hanging out with the guys lately. He's both sarcastic and thoughtful and that combo seems to keep the guys on their toes.

Everly and Maeve are here too, and so is Fable. As the owner—a friendly guy named Gage—guides us through how to mix an old-fashioned, Everly scoffs at Max's efforts to mix in bourbon. He looks amused as he stirs, but then the famously grumpy goalie turns to her with a stern look. "What is it, sunshine? Got a tip for me on my *cocktail?*"

Sunshine? I look to Wes, whispering, "He calls her sunshine?"

Wes shrugs. "Evidently."

"Not at all," Everly says to Max with a bright smile. "I'm just enjoying learning all about your new skills."

"You're surprised I can mix a drink?"

She gestures to his face. "I'm surprised you're not scowling."

"Consider me shocked too," Miles weighs in.

"Same here," Asher adds.

"And I have to agree," Wes adds.

"Looks like it's unanimous," Everly says.

Max harrumphs, almost like he's been caught red-handed being un-growly. He resumes mixing, and I keep wondering what's up with the two of them.

But I'll find out another time.

For now, I shake my cocktail glass, the ice clinking against the metal, and I'm happy, surrounded by friends who feel like family and with my guy by my side.

* * *

A few weeks later...

The view. Seriously, the view. "A little to the left maybe," I say.

Wes adjusts the frame and moves it slightly on the wall, then lifts the hammer again and smacks the nail behind it. "I think you just like watching me being handy," he drawls.

"*Maybe,*" I say. "I mean, the arm porn is good from where I sit."

He finishes hanging the artwork we both picked out, then asks, "Is this good?"

"It's perfect," I say, then pat the couch cushion. "Now come join us."

He walks over to the sofa, and flops down next to me and our newest addition. "Hey, Pancake," Wes says, then nuzzles the cutie—a Cattle Dog mix we adopted from Little Friends. He's item number one on our new list, which we're still building, but we have two items on it so far.

Ten Things To Do With Your Love
1. Adopt a dog.
2. Make a home.

We've crossed off number one. We're busy working on two, and the art on the walls is part of that. We framed the original list from Aunt Greta with all but number ten crossed out.

Now, he wraps an arm around me, and we enjoy the view of our new art together.

Number ten has always been something that shouldn't be crossed out.

It's something you should do every day.

It's something we do for each other.

10. Make someone happy.

THE END

Turn the page for a sneak peek of The Romance Line, Max and Everly's forbidden, enemies-to-lovers hockey romance that's coming to you in Kindle Unlimited in September.

And be sure to binge the **My Hockey Romance** series, set in the same San Francisco hockey world, starting with the spicy, hilarious, roommates-to-lovers Amazon Charts Bestselling romance **Double Pucked**, available in Kindle Unlimited!

For more Josie and Wes, click here for an extended epilogue or scan the QR code!

Turn the page for a teaser of Max's romance!

EXCERPT - THE ROMANCE LINE

Chapter 1
Max

Look, I can pull off pretty much anything in the clothing department, but this *might* be outside my wheelhouse. Especially since I definitely didn't pack a purple pair of underwear with little flowers all over the waistband and so little material that nothing is left to the imagination. Even mine, and I have a very active one.

Intrigued, I hold the scrap of purple fabric in front of me in my hotel room. Studying this less-is-definitely-more piece of lingerie, I have to wonder—who even wears this almost thong and also, does it hurt?

I should probably stop pawing around in this bag that's clearly not mine but looks just like it. Must have grabbed it in the lobby by mistake, and I'm guessing this suitcase doesn't belong to one of my teammates either. Not that there's anything wrong with that. To each his own and all. But this cornu-fucking-copia of lace and satin doesn't look like it would fit a pro hockey player.

There are only a handful of women traveling with the team on this road trip to Seattle. The athletic trainer, the team doctor, and the publicist.

My mind catches on that last possibility.

This can't belong to her.

It just can't.

Not straightlaced, rule-following, pantsuit-wearing Everly Rosewood. She's the kind of woman who owns exactly seven sets of cotton bras and panties, in the same matching shade of nude, same matching style, so she can grab and go at the crack of dawn all while devising new ways to torture me with press requests and promo shoot ideas.

No way does Everly own anything that's not navy, black, or beige. Best I return this bag to its rightful owner, pretend I never saw what's in it, and then never think about it again. Searching for the luggage tag, I find one attached to the handle and flip it over.

I freeze. Then, I heat up everywhere. We're talking inferno levels. This bevy of beautiful lingerie belongs to the team's publicist after all. The clever, mouthy woman who hates me. Yep, the one and only Everly Rosewood, who accomplishes more before her workday begins than most people do in a year. But this does not compute—she can't possibly dish out a list of promo duties in that teacherly way of hers while wearing a purple thong.

This is a test. This is clearly some kind of test. No, it's a downright moral dilemma.

Do I slam it shut or hunt around in her things a little more?

I need some distance from temptation. Spinning around, I pace toward the window overlooking the city of Seattle, rainy because of course it's rainy, and the arena where I'll be defending the net early tomorrow against one of the toughest teams in the league.

"All you have to do is zip up that suitcase, return it, and go the fuck to sleep," I mutter.

Great. Just great. Now I'm talking to myself. They say goalies are a little unhinged but this is next level even for me. I grip the windowsill, staring at the Space Needle lit up against the night sky, then I tear myself away, stalk right back over to the bed, ready—I swear I'm ready—to zip that suitcase all the way up and say goodbye to it.

Or, really, I'm almost ready.

I scrub a hand across my beard and gaze a little longer at the treasure trove of lace and satin, like a siren calling to me in the most tantalizing voice.

How do you think the slay-the-world-one-member-of-the-media-at-a-time queen would look in purple lace? Or in soft blue satin?

Does she have a date tonight? My jaw ticks. *Is she meeting a secret boyfriend in the rainy city tomorrow?* It ticks harder. *Does she—oh, hell—wear these every day to work under those pantsuits that drive you crazy?*

And it ticks the hardest.

I haul in a breath, trying to locate my moral compass. But it's hard to find right now. I try again with a pep talk. "All you have to do is reach for the zipper. Pull the teeth closed around one side, then the other. Done."

But I don't move. I stand here stupidly because all those sexy things are scrambling my brain. Taking up all the space in my head now that I know Everly Rosewood wears red lace panties, the color of my dirty dreams.

"Doesn't matter," I mutter. "It really doesn't matter what she wears." Squaring my shoulders, I get ready to perform the most herculean task—zip it up.

As I reach for the bag, my phone buzzes. Saved by the bell. I grab it from my back pocket at Mach speed, grateful for the distraction from a moral dilemma worthy of that vintage board game Scruples.

It's a text from my agent, Garrett. ***Been talking to Thrive about your sponsorship. Need to run some things past you. Let's chat when you return to SF.***

That has to be good. Why else would he text me late at night? Dude isn't going to text with bad news like, saying, *you lost your last sponsor less than a week into the season.*

So, clearly this is a good sign. I dictate a reply. ***Works for me. Maybe I'll even let you take me to that new kebab place on Polk Street and give me the good news.***

The bubbles dance for a minute. A long minute that should cool me off so I stop obsessing over this bag. Finally, Garrett's reply lands: ***Don't think I didn't notice you finagling a free meal. And sure. Kebabs will do. Just know this —I'm working hard to make this happen. I know you've got plans.***

I furrow my brow. Well, no shit. That's his job. He always works hard. Doesn't need to tell me that twice. But I'm not his easiest client lately, so maybe this is just his nice guy way of reminding me he's juggling all the broken plates I've thrown his way.

So I should take this exchange as a win, return this bag, and crash.

Except, what is that scrap of sinful red lace taunting me from the top of the stack of neatly folded blouses in the center of her bag? I shove the phone back in my pocket and then my curious fingers have a mind of their own. One look can't hurt. Fine, one touch. I snatch up the soft strap poking out of the blouses and fish out—what is this? A demi-bustier? A halter half bra?

I lift it to get a better view. It's sheer red lace, the color of a cherry, with the daintiest ruffle along the top. Maybe it's a bra of sorts. I don't even know. Then, with a new kind of reckless abandon, I reach for the next thing, and the next, and the next.

Until...what have I done? I've plundered her bag. Yep, I'm a lingerie pirate.

This is bad, man.

But this is also an opportunity. I smirk as I get to work neatly folding every single silky item.

An opportunity to give her hell.

I pack them all back up, except for this little red thing, and head to the door, like a good boy.

Well, not really. Because tonight, I've been a little bit bad.

Preorder: The Romance Line!

PS! Stay tuned for Fable and Wilder's holiday romance coming this fall to Kindle Unlimited in My Favorite Holidate!

DEAR READER

Dear reader,

Wesley's experience with dyslexia and the way he identifies himself primarily as "a person with dyslexia" and at the end as "a dyslexic" is based on extensive research into dyslexia, as well as insight and interviews from people living their best lives with dyslexia. Ultimately, everyone's experience of dyslexia, and how they talk about it, is unique to the individual as are their choices for the tools and technology they may use to navigate it. Wesley's strategies and feelings about reading and the tools he uses to read were informed by my conversations with people living with dyslexia and the stories they shared with me. In addition, Wesley's choice to usually identify himself with "person-first language," such as saying "I have dyslexia" was informed both by research into preferred language, but also the backstory I created for him and the media training he would have as an athlete today. However, at the end when he's speaking to the press, he specifically says "I'm dyslexic." That was a deliberate choice as his goals in that moment are to be intensely personal about this aspect of himself, and this felt like the most personal and intimate way for him to phrase the information he's sharing. This choice was also informed by my conversations with people who have dyslexia and the way they often refer to themselves by saying simply saying, "I'm dyslexic." However, Josie specifically uses person-first language ("he has dyslexia," rather than "he's dyslexic") in talking about his dyslexia. People with dyslexia often land on both sides of the conversation as to the language used, so my choice in mixing it up at the end was intentional, and based on conversations with people in the community.

I am grateful to my sensitivity readers for combing over this manuscript and helping me to present this side of his character authentically. Thank you deeply to Jacqueline and Bree, as well as Kate and Grace. Any mistakes are entirely my own. My goal was *not* to write a story about someone learning to live with dyslexia or learning to love in spite of it. My goal was to show positive representation and write a love story that happened to have a hero with dyslexia in it. I hope I succeeded, and I thank you for taking the time to read this story!

My best,

Lauren

I asked Jacqueline, one of my sensitivity readers, to compile a list of resources for this title and I am pleased to share this with you here.

From Jacqueline...

So, what is dyslexia?

According to the Yale Center for Dyslexia, individuals with dyslexia have difficulty with reading fluency, spelling, and learning a second language. However, these difficulties are not related to their overall intelligence. In fact, people with dyslexia are often fast and creative thinkers with strong reasoning abilities.

Prevalence: According to The Yale Center for Dyslexia, dyslexia is very common, affecting 20 percent of the population and representing 80-90 percent of individuals with learning disabilities.

The following resources may be helpful for people with dyslexia or those who want a better understanding of it.

1. State AT Resource Centers: Each state, the District of Columbia, and each US territory has state grant-funded assistive technology (AT) programs that provide AT demonstrations and loans. Click on the link below to find out more about your state program and resources they may have that can support individuals with dyslexia.

https://www.at3center.net/state-at-programs

2. Bookshare: Bookshare is an e-book library that has a huge collection of audiobooks and e-books, including textbooks and popular and acclaimed titles. The library is for people who have difficulty processing or comprehending printed text, seeing text in books or on a screen, or who have difficulty physically managing books or reading devices. Individuals can gain access to Bookshare after a professional with specific expertise, such as a teacher, librarian, assistive technology professional, reading specialist, or occupational therapist, confirms that

the individual has a qualifying condition, like a learning or reading disability such as dyslexia.

https://www.bookshare.org/

3. Don Johnston: Don Johnston is the creator of learning tools that support individuals with different learning styles and abilities. They provide free webinars on topics such as dyslexia and AT solutions that can be of benefit. Their products include Snap & Read, a reading support tool that reads text aloud, simplifies text, translates to more than 100 languages, and provides highlighting and note-taking supports. They also created Co-Writer, a word prediction tool. https://learningtools.donjohnston.com/

4. Text Help: Text Help creates digital tools for inclusive learners and workers. Their products include Read & Write, a literacy tool that can support people with dyslexia by reading text out loud, and by providing speech input and word prediction. They are also the creators of Equatio, a learning solution for math and science that allows math problems to be read aloud.

https://www.texthelp.com/solutions/people-with-dyslexia/

5. Understood: Understood is a non-profit organization that is a hub for people with learning and thinking differences. Their dyslexia resources include information on the signs of dyslexia at various ages, common myths about dyslexia, classroom accommodations and workplace supports, and a day in the life of an employee with dyslexia.

https://www.understood.org/en/dyslexia

6. Made by Dyslexia: Made by Dyslexia is a global dyslexia charity led by individuals with dyslexia. Their goal is to train schools and workplaces throughout the world to empower people with dyslexia. They also provide resources that highlight the strength of dyslexic thinking.

https://www.madebydyslexia.org/

7. C-Pen: The C-Pen is an AT device that scans and processes printed text, helping improve reading comprehension.

https://cpen.com/

8. Grammarly: Grammarly is an AT solution that provides assistance with spelling, grammar, punctuation, and clarity. It provides suggestions on how to improve written text. Grammarly offers a free and paid subscription.

https://www.grammarly.com/

9. Ginger: Ginger is another AT solution that serves as a grammar checker, sentence re-phraser, spell-checker, and online proofreader. They offer a free and paid version.

https://www.gingersoftware.com/accessibility

10. Google Voice Typing: Google Voice Typing lets users type and edit with their voice whilst using Google Docs. This feature is great for individuals with dyslexia, as it allows them to focus on content without being bogged down by spelling and grammar.

BE A LOVELY

Want to be the first to know of sales, new releases, special deals and giveaways? Sign up for my newsletter today!

Want to be part of a fun, feel-good place to talk about books and romance, and get sneak peeks of covers and advance copies of my books? Be a Lovely!

ACKNOWLEDGMENTS

Thank you to Maureen Herman for reviewing the entire manuscript, including the details about the library, and helping me finetune the specifics of Josie's career path as well as her focus on being a digital archivist, plus all the ins and outs of working at a library on a day-to-day basis. I am grateful for her eagle eyes and information mind!

I am grateful to Bree, Grace, Jacqueline and Kate for their insight. I am indebted to Sharon for checking all the hockey and guiding me through the sport. Thank you to Lo and Rae, Kim and Jill, and KP.

With gratitude to my author friends who I rely on daily — Corinne, Laura, AL, Natasha, Lili, Laurelin, CD, K, and Nadia, among others.

Most of all, I am so amazingly grateful to you — the readers — for picking this up! I hope you love Wes and Josie like I do!

MORE BOOKS BY LAUREN

I've written more than 100 books! **All of these titles below are FREE in Kindle Unlimited!**

Double Pucked

A sexy, outrageous MFM hockey romantic comedy!

Puck Yes

A fake marriage, spicy MFM hockey rom com!

Thoroughly Pucked!

A brother's best friends +runaway bride, spicy MFM hockey rom com!

Well and Truly Pucked

A friends-to-lovers forced proximity why-choose hockey rom com!

The Virgin Society Series

Meet the Virgin Society – great friends who'd do anything for each other. Indulge in these forbidden, emotionally-charged, and wildly sexy age-gap romances!

The RSVP

The Tryst

The Tease

The Dating Games Series

A fun, sexy romantic comedy series about friends in the city and their dating mishaps!

The Virgin Next Door

Two A Day

The Good Guy Challenge

How To Date Series (New and ongoing)

Friends who are like family. Chances to learn how to date again. Standalone romantic comedies full of love, sex and meet-cute shenanigans.

My So-Called Love Life

Plays Well With Others

The Almost Romantic

The Accidental Dating Experiment

My Favorite Holidate

A romantic comedy adventure standalone

A Real Good Bad Thing

Boyfriend Material

Four fabulous heroines. Four outrageous proposals. Four chances at love in this sexy rom-com series!

Asking For a Friend

Sex and Other Shiny Objects

One Night Stand-In

Overnight Service

Big Rock Series

My #1 New York Times Bestselling sexy as sin, irreverent, male-POV romantic comedy!

Big Rock

Mister O

Well Hung

Full Package

Joy Ride

Hard Wood

Happy Endings Series

Romance starts with a bang in this series of standalones
following a group of friends seeking and avoiding love!

Come Again

Shut Up and Kiss Me

Kismet

My Single-Versary

Ballers And Babes

Sexy sports romance standalones guaranteed to make you hot!

Most Valuable Playboy

Most Likely to Score

A Wild Card Kiss

Rules of Love Series

Athlete, virgins and weddings!

The Virgin Rule Book

The Virgin Game Plan

The Virgin Replay

The Virgin Scorecard

The Extravagant Series

Bodyguards, billionaires and hoteliers in this sexy, high-stakes
series of standalones!

One Night Only

One Exquisite Touch

My One-Week Husband

The Guys Who Got Away Series

Friends in New York City and California fall in love in this fun
and hot rom-com series!

Birthday Suit

Dear Sexy Ex-Boyfriend

The What If Guy

Thanks for Last Night

The Dream Guy Next Door

Always Satisfied Series

A group of friends in New York City find love and laughter in
this series of sexy standalones!

Satisfaction Guaranteed

Never Have I Ever

Instant Gratification

PS It's Always Been You

The Gift Series

An after dark series of standalones! Explore your fantasies!

The Engagement Gift

The Virgin Gift

The Decadent Gift

The Heartbreakers Series

Three brothers. Three rockers. Three standalone sexy romantic
comedies.

Once Upon a Real Good Time

Once Upon a Sure Thing

Once Upon a Wild Fling

Sinful Men

A high-stakes, high-octane, sexy-as-sin romantic suspense series!

My Sinful Nights

My Sinful Desire

My Sinful Longing

My Sinful Love

My Sinful Temptation

From Paris With Love

Swoony, sweeping romances set in Paris!

Wanderlust

Part-Time Lover

One Love Series

A group of friends in New York falls in love one by one in this sexy rom-com series!

The Sexy One

The Hot One

The Knocked Up Plan

Come As You Are

Lucky In Love Series

A small town romance full of heat and blue collar heroes and sexy heroines!

Best Laid Plans

The Feel Good Factor

Nobody Does It Better

Unzipped

No Regrets

An angsty, sexy, emotional, new adult trilogy about one young couple fighting to break free of their pasts!

The Start of Us

The Thrill of It

Every Second With You

The Caught Up in Love Series

A group of friends finds love!

The Pretending Plot

The Dating Proposal

The Second Chance Plan

The Private Rehearsal

Seductive Nights Series

A high heat series full of danger and spice!

Night After Night

After This Night

One More Night

A Wildly Seductive Night

Joy Delivered Duet

A high-heat, wickedly sexy series of standalones that will set your sheets on fire!

Nights With Him

Forbidden Nights

Unbreak My Heart

A standalone second chance emotional roller coaster of a romance

The Muse

A magical realism romance set in Paris

Good Love Series of sexy rom-coms co-written with Lili Valente!

I also write MM romance under the name L. Blakely!

Hopelessly Bromantic Duet (MM)

Roomies to lovers to enemies to fake boyfriends

Hopelessly Bromantic

Here Comes My Man

Men of Summer Series (MM)

Two baseball players on the same team fall in love in a forbidden romance spanning five epic years

Scoring With Him

Winning With Him

All In With Him

MM Standalone Novels

A Guy Walks Into My Bar

The Bromance Zone

One Time Only

The Best Men (Co-written with Sarina Bowen)

Winner Takes All Series (MM)

A series of emotionally-charged and irresistibly sexy standalone MM sports romances!

The Boyfriend Comeback

Turn Me On

A Very Filthy Game

Limited Edition Husband

Manhandled

If you want a personalized recommendation, email me at laurenblakelybooks@gmail.com!

CONTACT

I love hearing from readers! You can find me on TikTok at LaurenBlakelyBooks, Instagram at LaurenBlakelyBooks, Facebook at LaurenBlakelyBooks, or online at Lauren-Blakely.com. You can also email me at laurenblakely books@gmail.com

Made in United States
Troutdale, OR
08/26/2024

22339678R00276